FEARLESS
Hope

A NOVEL

SERENA B. MILLER

HOWARD BOOKS
A DIVISION OF SIMON & SCHUSTER, INC.

NEW YORK   NASHVILLE   LONDON   TORONTO   SYDNEY   NEW DELHI

Howard Books
A Division of Simon & Schuster, Inc.
1230 Avenue of the Americas
New York, NY 10020

First Howard Books trade paperback edition April 2014

HOWARD and colophon are trademarks of Simon & Schuster, Inc.

For information about special discounts for bulk purchases, please contact Simon & Schuster Special Sales at 1-866-506-1949 or business@simonandschuster.com.

The Simon & Schuster Speakers Bureau can bring authors to your live event. For more information or to book an event contact the Simon & Schuster Speakers Bureau at 1-866-248-3049 or visit our website at www.simonspeakers.com.

Interior design by Kyoko Watanabe
Cover design by Bruce Gore
Cover illustration © Pixelworks/ Steve Gardner; background imagery by Doyle Yoder and iStock/Getty

Manufactured in the United States of America

10   9   8   7   6   5   4   3   2   1

Library of Congress Cataloging-in-Publication Data

Miller, Serena B.
Fearless hope : a novel / Serena B. Miller.
p.   cm.
1. Amish women—Fiction. 2. Authors—Fiction. I. Title.
PS3613.I55295F43 2013
813'.6—dc23   2013038550

ISBN 978-1-4516-6037-1
ISBN 978-1-4516-6038-8 (ebook)
ISBN 978-1-4767-2786-8 (eShort)

To Derek Miller.
Thank you, Son, for the sacrifices you've made in serving our country, and for your continual insight, love, and encouragement.

Acknowledgments

Special thanks to my friend Pat, who shared the story of her mother-in-law demanding to be let inside the WWII German work camp so she could care for her son. My thanks to Mark Risner, a dairy farmer, for his tutorial on breeds and behavior of bulls. Thanks also to his young son, Matthew Risner, who personally demonstrated the behavior of a crazed bull. Thanks to Paul Stutzman, fellow writer and Mennonite, who helped explain the belief system of his church. Any mistakes made are all mine. To all my Amish friends in Holmes County—I can never thank you enough for all your patience, love, and trust. Endless thanks to Beth Adams, for her great editing skills, and Sandra Bishop, for her wisdom and strength as she steers her authors through the stormy waters of an ever-changing publishing world.

Now He was telling them a parable to show that at all times they ought to pray and not to lose heart saying, "There was in a certain city a judge . . . and there was a widow in that city and she kept coming to him."

—LUKE 18:1–3 (NAS)

chapter ONE

Hope Schrock had never met a bull she liked. This three-year-old Jersey eyeing her husband was no exception.

"Is he not a beauty?" Titus stood on the bottom rung of their board fence and admired the sleek, fawn-colored animal that the *Englisch* dairy farmer had delivered in his livestock truck. "He'll make many strong calves. Dairy farmers from all over the county will be lining up to pay me for his stud services. His granddam sold for eighty-five thousand dollars at public auction."

"Very impressive." Hope wished Titus had chosen a different way to add to their income. "How much did he cost?"

Titus ignored her question. "His granddam was judged All-American Grand Champion. Owning this bull assures us of a prosperous future."

The animal snorted, pawed the earth, and stared at Titus.

"I think he wants to eat you first." Hope gripped the hands of five-year-old Carrie and four-year-old Adam to keep them far away from the fence. "How much did he cost?"

Titus laughed and jumped backward off the fence. He was as agile as a young buck. Then he picked up Carrie, grabbed Hope about the waist, and whirled her around in a forbidden dance, giving her a quick kiss before he released her. Little Adam looked on, grinning at his father's foolish behavior. Titus could act quite *naddish* sometimes.

"This bull will help us buy a real farm instead of these two acres we're renting. We will build a wonderful herd of cows. In a few years we'll have one of the most prosperous dairy farms in Holmes County."

"Lord willing," Hope amended.

"True," Titus said. "Lord willing."

She adjusted her prayer *Kapp*, which had gone awry from Titus whirling her around. He had always been more openly affectionate than most Old Order Amish and she was not sure what to do about it. She enjoyed being loved by her husband, but his delight in her was sometimes embarrassing.

Now, however, they were in their backyard, a private place, assuming their *Englisch* neighbor, Mr. Lemon, wasn't looking out his window. The man did seem to spend an inordinate amount of time watching their comings and goings. She supposed it was because they were his first Amish neighbors. People did seem to stare.

Or Mr. Lemon might simply be lonely. They'd only just recently rented this place and hadn't gotten settled in with neighbors yet. It had belonged to an *Englisch* couple who had gotten too old to be left on their own. Their son, who lived in Cleveland, was renting it to them. He'd already sold off all the land except for the two acres that included the house and the small barn.

She and Titus had disconnected the electricity and brought in a generator. All this was apparently fascinating to Mr. Lemon, who watched from his back porch—much like her people bird-watched.

"Be careful!" She glanced over her shoulder, worried. "Mr. Lemon might be watching."

Titus smiled and laid a hand on her barely swelling stomach.

"With another babe on the way, Mr. Lemon might guess that your husband finds you irresistible." He nuzzled Carrie's creamy neck with his beard, making the little girl giggle.

"I am a blessed man," he said. "It is no small thing to have a fine wife, two healthy children, another on the way, and a strong new bull in my pasture."

Hope once again glanced at the animal. It had been shorn of its horns, but its massive neck and shoulders rippled with power. It was large for a Jersey. She guessed it to be nearing eighteen hundred pounds. Only a board fence separated them from all that simmering power.

"I do not like the looks of that animal," she said. "He has a wildness in his eyes that worries me."

"All bulls have wildness in their eyes," he scoffed. "You can't expect a bull to have eyes like a kitten."

"I suppose not." She hesitated, then asked, "How much did it cost?"

Yet again, her husband ignored her question. Whatever it had cost, she wished he had not purchased it. The feeling she got from the bull was malevolent in the extreme. She could almost feel its black thoughts focusing on Titus, and that frightened her. It was clear to her that the animal hated him.

"He's turning his side to you," she warned.

"And what does that matter?"

"My father taught me that bulls do that right before they attack."

"Why?"

"To let you admire how big and powerful they are."

"Oh, Hope." He laughed. "I respect your father's knowledge of livestock, but how could he possibly know—"

The bull charged.

Titus turned pale, and stood rooted to the spot with Carrie

in his arms. Hope screamed as the bull hit the top board with its massive head and bounced back, then shook the pain away and charged again.

"Oak." Titus was visibly shaken. "Good, solid oak. It'll hold."

"Hold or not"—Hope grabbed Carrie out of his arms and strode toward the house, pulling Adam behind her—"I want you to call the man you bought him from and sell him back."

"He won't let me sell him back," Titus called. "He gave me too good of a deal."

"How good of a deal? What did you pay for that animal, Titus?" Once she'd deposited the children inside the house, she came back onto the porch and stood her ground. She was not going to stop asking until he told her.

Titus's eyes did not quite meet hers. "Ten thousand dollars."

The amount took her breath away. It was every dime they had to their name! It had taken her six frugal years to save that much.

"Then sell at a loss." Hope's teeth were practically chattering from fear. Jersey cows were known for their gentleness, but Jersey bulls could be crazy mean, and this one was off the charts. She would never have agreed to the purchase if Titus had told her what he was intending.

"Please, Titus. Get rid of that animal. I'm begging you."

"He'll settle down. Eventually. You'll see."

"Titus . . ."

"I will *not* try to sell him back to the man I bargained with. I looked that animal over good before I bought him. For me to say that I want to change my mind because my wife told me to . . . well, I'd be a laughingstock."

"Better a laughingstock than injured or killed."

"Silence!" His voice grew stern. "I do not want to hear another word."

Titus was an easygoing, loving man, but he *was* a man and the head of their home. Therefore the final decision about the bull was his. He'd heard her protests, and chose to ignore them. There would be no more protests allowed. She swallowed her fear and her anger and went inside.

It was time to be an obedient wife, no matter how loudly her mind screamed that Titus had made a terrible mistake.

It was so frustrating. For as long as she could remember, she had enjoyed outdoor farmwork more than the domestic chores inside. Oh, she was competent enough in housework, sewing, and cooking. Her mother, Rose, had seen to it, but it was the running of a farm that fascinated her. It always had.

There was an age gap between her, the eldest, and her two younger brothers and two sisters. Because of that, she'd gotten to spend more time than most with her father as he worked his land and cared for their animals. He had often commented about what a wonderful farmer she would make . . . if she were a man.

If she were a man, Titus would have listened to her. Because she was a woman, her kind and loving husband frequently dismissed her advice. It was not fair, but she had learned to accept it. Like so much that her people did and believed, it simply was the way things were and always would be.

It was difficult to do her housework, though, knowing that Titus was outside going about his chores with that animal watching him. She kept glancing out the window, nervous as a cat, checking, wishing Titus would come inside where it was safe.

The window over the sink overlooked the farmyard. From there she could see the barn, the pasture, the chicken coop, and even the lean-to in which they kept the family buggy.

She could also see the bull, and he was still upset. At the moment, he was on his front knees pounding his head into the ground in anger. She'd seen other bulls do that and it always frightened her. One local farmer had been crippled when he tried to run away from a charging bull. He tripped, fell, and was nearly pounded to death.

She gave Carrie and Adam their Saturday-night baths, tucked them into bed, and had just set the supper dishes in the sink when she saw Titus entering the small pasture with a rope in his hand. She did not know why he felt the need to go in there, especially while the bull was still riled up, but she knew it was a mistake. A fatal mistake.

From her kitchen window, she screamed a useless warning as that thundering, flesh-and-blood locomotive tore across their small pasture, straight at Titus.

She went running out the back door just as it knocked him over and began to pummel him with its massive head. Titus was not a large man. He looked like a rag doll to her as she leaped off the porch. Then she heard a gunshot.

Mr. Lemon shot the bull again and again, trying to keep it from further savaging her husband's crumpled body.

"Cardboard characters. Predictable plot. Drivel disguised as dialogue. I expected better from a Nate Scott novel."

Logan Parker, aka "Nate Scott," gulped down his shock and dropped the *New York Times* onto the floor. The review felt like a sucker punch. He had gotten a handful of bad reviews in the past, but like most authors, he had trained himself to ignore them. The enjoyment of books was a subjective thing. People had different tastes. What one enjoyed, another person might hate.

Ignoring reviews was part of his job. If his self-esteem rose and fell on the basis of a good or bad review, he would never have been able to write the past twenty-three novels, nine of which had risen to *New York Times* bestseller status.

This last one had netted him an advance that was more than some people made in a lifetime. "Nate Scott" was a name publishers were willing to bet big money on, so why did this one review hit him so hard?

Perhaps it was because this particular reviewer was a friend and someone whose opinion he respected. More likely, it was because it verified what he already suspected. The characters of his latest novel *were* cardboard. The plot *was* predictable. The dialogue *was* drivel.

He rose from his chair and paced the floor. He wanted a drink. After that review, he *needed* a drink. Unfortunately, it was only eight o'clock in the morning and his personal discipline involved having nothing stronger than coffee until noon. As long as he could wait until noon, he felt like he was still in control of his need for alcohol.

He sat back down, picked up the newspaper, and read the review again. It still stung. Deep down, he'd known his writing was tanking and this confirmed it. Somewhere along the way, he'd lost something critical to his writing and he did not know how to get it back.

There was a bit of magic involved in writing well, a sort of self-hypnosis that a good fiction writer fell into when the "movie" began to play in his head—that moment when his fingers could hardly keep up with the plot and dialogue. There was an addictive being-in-the-zone feeling that beckoned him to his home office every morning.

Or at least it used to. These past two books were dogs. He had hated the process of writing them. Which was lethal to a career.

He rose again and opened the door to his personal liquor cabinet. A small shot of whiskey might help take some of the edge off the gnawing feeling that at the ripe old age of thirty-four, he was a has-been.

Noon, he told himself firmly and shut the cabinet door. In his mind, if he could just wait until noon to take his first drink, he would continue to prove to himself that he wasn't a drunk. He locked the cabinet against himself, put the key in his pocket, and tried to forget that the key was there. In his earlier days as a writer, after his young wife, Ariela, died, he had not needed alcohol to deaden the pain. Instead, he quit his job as a journalist, and holed up in their small apartment, writing obsessively out of the darkness of his soul in order to hang on to his sanity. He was as shocked as anyone when his bleak, psychological thrillers began to sell . . . and sell well.

Now he was locked into a genre he was sick of, but he was making entirely too much money to quit. He continued to limp along, putting words on paper, hoping no one would notice that he had lost interest in something that had once been his passion.

It was then that he had fallen back upon the hack writer's crutch. He was drinking heavily and his fiancée, Marla, kept riding him about it.

"What are you still doing back here, Logan?" Marla entered his office sanctuary and proceeded to open the wooden blinds, allowing sunlight to stream in. She was always doing that, and Logan hated it. He squinted, a little hungover from the night before, shielding his eyes from the bright light with his hand.

"You have that meeting this morning," she said. "And I have to get to work."

Brunch with his agent. He'd forgotten. What a jolly meeting *that* was going to be after this morning's review! His agent tended to be a little on the morose side even when things were going well. He was also a teetotaler, which Logan had recently begun to find annoying.

"You're going in on a Saturday?"

"Saturday is the only time this client can meet with me," she said. "Don't worry, I'll be back early."

The open blinds revealed a view of Central Park that would make even the most jaded Realtor salivate. He had worked hard for this view. It now occurred to him how little he enjoyed it.

"Did you take your meds this morning?" Marla stopped fussing with the blinds and studied him, her head tilted to one side.

The question bothered him. Marla was very big on medication. She had a doctor who, from what Logan could see, happily prescribed a pill for anything—real or imagined. She had recently talked him into taking an antidepressant because she said he had been acting more "down" lately than usual.

Well, she was right. He was down. Very down.

Perhaps that was why there were a *lot* of bad people in his novels. He had found the act of thinking up new ways to kill them quite therapeutic.

"Yes," he grumped, "I took my meds."

"Good," Marla said, brightly. "So did I."

That would be the weight loss pills that Dr. Have-Prescription-Pad-Will-Travel had given her recently. He really didn't think weight loss pills were healthy for Marla. Sometimes he secretly compared her to one of those plants that thrive on air alone. Marla did not cook, nor did she eat more than a few bites of food a day.

On the other hand, she managed to hold up her end of the interior design firm where she was angling to become a partner. She believed that she needed to be thin to be taken seriously in her field.

She had recently set a wedding date for next October. He did not remember proposing to her, but for all he knew, he might have done so one drunken evening. He'd been losing his memory recently, which was a worry.

He was grateful for Marla. She was beautiful, competent, and cheerfully took care of the details of their life, freeing him to concentrate on his books. She had also been his wife's room-mate and closest friend when they were all in college together. Ariela had majored in political science. He was set, at that time, on becoming an investigative journalist. Marla had been the artistic one of the three. She had redone her and Ariela's dorm room to the point that other students began to rely on her style and creativity. The three of them had joked about how Ariela was going to change the world, he was going to write about it, and Marla was going to make everything pretty.

Marla had mourned with him during the darkest days of his grief. Becoming a couple and living as a couple had evolved slowly over a period of several years. It might not be a grand passion, but Marla was a comforting presence in his life and he appreciated her.

What he did not understand was why she bothered with him at all. Living with a writer was no fun, especially during deadlines. He felt lucky that someone as attractive and intelli-gent as Marla cared enough about him even to stick around, let alone be willing to marry him.

He wished they could spend more time together, but Marla was climbing the very slippery slope of becoming a well-known interior designer in New York City, and he was trying to hang on to his slot as a bestselling author.

Hanging on that slot was assuredly not easy. There were many hungry young writers snapping at his heels. It was fright-ening to wonder if he would have to retire before he was forty because he was already used up. What on earth would he do with himself if he could never write well again?

He sat, sunk in his own misery, while he watched Marla flit around his office, straightening up and moving decorative items a fraction of an inch here or there. Ever since she started taking those weight loss pills she seldom sat still. Of course, she also had a big hand in decorating his office, and she did not want the effect spoiled by his tendency to scatter notecards, pens, and piles of research books about.

He ran a hand over his unshaven face. Being around Marla always made him feel a little grungy. An early Saturday morning and she was already in full makeup and heels. Her hair was done in an elaborately disheveled bun. Her skirt was so tight it looked uncomfortable, but he knew she didn't think twice about comfort if it meant looking good. For lunch, she would purchase a bagel with cream cheese from a street vendor, take two bites, and drop the rest in the nearest trash can. He'd seen her do it dozens of times. It worked well for her. Marla was a head-turner. Every man he knew envied him.

Speaking of food, he needed coffee.

He wandered into the kitchen and grabbed a jar of instant Nescafé. The shiny, new latte machine was too complicated for him to manage this early in the morning. He tended to need a cup of coffee before he was alert enough to *make* coffee.

"By the way . . ." Marla's high heels clicked smartly on the tile floor as she walked into the kitchen, where she plucked the instant coffee out of his hand and put it back in the cupboard. "I have to go to Ohio this week."

"Ohio?" This got his attention. The Midwest wasn't exactly Marla's cup of tea . . . or his. "Why on earth would you want to go there?"

With relief, he saw that she had switched on the coffee machine monster and was preparing to make him a cup of hightest. He sat down at the table and waited expectantly.

"A client is insisting on Amish-made goods only. Apparently she's addicted to those Amish romance novels everyone is reading these days. My boss decided one of us should go to the source. Apparently there are Amish furniture factories in Ohio. She thinks it might save us several thousand to deal directly with them."

"And you drew the short straw?"

"Yes, I did. Do you want to come with me?"

"To Ohio?" He grimaced. "Not particularly."

"By the way, I was up early this morning and I read the review." She sprayed something on a cloth and started polishing the counter. "I know why you are in such a foul mood. It might do you good to get away for a few days."

He took a sip of black ambrosia. Ohio was the last place on earth he wanted to go.

"No."

"But I don't want to go alone," Marla said. "My birthday is coming up next week. You could consider it an early present. You won't have to get me another thing."

"Promise?" he asked.

"I promise. Just come with me. That will be present enough."

He considered the offer. Driving her to Ohio seemed like a small price to pay to avoid having to shop for a gift. He hated wandering around department stores trying to find something she'd like. "Sure," he said, staring into his coffee cup. "Why not? When do you want to leave?"

chapter TWO

Like most wives, Hope Schrock had wondered what it would feel like if she ever had to bury her husband. Would she be stoic and strong, or would she fall apart?

Being Amish, she knew she would be expected to bow to God's will, but deep down, she could not imagine continuing to breathe without the man she loved. She expected to feel a blinding grief from which she would never fully recover.

Now that which she had feared had come to pass. Titus was gone. She was a widow, her children fatherless, but her mind was not reacting like it should.

The blinding grief had not hit. So far, all she felt was a wild and raging anger . . . at Titus. Oh, how she would love to give that man a good talking-to!

This made no earthly sense, but the fact remained—she could not will away the fury that smoldered in her breast. Oh, how badly she wanted to tell Titus that she was not a child or stupid. She had known what she was talking about when she begged him to sell that bull. If he had only listened!

Bishop Schrock, her father-in-law, walked through the door. She kept her eyes down, fearful that he would look into her heart and see the anger she felt toward his son. Her father-in-law had his own great grief to carry. He did not need to deal with her anger on top of his own sadness.

Titus had been such a happy-go-lucky person, especially for one with roots deep in the Amish faith. He always looked on the bright side of things. It was as though he thought nothing bad could ever happen to him or his family. It was probably that very optimism that killed him. Or his pride.

Yet again, she remembered how he had sent her back into the house when she begged him to send the bull back, and her anger welled up yet again.

This was not good with Bishop Schrock approaching her. He and his wife had always been kind to her, and the last thing she wanted was to hurt either of them.

"You know you are welcome to move in with us," he said. "Thelma and I have plenty of room. We would welcome having young ones beneath our roof again."

"Thank you." She twisted a handkerchief around and around a finger. "But I would like to stay in the house that Titus and I shared together. I am grateful for your offer, though."

It was the truth. She *was* grateful, but as kind as the Schrocks had always been to her, she did not want to live with them.

Little Adam tugged at her apron, wanting to go to the bathroom. At four, he was much too young to grasp the fact that they had just put his father in the ground.

Tears started in Hope's eyes when she thought about Titus, only four days earlier, sitting in the front yard, enjoying the sight of Adam playing with a toy tractor.

Her mother, Rose, caught the little boy up in her arms and took him out. Adam had been difficult to potty-train. Her mother knew it was critical to get him out of there before he had an accident.

A wave of morning sickness hit just as her twelve-year-old

sister asked if she could bring her something to eat. Hope shook her head and forced the bile down that was threatening to crawl up her throat.

What a mess you've left me in, Titus. I should be home right now with my feet propped up and you bringing me tea and crackers! Her mind skittered around as she wondered what to do about the future. A young *Englisch* widow would probably hire a babysitter and go searching for a job that would support her family. The fact that Hope was Amish severely narrowed her choices, even though she sometimes dreamed of what she would do if she were free to choose any career she wanted.

She had been smarter than Titus in school, quietly besting the whole class in every subject. Her math skills were excellent, as were her reading and writing. Her father, Henry, was an especially skilled farmer, and because of him, there was little she did not know about running a farm or caring for livestock. Deep down, she knew there was really only one career she had ever wanted—in her heart she took after her father, a farmer who loved growing things. Unfortunately, knowing how to run a productive farm was not going to be of any help to her. Except for the two acres they were renting, she had no land of her own, and there wasn't exactly a Help Wanted section in the local newspaper for Amish women wanting to work as fieldhands or farm managers.

Myron, one of the older teenage boys from their church, walked up and stood solemnly in front of her.

"Titus was a *gut* man." He held his black hat loosely in his big farm-boy hands. "Everyone liked him."

"*Ja*, he was well liked," she answered.

"I will care for your yard-mowing come summer," he said. "Do not worry about that."

She nodded her acceptance, unable to speak without choking up. These were her people. They did not ask what they could do . . . they simply did it. She knew that Myron would be as good as his word once the grass began to grow.

"Your husband is in a—a better place." Paul Troyer stumbled over the simple words. "He is . . . with Jesus now."

Poor Paul. She felt sorry for him. Only a month ago he had nearly fainted when he'd opened the hymnal he had selected by lot and found the paper telling him that he had been chosen to be their next minister. Such a heavy burden on his shoulders for the rest of his life. Ah, well, the Lord knew best.

Hope tried to concentrate and take comfort from the words that were being said by the various people who spoke to her, giving condolences. Everyone in the church knew and cared about her circumstances. Her children would not go hungry. The church's alms would give her some measure of cushion while she tried to figure out what to do.

From across the room, she saw one man eyeing her, and she wished he would stop. Abimelech Yoder was recently widowed and was openly searching for a new wife to finish raising his children. She would never be desperate enough to move into Abimelech's house. He was at least fifteen years older than she was. Besides, she never cared for the man and always pitied his overworked wife.

Adam and her mother came back and the child sat more patiently now that he had gotten his trip to the bathroom. Carrie was being allowed to play dolls quietly in the corner with some older girls who were being kind to her.

"Where is Daddy?" Adam tugged on her sleeve and asked the heart-wrenching question in German, which at his age was the only language he knew.

"*Daed* got hurt," Hope whispered back. "He will not be with us anymore."

Adam looked at her with innocent blue eyes.

"Does Daddy need a Band-Aid?"

The question broke her heart anew. There was simply no way that this sweet child could understand what had happened, and he shouldn't have to. Titus had been strong, young, and brave. He should be out mowing hay right now instead of lying in the ground.

Oh, she was so angry!

How were her children supposed to deal with such loss? Apparently, Adam intended to deal with it by resurrecting the thumb sucking he'd put away for nearly three years.

They were quite the bruised family, they were.

She was aware that the Lord did not promise anyone a trouble-free life. With a history of ancestors martyred for their beliefs, she did not come from people who expected an easy path.

So why was she bothering to question the pain she felt?

Once, she had overheard an older woman say that truly deep faith was forged on the anvil of misfortune and tragedy. Hope did not want to believe this. She did not want to possess a deep faith if this was the price one had to pay. Shallow was good. All she wanted was a happy life with her family intact.

In the back of her underwear drawer, in a jelly jar, she had accumulated fifty-three dollars and ninety-two cents. She knew the exact amount because she had counted it only last night. It was money she had been saving to purchase new work boots for Titus for Christmas.

How did a woman raise two children on fifty-three dollars and ninety-two cents? It wouldn't last a week.

Bishop Schrock and Thelma would help all they could, but she did not want to live off them and the church indefinitely. In the past, her parents could have helped, but they had their own problems these days. Her father had lost the fine farm he had inherited, by developing a weakness for gambling.

Lord, you are going to have to take care of us. I cannot do it.

She waited for a feeling of security and faith to fill her heart, but it did not come. Instead, her mind ran around again like a small rodent searching for food. Fifty-three dollars and ninety-two cents. Adam needed shoes and so did she. How would she pay the five hundred dollars' rent on their home? What if their horse needed the vet? Or her cow? How would she pay for propane to heat the house? How would she pay for kerosene to light their nights?

"You are young and a hard worker." Missy Bylar smiled and patted Hope's hand. "You will soon find someone else."

Hope flushed at Missy's words. Titus had been in the ground less than an hour and this woman was talking about finding someone else? As though Titus were some sort of pet dog she needed to replace? She bowed her head, unable to speak without making a sharp retort. Missy, her duty to speak to the grieving widow accomplished, excused herself and went to fill her plate with funeral food.

Hope didn't care much for Missy. The woman always seemed so self-satisfied with her wealthy husband, huge, comfortable house, and her six children, whom she cared for with the frequent help of two hired girls from their church.

It was rumored that Missy and her husband even kept an *Englisch* driver on retainer to take them wherever they wanted to go whenever they wanted to go there. The only time she ever saw them in a buggy these days was when Hans drove the family to church.

Missy's husband had inherited a thriving Amish furniture store and managed it well. With the massive influx of *Englisch* tourists into Holmes County in recent years, they had become quite prosperous.

Hope tried to be charitable, but she wondered if Missy would be quite as cheery if all she had in her underwear drawer was fifty-three dollars and ninety-two cents.

The table spread in the front room had a generous supply of casseroles, noodle dishes, and cooked meats and vegetables. The people carried on a low conversational buzz that to Hope's anguished ears sounded a great deal like the buzz of flies. Every now and then, the buzz was punctuated with a laugh.

How could they laugh when her world had fallen apart?

An elderly *Englisch* woman took the empty seat that Missy had vacated. Hope knew her slightly. She was Elizabeth Conners, the grandmother of the *Englisch* nurse that Levi, her first cousin, had regrettably left the church in order to marry.

"It's a lovely day for a funeral, don't you think?" Elizabeth said.

A lovely day for a funeral? What an odd thing for the old woman to say, even if she was *Englisch* and probably didn't know any better.

"The day we buried my husband was so rainy." Elizabeth seemed to be completely at ease chatting with her. "It was lightning and thundering, which matched the climate of my heart, but it made it awfully hard on the people who went with me to the cemetery." The old woman patted her hand. "You'll have to forgive everyone for talking and eating and laughing as though they are at a picnic. It is not *their* hearts that are breaking. If you'll notice, it's only the younger ones, who haven't yet experienced grief, who laugh. Those of us who have been in your shoes know better. How are you doing, dear?"

"I wanted him to return that crazy bull that killed him," Hope exclaimed. "But he refused."

Her words burst out so suddenly that even she was surprised. It was the first time she had said a disloyal word about Titus out loud. She glanced sideways at Elizabeth to see if she was shocked.

"Of course you were wiser about the danger than him,"

Elizabeth said. "Young women are almost always smarter about such things than young husbands."

It was comforting to have someone agree with her.

"I've actually given the subject some thought," Elizabeth continued. "I think perhaps healthy young men tend to feel immortal because they are so very physically strong. They do not know how quickly one can become helpless and vulnerable. It makes them act a little foolishly sometimes."

This made a bit of sense to Hope—at least, it made more sense to her than some of the platitudes quoted to her so far.

"If I were you," Elizabeth said, "I believe I might be wanting to give that young man of yours a good talking-to right about now, except for the inconvenient fact that he can no longer hear you. He has gone on to glory, leaving you to muck about here on earth without him. My guess is, you might be in need of a little help right now." Elizabeth reached into the pocket of her dress and brought out two bills and pressed them into Hope's hand. "For the children."

"I cannot take this," Hope said.

"It's a gift, dear." Elizabeth said. "From one widow to another. And if you ever feel like you need to have a good cry, come to my home and talk to me. I'm *Englisch* . . . and I don't count."

"There you are, Grandma!" Grace, her cousin Levi's *Englisch* wife, walked in. "Are you ready to leave?"

Grace had worn a simple, long dress to the funeral, and Hope appreciated her cousin-in-law's small sacrifice. The gossips said that Levi's wife was reputed to practically live in jeans and it was also reported that Levi strongly disapproved. Watching those two strong-headed people who came from such different lives try to keep a marriage together had provided a great deal of entertainment for the local Amish community. Many felt sorry for her aunt Claire, who was Levi's mother. Daughters-in-law were hard enough, but an Amish woman with an *Englisch* daughter-in-law was to be pitied.

"I'm ready." Elizabeth stood. "I've said what I wanted to say."

Grace held Lizzie, her baby girl, in her arms. Lizzie was about a year old. She had curly blond hair, and was sound asleep in the crook of Grace's arm, dressed in a darling pink dress. Hope liked Grace, but most of her people were surprised that Levi's marriage to the former *Englisch* military nurse had survived at all.

Grace bent over and whispered, "How far along are you?"

Hope was startled. Even her own mother did not yet know of her pregnancy. "Barely two months."

"Claire and I will be opening our home birthing clinic in another week. You can be our first client if you want."

"You and Aunt Claire are working together?"

"Yes, in Elizabeth's old house."

This information was so startling that it almost knocked all other thoughts out of her head. Grace smiled at her surprise. "You should come see us."

As the two women left, Hope opened her hand and saw that she was holding two one-hundred-dollar bills. She doubted that Elizabeth could afford this gesture, but she was grateful as she stuffed the money deep into the pocket of her dress.

Her mother put a gentle hand on her shoulder. "You must come and feed yourself."

"I am not hungry," Hope confessed. "I cannot swallow a bite."

"You don't have a choice." Her mother's voice, usually so kind, had a barb to it. "You are a mother. You will chew, swallow, and smile at your children while you do so. You must reassure them that even though they have lost a father, they have not lost a mother."

The tone of her mother's voice felt like a slap, but her words were wise, and Hope knew it. Her eyes filled with tears that she wiped away as she rose to try to find something she could keep down.

"You are right, *Maam*," she said, with respect. "I will be strong for my children."

chapter THREE

"So, what do you think?" Marla laid her hand on a cunningly crafted computer desk.

What he thought was that it seemed strange to find Amish-built furniture designed for TVs and computer desks. From what he understood, the Amish did not allow televisions or computers in their homes. How could they justify creating so much well-designed furniture for items that were forbidden?

Since Marla was going to be making such a large purchase, the furniture store owner went out of his way to show them around. To prove that his furniture was, indeed, completely Amish-made, the owner took them to the workshop in the back where bearded Amish men created the lovely pieces he sold.

Logan watched these somber craftsmen concentrating on their work, and he felt a small kinship. He put that much thought and intensity into his craft as well, making sure that every plot point dovetailed perfectly into the next. He always polished each manuscript until it shone—except, perhaps, for those last two.

It had been a bad year.

Off in a corner, however, was a young Amish man working on something different than the others. In front of him was a massive, old-fashioned chifforobe that he was polishing with a soft rag. Logan knew the instant Marla saw it because of her quick intake of breath.

"I have to have that!" she whispered.

The chifforobe was hand-polished cherry with carvings on the outside and multiple drawers of varying sizes within.

It was amusing to watch her try to talk to the creator of the piece. The young man mumbled monosyllabic answers and stared at the floor. Marla did not seem to realize that every man in that room was trying to avoid looking at her.

The short skirt, formfitting blouse, and four-inch heels were not the sort of outfit these men were used to. Marla was partial to bright red lipstick. With her pale skin and expertly made-up pale blue eyes, she would not soon be forgotten by these furniture makers.

The older men studiously stared at whatever piece they were working on. The younger men stole quick, surreptitious glances. One teenager stared openly at her, his mouth hanging slightly open. An older man quietly smacked the boy on the head, causing the boy to avert his eyes and reapply himself to his work. Logan could hear the collective sigh of relief when he and Marla left the workshop.

An hour later she had concluded her business with the owner and they drove around Holmes County to see the sights.

"Rolling farmland, lots of cows, horses and buggies," she said. "It's beautiful, and quaint, but I think I'd go nuts from sheer boredom after a while. I'm looking forward to going home."

"What?" he pretended to be surprised. "You don't like fresh air, rolling hills, and German cuisine?"

"I like the smell of New York," she said. "I like concrete. What on earth do people *do* here? I'd go stark raving mad inside of a month."

"You'd make Amish girlfriends. You'd learn to quilt and milk and raise vegetables." He couldn't help teasing her. Marla was a city girl through and through.

They were on their way to Holmes County Pottery, where Marla planned to purchase several hand-thrown pots her firm's client had requested, when Logan accidentally took the wrong fork in the road.

"Holmes County Pottery is the other way," Marla said, glancing at the map she had lying on her lap. "You took the right turn instead of the left back there."

"Sorry," he said. "I must have been daydreaming. For some reason I thought I was supposed to go down this road. I'll turn around as soon as I find a good spot."

One mile later, he had not only found a place to turn; he'd seen a house that looked so familiar, a small shock went through his body. A two-story farmhouse sitting atop a hill. It was plain, square, and white, but even though it was late fall, he had a vision of pink roses growing up one side. A grape arbor with two benches stood near, covered with denuded grapevines. The yard had a white fence that set it off from the surrounding pasture. A long lane wound up to the house with its large front porch. What appeared to be a small fruit orchard grew on one side.

It was not that special, at least not in Amish country, but he could not take his eyes off the place.

"Watch out!" Marla cried.

He jerked the car back onto the road, narrowly missing the ditch.

"What's wrong with you?" Her voice was shaking. "Have you been drinking again?"

He slowed to a crawl so that he could look without putting their lives at risk. "It's that house."

"What about it?"

"It seems strangely familiar. And no, I haven't been drinking."

"I thought you said you'd never been to Ohio."

"I haven't."

He drove past it slowly. One field over was another square, sturdy-looking house with a For Sale sign on it. He pulled into the driveway and sat looking at it. It, too, felt familiar. This made no sense. What was it about these two houses that made him wish he could go knock on the door?

There was nothing special about either of the houses, but even the lay of the land had a profound emotional effect on him.

At that moment, a middle-aged woman dressed in bib overalls and dirty Crocs came walking up the driveway and motioned for him to roll down his window, which he did.

"Can I help you people?" the woman asked.

"I'm sorry," he said. "We were just looking for a place to turn around and I stopped for a second to admire the house."

"It's a nice old home." She brushed some straw off her bibs. "I'm Verla Grayson, the Realtor in charge of this place. Sorry if I look like something the cat drug in, I was helping my husband birth a calf down at our place and just walked up to check on things. If you want to look around, I have some free time and a key."

He glanced at Marla, who had a bemused expression on her face. She was not used to seeing Realtors dressed in bib overalls.

"Do you mind going in?" he asked her.

"I don't see the point." Marla checked her watch. "But we do have some time left before the pottery store closes."

He was grateful. Marla could be quite gracious when she tried, but he already knew that the Realtor would be a highlight of Marla's next luncheon with her girlfriends. She was not a cruel person, but she loved to make people laugh, and was probably already figuring out exactly how she would tell this story for its greatest effect. He was fairly certain the whiff of cow manure emanating from Verla would figure prominently in the recital.

"So, are you two kids in the market for a house?" Verla dug a key out of the side pocket of her bibs.

Logan wondered what he should say. That the house had practically called his name from the road? That he felt like he had a connection to it even though he'd never set foot in Ohio before? It sounded too weird, even to him, who made a living by making up stories.

"Up until a few minutes ago, I had no idea we were looking for a house," Marla said. "But I guess I was wrong."

He stood on the front porch gazing around while Verla unlocked the door. The familiarity of everything was striking. He felt as though he had spent time right here on this porch. Except he hadn't. There was no way he could have.

"Oh, come look, dear," Marla called. "A huge kitchen. I would be able to do all my cooking and canning in here."

"Of course."

There wasn't a whole lot else he could say. Marla did not cook, and she didn't have the faintest idea how to can. Her expertise with their coffeemaker and microwave was as far as it went. If a man wanted to be with Marla, he needed to be prepared to spend lots of time in restaurants.

He felt mildly dizzy from the strange familiarity of the house and grasped the railing tightly as he followed the women up the stairs.

"Five bedrooms!" Marla exclaimed, still playing the happy homemaker. "Just think, Logan, each of our children can have a room to themselves and one left over for a nursery."

Verla beamed. "You have three children *and* you're expecting?"

Marla smiled modestly and laid a hand on her flat stomach. "I'm due in seven months."

Logan didn't know whether he wanted to laugh or shake her. When Marla got in a certain mood, she sometimes didn't know when to stop.

He followed the two women into one of the upstairs bedrooms. Verla, encouraged by what she interpreted as Marla's enthusiasm, became quite excited.

"Just look at this view!" she crowed, waving a hand with as much pride as if she'd created the countryside all by herself.

He looked, and was dumbfounded. This view, too, felt familiar. Very familiar. From here, he could see the other house that had made him nearly swerve off the road.

The feeling of déjà vu was so strong, it was nearly overwhelming. It made him wonder if he needed to talk to a psychiatrist when they got back to New York.

The rooms were empty of furniture, but one felt more familiar than any of the others—the smallest bedroom. He could have sworn that he had stared at that particular water stain on the high ceiling before.

The been-here-before feeling was not at all unpleasant. In fact, it was the exact opposite. He felt a peace here that he had not experienced in a very long time. He gave a huge, involuntary sigh as he felt the perpetual knot in his stomach relax. Perhaps his writer's muse was trying to tell him something.

"This would be a wonderful place to write," he said, wistfully.

At this, Verla turned her sales pitch up a notch. "Property in Holmes County just keeps climbing. Everyone wants to move here. With a few improvements, you could probably resell this place in a couple years at a nice profit, especially with the two hundred prime acres that come with it."

"How much?" he asked.

Marla shot him a surprised look.

Verla named a price. He did some quick calculations. He could afford it if he cashed in some stocks.

Of course, he wasn't serious about buying it. Not really. And yet the idea of living here did hold a certain attraction. "Would you like to own a house in the country, Marla?"

She smiled. "You're joking, right?"

"Not entirely."

"We need to talk," Marla said to the Realtor. "Could you give us a minute alone, please?"

"Of course." Verla left the small room, closing the door behind her.

"Have you lost your mind?" Marla asked. "This place doesn't even have *electricity*! It is a million miles from *anywhere*!"

She was absolutely right.

"I know." He shook off the longing to possess the house. "The idea is ridiculous. It's just that I'm in such a slump and for a moment there—just for a moment—I had this crazy thought that maybe this house could help me find my way out of it."

Hope lay in bed, staring out the window. Her two children were coloring quietly on the quilt beside her. They were good children, made more so by her strange mood. Every now and then, Carrie looked at her with worry written on her little face.

"Momma's okay," Hope soothed. "Just tired. Go ahead and color."

They weren't used to seeing her lying abed in her nightgown this late in the morning. They were used to her being up, the cow milked, and breakfast on the table. Sometimes she would have already put a line of clothes out to dry before they awoke.

"Mommy?" Carrie said. "Daisy-cow is crying."

"I know."

The truth was, she had been trying to ignore the sound of their old cow bawling for the past half hour. She simply couldn't face getting up, getting dressed, and going out to milk her.

"Mommy," Adam echoed his big sister, tugging at her sleeve. "Daisy . . ."

She pushed his little hand away. "*Nah schtopes!* Stop it!"

He recoiled and looked at her with startled eyes. His lower lip trembled and he crawled off the bed and ran into the kitchen. She could hear him sobbing and she hated herself for her momentary show of impatience.

With Adam crying and Carrie looking like she was about to start, plus her cow bawling to be milked, all she wanted was to give up. She wasn't ill, she was just so tired! Tears welled up in her own eyes. All she could think about was Titus and how desperately she missed him. The anger at him that had gotten her through the first days after his death had leaked away, leaving her as lifeless and limp as a busted balloon.

And then God sent an angel.

She heard the front door open and a familiar voice comforting Adam in the kitchen, then . . .

"*Vas ist letz?* What is wrong in this house?" Claire burst into Hope's bedroom with Adam in her arms, his face buried in her shoulder, and his shoulders shaking as he sobbed.

"*Musht hilve?* Do you need help? I bring an apple pie over, and find this baby upset, your cow in pain, and you still in bed."

"I didn't hear your buggy," Hope said.

"No wonder, with all the racket inside and out. Are you ill?"

"No."

"Then you are giving in to your grief. That will never do. You're stronger than this." Her aunt's gaze was sympathetic but her voice was no-nonsense. "You cannot let yourself give in to it. You know that, right?"

"I'm tired."

"I don't care." Claire's voice cracked like a buggy whip over her head. "You may *not* stay in bed, no matter how bad your heart aches. You *must* get up. You *must* take care of your home.

A mother *must* care for her children. It is the only way. You do *not* have a choice. You may *not* give into this. Get out of that bed right this instant!"

A strangled moan came from the barn. Daisy was in real pain.

"And to let a poor animal suffer like that!" Claire clucked her tongue. "That is not like you. I will go tend to Daisy. You get dressed. Do you hear me?"

"*Ja.*" Hope glanced away, thoroughly ashamed of herself. "I hear."

Claire sat Adam on the bed and held out her arms to comfort Carrie, who flew into them. The little girl's arms clung tightly to her great-aunt's neck as they left the room together.

"I'm sorry, Adam." Hope gathered him to her. He stopped crying the minute she started to rock him in her arms. With Claire milking Daisy in the barn, the cow stopped bawling, too.

Hope, however, was still in pain, trying to absorb the full sting of her aunt's anger, and yet who better to pass judgment? Claire had also been widowed. She had somehow risen above her grief and begun making a living as a midwife for her family. Now she was known far and wide for her skill. No Amish or Mennonite woman in the Mt. Hope area wanted to give birth without Claire at their side. If anyone had earned the right to criticize a woman lying abed from grief, it was Aunt Claire.

Hope obeyed her aunt. She rose and got dressed.

A half hour later, Claire came into the house and Hope heard her straining the milk. Then she heard her open and close the refrigerator, putting the fresh milk inside. A few seconds later she heard her washing out the milk pail and answering Carrie's chatty questions. Hope finished pinning her hair up, positioned her prayer *Kapp* on her head, and went out to face her.

"Are you feeling better?" Claire asked as Hope entered the kitchen.

"*Ja.*"

"Good!" Her aunt nodded approvingly and began slicing the pie she had brought. "Then perhaps you have an appetite?"

It was healing to have her aunt fuss over her. The pie was delicious.

"What are your plans for the day?" Claire asked.

"Plans?"

"Before I leave here, I want to know that you have plans to do something besides go back to bed. Maybe something you and the children could enjoy together?"

"Like what?" Hope couldn't think of one thing she wanted to do.

Claire paused in washing dishes and gave the question some thought. "It would probably do you good to get out of the house and into the sunshine. It's a lovely fall day. Perhaps a picnic?"

"A picnic." Hope felt no enthusiasm.

Claire dried her hands, cupped Hope's face in her palms, and looked deeply into her niece's eyes. "A picnic with your sweet *kinner* who are also grieving. You are strong. You can do this, *ja?*"

"*Ja.*"

Claire left after helping her gather together a few sandwiches and a thermos of cold milk. Hope grabbed a sweater, dressed the children in warmer clothes, hitched her horse to her buggy and loaded them in.

She *would* be strong for her children.

"Where do you want to go for our picnic?" she asked.

"Can we go play on the swing you had when you were a little girl?" Carrie asked.

The swing had hung from a sturdy, giant oak tree at her childhood home for as long as Hope could remember. Their family no longer possessed the old home where five generations of her family had lived, but it had come back on the market recently and Verla had told her it would be okay for them to visit while it was unoccupied.

It was also the last place Titus had taken them on a family outing, only days before his death.

Undecided, she held the reins of Copy Cat, the strong-willed horse with which Claire had recently gifted her.

"Please, Mommy?"

It was barely two weeks ago that the four of them were there. Titus had played with the children and made her laugh. She had told the children stories about growing up on the farm. How happy they had been together!

It would be painful to go back there so soon, remembering the family day they had enjoyed, but then, everything was painful these days. She turned Copy Cat's head toward the house her mother and father had once owned. The horse kept up a brisk trot in the early-November weather. The fresh air and sunshine did feel good. She felt her heart gaining courage as she made this small journey with her children.

No one would ever catch her lying abed and feeling sorry for herself again.

chapter FOUR

Logan could not get the Amish house out of his head. It was so much on his mind, he even brought it up during his business lunch.

"I don't get it." His agent, Harry Drummond, dabbed at his mouth with a napkin. "If all you want is a country retreat, there are plenty of farmhouses closer than Ohio."

"True." Logan drained his wineglass and refilled it from the bottle he'd ordered. "But this place felt . . . right."

"You actually think living there might help you write?" Harry was a small, wiry man with penetrating gray eyes that were famous for seeing through authors' excuses.

"I don't know," Logan said, "but it's worth a shot. I haven't been able to compose a decent paragraph in weeks."

"Then by all means buy it."

"Seriously?"

Harry leaned back and studied him. "Seriously."

"Why are you saying that?" Logan asked. "Even I don't think it's a good idea, and I'm the one who wants to live there . . . at least part of the time."

"I have some news that might impact your decision." Harry

quietly dropped a bomb. "Your publisher is debating whether to extend another contract to you."

Logan was flabbergasted. "I'm a bestseller . . ."

"Not anymore." The agent took a sip of water, the only beverage Logan had ever seen him drink. "Your last two are not earning out your advances. In this economy, even a large publisher can't afford to take a hit like that for long. If this next one is no better than the last two, I'm afraid you're going to find yourself writing advertising copy in a cubicle."

Harry's voice was quiet, but his words were so harsh, it felt like he was shouting.

"I've known you for a long time, Logan," Harry continued. "I helped you build a career. I watched you bury your grief over your wife's death beneath a layer of well-written books. You've been a writing machine, and an excellent one, but from what I can see, the writing machine is broken. You're burned out. I'm now watching a good writer bury himself in a bottle."

Fear clutched at Logan's heart. "I'm not an alcoholic."

"Maybe not." Harry glanced at the nearly empty wine bottle sitting between them. "But I'm convinced you're halfway there."

It was true, and Logan knew it.

"Here's a thought." Harry carefully folded his napkin and laid it on the table. "The brain is a lot like a computer. Sometimes it needs to reboot. I'm thinking that this longing you've developed for the Amish farmhouse might be your mind crying out for a rest. I find it interesting that you would be so drawn to a place where you won't have easy access to electricity or the internet."

Harry had a point. The feeling of peace that had overtaken him in that house was profound. Was it nothing more than his mind begging for rest?

"I suggest that you buy the place. Take a couple months completely off. Don't touch your computer. Read other people's books. Old books. Take some time to regroup."

Harry rose from the table. Lunch was apparently over, the meeting adjourned. His agent was a busy man.

"What about my deadline?"

"I'll talk them into pushing it back." Harry pulled a sizable tip from his billfold and tossed it on the table. "Who knows? If this works out for you, I might send my other stressed-out clients over there. Perhaps I'll take a sabbatical and visit you."

"You have New York City in your veins." Logan smiled. "You would hate it in Holmes County."

"I don't know about that." Harry did not smile in return. "I get tired of the rat race, too. Going completely off the grid for a while sounds pretty good to me. Give it a try. Let me know how it goes. And it would be wise to get yourself dried out while you're at it."

As Logan watched the dapper little man walk away, he felt a sense of desperation. Harry was a polite, mild-mannered man, but he was *not* a friend to his clients. He could make or break a career, and he did not bother with authors who did not produce. A quietly spoken suggestion from Harry was as good as an ultimatum.

He had been warned. If Harry Drummond dropped him as a client, the whole publishing world would be watching and taking notes.

"I thought we were finished with this," Marla said. "You're not a farmer, Logan. You've never even had to mow a yard. What are you going to do with two hundred acres of Ohio farmland?"

"It isn't about the farmland. It's about my career. Harry

thinks buying the place as a sort of writer's retreat might help me get back on my feet."

"You have a nice office here . . ."

"Marla, I've paced the floor, stared out the window, walked around Manhattan, and written two of the worst books of my career here. I'm burned out, and I'm drinking too much. Something needs to change. I think going there for a while might help."

"Couldn't you just rent a room somewhere? Or stay in a hotel?"

"I could, but I don't want to." He struggled to explain without hurting her feelings. "I felt a peace in that house that I haven't felt before. It's hard to describe, and even harder for me to understand, but the déjà vu I felt there was nearly overwhelming. It was as though the very house itself was trying to welcome me. The second I walked in . . . I felt as though I had come home. I've not had that anywhere I've ever lived. I want to see if I can hang on to that feeling long enough to start writing well again."

In spite of his attempts to explain, she took it personally.

"Is it me?" she asked. "Am I the problem?"

"No, honey. It isn't you. I'm the one who's the mess."

"But it's such a huge step. I mean, buying a house?"

"Which we can sell at a profit in a couple years," he said. "It might or might not help me salvage my career, but you heard what Verla said. Property values are steadily going up in that area. Buying a house in Amish country isn't exactly a bad investment."

"Logan . . ." Marla's voice became soft and careful, as though addressing an invalid. "I have the name of an excellent psychiatrist . . ."

"I promise you," he said, "if this doesn't work, you can hook me up with any shrink you want."

"If you have to do this, I'll try to understand, but"—Marla took his hand in hers—"I'll miss you terribly."

"You'll come visit on the weekends, or I'll come here. A lot of couples have long-distance relationships."

"And a lot of couples break up because of it."

"And a lot of couples break up who are together constantly. Creatively, I'm dead in the water right now, Marla. If I can't get past this slump, or writer's block, or whatever it is, you aren't going to want to be around me anyway."

"You really think this will help?" she asked.

"I have no idea," he said. "But I have to try something. I can't just keep doing what I'm doing."

"Living with a writer is such an emotional roller coaster." She heaved a sigh. "You're up, you're down, you're sideways. Really, Logan. Some days you act like you're the worst writer in the world, then there's an award or a great review, and you think you're God's gift to literature. Then, about half the time we're together, you act like you're in another world."

"Half the time I *am* in another world . . . the one that I'm making up."

"Well . . ." She smiled. "At least you're seldom boring."

"So, I can call Verla?" he asked.

"How long do you expect to stay?"

"Harry said he'd push my deadline back a couple months, which gives me eight months before it's due. I'll work on getting the house fixed up, and after I'm finished with the book, we can spend long weekends there together from time to time. Maybe Verla could help us rent it out during tourist season. Who knows?" he teased. "Maybe you'll fall in love with the place and want to move there and run a bed-and-breakfast."

"A bed-and-breakfast? Me? Now I know you're delusional."

He grinned. "I'll admit, there's a downside to running a B&B. I suppose people actually expect you to cook them breakfast."

"I'll agree to this purchase under one condition," she said.
"What's that?"

"Promise me you won't drink while you're there."

He hesitated. Could he promise such a thing?

"I'll do my best."

"Your best isn't good enough. I know you keep your promises. Promise me that and I'll agree to the house."

He took a deep breath. "I promise."

She handed him the phone. "Now you can call Verla."

"Is Deborah Parker in?" he asked.

The receptionist was young, new, and wearing what some people called a "power suit." She regarded him with open suspicion. Probably a prelaw student working her way through college. That tended to be this law firm's preference. "Do you have an appointment, sir?" The tone of her voice suggested that she was not at all pleased with his presence.

"No, but if she's not with a client, she'll see me."

She frowned. "Ms. Parker is working on an important case and asked not to be disturbed."

"Trust me." He bit back a grin. "It's okay to disturb her. Just tell her Logan's here."

She cocked an eyebrow "Do you have a last name, sir?"

"Yes I do. It's Parker."

"As in . . . ?"

"I'm her son."

"Oh!" The girl scrambled to announce his presence. Within seconds he was seated across the desk from his mom.

His mother had long ago lost the need to wear anything remotely resembling a power suit. Deborah Parker, attorney-at-law, had built such a reputation of brilliant and ethical work over the years that she could get by with wearing pretty much anything and no one ever complained. Today it was a long, flowing skirt, flats, and a loose-fitting pastel blouse. A beaded necklace made by the young daughter of one of her good friends was her only decoration. Her blond hair was short and sticking up today because she had a tendency to run her fingers through it when she was concentrating. She looked cool and comfortable and he felt an intense pride in her and what she had accomplished as a single mother.

"Who's the new watchdog?" he said. "Seems devoted to her work."

"Isn't she ferocious?" his mother agreed. "Give that girl a few years and I'll be trying cases against her . . . and losing."

"You? Lose a case?" he said. "I doubt it."

She chuckled. "It has been known to happen."

"Rarely."

"True." She stood and adjusted the window blinds to keep the sun out of his eyes. "There. That's better."

His mother was reputed to be the best criminal lawyer in the city. It was his opinion that she was also the best in the state. She had a razor-sharp mind and the tenacity of a pit bull.

"I came to get you caught up on my plans," he said. "I'm driving back to Ohio tomorrow to buy that house I told you about."

She was jotting something on her desk calendar as he said that. He saw her hands still and a fleeting look of pain cross her face. "You're sure about this?"

He told her about his conversation with his agent.

"I'm sorry you're having such a struggle, Son," she said. "But if this is what you need, I hope it turns out well."

"Will you come visit?" he said. "It might be good for you to get away, too."

"I—I can't promise anything." She averted her eyes.

"Is something wrong, Mom?"

"Nothing I can't deal with." To prove it, she turned on her megawatt smile.

He felt uneasy, but didn't press. His mother would tell him if something was wrong . . . or she wouldn't. Prying never did any good with her.

"The place has five bedrooms. I'll make sure one of them is yours."

"Thank you, dear," she said. "You can buy a lovely Amish quilt for my bed."

chapter FIVE

Logan fit the old-fashioned key into the front door and turned the lock. The door swung open and he stepped into the bare living room. *His* bare living room. The house seemed to quietly welcome him just like before.

He laid the new deed on the mantel and wandered into the kitchen, hands in his pockets, probing his heart to see if that feeling of peace he'd experienced the first time he'd entered the house was still there, and it was.

He closed his eyes and took a deep breath. Even the scent of the old house seemed familiar. He got the sense of hundreds of family meals eaten in this kitchen, of heads bowed, hands clasped. For a moment, he could almost hear the echoes of children's voices from the past.

When he was a little boy, his mother had taken him to mass once a week at St. Patrick's Cathedral in Manhattan. They always stayed in the back, and he always sat beside her on the pew while she prayed. She was not Catholic, and she didn't go to confession, but she told him that sitting quietly inside that beautiful church for a while was enough to get her through the week.

He had asked her once what she prayed for. She smiled, ruffled his hair, and told him that she prayed for him . . . and for forgiveness. As a child, he could not imagine anything his sweet mother might have done that could possibly need to be forgiven. As a teenager, he decided that she probably felt guilty for having given birth to him out of wedlock. As an adult, he saw a woman who smoked too much, worked too hard, was frequently impatient with people who wasted her time, but who would fight ferociously for her clients . . . or for him. He clearly saw her flaws, but he loved her. They could talk about practically anything. No subject was taboo, except his father. He was no closer to learning the man's name than he had ever been. He had given up trying to pry it out of her.

It had been many years since he'd gone to St. Patrick's, but she continued to go weekly. He had once asked her why she went when she wasn't even Catholic.

"There are places on earth that feel holier than others," she had said. "Some people feel inspired by the Grand Canyon, or in a great redwood forest, or standing beside the ocean. For me . . . it's right here in the middle of the city." She had glanced up. "These beautiful, soaring ceilings, these gorgeous stained-glass windows. The quiet. The candles. It feels holy to me, and healing."

Then she'd tucked her hand in the crook of his arm and they had walked out. She always stopped, held her head high, and breathed deeply when they emerged from the church. It was her way of preparing herself for another week of putting criminals behind bars, or keeping innocent people free.

He thought about that conversation now as he stood, alone in the echoing stillness of the old house. It, too, felt holy to him . . . and healing. It felt like he belonged here.

Coming here might not be the magic cure he needed to get over this emotional bump in the road that was keeping him from writing well, but it felt good to be here, and for now that was enough.

• • •

Over the next few days, he furnished his rooms with the solid Amish-made furniture he had admired on his first trip. Lehman's delivered a propane stove and refrigerator. Verla's husband showed him how to light the gaslights. He picked up utilitarian dishes and linens at Walmart.

Within a week, everything necessary to basic living was in place. Kerosene lamps on the tables; firewood bought cheaply from an Amish teenager who was selling it door-to-door from a horse-drawn wagon. The boy's name was Simon, a good-natured young man who stacked it neatly behind the house at no extra cost.

"I used to work for the man who lived here before you," Simon said while waiting in the kitchen for Logan to get the cash to pay him. "I helped him put up hay in the summers. He was a *gut* man."

Even after he was paid, Simon did not seem in a hurry to leave. Logan noticed him eyeing some day-old doughnuts left out on the table.

"Would you like some doughnuts?" he offered. "I'm afraid they're a little stale. I was planning to throw them out."

Simon fell upon them as though he had not eaten in days. Of course, teenage boys tended to get hungry easily, but still, he ate as though he was starved.

"Would you like some coffee?" Logan asked. "It's left over from this morning."

Simon nodded and took another huge bite of doughnut, practically swallowing it whole.

With no microwave, Logan heated the coffee up on the stove. It was boiling hot when he served it, but Simon slurped it down anyway. Then he stared longingly at the last two dough-nuts.

"Please," Logan said. "Help yourself. I don't plan to eat them."

He did not have to ask twice.

Slightly unnerved by the boy's hunger, he added an extra ten dollars to the small amount Simon had charged.

"For stacking it," he explained. "That wasn't part of the deal."

"But you fed me," Simon protested.

"That's okay." To his own surprise, he found himself adding, "If you get hungry again, you're welcome to come back."

"Thank you!"

In his opinion, Simon's gratitude was more heartfelt than a half dozen stale doughnuts warranted, but Logan liked the boy and hoped he'd stop by again.

He was finding it hard to live for even a week with nothing but isolation and silence. He had worked so hard for so long that it felt strange not to be sitting down at his computer every morning. It felt even stranger not to check email or fuel other social media outlets with his words. Marla had strictly forbidden him to even use his smartphone unless it was to contact her or his mother.

"Take time off," she had said. "Like Harry advised. Then knock 'em dead with this next book."

The problem, he was finding out, was he didn't know what to *do* with himself if he wasn't writing.

He had thrown himself into his career so totally and obsessively for so long that he had no hobbies and, although in possession of many acquaintances, he had virtually no close friends.

Logan cast about in his mind, trying to come up with something to occupy his time, and chose something so uncharacteristic that Marla would have been shocked. He decided his house needed to look more like a home and spent several more days doing little except roaming around the area shopping for things that were not at all necessary, but that he just *liked*.

He bought bright-colored hand-loomed throw rugs in craft stores in Berlin, and several huge, Amish-made baskets from a roadside stand, which he used as side tables. He bought peaceful landscape prints from a local photographer by the name of Doyle Yoder for his walls. At the pottery place he and Marla had visited, he bought a dozen hand-thrown pots. He stopped at a house advertising homemade quilts and looked through dozens sewn by an elderly Amish woman whose fingers, he noted, were knotted with arthritis. He wondered, as he purchased five of the finely made quilts, what it had cost her to make the tiny stitches.

Each item gave him a sense of satisfaction as he placed it in his house. He was no decorator, but he cherished the feeling of humanity with which he filled his home by purchasing things that local artisans had lovingly created.

The final touch involved combing antiques stores and rescuing dusty, forgotten books. Harry had suggested he read other people's books, old books. He liked that idea. Old books, instead of trying to keep up with the latest bestseller, the latest copy of *Publishers Weekly*, or yet another research book.

The windows he left bare, except for piling stacks and stacks of old books upon the sills. It seemed odd not to have Marla, with her interior design expertise, here to help him, but in a way he was grateful that he was getting to create an environment that was all his own. The things he purchased felt right for this old house, and right for him.

In this way, he acquainted himself more intimately with the countryside and its people. Even though it was a constant battle, he kept his promise to Marla and did not drink or keep any alcohol in his home. Instead, he discovered overgrown paths on his land and took long walks whenever the desire to drink threatened to overcome him. As he climbed the hills and explored the paths, he was astonished at how out of shape he had become. He also marveled that the very land itself seemed to welcome him—just as the old house had.

Today he was discovering that nearly all of Holmes County closed down on Sundays. The Amish restaurants, upon which he depended heavily for sustenance, were closed. Pretty much everything was closed. There was little to do on a Sunday in Amish country except to go to church, or visit with family and friends.

He had neither family nor friends living here, and he most certainly did not have a church.

Today he felt like a complete alien driving through the streets of Berlin, Ohio, with its shuttered windows and Closed signs on all the small businesses.

As he drove past one farm, he saw about forty black buggies parked outside in a pasture. Streaming from those buggies was a line of black-clad Amish men and women, along with many children. They were in family-type clusters, talking with one another as they walked together. He thought how close the friendships must be within this group of people who had probably gone to church together all their lives.

As he watched this, it hit him how terribly lonely he felt, and he suspected he had been lonely for a long time. As an only child, he had learned to keep the loneliness at bay by making up stories with which he kept himself entertained. As an adult he had continued to do so—and gotten paid for it.

His love for Ariela, and her love for him, had made the loneliness go away for a while. The day he met Ariela, he knew he had found his other half, the person who could fill all the empty spaces. With Marla—although he was grateful for her presence in his life—things were different.

He wished he had the right to stop, park, and walk into that barn with that group of people. Had Marla known what he was thinking, she would have laughed and texted her friends about the latest funny "Logan story." His fiancée seemed determined to present him to her friends as a rumpled, mildly attractive, absentminded writer. It had become a sort of shtick within her circle.

He slowed down as he passed the people going in to church. Then he turned around and pulled over at a wide place in the road. Just close enough that he could watch, far enough away not to be obtrusive.

In the distance, he saw a young woman with two children in tow. A little boy and girl. As she came closer, he saw a sadness in the woman's face that caught at his heart. His writer's mind wondered what tragedy might have happened to cause such sadness. There was no father within that small family group. Had he left her and the children? Had he died? Or was he simply at home ill? He felt a stab of empathy for the two children. There had been no father in his family group, either, when he and his mother had walked to church.

It occurred to him that the heroine in his latest novel, a psychiatrist who specialized in sociopathic behavior, needed to be made more multidimensional. Perhaps he should give her a deceased husband and two small children. That would ramp up the tension when her unhinged client turned into a midnight stalker. He grabbed his smartphone and recorded the idea before it could slip his mind. Perhaps he would give his heroine that innocent-but-sad expression the Amish woman wore. She drew even closer and he saw that she was quite beautiful in spite of wearing no makeup. Perhaps he would give the psychiatrist the same appearance. Could she have a devoutly religious background? He definitely didn't want any more reviews accusing him of writing "cardboard characters."

It was the first time he'd felt the tiniest spark of creativity in weeks, and it flickered out way too soon. His thoughts were interrupted by the buzz of his cell phone.

"So what are you doing today?" Marla said. "Playing cow chip bingo like I saw on TV?"

"Cow chip bingo?"

"It was on a program called *Amish Mafia*," she said. "Have you seen it?"

"I don't have a TV here, Marla," he said. "You know that."

"Sorry. I forgot. So, how *are* you doing over there in Amish land?"

"Fine."

"You're lying."

She knew him entirely too well. "You're right."

"That's what I was afraid of. Tell me what you've gotten accomplished so far."

Marla was a task-oriented person. He had discovered early on that if he didn't have a task, she would assign him one.

"I've pretty much finished putting the house together."

"Good for you!" The tone of her voice reminded him of a schoolteacher encouraging a kindergartner. "Have you done any writing?"

"Honestly? I've not written a word since I got here. I'm giving Harry's advice a shot for a while."

"I'm almost afraid to ask, but . . . how's the drinking?"

"I made you a promise, Marla, and I'm keeping it."

"Good boy!" Again with the encouraging teacher voice.

He appreciated her encouragement, but he felt a flicker of resentment. He was not a child.

"One of my friends asked me how you recharge your laptop and cell phone with no electricity? What should I tell her?"

"I'm not using my computer yet, but when I do, I'll charge it with my car battery."

She laughed. "I can just see you tromping outside in the rain some night when your laptop dies on you."

"Verla says that's how the Amish teenagers keep their cell phones charged, with a car battery."

"You are living among such interesting people."

"I think so," he said.

"I was joking."

"I wasn't."

After a few more comments, they hung up. There really wasn't much more to say. In-depth conversations were not a big part of their relationship.

chapter SIX

Logan awoke to the sound of a rooster crowing at the farm next door. He cracked open an eyelid. The sky was growing lighter, but it was barely dawn. This rude awakening, he had discovered, was going to happen every morning. He burrowed back down into his pillow, but the rooster was an insistent alarm clock that he could not shut off. He now knew from experience that he might as well give up.

A few minutes later, he was bundled in a sweater and jeans against the chill of an autumn morning, with a steaming cup of coffee in his hand, sitting on a porch rocker. The sound of the rooster was no longer an irritation, but part of the joyful cacophony of the world around him awakening.

The mist-covered, rolling farmland was a feast to his eyes, and the covered porch felt like the arms of a good friend enfolding him. He settled back and allowed the peace of the place to seep into the raw cracks of his soul.

There was no doubt about it, he loved it here.

The coiled spring that seemed to be so tightly wound inside him felt as though it were loosening a little more each day. He'd slowly begun to cut down on his depression medication and was feeling no ill effects. Although it was still a struggle, especially in the evenings, his desire for alcohol was diminishing with each day.

He had not experienced a feeling of peace this deep since before his wife had died.

Ariela would have loved it here, too.

He allowed the feeling of grief to linger only a moment before he gently put it aside. Ariela had been a generous person. She would want him to enjoy this lovely place with or without her.

It had been nearly a month, and he still had not overcome his inability to write again. It was the first true writer's block he had ever experienced, and it was brutal. His New York editor contacted him to inquire how the book was coming, and was not amused by the news that he had chosen to bury himself here. He had built his career within easy reach of everyone who was anyone in the publishing business. He also had built a reputation for meeting deadlines on time with quality work. As Harry had pointed out during their lunch together, he had been the perfect, uncomplaining, writing machine, churning out bestseller after bestseller, until the perfect writing machine had broken down.

Now he was desperate to fix that machine and didn't have a clue how to do it.

No writer's trick he knew would prime the pump, and he was starting to get scared.

"Thelma and I want to help." Bishop Schrock handed Hope an envelope filled with cash. He had stopped early in the morning on his way to work. She was glad that she had already milked the cow and hung out her wash. It would have been humiliating had he found her in the same shape that Claire had.

With reluctance, Hope accepted her father-in-law's gift.

"You are our daughter. You are raising our grandchildren,"

he said. "Neither we nor the church want you to be in want. There will be more money when you need it."

"I am very grateful," she said, "but I wish we did not have to take this."

"Don't worry right now about finances. You should concentrate on these children and keeping yourself strong and healthy so that you can care for them."

"Thank you, Bishop," she said.

It felt so strange to be on the receiving end. She and Titus had frequently given what they could for others. It was the Amish way, to share with those in need. They had been happy to help.

Now she was learning that having to be the taker was much, much harder for her than being the giver.

As willing as she knew her people were to help widows and orphans, the last thing she wanted was to live on alms from the church forever. She was young and healthy and a hard worker. From what she could see, she had two choices: either find a job fast, or marry someone who would support her. The last choice, in her opinion, was not an option. Unfortunately, there had been one inquiry along that line already, even though she had not yet needed to flip the calendar to a new month following Titus's death.

Abimelech Yoder, whom she had caught staring at her after Titus's funeral, had already brought up the possibility with her father. He was a decent enough man, she supposed, and obviously desperate to place a mother in that kitchen, but she did not love him. She would never love him.

The bishop had brought some brightly colored balloons, which he now blew up for Adam and Carrie. Then he said good-bye, leaving each of the children happily clutching a balloon.

After he left, she tucked the envelope of money away in her

underwear drawer, determined to make it last as long as possible. She fixed the children breakfast, then sat down at her desk, pulled out some plain three-by-five cards, and started making up little advertisements to put in some of the shops in Mt. Hope. She knew how to clean house, cook, and sew. She hoped there would be an *Englisch* woman willing to hire her for a few hours each week.

She did not know many *Englisch* women well, but she had heard that many of them were not particularly skilled in these areas, while Amish women were taught how to keep a house from childhood on. Hopefully, whoever hired her would not mind so much if she brought two well-behaved children with her. She also hoped they wouldn't mind too much when they found out she was pregnant.

The little card looked bare to her after she had printed her name, the type of work for which she was looking, and the phone number in her shanty. She found some colored pencils and created a small, colorful border around the card, hoping it would make it stand out from other advertisements. Five cards were finished before the children interrupted, wanting to go outside and play.

As she helped them into their warm, outdoor clothes, she gave thanks to God for her loving church and her healthy children. Then she asked God for a special favor. Would He please bless her little cards with success? Would He please allow them to attract the attention of just the right person? Someone He would choose? She did not mind working hard, but she hoped that she could find employment with someone who would at least be kind.

The house was furnished. He felt rested. The deadline was still a worry to him and he felt weird not writing. So, he decided to ignore Harry's advice. He recharged his laptop and got back to work. Or at least he tried to.

It was a mistake.

There was a time when he had thought that writer's block was nothing more than the excuse of a lazy writer. Now he regretted ever having held that opinion. Writer's block was real and it was deadly. Harry had bought him some time, but the fact remained, if he didn't produce a book soon, he would have to give back his advance and possibly even face legal action.

The minute he sat down in front of his laptop, a feeling of dread came over him, so strong that he jumped out of his chair as though the laptop were a snake ready to strike. He paced the floor until he could face touching the keyboard again. Found out again that he couldn't do this.

He had never experienced anything remotely like it before. A professional writer doesn't wait for the mood to strike. For him, at least in the past, the "mood" struck at precisely eight o'clock in the morning, because he had deliberately trained himself to sit down and write from eight o'clock in the morning until one o'clock in the afternoon. Every day. Rain or shine. Seven days a week. Period.

He usually kept the television on low for background noise. He found the muted sounds comforting. They helped him relax and concentrate. His writing routine then involved stopping, eating a quick lunch in front of the TV. When he had been at his best, he had always taken a long walk so that his body would not atrophy. Then a fifteen-minute nap to ease the switch from creative brain to analytical brain. The afternoon was spent self-editing, doing research, answering e-mails, writing blogs, doing PR, and dealing with the business of being a full-time writer. He broke from that only when Marla got home from her job. Then they would go out to dinner and come home to watch television until they fell asleep.

He was ashamed of the loneliness he was experiencing now. He had never realized before just how much television supplied his need for human interaction. Or how much he had depended emotionally on Marla's coming home each night.

After the fourth attempt to write a complete sentence without breaking out in a sweat, he gave up and put the laptop away. He was in even worse shape than he had thought. Perhaps Marla was right. Maybe he *did* need a shrink.

chapter SEVEN

He was wasting time wandering around, poking through an antiques shop he'd noticed in Mt. Hope. He was loafing again, since it didn't seem like he had a choice in the matter. Right now, he was fairly certain that he couldn't force himself to write even if one of his characters held a gun to his head.

He was certainly not a stranger to antiques stores. Marla sometimes dragged him along with her while hunting for unique items to use in her decorating business.

This particular antiques store was better than average. Higher-end items. These things were not just old, they had been expensive before they became antiques. Even Marla would have approved. He made a mental note to bring her here when she came to visit.

The place resembled a Victorian home more than a store. He had almost missed the weathered sign halfway hidden behind the lilac bush.

They had quite a collection of old books. Many of them were religious, which did not surprise him, considering his geographical location. It stood to reason that in a town that practically rolled up its sidewalks on Sunday, there would be lots of religious books. He stood looking at the confusing array of titles and shook his head. When it came to religious books, he had no idea how to tell which one might have value and which one would not.

That's how he felt about organized religion in general. He sometimes longed for the comfort of faith, but how on earth could one ever discern truth from fiction? The good and honest from the bad and dishonest?

Something caught his eye on the top shelf: a slender, dark-grained leather case with a latch. He pulled it down, finding it surprisingly heavy. He laid it on a round, claw-foot table near the window, flipped the latch, and lifted the cover.

To his surprise, nestled inside the case was a maroon red, jewel-like, portable typewriter, unlike any that he had ever seen. The ribbon appeared to be intact. He gave one key an experimental tap and was pleased with the smooth action.

The noise brought the proprietor, an elderly woman who looked entirely too fragile to be working at a job. She resembled an old-fashioned librarian, birdlike in her frailty, her gray hair in a classic bun. He judged her to be in her very late eighties or early nineties.

"Isn't it lovely?" she said. "Ever since my nephew brought it here from an estate sale I wished it could talk. I think it would have quite a lot of interesting stories to tell."

"What do you know about it?" he asked.

"That's a portable 1934 Smith & Corona Super-Speed Silent. The family said it once belonged to a relative who was a newspaper correspondent during World War II. It was quite expensive in its time, and considered to be of the highest quality."

"It's beautiful." He ran his hand over the smooth, glass-like finish.

"I can find you a sheet of paper to try it out if you wish."

"I would appreciate that."

It did not take her long to find some blank computer paper, which she rolled into the platen. She seemed very familiar with the workings of manual typewriters and he was grateful because he had never used one before. Their time had been long past when he entered high school.

"Now," she said, "you can try it out."

She watched over his shoulder as he attempted to use it. At first it seemed awkward and difficult compared to the minimal effort it took to touch the keys on his laptop, but soon he fell into a rhythm and the muted clackety-clack of the keys delighted him. It made him feel as though he were a "real" writer instead of someone who simply created blips on a screen.

"During the war, it was nearly impossible to get a typewriter," she said. "The military was using every available one, and some of their manufacturing companies were pressed into service to make weapons instead. This instrument would have been a rarity and highly valued. My guess is that the correspondent would have protected it with his life."

"Do you remember the war well?"

He assumed she was old enough to have gone through it, but it was a little hard to judge her age. She could have been anywhere from seventy to a hundred. She had that timeless quality that some women acquire.

"Oh, my dear boy. Do I remember it?" Her shoulders straightened. "I helped *win* it!"

There was something in the tone of her voice and the pride in her eyes that made him think she had lived it in ways that most people her age had not.

He loved hearing other people's stories. With plenty of free time on his hands, he probed further.

"How did you live it?" he asked. "Did you grow a Victory Garden? Deal with rationing? Lose a sweetheart or a husband to the war?"

"Oh no. None of that. Stay right here and I'll show you something."

Intrigued, he waited until she came back carrying a small, velvet box and handed it to him.

"Open it."

He did. Inside was a gold medal with the picture of a woman pilot embossed on the front.

"Is this what I think it is?" he asked, in awe.

"A Congressional Gold Medal. The highest honor awarded to a civilian. I did a great deal more than grow a Victory Garden during the war. I was a WASP. The Women Airforce Service Pilots. I flew the planes!"

He had read about the civilian women pilots who had ferried various airplanes, including giant bombers, from the factories to the war effort, freeing more male pilots to be in combat.

"You were a WASP?" he said. "What did you fly?"

"I flew nineteen different types of planes, including B-17s, B-25s, P-47s, and P-51s. I received this medal only four years ago. It took an act of Congress and a presidential signature to make it happen, but we were finally recognized for our service to the country. Thirty-eight of us died while ferrying those planes. I remember having to take up a collection to get the casket of one of our pilots back to her people in Kalamazoo. The government didn't recognize us as military. We paid our own way there and our own way back home, or, as in the case of my friend, other people had to pay it for us."

"You don't sound bitter about it." He inspected the medal. The workmanship was beautiful. "I would be angry if I'd had to wait so long."

"That was just how it was back then." She lifted bony shoulders in a shrug. "Our records were closed for thirty years. Historians couldn't get into them. No one knew. Some people thought it was an empty boast when I told them what I had done in the war. They thought I was making it up, but I wasn't."

A story began to form in his mind.

"Do you have more blank paper?" he asked. "I'd be happy to pay."

"Of course." She returned with a small stack. "Feel free. I don't get much company in here."

She patted him on the shoulder like a doting aunt, then left to take up her hopeful perch on the stool beside the old-fashioned brass cash register.

He was vaguely aware that people came and went in the store, but he was too busy playing with his new toy to be bothered by them. The few customers seemed to realize that he needed to be left alone.

After a while he stopped typing, pushed back his chair, and blinked. He had been deeply immersed in the story world he had been creating. Surrounded by antique furniture and doilies, he had been transported to an entirely different time, and the words had simply poured out of him.

The paragraphs were filled with typos and strikeovers, but the antique instrument had caused a WWII story to begin to form the minute she had told him about its history. He felt, as he sat there, as though he were the correspondent who once carried and used this machine. His few years working as a wet-behind-the-ears journalist on the streets of New York City had given him some insight into what it might be like to be a young war correspondent who was scared silly, but equally determined to make one's mark on the world. He could also imagine this lovely older lady as the beautiful young woman she must have been as she climbed behind the controls of a bomber. What courage that must have taken!

He took a rest and read over what he had written. It was good. A little different from the stories he was known for, but good.

He walked around the table, nervous as a cat, putting his hands in his pockets and then on top of his head. Could something as simple as an antique typewriter be the key to opening up the well of creativity within him that had gone dry?

Authors are every bit as superstitious as professional athletes. Most have their little rituals, favorite candles, special writing socks, certain music. One writer he knew could write only with a pet parrot sitting on top of her head.

On the left-hand side of the maroon typewriter were five completed pages. It was satisfying to see his work lying there in such a tangible form. He seldom bothered to print out pages from his computer. They went straight from his keyboard to his editor, electronic submissions so insubstantial that months of his life could be deleted with a keystroke.

"May I?" the old woman asked, indicating the pages of writing.

"Be my guest."

For some reason, it felt like the very first time he had ever allowed someone to read his work. The same new-writer nervousness. Would she like it? Would she laugh? Cry? Be bored? Criticize?

She did none of these things. Instead, she read to the end and then looked up at him almost in wonder.

"Where did you learn to write like this?"

He had not told anyone in Holmes County what he did for a living. Fame created a wall once people knew who he was, and he did not want to erect that wall between himself and this sweet lady. He just wanted to be treated like everyone else . . . and write.

For the first time in ages, he just wanted to write!

"My name is Logan Parker," he said. "I—I just like to dabble."

Actually, that was pretty close to the truth. "Dabbling" was an exaggeration, considering how little he had actually written these past few weeks.

She looked deeply into his eyes. "You should be a writer, young man," she said. "You have a gift. And it is a sin to waste such a God-given talent."

Her attempt at encouragement brought a lump to his throat. It took him back to when he first began to write—when the dream had been fresh and clean and not sullied by the realities of trying to move massive quantities of books.

"I'd like to purchase this typewriter." He reached for his wallet. "How much?"

She didn't answer. Instead she cocked her head to one side. "I don't believe I shall sell it to you."

He noticed a price tag, handwritten in an old person's unsteady hand, dangling from the handle. It read $300.00.

He pulled out his wallet and tried to hand her three one-hundred-dollar bills, but she put her hands behind her back.

"No," she said. "I'm sorry, Mr. Parker. It is no longer for sale."

He was puzzled. Could she be suffering from dementia?

"I don't understand."

"I won't sell it to you, but I *will* rent it to you," she said. "My name is Violet Hanover. I used to teach high school English at Garaway High School. I am afraid that if I let you walk out that door with this instrument under your arm, you will never come back and you will never finish this story. If that were to happen, I would be devastated because . . ." She beamed at him. "I cannot wait to see how it turns out."

Bless her heart.

"I might even be able to give you a few pointers from time to time," she said. "I'm an awfully good proofreader."

He just bet she was.

He was intrigued. It had been a long time since anyone had shown any interest in his writing except to wonder how soon he could crank out the next book.

"What do you mean, you'll rent it to me?"

"Do you have a day job, Mr. Parker?"

"Not exactly."

"Perhaps you could come here every day?" Her smile never wavered. "Let's say around one o'clock." Her voice had taken on the echoes of the teacher's voice she might have used when dealing with a promising but recalcitrant student. "I shall have a cup of tea waiting for you. You may sit here at this table and type until the store closes at three."

"How much do you want for rent?"

"Your rent, Mr. Parker"—her faded blue eyes twinkled again behind her thick glasses—"is to let me read whatever you manage to write each day."

"But you will have customers."

"And I shall tend to them. But no one will be allowed to purchase this writing instrument from me."

This was one of the strangest offers he had ever received as a writer. To sit in this out-of-the-way antiques shop tapping away at an old typewriter while a ninety-something former girl pilot brought him tea.

He loved the idea.

Writing on a state-of-the-art computer in the silence of his old farmhouse was certainly not getting him anywhere. Instead, he would give this a try for a day or two. If things went well, he would have learned a new method of getting over writer's block. If things went badly, well, he couldn't be in any worse shape than he already was.

"I'll be back tomorrow," he said. "At one o'clock. I'll bring some Earl Grey tea. That's my favorite."

"Don't bother. I just happen to have quite a stash of excellent Earl Grey. I'll see you tomorrow." Then she made a comment so adorable and old-fashioned that it made him smile long after he left. "Make sure you have your thinking cap on when you come back in here, young man! I shall be expecting great things from you."

chapter EIGHT

"May I put this on your bulletin board?"

The Amish woman was dressed in a dark green dress and was holding hands with two cherubic children. She dropped one child's hand long enough to give a card to Violet.

"What is it?" Violet asked.

Logan ripped a sheet of paper out of the old typewriter and added it to the growing pile of manuscript pages in front of him. This was the most prolific he had been in ages—as long as he was writing on the antique typewriter. He and his laptop were still at odds.

There was something about working here, with people coming and going, that was energizing. Sometimes he listened in on the conversations swirling around him, but more often the voices of customers became background noise as he immersed himself in the culture of 1942 Germany.

"I'm looking for work," he heard the young woman say.

He felt sorry for Violet. As tenderhearted as she was, it would be hard for her to turn the woman down. He doubted that there was enough work here for Violet to hire her.

The story was going well and he was excited. He had gotten books about World War II out of the library and ordered more through a local bookstore. Each night he read copiously and each day he spent sitting at this table spinning a story unlike any he had ever written. For several hours a day, he looked at the world through the eyes of a frightened, twenty-two-year-old war correspondent who was falling in love with a courageous young girl pilot.

Sometimes people stopped to chat. More often they respectfully didn't.

His deadline for the next sociopathic thriller for his New York publisher loomed, but he put it aside as he indulged himself in the story that had grabbed him by the throat and would not let him go. He had stopped coming in at one o'clock. Instead, he came in as early as the store opened in the morning and stayed until it closed.

Violet was as good as her word. She proofread, made insightful comments in the margins of his manuscript, provided him with pots of tea, and helped him with historical accuracy. In return, he frequently treated her to dinner at one of the local restaurants.

The Amish woman lifted the youngest child, a little boy, onto her hip. "I'm looking for work cleaning houses."

Logan's ears perked up. A housecleaner? Ever since he'd started writing on a consistent basis again, his house was falling apart. Clothing, dishes, papers, books were stacked and toppling over.

"And I also cook."

She cooked? "Oh, honey," Violet said. "How can you clean houses and cook for other people with those two children?"

"They are *very* good children," the Amish woman said.

Logan lost interest. A woman who planned to drag two children along with her couldn't possibly do a decent job. If he hired her, the children would probably tear the place apart.

On the other hand, the older child, even without her mother

holding her hand, was standing perfectly still, looking up at Violet, being as good as gold. The little boy astraddle his mother's hip, with his little suspendered pants and minuscule Amish hat, was adorable.

Although the woman and her children had their backs to him, there was something familiar about them.

Violet looked at the little card she still held in her hand. "Why are you looking for work, dear?" she asked kindly. "Has your husband lost his job?"

"My husband is gone," Hope said. "He was killed by a bull."

"Oh!" Violet glanced up from the card. "You must be Henry and Rose Miller's eldest daughter. I heard about your loss. Such a tragedy! Doesn't the church have alms to help you?"

"*Ja*, but I want to do my part. I'm a hard worker and my small house does not take much time to clean. I have several hours to spare each day."

She turned slightly, and he realized that this was the pretty Amish woman with the sad face he'd seen walking to church with her children.

He'd guessed right. She was a widow. His heart went out to her. Having someone to sweep, wash dishes, and tidy up really would be helpful. The children seemed quiet and obedient.

"I could use some help," he said.

She turned to see who had spoken.

"You?" she said. "You would hire me to work for you?"

"Yes," he said. "Would that be a problem?"

There was a long hesitation while she considered. "How many hours?"

"How much time would you like?" he said. "My house is a mess. You said you can cook, and I'm getting tired of eating every meal in restaurants. If you want to come over a few hours each week, I'd be obliged."

She turned a questioning gaze to Violet as though she was not at all sure what to think about this offer.

"He's quite nice," Violet reassured her. "And he spends most of the day in here working on his book anyway."

"Your wife does not clean or cook?"

It was interesting that she immediately assumed he had a wife. He supposed that was because most Amish men his age would be married, but he had no desire to discuss his relationship with Marla. The situation was a little complicated to explain to an Amish person, especially since it did not fit into their moral code. In fact, he was beginning to regret ever having looked up from his typewriter. This could be a mistake. The woman was a little too attractive for comfort. Having her working around his house could be distracting.

"My . . . wife is presently living in Manhattan," he explained. It was close enough.

"She does not live with you?" There was suspicion in the woman's voice.

"She has a job there," he answered.

"He is writing a book." Violet beamed like a proud mother. "It is very good."

The woman was uninterested in his writing. She had gotten stuck on the fact that his "wife" was living in another state.

"Why does she not live here with you?"

"I enjoy living here, and she does not." Slightly annoyed that he was expected to explain anything about his living arrangements at all, he was brief. "We've worked out a temporary compromise."

He had not expected to get the third degree. That was one of the disadvantages he was discovering about living in a small community. People actually seemed to think that they had a *right* to information about one another's lives.

"My name is Hope Schrock. I will clean the house for you."

Hope sounded as though she were bestowing a favor upon him. "You will be pleased."

Her confidence was amusing. This was a woman who seemed to know her own worth.

"Let's start out with a couple hours a day," he said. "We could try it for a week or two and see how things work out."

"I can bring my children?"

"If you can wash the dishes and do a little laundry and sweeping with your kids around, it doesn't matter to me. How much do you charge?"

She named an hourly wage that he thought ridiculously low, to which he readily agreed. The relief he saw on her face transformed her. She smiled and her smile lit up the room. The woman even had a dimple in her right cheek. "You will not be sorry," she said. "I am a *gut* worker."

"I'm sure you are." He wanted to get back to the scene he had been writing before it grew stale. He rolled a new piece of paper into the typewriter.

"I can start tomorrow?" She sounded hopeful.

"Sure. That's fine, whatever you want to do." He wrote out the address on a piece of paper. "Here's where I live."

She glanced at it and turned pale. "Are you sure this is where you live?"

"Of course I'm sure." He frowned, wondering what the problem was. "Why do you ask?"

"Because that was my parents' home for many years. I grew up there. I did not know it had been sold."

"I've not lived there long," he said. "The back door is unlocked whenever you want to go over."

"*Ja*," she said. "The lock never worked too *gut* on that door anyway."

He did not hear her. He had already gone back in time to 1942 and didn't notice when she left the store. He barely registered the fact that Violet had brought a fresh pot of Earl Grey to the table.

"I didn't realize you'd bought Henry and Rose's place," she said. "You might want to know how they lost it, if Hope is going to be working there—it was a terrible thing in this community."

He looked up from the typewriter. "I'm listening."

"Henry was one of the finest farmers around, and that's saying something. Then an *Englisch* friend took him to a horse race over near Columbus. Henry always loved horses. The track also had a casino attached. Henry started disappearing for days at a time. Rose didn't know what to do. She thought he was having an affair, and was so ashamed, she didn't tell anyone for a long time. She didn't know he'd gotten addicted to gambling. No one figured it out until he was in such deep debt he lost everything—including the farm. It caused quite a stir around here."

"It's hard to imagine an Amish man getting addicted to something like that."

"An Amish man can get into the same trouble anyone else can." She walked back to her stool at the cash register. "If someone's willing to drive."

chapter NINE

H ope had not been inside the house since her mother and father moved out, and she was curious to see what sort of state it might be in. How strange it would be to clean this house with which she was as familiar as her own body.

The fields were looking quite ragged, she noticed as she drove her buggy up the driveway, and it pained her that apparently no one would be farming the fine acreage.

It was natural, she supposed, to feel some resentment toward the man who had purchased the home she had loved, but it was unfair, and she chastised herself for her uncharitable thoughts. He did not know the history or the heartbreak behind the fact that he was living there instead of her parents.

Of course, *Englisch* choices and ways were a mystery. She did not understand so many of the things they did. Frequently, she wished they would all just go away and leave her people alone, except that they *did* bring much income into the area!

They also brought their loud music and fast cars. When driving her buggy with her children inside, she often fantasized about what life would be like without the foul-smelling *Englisch* cars constantly passing her as she tried to go about her errands. Hills were the worst. She could not force her horse into a trot on a hill, which meant that she could not hurry. When a car drew up behind her, they could not safely pass because they could not see over the hill, so they were forced to idle behind her as her poor horse labored up the hill. There was nothing she could do about it.

Sometimes the *Englischer*'s need for speed overcame their good sense and they passed her anyway, blindly, not knowing if there was a car coming toward them at all. She had experienced many close calls.

Yes, a world without *Englisch* would be so much easier. It would be even better if the whole world was Old Order Amish like herself and her family. What a wonderful world that would be! Life would be so simple and pleasant!

Of course, then there would also be no doctors to care for them when they got sick. It was a puzzlement.

It was also a puzzlement why a grown man would sit around typing stories all day. And for him to use an old antique typewriter in order to do so! Even the Amish had access to word processors. One of her cousins was a scribe for *The Budget*. She wrote a small column about her church settlement every week on a word processor her husband had purchased for her. The cousin said it worked much like the *Englisch* computer except that it did not have the capability of accessing the evils of the internet.

Her cousin explained that she had heard rumors of terrible things on that internet. She had whispered—the children were within earshot—that some *Englisch* men used it to look at dirty pictures. This was much more than Hope wanted to know. She was grateful to have a culture in which her children would not be exposed to such things! She wanted them to have a wholesome life, one dedicated to God, not one in which there were so many questionable things bombarding them.

That was the reason she chose to leave the children with her mother the first time she entered this *Englisch* man's house. Who knew *what* sort of things he might have lying about! Better not to bring tender young eyes into this place until she found out what kind of a man she would be working for.

She had stopped at her in-laws' last night to get permission from the bishop to take this job. Bishop Schrock said that he would not forbid her, and that he respected her desire to provide income for her family, but to let him know if she ever found herself uncomfortable working for this outsider. If so, he would try to find her a different position.

Today she would find out if this job was something that she, in all good conscience, could do.

As she entered the kitchen where she remembered her grandmother rolling out pie dough, it felt so familiar. The place was filled with so many good memories. It was, however, very messy. Nothing seemed to be in its rightful place and there were books scattered everywhere. In addition . . . it smelled bad.

Logan Parker apparently did not know how to wash a dish! The counter was stacked high with unwashed dishes as well as take-out containers. The trash can was piled high with more take-out containers. A dishcloth lay moldering in the corner of the sink, along with a pot that had some burned beans stuck to the bottom.

Did he not realize that dirty dishes attract mice? This was an old house with many secret ways for mice to crawl in. Where mice could enter, so could snakes! Snakes love little rodents. Her mother had fought mice expertly with traps *and* by never, ever leaving food where they would find it.

She was surprised that he had not had electricity brought in. That was the first thing most *Englisch* people did when they bought Amish family homes. They almost always had the solid, honest houses wired for electricity.

She opened the propane-fueled refrigerator. It was not well stocked, but there were some odds and ends of vegetables and her employer had a small roast in the freezer. It also looked like he'd spilled some tomato juice and neglected to clean it up.

This was interesting to her and validated her opinion of men in general, which was that they were not suited to keep house. Most were, from what she'd seen, slobs at heart unless they had a good wife to keep them on their toes.

Leaving the kitchen, she strode into the front room and saw that it was overflowing with newspapers, coffee cups, and scribbled-upon papers. Books were scattered everywhere and many had pieces of paper sticking out of them. Who had time to read so many books? Probably not someone who would care for the land like her father had, or as she could have, if given half a chance.

She mounted the stairs with great purpose. If she had ever seen a person who needed a housekeeper, it was this *Englischer*!

It felt awkward entering his bedroom, but she assured herself that cleaning this room was part of her job, just like any other room in the house. It was as bad as she expected. Clothing was strewn everywhere. The bed was unmade and looked like it had been unmade for a very long time. Socks. Underwear. Scattered around on the floor.

She picked up the man's underwear with two fingers and held them at arm's length. Goodness. This was much more than she had wanted to know. Who wore red boxer shorts that had pictures of a drunken Santa Claus holding a beer bottle on them? Was this normal behavior? She dropped them back onto the floor with a shiver of disapproval. The only thing she liked about this room was the scent. Logan Parker used some sort of cologne or body wash that was *very* masculine and pleasing.

Then she entered what had once been her old bedroom,

which overlooked the fruit orchard and had always been a special sanctuary for her.

What she saw when she entered was a shock. It looked like a crazy person had been here! It was completely bare except for a kitchen chair in the middle, and beside it, a card table with a box of colored index cards, pens, and a tape dispenser.

The chair and card table were not a shock. What shocked her was that three of the walls were covered with index cards. The *Englischer* had even drawn upon the wall, itself, in pencil.

She went up to the wall and began to read. There were numbers written all over it. A series of cards were lined up underneath each penciled mark. The notes were so cryptic she could make no sense of them. Beneath the number *23*, she pulled one off the wall and read it. "H/h discovr jewels/airport lockr/chase w/rent-a-cop." She attached it back on the wall and read another: "Beach/low tide/crab bite." Another card read, "Parachute/damaged. Freefall/deliberate?"

This wall made absolutely no sense. She had never seen anything like it in her life. She hoped it did not mean that she was working for a crazy man, but one never knew with *Englisch* people! Some did very strange things. She closed the door firmly behind her.

Another bedroom had apparently been intended as a guest room. Everything was new and untouched, including the bed, which had an exquisite quilt upon it. She looked closer at the quilt and its tiny, tight stitching. Unless she missed her guess, that was Sharon Hochstetler's work. The fact that Logan had bothered to purchase a true Amish quilt instead of the cheaper, badly sewn foreign quilts that stores like Walmart carried, pleased her. The other two bedrooms were about the same. It looked as though this man had hoped to have company, but had not had any yet. Perhaps his New York friends had not wanted to come. If so, she felt sorry for him. He had gone to the effort of purchasing furniture and bedding, but it was apparent that he was living here very much alone . . . and, with the exception of the untouched guest bedrooms, in squalor.

Well, if he wanted her to clean, she would clean. Her mother had taught her from the cradle up how to keep a house nice.

Starting with the kitchen first, she emptied the sink of dishes, filled it with soapy water, rolled up her sleeves, and started to work. He had hired her for two hours a day. If she worked quickly, she could get a terrible amount of work done in two hours. If he was pleased, by the end of the week, she would have made more than enough money to purchase groceries and the new shoes she so desperately needed. She could hardly wait to retire the ones she was wearing.

In a kitchen that had once belonged to her great-great-grandmother, she pulled the roast out of the freezer to thaw, and then did what her mother had taught her how to do so well—she made the house sparkle.

chapter TEN

"Violet tells me that you're writing a story set in World War II?"

The gentleman was nearly bald, quite elderly, carried a cane, and walked with a limp, but he held himself like a soldier as he stood at the table where Logan was typing.

"I am."

One of the best things about working in Violet's shop was that he was seldom completely alone. Since he kept telling himself that what he was writing here was only a method of priming the pump for his "real" books, he didn't mind a few interruptions. In fact, he was enjoying this way of meeting a few local people. Some were apparently fascinated with the fact that Violet had an outsider from Manhattan writing a "book" on her antique typewriter.

"You got time to hear my story?"

"Of course," Logan said.

The old man sat down, grimacing, with one leg stretched out straight in front of him. "I just want someone who knows how to write to hear a certain story before I die. My name is Frank Young, by the way." He reached out and shook Logan's hand. "I was one of the soldiers who helped liberate one of the German work camps during World War Two."

Logan sat up straighter. "I've seen pictures. They're pretty hard to forget."

"If you think looking at some black-and-white photos is hard, try being there. The sounds, the smells . . ." Frank shook himself. "Takes a lifetime and it still doesn't fade, but that's not the story I wanted to tell."

"Frank!" Violet walked in from the back room. "I didn't know you were coming today. Can I get you some tea?"

"Sure!" He winked at Logan. "Just make sure to stir it with your finger."

"Oh?" She seemed puzzled. "Why?"

"'Cause I like a little sugar in my tea."

"Oh, you stop, now!" Violet gave Frank a little slap on the shoulder.

He grinned devilishly at Logan as she went into the back room, where she had a small kitchen.

"You should have seen that girl when she was twenty," Frank said. "I wasn't the only young man around here turning handsprings hoping she'd notice me."

"What happened?"

"She fell in love with my brother after the war and made him a real good wife." Frank gazed off toward the kitchen. "You should have seen her behind the controls of a plane, mister. Hands as steady as a rock. But that's not the story I came to tell."

Instinctively, Logan reached for the notebook and pen he always kept in his back pocket. He never knew when he'd need to jot down notes or ideas. This man's story sounded like it might be jotworthy.

"I got plenty of time to listen, Frank," he said.

"There's not really a lot I want to tell," Frank said. "Don't *want* to remember most of it. Would rather forget some of the images that got stuck in my head, but I was one of the soldiers who had the honor of giving on-the-site medical care to the people we liberated. I was raised Mennonite and had been a conscientious objector at the beginning of the war, so they gave me some training as a medic. By the end of the war, I had a gun in my hand and was glad to have it. Once I got over there and saw what was happening, I couldn't remain a C.O."

"Here's the tea." Violet had brought out a tray that also included store-bought cookies. She gave Frank an arch look. "*And* the sugar bowl."

The old man chortled as he shoveled two heaping tea-spoons of sugar into his teacup and Violet went to speak to a young couple who had just come in and were standing in front of the cash register holding an antique doll cradle.

Logan found himself reevaluating old age. It looked to him as though some embers sometimes never went entirely out. Even at ninety-something.

"It was one of the men we rescued at another German work camp who told me about it, once he got some food down him and he thought he might live." Frank took a slurp of his tea, then cradled the cup in his hands and leaned forward. "Of all the things he had experienced in that terrible place, it was the memories of his sister that he couldn't shake."

"What kind of memories?" Logan clicked his pen and held it poised over his notebook.

"He and his father, his sister, and her little boy were put in one of them cattle cars headed for a work camp. Packed in like sardines. Couldn't sit. Had to stand. The train stopped for some reason, and that's when they found out that the old man had died. Too crowded in that railroad car for him to fall to the floor. The brother and sister asked permission from one of the guards to be allowed to carry their father off the train. Guard must have been softer than most. He actually let them drag the old man's body to a local church's steps.

"They were Catholic, arrested because they had been caught helping Jews, and there was a Catholic church in that little town. They managed to pin a note to the old man's coat, hoping a priest would take care of it. The guard made them keep the little boy with the others back at the train. Probably figured they wouldn't try to escape if the child was left behind. The brother and sister heard the train start up, and the next thing they knew, it had pulled away. The brother said all *he* could think about was how lucky they were that the guards had forgotten they were there and that now they were free and could escape."

Frank took another slurp of tea, then pulled out a red bandana and wiped his eyes that had begun to water.

"Are you okay?" Logan asked.

"Oh, don't worry about me." Frank blew his nose. "I'm all right. Old men cry easily. Too many memories." He stuffed the handkerchief into his back pocket and cleared his throat before going on. "My friend, who was nothing but skin and bones, said that all he could think about was getting away. The problem was, his sister wasn't interested in running away. She wanted to find her boy. So she started walking down those railroad tracks, going the same direction as the train. She said she was going to walk them tracks until she found her child or she died trying."

Logan laid the pen on the table. He didn't need to take notes. This was not a story he would ever forget. "What happened then?"

"The brother kept following along behind her, begging her to give up, trying to convince her that all she was doing was sacrificing herself. He told her the little fellow wasn't going to survive anyway—he was a sickly sort of boy—and that at least she had a chance to get away. He even told her she could have other children. That was the part he hated the most, having said such a thing to her."

"Did she listen to him?"

"No. She just kept walking and walking. And the brother kept begging and begging. The farther they got, the more danger he knew they were in, and he finally gave up and left her. Started going the other direction. Trying to save himself. He said she never once looked back. He stopped a couple times and watched her. Said he'd never forget what she looked like, all by herself, a young mother walking down the middle of those train tracks. Determined to find her child no matter what."

Logan leaned back in his chair and shook his head. Who could fathom a mother's love? While Frank took another drink of tea, Logan's thoughts roamed to his own mom. Under the same circumstances, would she have done that for him? There was no doubt in his mind that she would have. Deborah Parker could be a tiger when it came to her only child.

"The brother was eventually recaptured and taken to the same camp. Running away hadn't done him a bit of good. After he got there, he found out the rest of the story."

"Which was?"

"She made it to the camp. This was later in the war, and by that time everyone pretty much knew what those camps were used for and that people going in never came out again. But when she got there, that young mother pounded on the doors of that German work camp and demanded to be let in."

"I imagine the guards were a bit surprised?"

"A mother pounding on the gates of hell to get to her little boy? I imagine so."

"Did they survive?"

"That's the strangest thing. They did. Somehow, that mother

and her boy managed to survive. I always figured it was sheer willpower or maybe pure luck on her part. The war was starting to wind down and the Germans were losing. It was starting to look like every man for himself. She somehow managed to bribe a guard to turn his head just long enough to allow her to escape, carrying that child on her back. She didn't have a dime to her name or extra clothing, or food. She walked until her shoes fell to pieces and then she walked until her feet were bloody pulp, but she survived. She eventually got herself and the boy to America. Rest of the family was gone. After the war ended, I made it my business to help the brother find them. Took me a long, long time."

"Where they okay?"

"The brother never did all that good. The doctors thought it was because of the starvation, but I always thought it was because he couldn't ever forgive himself for being a coward."

"He shouldn't have blamed himself."

"That's what I told him, but he never got over any of it. Drink finally took him. He wasn't all that old when he died."

"Where's the boy now? Is his mother still alive?"

"No. I buried her twelve years ago today."

"You?"

"Couldn't let a woman like that get away from me, now, could I?"

Logan was stunned. "And the boy?"

"Finest son a man could ever ask for."

Frank used both the table and the cane to pull himself up. "Violet says you're a good writer. Maybe even a great one. I thought it was worth a shot to see if my wife's story would be of interest to you . . . even if you only write fiction."

Logan stood when the old man did. Not to assist him—he had a feeling that Frank would not welcome any assistance as long as he was capable of navigating on his own. It was just the respectful thing to do. He would never forget Frank, or his story. He also knew that the plot of the book he was playing around with had just taken a sudden, and major, turn.

Logan was so distracted by Frank's story he nearly forgot that he had hired a housekeeper that morning. He hadn't expected her to start the job that very day, but when he walked through the door, he discovered that his house smelled fresh and clean, the sink was empty, the dishes washed and put away, and . . . to his utter astonishment . . . a stew was slowly simmering at the back of the stove. He had not been aware that he possessed the ingredients to make a stew.

He went upstairs and saw that his unkempt bed had been made. In fact, he turned down the covers and there were fresh sheets on it. The bathroom sink and tub, which had been grungy, were sparkling.

He found a bowl, ladled some stew into it, and selected a research book to read while he ate. If this was what Hope Schrock could do in two hours, life was going to get much, much simpler.

chapter ELEVEN

"This is the room you slept in when you were a little girl, *Mommi?*" Carrie held the dustpan for her to sweep the few bits of dust that had accumulated.

"It is."

"I like this room," Carrie said.

"I once saw a cat chasing a dog from that window."

Carrie looked up at her from where she was concentrating on her important task. "Cats don't chase dogs."

The little girl had a five-year-old's conviction of how the world should be.

"Well, this was a very brave cat, and the dog was very cowardly. He had gotten entirely too close to the cat's new kittens and the mama cat did not like that."

It was Hope's second day of employment. She had decided that in addition to her overall cleaning and straightening, she would concentrate her efforts on one room per day until she'd been through the entire house. Then she would start all over again.

As she chatted with her daughter in their Germanic native tongue, she was startled out of her thoughts by the sound of a man clearing his throat behind her. She whirled around and saw her new employer, Logan Parker, in the doorway.

"I'm sorry," he said. "I didn't mean to frighten you. When I saw your buggy, I thought I should come and let you know I was here."

He was leaning against the door frame in a casual way with his hands in his pockets. Now he pulled himself away, came over to where she and Carrie were standing and knelt down in front of her little girl.

"Hello," he said. "I don't believe I've had the pleasure of meeting you yet."

Carrie sidled away and hid behind her mother's skirts.

He stood up and asked, "Did I do something wrong?"

"She does not understand you," Hope explained. "We do not teach our children English until they go to school."

"Oh." He mulled this over. "Why?"

It really wasn't something she'd ever pondered. "That is just the way it has always been."

He thought this over, then said, "You had a little boy when I met you in the antiques shop."

"That would be my Adam. He is with my mother today."

"You have beautiful children."

She brushed his compliment on their beauty aside. "They are *gut* children."

"I appreciate the work you did yesterday. Is there anything you need that I can get you? Special cleaning supplies maybe?"

She thought this over. His home was fairly well stocked with what she needed. Those few things he didn't have, like good cleaning rags, she brought with her.

"You might get some groceries in if you want me to cook for you."

"Are you sure? After eating yesterday's stew you fixed, I was under the impression that you might be a magician who could conjure food out of thin air."

She frowned, unsure of what he was saying. "Are you making a joke?"

"Not at all," he said. "I meant it as a compliment. If you want to make me out a grocery list each week, I'll be happy to get whatever you want."

"That would depend on what you like to eat," she said.

He shrugged. "I don't care. If you fix it, I'll eat it."

Ah. A man who was not picky. That was always a good thing.

The room was without blinds or curtains and sunshine flooded it. They stood for a moment, facing each other, taking each other's measure. She saw a nicely built man with gray eyes and dark hair that needed cutting. He wore a blue pullover sweater with the sleeves pushed up, khaki pants, and black wire-rim glasses. He had a habit of kicking his shoes off at the door. There were several pairs lined up in the kitchen, and he was in his stocking feet. Considering the fact that it was her job to keep his floors clean, she appreciated this thoughtfulness.

He was, she decided, a casually handsome man—which was a matter of little importance compared to the fact that she saw genuine kindness in his face. She did not feel threatened by his presence and that was a very good thing because she very much wanted to keep this job.

Logan had stopped for only a few minutes to pick up some notes he had forgotten to take along on this latest chapter of his WWII novel. He knew Hope would prefer he stay away while she was there, and he agreed. Her people would not approve of seeing his car and her buggy parked there together side by side.

Violet had warned him that Hope would be risking censure if she was seen spending time alone with him.

It was certainly a different mind-set than what he was used to, but he could respect the fact that in this community, a young, widowed Amish woman would have to be careful.

Unfortunately, he thought it best that he stay away for his own sake as well. The image of Hope and her little girl together had been a riveting one. Perhaps it was only the quaint, old-fashioned clothing, or the musical sound of her voice as she had talked with her child, but he had found himself transfixed.

Maybe it was only the way the sunlight came streaming through the window, but it had seemed to him that her lovely skin practically glowed with health. Her eyes were rimmed with thick, dark lashes and perfectly formed brows. Her lips were naturally a deep pink and needed no artifice. Everything about her was lovely. She was one of those rare women who did not need so much as a touch of makeup to be beautiful.

As he seated himself once again at his table in the antiques shop, he had trouble concentrating. The image of his new housekeeper kept coming to mind . . . which was quite disconcerting.

It was especially disconcerting because this was exactly what had happened to him the day he met his wife. He had not been able to get Ariela's face out of his mind for days after meeting her in a journalism class at Columbia.

His young wife had been the direct opposite of his new housekeeper in almost every way, though. Ariela had been in the Israeli army, and during that time she lost most of her family when a stray Palestinian rocket had landed in the midst of a wedding celebration. Her only close relative left was an uncle who had been ill and stayed away that day. Ariela was strong and brave and loudly opinionated, usually more than his match in any political debate, and Logan had adored her.

He had loved her so utterly and wildly that watching her waste away had almost destroyed him.

Marla was an excellent choice for him at this stage in his life. He cared deeply for the woman, and was grateful for her presence, but it did not feel as though his life force would melt away if he ever lost her, and this was a very good thing. He never wanted to hurt that badly again.

His sudden, intense attraction to the Amish woman was puzzling, and he knew this was definitely something he would have to monitor and avoid. It would be best if he stayed away from Hope Schrock as much as possible.

Hope had to pass Aunt Claire's new birthing clinic on her way home. There had been quite a flurry of activity there as they got the clinic set up and remodeled. She decided to stop and see if they had settled in yet.

Her cousin Levi, Grace's husband, was replacing a porch step when she stopped. He waved a hammer in her general direction in greeting.

"If you came to talk to Mom or Grace, they're over at Prudence Miller's place."

"Oh? Her baby must have come a little early."

"It did. Grace got the call this morning." He laid down his hammer and wiped his forehead. "I'm going in for some lemonade. Do you want me to bring you out some?"

She rarely got a chance to talk to Levi anymore, although they had been close as children. "I would like that."

He came back out with three glasses and a plate of cookies.

"Grace made these," he warned. "I'm not guaranteeing anything. She's still learning."

"How are things going between the two of you?"

"We still have an occasional bump in the road, but the

thing that we were having the most problems over has been resolved."

"And what was that?"

"It was her insistence on working at the Pomerene Hospital ER after the baby came. I did not think it would be good for our family for her to work so far from home and be gone from our daughter for so many hours. She felt like I was trying to control her. We could not find a way to agree."

"And now?"

"Grace's grandmother, Elizabeth, solved the problem for us when she moved into my old apartment at the farm and turned the house over to us for this clinic. It was entirely her idea. She pointed out to my mother that going into partnership with an experienced nurse-practitioner would greatly enhance the quality of safety she could provide for the women she cared for as a midwife. Then Elizabeth sold Grace on the idea of how important this work could be to the women of this area." He took a sip of lemonade. "I kept my mouth shut, let the women sort it out. I built whatever they wanted me to build, and remodeled whatever they wanted me to remodel. My stepfather, Tom, has been a big help."

"Aunt Claire seems happy in her new marriage."

"Tom is good to her, to all of us. Ever since he came back to Holmes County, got back in touch with his Amish roots, and married my mother, things have gotten a lot better around here."

"Do you ever miss being Amish? Do you ever regret leaving?"

"I don't regret leaving the Swartzentrubers. Their *Ordnung* was so restrictive I felt like I was in a straitjacket." He drained his glass and tossed the ice cubes over the porch railing. "We've started visiting some of the Mennonite churches around here. I'm trying to see if there is one where Grace can fit in and feel comfortable."

"You've given up a lot to be with her," Hope said. "You must love her very much."

"She's my other half."

For some reason, that statement hit her hard and she had to fight to hold back the tears. It was like this for her sometimes. Her loss would suddenly, and completely, overwhelm her.

"Hope," Levi said, "I'm so sorry. I know it hurts having Titus gone."

"There is pain." She put an arm around Carrie. "But we are making it through. Carrie helped me clean house for the *Englischer* who purchased my parents' home. She is turning into a big girl."

"And a good worker."

"Yes." Hope wiped her eyes, nibbled the edge of one of Grace's cookies, swallowed, and laid the uneaten cookie down on the porch swing where she and Carrie were sitting. The taste had been a shock.

"Not so good, huh?" he said.

She tried to be diplomatic. "It could use a bit more sugar."

"Grace is on a mission to eliminate sugar from our diet." He took a tentative bite, made a face, and put it back on the plate. "Yes, that is about what I was expecting. Sorry."

As she rose to go, Hope reached over and covered Levi's hand with her own. "I am happy for your happiness, Cousin."

"If you need anything done around your house, you know you can call me."

"Yes," she said. "And knowing that makes my mind much lighter."

Their short visit over, she trotted her horse down the lane to the main road, and Levi went back to fixing his steps. The short visit had done her a world of good. She felt sorry for anyone who lived in a place where they had no family.

chapter TWELVE

Hope was appalled to see Abimelech Yoder drive into Logan's yard while she and Carrie were sweeping the porch.

"What a *gut* mother!" the widower said, climbing down out of his buggy.

"Abimelech!" she said. "What are *you* doing here?"

"You are not glad to see me?" He sounded hurt. "I was driving past. I saw your buggy and wished to speak with you."

"But why here?" she said. "I saw you at church only this past Sunday."

"It is difficult to talk with you privately when you are surrounded by others." He nervously tugged at his beard, a habit which she'd noticed was getting worse lately.

"I apologize, but I have much work to do." She busily resumed sweeping the dead leaves that had fallen onto the porch, hoping he would take the hint and go away.

The fact that he had come to her employer's house uninvited was a little frightening. She trusted the men of her church, but Abimelech had been staring at her so openly during their last fellowship meal that she felt quite nervous having him near her while she was alone.

Abimelech scowled. "I hear that some rich *Englisch* man bought your father's farm and hired you to . . . keep house for him."

She blushed. The term "keeping house" was a borderline term. It could mean that she was simply doing the man's housework, or it could mean the unthinkable—that she had moved in and was living with him.

"I am employed to clean and cook," she said. "He is rarely here."

"And he pays you well for this . . . cooking and cleaning?"

Again—Abimelech's voice sounded as though he was saying one thing and meaning another.

"Well enough that I have not had to take alms from Bishop Schrock in over a month."

"If you married me, you would not have to take alms at all, nor would you have to work for this *Englisch* man in a house that should still belong to your family."

She gasped at his blunt mention of marriage, then decided to ignore it. "My father allowed the sin of gambling into his life and lost the farm. It was for sale. The *Englischer* had a right to purchase it."

She could not believe she was defending Logan to one of her own, but her employer had treated her kindly. He was innocent of her father's failure. That was on her father's shoulders.

There had even been a very nice bonus in the envelope Logan had left on the kitchen table last week!

"I am a good, steady worker with a large house and a roof that does not leak. My farm is productive. My children are under my control and not problem children. I am of your faith. I can help you raise your small children. You should quit this job and marry me."

"I do not love you," Hope said. "I will not marry you. It is that simple."

Abimelech then did something that she would never have believed could happen back when he was simply her father's friend who came to visit with his wife and children from time to time. Back when she was not much more than a child herself and paid little attention to the grown-ups. He allowed his eyes to look at her from the top of her head to the bottom of her feet and then back up again. The look in his eyes was not love, it was something else, and the realization that he was not a good man made her flinch. The air around them seemed to become thick with an emotion that closed her throat and made her want to cover herself.

Thank goodness Carrie was with her. Had there not been an innocent witness in that little girl's eyes, she wasn't sure what Abimelech might have done or suggested.

The little girl was too young to understand what was going on, but Carrie's sturdy little heart made her come take her mother's hand and stand protectively beside her. Hope held tight to her broom with her other hand, wondering if she would have reason to use it as a weapon.

When her daughter moved to stand with her, Abimelech seemed to come to himself and had the grace to look away.

"I have been too long without a wife," he muttered before walking away.

The minute he left the porch, she dropped the broom, picked Carrie up in her arms, and flew into the house, then locked all the outside doors. The lock on the back door had never worked properly, if one tried to secure it from the outside, but her father had installed a large screen-door lock-and-eye on the inside for securing the house after their family had all gone to bed. This she shoved down into place, and then collapsed into a kitchen chair.

If Titus were alive, Abimelech would have *never* dared look at her like that!

Carrie crawled onto her lap and hugged her neck. "I am scared, *Mommi*."

"Oh, little one . . ." She smoothed back her daughter's hair, realizing that she had frightened the child with her frenzied locking of doors.

"Abimelech would not hurt you . . . or me." And then, because she tried very hard to always be honest with her children, she added, "At least, I hope not."

"I will ask Grandpa to make him stay away from us," Carrie said stoutly. "Everyone must obey Bishop Schrock."

"That is true," she soothed the little girl. "But let's not worry about that now."

Actually, the knowledge that Bishop Schrock and the other men of their church would not allow Abimelech to bother her if they knew that he had been inappropriate in his behavior was a comforting one. As was the knowledge that her father would have a few words to say to the man as well if she told him what happened.

She was not without resources to keep this man out of her life and would not hesitate to use them.

"I shall pray that he finds a wife, soon," she said. "But that wife will not be me!"

Logan was surprised to find two buggies in his yard instead of only Hope's. In fact, he was a little surprised to find her buggy there at all. Having her work for him was rather like employing a ghost. Hope had apparently adjusted her schedule to be gone whenever she thought he might be home. Sometimes he suspected that she turned around and went home whenever she saw his car at the house.

It was a bit of a surprise to see a strange Amish man tearing past him, whipping his horse into a canter within seconds of leaving the driveway.

This was odd. He had not seen anyone here make a horse go faster than a quick trot while pulling a buggy. The man was obviously angry, and what on earth had he been doing at his house?

As he got out of his car, he was perplexed, curious, and more than a little concerned.

Finding his own back door locked, he knocked. This was highly unusual. He'd taken some pride in living in an area where doors could still be left unlocked. "Hope? Are you in there? It's Logan. Please let me in."

A flustered, embarrassed, red-faced Hope opened the door. It was apparent that she had been crying.

"Hope—what's wrong?"

"I'm sorry, I—I—"

"What happened here? Who was that man I saw?"

"Abimelech Yoder. He wants to marry me. And I refused him. That is all."

Her embarrassment was almost too painful to watch.

"Abimelech Yoder." He turned the name over in his mind. "He's the man who just left?"

"*Ja.* I'm sorry. It won't happen again. I was just sweeping the porch when he came and started . . . proposing to me."

"Wait a minute." Logan felt immediately protective. "That man came onto my porch, uninvited, and frightened you?"

"He is a friend of my father's," Hope said. "He was used to coming and going at our home."

"Except that it isn't your home anymore. Doesn't he realize that?"

"He knows, but he wanted to talk to me alone and he lives nearby."

"Sit down." Logan pulled a chair away from the table, took

her arm, and gently led her to it. He noticed that she was trembling.

It seemed so strange to have her actually sitting here. He had laid eyes on her only once since he'd hired her. All he ever saw of her was the evidence of her hard work.

The house was always clean these days, and it smelled amazing. Thanks to Hope, his house ran as much like clockwork as a house without electricity could run. He did *not* want to lose her, and he deeply resented the man who had so obviously upset her.

Now the lovely Amish housekeeper was sitting in his kitchen with tears shimmering in her eyes, and her little daughter looking on with concern, a miniature of her mother, same dark blue dress, same little *Kapp*, same bare feet.

"Can I fix you something? A cup of tea maybe?" That sort of thing sometimes helped Marla stop crying.

Hope choked out a laugh. "I think I am the one who is supposed to be getting the tea around here! I will be fine."

"Right." Logan turned on the stove, lit the burner, and placed the teakettle on it. "I'm going to take that as a 'yes.' Don't get up. Let me take care of you for a change."

At home in Manhattan, he would have simply put a cup of water in the microwave. Using the old-fashioned teakettle still gave him fresh pleasure each time. There was something about the process of actually boiling water for tea that he enjoyed.

"Here." He poured the hot liquid over a tea bag, then placed it, a container of milk, and the sugar bowl in front of Hope. "Now tell me what's going on."

"Abimelech Yoder is a widower with eight children and a good farm." She gave a deep sigh. "He and his older children also run a small store. He feels that he needs a wife. I am without a husband and he thinks it would make good sense for me to marry him. He seems to be angry that I am refusing him."

"How long has your husband been gone, Hope?"

"Two months now."

"Only two months?"

"*Ja.*"

"You barely know your own name if it has only been two months. Let alone have someone trying to talk you into marriage! I'm surprised you can function at all. Are you sure you even feel like working here?"

"I have children. I *must* function." She tilted her head and studied him. "You sound like a man who has known grief."

He seldom talked about Ariela, but somehow, it felt right to confide in this Amish widow.

"I was married before. I loved her with all my heart."

"What happened?"

"Leukemia."

There was no need to say anything more. A world of explanation was attached to that one word.

"I am so very sorry! How did you stand it?"

"I was not terribly sane for the next couple of years. It took a long time for me to recover and sometimes I'm not entirely sure I ever did."

She thought this over. "Sometimes I fear that I will never recover, either. I loved my husband so very much. From the time I was fourteen I knew I wanted to marry him."

He sat down at the table across from her. "It will get a little easier with time."

"It is very hard right now." She cradled her teacup in her hands. "Especially when Abimelech is being so pushy."

He drummed his fingers on the table. "I don't know much about the Amish, but is it normal for your people to marry so soon after a spouse's death?"

"No, not at all. We are the same as your people that way. But that is not the biggest problem to me."

"What is?"

"We Amish marry for love, and I do not love him." She stared down at her hands, which she now folded in her lap. "I will *never* love him."

"Then he is never to come here and bother you again." He felt anger building inside while he watched her. She was not a large woman, and delicately made. The thoughts of that rough-looking scarecrow of a man frightening her made him want to bash his face in.

"My father and the bishop will take care of it," she said. Then she added in a small voice, "At least I hope so."

"Keep the door locked from now on when you're here."

"I think that might be a good idea." She looked up and there was worry in her eyes. "You will not fire me because he was here?"

"Fire you?" He was shocked. "After the good job you've been doing? Of course not!"

"You think I have done a *gut* job?" Her face lit up with such a grateful smile that it made his heart ache.

"You've been doing a wonderful job. I don't know how I got along without you."

She glanced around. "I love this old house. It is a pleasure to my heart to care for it."

"Your grandfather built it?"

"My great-great-grandfather built it." She seemed to suddenly realize that she and Carrie were alone with him, and stood up nervously. "It is getting late. I should leave. Carrie . . ."

"Do you feel well enough?" he said. "I could drive you if you aren't."

"I am fine now. I must go. It grows late. I have a cow to take care of."

"I have an empty barn," he said. "Would it be easier for you to keep the cow here?"

"You would pay me to milk my own cow?" There was amusement in her voice, and he was glad to hear it. She was getting over her shock from the man's rough proposal.

"Sorry," he said. "I don't know how much care a cow needs. I suppose that was a stupid thing to say."

"No," she said. "It was very kind and thoughtful, but I must go now."

"I understand."

Then, instead of leaving, she abruptly sat back down, twisting her apron in her hands, her eyes downcast.

"You have been so kind to me that I am ashamed of not telling you something I should have told you when you first hired me."

He smiled to reassure her. "I can't imagine you having too great a sin to confess. What should you have told me that you didn't?"

"I—I'm pregnant," she said. "I did not want to tell you that first day because I was afraid you would not hire me if you knew, and I badly wanted to work in this house that I knew so well. I thought if I showed you what a *gut* worker I was first, you wouldn't mind so much when you found out." She glanced up at him quickly. "I did not lie. It was not *really* a sin."

"You're pregnant?"

"A woman's eyes would already have seen. If you want to fire me now, I will understand."

"You're pregnant?" He was a bit flustered by her confession. He knew next to nothing about pregnant women. Weren't they supposed to be fragile?

"That is what I said." She stopped twisting her apron. "Is this a big problem to you?"

"No. No problem." At least he hoped not. "Do you feel all right?"

"I feel fine. May I continue to work here?"

"Of course, as long as you like, but I don't want you to overdo. The baby must come first."

"*Ja*. Babies must always come first. But I will be fine."

"A baby," he said with wonder. "I've not spent much time around babies."

"A good baby isn't much trouble," she said. "I should be able to do my work again soon after it comes. I will need to bring it with me, of course."

"Of course you will. How far along are you?"

"Three months. I am due in May."

He quickly counted the months. If he kept to the timetable he and Marla had agreed upon, the baby would be about two months old when he left. Instead of relief at the thought of leaving Hope and her baby behind, he felt a surprising stab of disappointment.

While he pondered this, Hope rose from the table, carried her teacup to the sink. She rinsed it out and set it to drain.

"Thank you for understanding," she said as she left with Carrie in tow.

He watched in the direction she had gone for a long time after her buggy left his yard. How strange would it feel to have a baby in his home? Somehow he got the feeling that the old house was pleased with the fact. It was the kind of house that had been built to shelter babies.

He wished he knew what was in her head. As a writer, he was used to putting himself inside people's heads, seeing out of their eyes, hearing out of their ears, but he couldn't begin to imagine what went on in this Amish widow's mind as she faced bringing another life into the world. What did she think about? How tenuous was her financial survival? She had looked so scared for a moment when she had asked if he was going to fire her.

He realized that yet again, there was something that smelled delicious simmering on the stove. He glanced into the skillet and found a hash in which she had used up the leftovers from yesterday's roast, turning them into something wonderful as usual. She didn't have to scrimp like this—he was able to afford enough food that she didn't have to use up leftovers. He took an exploratory taste. Sure enough, like everything else she made, this, too, was scrumptious. He hoped she had fed herself and the little girl as well. He would make sure to bring in more groceries. So many that she would have to take extra food home with her.

chapter THIRTEEN

S unday services were a challenge to Hope with Abimelech Yoder glowering at her. They were having church at Hans and Missy's house, and even though the couple had a house large enough to fit in all the benches from the church wagon, it was still a tight squeeze for thirty-eight families. They were crowded together, women on one side, men on the other, facing one another as usual, so it was no trick for Abimelech to stare at her.

She sat with face averted when the preacher stood in the middle of the group. When he moved to one side or another, it was possible for her to look up and allow her black bonnet to block her gaze just enough to avoid Abimelech's eyes.

As she wrestled with her discomfort at being stared at, she felt rivulets of sweat roll down her back. She didn't know if it was nerves or the moist heat being thrown off by so many bodies.

Like many Amish houses in Holmes County, Hans and Missy's had a wraparound porch that provided acres of tin roof for the rain to ping against. Adam squirmed beside her and she patted his leg as the rain increased to a roar against that roof. Thunder rolled in volleys through the windows, which had been opened to relieve some of the heat inside the house. Even though it was December, all the bodies packed into the house made it uncomfortably warm. Then the wind picked up and ruffled the pages of Bibles opened on the laps of those who were not holding small children.

The preacher was visiting from another church district. He had a good voice and plenty of volume, which he cranked up in order to be heard. It was as though he and the storm were having a duel to see who could be the louder as lightning crackled in the sky. Adam jumped with each strike and hid his face in her lap. Hope, sitting with her mother, Rose, gathered Carrie against her side. The two women exchanged worried glances.

There had not been enough stalls to put all the horses in Hans and Missy's barn, and even though it looked like rain when Hope drove in, she was too late to get a spot. She had tied her horse to a fence post and hurried inside, leaving the door of her buggy rolled open. This was regrettable—there would be wet seats for her and her children on the way home!

The thing she most hated was that her poor horse was standing outside in all of this. Horses were, of course, used to being outside in all sorts of weather—but she blamed herself anyway.

If Titus were here, he would have taken care of the horse while she ushered the children inside. It had been so wonderful to have someone to do things like that.

The Lord had been wise in creating a mother and a father for a family. It was so difficult trying to be both. It hit her anew that Titus would never be coming back, and she choked back tears, determined not to allow the children to see her cry. They missed their father terribly, they did not need to be worried by their mother's tears.

She realized Abimelech was struggling with the same problem. He, too, was trying to be both father and mother to his

children, as well as apparently wrestle with being a man in need
of a woman. There were a handful of other widows in their congregation, but all were well past the age of raising his children.
Unfortunately, she was the only viable candidate from within
their church for him to court.

The preacher was apparently finished because suddenly
everyone was singing. She had not heard a word the man had
said. Her thoughts were too busy, tumbling over one another,
remembering how thrilled she was to say yes to Titus's proposal.
With Titus, it had never been an issue whether or not to marry
him. She loved him passionately and had happily gone into marriage with him.

Was it possible to marry someone for whom you felt no love
and yet manage to create a good marriage and family? She had
always wanted a large family, and in order to have more children, she would have to have a husband. What if Abimelech
was the only possibility that ever came along and she waited too
long?

Her options were quite limited when it came to potential
husbands. He would have to be Amish. She would never allow
her children to be raised by an outsider, to bring strange teachings into her family. Abimelech would be considered a catch in
many Amish women's minds, but the thought of him touching
her made her shudder.

In some ways, *Englisch* women had it so easy. They could
marry whomever they chose. There were no restrictions on
them. They divorced and remarried at will. She couldn't imagine such a thing for herself. The idea of marriage being for life
was too ingrained within her.

A visiting preacher had once said that the divorce rate
among the Amish was less than one percent, while the divorce
rate among the *Englisch* was closer to fifty. That meant that half
the *Englisch* people she saw on the streets had been married and

divorced, in spite of the fact that the Bible said there was only one reason to divorce—infidelity.

The idea of one spouse being unfaithful to the other felt so alien to her. She would never have cheated on Titus. The man didn't exist who could have enticed her away from her husband and children.

The *Englisch* lived strange lives.

Just like that *Englisch* man she worked for. How strange that he and his wife lived separately most of the time. She couldn't imagine Titus ever having allowed such a thing.

The call to prayer came and she slid down onto her knees and bowed her head, one arm around Adam to encourage him to kneel as well.

In that blessed, silent time of prayer, she prayed for her children, her mother and father, her younger brothers and sisters, Levi and Grace and their new little one, her church, Abimelech Yoder as he, too, struggled to care for his children alone, and lastly, her employer, Logan Parker, who appeared to be a decent man even if he was *Englisch*.

A rustle in the crowd alerted her to the fact that the silent prayer was over. Soon it would be time to eat and enjoy fellowship together. It would be awkward for her with Abimelech there, but the thing about being Amish was that you couldn't really ever escape being around someone you were uncomfortable with if they were part of your church.

The rain stopped soon after services ended, and the sun came out. As quickly as possible, she left her children with her mother and went out to see to her horse and buggy. The horse seemed none the worse for wear from his impromptu bath— but the inside of the buggy was soaked, just as she'd feared.

"You might need this." Bishop Schrock handed her an old towel. His buggy was next to hers.

"Thank you so much."

The bishop grew solemn and cleared his throat. "I saw Abimelech Yoder watching you this morning."

She averted her gaze. "I saw that, too."

"It is early days yet. Do you welcome his attention?"

It was difficult having to speak about a man's attention toward her with the bishop, and the fact that he was her father-in-law made it even more awkward. Although she'd comforted herself with the thought that the bishop and the men of the church would protect her from Abimelech's unwelcome attention if need be . . . the reality of talking openly about it was highly embarrassing.

It wasn't the Amish way to speak badly about someone, so Hope was careful with her answer. "He is a good farmer."

The bishop smiled and repeated his question. "Do you welcome his attention?"

She wiped down the seat of her buggy. "He has many children in need of a mother."

"Speak your heart to me, Daughter," the bishop said. "Will you ever welcome his attention? I heard that he paid you a visit at the *Englisch* man's house the other day. He was seen driving away in great anger."

She didn't even bother to ask how the bishop had come by such information. Her father-in-law seemed to have eyes everywhere when it came to the members of their church. She sighed and turned around. "No. I do not. Even if I live forever with no husband, I will never welcome Abimelech Yoder's attention."

"Then I will take care of it." The bishop's jaw was clenched as he strode away.

Hope felt sorry for anyone who was part of a church district not overseen by Bishop Schrock. He was a true shepherd, not only in name, but in his deeds. The Lord had given them a great gift when Bishop Schrock was chosen by lot to become their leader.

• • •

Logan was once again struggling to get some pages finished on his latest thriller. It wasn't great writing, but he was at least able to push the plot along. It was Sunday and there was no place to go and nothing to do. The antiques shop and all the other shops were closed, and so were the restaurants.

There was nothing to do except wrestle with his laptop and get his word count up. Two thousand words was the assignment he had given himself this morning. He'd achieved that, but they were not particularly good words. With the word-count function at the bottom of the screen, he had to fight to keep himself from checking his progress every few sentences.

If he *ever* got this last novel in the series finished, he might never begin another one. The only writing he seemed to enjoy these days was the WWII story he had started at Violet's, which he pounded out on that antique typewriter, where there was no word count to check, only the satisfaction of completed pages piling up.

Word had gotten out soon after about what he was doing, and other elderly men and women began to come in to see him. They sat at the round claw-foot table, drinking Violet's tea, and told him their stories. To his knowledge, none of them knew that he was a professional writer, and yet their need to tell their stories was so great, they didn't seem to care. They simply seemed grateful for a listening ear. They liked having someone pay attention to the fact that their lives had mattered.

"I was a nurse in London." One precious lady in her late nineties had chatted with him only yesterday about her experience in the war. She'd lain propped upon pillows on her bed at the nursing home, gazing at a picture of her husband that someone had hung for her on the opposite wall. She had been a war bride whom a local soldier had brought back to Holmes

County, and she still had a lovely English accent. "I worked at the hospital during a time when the German bombers were being quite . . . energetic."

"How did you feel about everything that was going on?" he asked.

"Pardon?" She leaned forward to hear him better.

He repeated his question. "How did you feel about the air raids, the rubble, the danger?"

"How did I *feel*?" She glared at him with faded blue eyes. "There was no time to *feel*, young man! We had too much *work* to do! If we had stopped to *feel*, we would never have won the war!"

His fingers flew, trying to get the strength and dignity of that woman's conversation down on paper.

As he worked, and his typewriter story grew and deepened, the less interested he became in the novels that had made him famous. Still, he labored on, trying to fulfill his contract. Punching words into his laptop each evening. Following the script. Following the template. His heart just wasn't in it.

There was no script or template for the WWII story. It was creativity at a level he'd never experienced before. Blending the old with the new. Fictionalizing people's real-life experiences, but remaining true to the values they had expressed.

What had once represented a sort of playtime and a way to get past his writer's block was quickly becoming an obsession. The stack of pages accumulated on that old claw-foot table.

The more people he talked to, the more a part of the community he felt he was becoming. The older generation had families who began to recognize him and greet him on the street and in the stores. He wasn't Nate Scott to them. He was just Logan Parker, a slightly eccentric outsider whom Violet—a woman who had taught English to half the people in the county—had taken under her wing and thought might have the potential to become a good writer. If he really applied himself.

He was thoroughly enjoying his new life . . . except for the book that was due soon, which he did *not* want to write.

Two thousand words were plenty for one day. Now what could he do? Normally he would have worked around the house, except that Hope had already taken care of everything. All was tidy. All in good repair. Even the mousetraps were set.

The girl seemed happy to have so much as a spoon to wash these days. He would have to work even harder at giving her something to do. It was a strange situation to be in. He had begun to deliberately scatter things around just to give her something to pick up and put away. He didn't want to lose her, and he was fairly certain she was the kind of person who would not take money without first doing what she considered an honest day's work.

The rain had finally stopped. He decided to take a long walk. This January had been warmer than normal, and exceptionally rainy.

He came in an hour later from a long tromp in the woods, exhilarated from the exercise. Hiking on his own property was much more fun than walking on a treadmill in the gym.

At the door, he stopped to wipe the mud off his feet and then thought better of it. Tracking in dirt might give Hope all of ten minutes of mopping to do tomorrow.

He pulled off his damp sweater. He hadn't talked to his mother in a couple of weeks because she was involved in a high-profile case that was keeping her and her firm ultrabusy, but she usually gave herself a break on Sundays if at all possible, no matter what else was going on.

He glanced at the clock on the wall. It was eleven o'clock. If she'd gone to St. Patrick's this morning, she would be back by now and having her second cup of coffee. When he was younger, she would have spent part of the morning with several Sunday newspapers scattered about, but these days she read her *New York Times* and *Wall Street Journal* online. It should be a good time to call. He went out on the front porch, where the reception on his cell phone was best.

He had continued to come up against things that felt familiar to him, curves in the road where the feeling of having been there before would hit yet again, the inside of the country store in nearby Trail, where he stopped to purchase some of their famous bologna. He had begun to wonder if maybe he *had* been here at one time during his childhood. It was the only thing that made sense. It was normal for a person to have déjà vu from time to time, but not this often or this intensely.

He had even slowly worked his way off his antidepressant medication, wondering if it had been somehow causing this—but the feelings of strange familiarity still did not go away.

The sound of his mother's smoky drawl made him smile. She had given up cigarettes years ago, but all that smoking had left a permanent roughness to her voice. She tended to speak slowly, and with a certain built-in sarcasm. It worked well in the courtroom, and made her stand out in a city that moved and talked fast. With him, though, there was never any sarcasm. She was all mother, all the time. As he'd grown older, she'd become one of his closest friends.

"Logan. It is *so* good to hear from you." The instant she realized it was him, a smile wrapped itself around her words.

"Is the case going well?"

"We won!" she crowed.

"Congratulations." The woman was deadly when it came to protecting her clients.

"So how are you getting along?" He heard her take a sip of coffee.

His mother had a need for coffee that rivaled even his own.

In fact, sometimes he thought it rivaled normal people's need for oxygen. She said it took the place of cigarettes.

"Getting words down on the page as usual." It was his stock answer, but evidently she heard something in his voice that made her dig deeper.

"What's wrong?"

"Can you remember if I was ever in Holmes County as a child?"

There was a long silence on the other end of the phone.

"Mother? Are you still there?"

"I'm still here, darling," his mother said. "I'm just trying to remember. No, I don't think so."

"Did Grandmother ever take me on vacation here by any chance?"

"My mother?" She gave a throaty chuckle. "Hardly. If your grandmother took a vacation, it was always to Europe."

His grandmother had been a painter, and had spent a great deal of her time in Paris. He, too, could not imagine his grandmother bringing him here.

"Why do you ask?"

"I think I mentioned to you when I told you about buying the house that it felt familiar?"

"You did."

"It's still the strangest thing, Mom," he said. "I feel like I've been here before."

"It's called déjà vu, dear."

"I know, but this feels . . . different."

"I'm sorry, but I've never been in Ohio in my life," she said. "As far as your grandmother? I doubt we could have paid her to go there. The Midwest wasn't exactly her thing."

"No." He smiled. "French sunsets were her thing."

His mother laughed. "I still have several of those paintings of hers in storage if you'd like a few for your house."

"Several?"

"Um . . . maybe thirty."

"One thing about Grandmother," he said. "She was as prolific as she was eccentric. Too bad she wasn't a particularly good painter."

"I miss her, terribly."

"Me, too."

"You did have a good childhood, didn't you, Logan?" There was an unfamiliar catch in his mother's voice. "I mean, you did have a happy life in spite of having two nutty women raising you?"

"Mom," he said, sincerely, "I had a great childhood. You were always so good to me. Grandmother, too. I never lacked for anything."

He could hear his mother sigh with relief and he wondered if age was finally catching up with her. It was rare for her to need reassurance.

"Is there something wrong, Mom?"

"No, dear. I just miss you, that's all, but I'm glad you're enjoying your new home."

"It's beautiful here. I'd love for you to come for a visit."

"You know what? I might just do that pretty soon. I've got a few more cases to get off my desk first." Her voice grew stronger. "Now, you get back to your writing! I need another Nate Scott novel to read."

chapter FOURTEEN

"I s Nate Scott your favorite author?" Hope asked.

He was deep into a book he'd purchased about WWII artillery. "Why do you ask?"

"You have an awful lot of his books lying around. I read a few pages."

"What did you think?" He waited, curious about her answer.

"I did not like it much."

He winced. Now even his housekeeper was giving him bad reviews. He might as well tell her the truth.

"I'm Nate Scott."

"You have a fake name?"

"A pseudonym. A lot of authors do that."

"You wrote all those books?" She digested this. "Why?"

"Because that's what I do. That's how I make my living. That's who I am."

"Oh." She thought it over. "Is that the reason for the crazy room?"

"The crazy room?"

"The one with all the colored note cards taped to the wall with strange things written on them?"

"That's the method I use to structure a book."

"Oh." She looked confused.

"I tape the plot to the wall where I can look at it and think about it and change it."

"Oh." She thought this over, too. "That is your job? Making things up?"

It was obvious that she did not think much of his method, his books, or the profession he'd chosen.

"That's how I make my living. I knew from the time I was a child that I wanted to be a writer. It's worked out well for me."

"That's nice."

He had been around her long enough to know that when she used the word *nice* she was just being polite. To her, being a writer was probably synonymous with being lazy.

"Isn't there anything you ever wanted to do since you were a child, Hope? I mean, something in addition to being a wife and mother?"

"*Ja.*" She seemed uncomfortable with the question.

"What was it?"

"You will laugh at me."

"I would never laugh at you."

"I always wished I had a farm to run." Her voice was shy. "A place where I could be in charge. I always thought I would make a very good farmer, but my father told me it was not an appropriate thing for a girl to do. I think he was probably right."

"I don't think that's true anymore."

"It is. Women grow vegetable gardens and mow yards, but I've never known an Amish woman farmer unless she was help-ing her husband." She seemed to lose interest, or perhaps she was embarrassed for having voiced her dream. "You must tell Violet who and what you are."

"I will. Soon. It's just that she assumed . . . and I didn't want to hurt her feelings, and then one thing led to another."

"One thing always leads to another. That is why we are taught by our preachers not to let Satan get a toehold."

"You're right. I'll tell her tomorrow."

Hope nodded approval. "Good."

Violet was not nearly as surprised as he expected her to be, and much more excited than he'd ever dreamed.

"I knew you had talent!" she crowed. "Just wait until I tell my friends!"

"What are you going to tell them?" He felt a little nervous about her enthusiasm.

"Why, I'll tell them that all these stories you've been collecting from us are going to get published!" Her forehead creased in thought. "You should probably hurry, though. Frank's heart has been acting up."

He had expected her to be upset, or mildly disappointed in him. It had not occurred to him that she would assume this would mean automatic publication. All he'd been doing was using these stories and that old typewriter to overcome his writer's block and get to know the community. Now she was expecting immediate publication? This might have been a mistake.

"When will our book be finished?" she asked eagerly.

"Soon." He felt sick at heart. This work he'd been doing here was not serious writing. He was writing a WWII love story, for pity's sake. No one wanted to read a love story by Nate Scott. The fans would be so disappointed. "Maybe in a month or two."

"I'm very excited," Violet said. "But hurry. None of us is getting any younger, you know."

Looking at her eager face, thinking about how hard it was going to be to convince his agent to represent this novel, the chapters he still had to write and edit on the book that *was* due, not to mention all the people in his life right now . . . well, it made him wonder what on earth he'd done with all his free time back in New York.

At least he was writing again, and unless he missed his guess, he thought there was a chance that he was writing well.

"So, anything interesting happen at work?" he asked.

Marla and he tried to talk several times a week, but it seemed to be getting harder and harder to find anything to talk about.

"Not really," Marla said. "Same old, same old. What about you? What did you do?"

"I got my word count in for the day," he answered. "The writing is getting a little easier. Oh, and I took Violet over to Keim's Lumber in Charm at lunchtime today. She wanted to get a special telescoping tool they carry there for picking apples off trees. The apples have already been harvested for this year, but Violet saw in the newspaper that the tool was on sale and wanted one for next year."

"Didn't you tell me she was in her nineties?" Marla asked.

"Early nineties."

"*She's* awfully optimistic, don't you think?" Marla laughed. "Thinking she'll actually be around next year to use it!"

Her comment struck him as a little cold-blooded. He thought it valiant and sweet that the old woman still hoped to harvest her own apples off her own trees next fall. Of course, Marla didn't know Violet enough to care about her, and that was part of the problem. Marla didn't know any of the people he was coming to talk about and trying to describe to her.

An awkward silence fell. There had been more and more of these lately.

He tried to come up with something about his day that would interest her.

"I bought two little matching tricycles at Keim's Lumber today for Hope's children," he offered. "One was pink and the other one was blue. I saw them in the toy section while Violet was purchasing her apple picker, and I couldn't resist."

"Oh?" Marla seemed surprised. "You're buying toys for Hope's children now?"

There was something about the sound of her voice that made him wish he'd not mentioned it.

"Well, they are such good children and they have so little. You should have seen them. They were so happy with those little trikes."

"That doesn't sound like a good idea. What will that do to the floors?"

"The floors are wood and pretty scarred already. There's not much children can do to hurt them. Besides, I didn't care."

"You just sat there working while your housekeeper's kids rode all over your house?"

"They didn't stay long after I got home today. Hope was almost finished with her work, but she made a little post office game of giving the children items to put away. You should have seen those two little ones pedaling all over the house pretending to deliver the mail. It was cute."

"Oh." Silence.

"I'm discovering that the Amish are very intentional about teaching their children to work. Violet's been telling me about it. They start early and incorporate it into everything they do. Fascinating to watch. I can't believe the things little Carrie can already do in the kitchen."

"Yes. Interesting." More silence.

He could tell he'd said something wrong, but for the life of him he didn't know what.

"What did I say?" he said. "Don't sit there and brood, Marla."

He heard a sniffle on the other end.

"I'm afraid you're going to start hounding me to have children again."

He closed his eyes wearily. Apparently they were going to rehash an old fight—one they'd never resolved. Just because he'd purchased tricycles for Hope's children and had been foolish enough to think Marla would enjoy hearing about it.

"I've never 'hounded' you about that."

"But you *want* them." She made it sound like an accusation. He didn't deny it. "I wouldn't mind having a child."

"I'm not the motherly type, Logan. You know that, plus I've worked too hard getting to where I am to jeopardize it by having a child. I thought you understood."

"I accept the fact that you don't want children, but I've never understood," he said. "Mom built a pretty amazing career after she had me, and she was single."

"I'm not your mother," Marla said. "And that's unfair."

"You're right, and I apologize." He admitted defeat to himself. It was wrong for him to try to talk Marla into having a family that she didn't want, but sometimes he wished she'd told him before they had started building a life together.

Then a thought hit. Maybe the reason Marla didn't want children was because she'd never spent much time with them. It might help if she could be around Hope's two children for a bit, and see how adorable they were.

Besides, this business of trying to keep a relationship going with phone calls alone wasn't working, and Marla had been especially busy at work lately. Too busy to come for a visit, she said. He was reluctant to go to New York if she had no time for him. In fact, the more time he spent here, the harder it was to contemplate moving back at all. He liked the peace and quiet of the countryside and it seemed to be agreeing with him. His creativity was coming back, and his desire to drink was no longer overwhelming.

"Are you ever going to have any time off?" he asked. "We need to spend some time together."

To his surprise, this time she agreed.

"You're right," she said. "I think it's high time I came for a visit."

Hope was as nervous as a cat. Logan's wife, Marla, was coming for a visit. She would be here in an hour. Housekeeping for a man, especially one as absentminded and kind as Logan, was easy. Being under another woman's watchful gaze was something else entirely. Would her housekeeping be up to the *Englisch* woman's standards? Would the supper she had fixed be all right?

Verla had told her that Logan had three children and another one on the way, so she had stripped the beds and washed and dried the linens, even though no one had slept in them since they had been taken home from the store.

Logan purchased extra food, although he acted a little uncomfortable when she asked him about what the children liked to eat.

"They probably won't come," he said. "Marla isn't fond of . . . traveling with them."

His unease about talking about his children worried her. The man seemed downright miserable whenever she brought up the subject. She wondered what was wrong. A father should show a little more pride in his children.

"Hope?" He sounded nervous. "Before Marla gets here, I need to tell you something, and I'm not sure how to go about it."

This did not sound good. She was tossing a salad to go with the rolls. She paused in her preparations. "I am listening."

"You keep mentioning my children . . . but I don't have any."

"But Verla said . . ."

"I think I know exactly what she said, and I know why she

said it. Marla has a wicked sense of humor sometimes when she gets in a certain mood. She was annoyed with me the day Verla first showed me the house and she pretended that we had three children at home and that she was pregnant. None of that was true. It was a sort of . . . game to her."

"Marla is not a truth-teller?"

"Sometimes she goes a little overboard . . ."

A car pulled into the driveway. Logan went outside and Hope stayed discreetly in the house so the husband and wife could greet each other in privacy.

"Hello, darling!"

Hope heard his wife's voice for the first time.

"Hi, Marla. I'm so glad you came."

Hope heard the trunk slam as he got the luggage. She busied herself at the sink, not wanting either of them to think that she was eavesdropping. Adam sat on the floor of the kitchen, playing with pots and pans. Carrie sat at the table cutting out brightly colored birds from a child's workbook that Hope had found in a thrift store. She had taken extra care with the children's clothing that morning, wanting them to look nice for Marla. She noticed that Adam still had a bit of bread and jam clinging to his face, and quickly took a damp cloth to it.

"I'd like for you to meet my housekeeper, Hope, and her children, Adam and Carrie," Logan said. "Hope, this is Marla."

She glanced up from washing Adam's face and saw one of the most astonishing-looking women she'd ever met. Marla was nearly as tall as Logan, and sleekly beautiful in the same way that women on the front of glossy magazines at the grocery checkout counter were beautiful. Adam's eyes went round and his mouth hung open looking at her.

"Hello, Hope." Marla held out her hand, as though for a handshake.

"Hello." Hope felt shy and tongue-tied.

It felt strange shaking hands with another woman. That was something men did. A nod and smile would have been her preference. Marla's hands were soft and smooth. Hope knew that hers were rough and callused from work. Marla's fingernails were long and polished dark red.

Logan's wife wore white jeans so tight they looked like they were painted onto her long legs. Logan helped her off with her coat, and Hope saw that she wore a tight black sweater that didn't quite reach the top of her jeans, along with black high heels and silver earrings. Her reddish hair was tossed about like someone who had ridden too many miles in a buggy without a bonnet, but Hope suspected the messy style was deliberate. Her eyes were heavily made up, and those eyes now calmly looked Hope up and down, and dismissed what they saw.

Hope, in her simple brown dress, felt like a small, plain wren beside an exotic bird of paradise.

Marla turned to Logan. "It's been a long drive. I'm tired, I have a headache, and I want to lie down."

"I'll bring you something," Hope offered. "An aspirin? Some tea? I have a nice pot roast ready if you're hungry."

"Thank you," Marla said. "But I couldn't eat a thing and I brought my own medication."

With that, Logan's wife headed toward the stairs.

Hope tried to be charitable. Her headache must be very bad indeed for the woman to have been so dismissive.

Hope watched Logan follow his wife upstairs with her expensive-looking luggage. Then she glanced down at her beautiful children. Marla had not even acknowledged them, nor Hope's efforts in preparing a nice meal for her. Still, some people did not travel well.

Logan hesitated on the steps and glanced back at her.

"Thank you for all you did, Hope. We'll enjoy your meal later."

"I will straighten the kitchen before I go."

Disappointed in the woman she had thought might become a friend, she carefully put away the dinner to which she had given so much time and thought.

Logan took Marla's suitcases to their room and was surprised to find her standing near the window, flipping through a fashion magazine she'd brought with her.

"How can you bear not having electricity?" she complained. "I have to stand here by the window just to have enough light to read."

"I thought you had a headache."

"Oh that. I'm fine. I just haven't seen you for weeks. I didn't feel like standing around making small talk with some woman in a bonnet."

Your wife is not a truth-teller? Hope's quaint statement came back to him. Marla did bend the truth from time to time in small ways if she felt like it.

"She worked really hard making a nice supper for you," he said. "It would have been nice if you'd thanked her."

"She's your housekeeper." Marla was unrepentant. "That's what you pay her to do. Besides, I don't eat red meat anymore."

"You didn't even notice her children. She had dressed them in their Sunday clothes for you."

"Of course I did. I noticed that the boy needed his face washed. What had he been eating, anyway?"

"Yesterday she brought some strawberry jam she had made last spring, and made homemade bread today. She'd given him a piece of it. Since when did you stop eating red meat?"

"Weeks ago. If you had been around, you'd know." She sat down on the bed, took off her high heels, and glanced appreciatively around the bedroom. "Nice furniture, Logan. You've certainly been busy."

"I told you I'd bought it."

"Yes, but knowing you I half expected you to be sleeping on an air mattress and eating off paper plates. Why, you've become downright domestic. This is not nearly as awful as I would have expected. Or did your cozy little housekeeper pick all this out for you?"

That was Logan's first indication that Marla was angry.

"Are you insinuating something?"

"All I'm saying is that you certainly have a nice little setup here."

"Hope is a decent, moral woman. A widow trying to make a living for her children."

"Then you would be quite the catch, wouldn't you?" Marla's eyes narrowed.

"I would never lay a hand on her," Logan said.

"Interesting that you would mention that so quickly." Marla flung down the magazine. "I'm guessing you would like to, though, wouldn't you?"

Alarm bells rang. Marla was capable of escalating an argument into a fever-pitch fight in seconds. They didn't fight often, but when they did, she had no control whatsoever over her tongue. Some of the words Marla was capable of throwing at him were not words those innocent children downstairs deserved to hear. Nor did their mother.

"Be careful what you say, Marla," he warned. "Before you say another word, let me go send Hope and the children home. Then we can talk."

"Your first thought is about your housekeeper?" Marla's voice turned deadly. "Let me tell you something . . . "

• • •

The photograph drew her to it like a magnet. Hope tried to look away, but couldn't. It was a picture of Logan and Marla on a beach. Logan was wearing baggy blue swim trunks, but Marla was very tan and lean and wore only a small, white bathing suit that Hope knew was called a bikini. Marla had struck a pose with one hand on her hip, and the other around Logan's waist. One slim leg was stuck out, and her chin was tilted as though proud of having such a beautiful body.

Hope could not imagine allowing someone to take such a picture. Why, the woman was wearing clothing that covered much less than the underwear Hope discreetly purchased at Spector's in Mt. Eaton, after making certain there were no men in the store.

The *Englisch* were such a puzzle. Why would any woman allow herself to be seen in public in such an outfit? Let alone allow a picture to be taken and then framed and displayed.

"Mommi?" Adam called to her from downstairs.

She jumped and put the picture facedown on the side table so that Adam could not see it if he should walk in. Her son should not be looking at pictures of half-naked women, even if he was only four.

She did not like Logan's wife very much, and selfishly hoped she wouldn't be coming to visit him often. The meeting yesterday had been such a disaster. Logan and his wife had argued, so Hope had gotten the children in the buggy without even putting the food away. She did not need the job so badly that she would allow her children to hear such words!

It was Monday morning, and Marla was gone. She had not bothered to wash up their dishes. The bathtub had not been wiped out after her bath. Two days' worth of damp towels were scattered all over the bathroom floor. There was makeup spilled in the lavatory. It was as though she had tried to leave Hope as much work as possible.

Presumably, this photograph was a gift left for Logan to

remember her by. Hope had seen Logan for only a few minutes earlier this morning, but she noticed that he was in a foul mood.

None of this was any of her business, but she could not help but take note and wonder about those two. The *Englisch* had their television and picture shows to watch, the Amish had each other and the *Englisch* to watch. Logan and his wife would be entertaining if it weren't for the fact that she liked the man she worked for and thought he deserved better.

Only last week he had purchased two small tricycles for Adam and Carrie to play on. One pink. One blue. He made no big to-do over it. He had simply brought them home with him.

"I was at Keim's and I saw these. I thought they might help entertain the children while you work," Logan had said. "They are such good children. I thought they should have a reward."

The Amish did not necessarily consider good behavior something to be rewarded. Good behavior out of children was something to be expected, not bribed, but they did give and receive occasional gifts, and so she thanked him.

She was grateful that Logan had been thoughtful enough to purchase something that would not go against their culture. A handheld video device for her son would have caused her to make an embarrassing refusal, but a little tricycle? That was not a problem. She wondered if he had figured it out all by himself or had asked someone for a suggestion. Either way, it warmed her heart that he had been so thoughtful.

Of course, it would never do to spend too much time thinking about him. In fact, after hearing part of their argument, she suspected he would soon sell the house and move back to New York.

It was her opinion that Logan's wife was very spoiled and more in love with herself than with her husband. If *she* were married to someone as handsome and kind and thoughtful as Logan, she would *never* speak so angrily to him!

Where had *that* thought come from? She put that idea away and quickly asked God for forgiveness. It was a terribly sinful thing to imagine being married to another woman's husband.

"Go outside and play, Adam," she called. "I will be down soon."

Satisfied that his mother was within easy reach, he happily obeyed.

She went downstairs and was folding up blankets that had been left strewn about on the couch when she heard Logan's car pull into the driveway.

She tried to hurry with the straightening up because she didn't like to stay once Logan arrived, but the dishes were not done, and she wanted to put some of the good bread she had set to rising to bake in the oven. It was very inconvenient when he came home early.

She heard him outside talking to the children and smiled as she heard them trying to speak to him in English.

He came into the kitchen where she was starting the dishes to soak. "I brought some gummy bears for them from Violet's shop. I hope you don't mind."

"Children like sweets."

"What about their mother?" He produced a large package of Coblentz chocolates from behind his back.

He was smiling, but his smile faltered when she merely stood there with her hands in the suds.

"Don't you like chocolate?" He seemed genuinely puzzled.

She dried her hands on her apron and reached for the box, a little unsure what to do about this. Chocolates were a gift that a man gave to his wife or his sweetheart. She was torn. Coblentz chocolates were also a local delicacy. They were delicious . . . and expensive. She rarely got any. It was a hard gift to turn down.

"Thank you," she said. "I do like chocolate very much, but it is not an appropriate gift to give your housekeeper."

"Huh?"

She laid the chocolate box on the table and turned back to her dishes. Her face was burning. She should not have said anything.

"Hope?"

"*Ja.*"

"You have worked for me several weeks now, and you have done an excellent job. Beyond excellent. But sometimes you act as frightened as a rabbit when I'm here. Have I done something wrong?"

She scrubbed at a pot. Marla had apparently tried to make oatmeal and burned it. The pot might not ever be the same. "No."

"Have I frightened you in any way?"

"No."

"Then enjoy the chocolate. I don't mean anything by it. I just thought you would enjoy it. And . . . I also wanted to apologize about Marla. She can be pretty high-strung sometimes."

"Thank you." She continued to work on the dishes and did not look at him. "But it is not necessary for you to apologize for someone else's behavior."

"Marla's a city girl. Being in the country isn't easy for her. She doesn't know what to do with herself."

She could start by picking up her own towels, Hope thought.

"It is fine."

"Thanks for understanding." He left and went upstairs.

Tonight she would allow herself to enjoy some of the chocolate, but not while she was here. The way she figured it was that she had earned it.

A few minutes later Logan came thundering down the stairs dressed in nothing but running shorts, a sweatshirt, and tennis shoes. She quickly turned away. She was not used to seeing so much of a man's legs. Seeing him in bathing trunks in a photo was one thing, but to be standing there only a few feet away—well, she hoped no one saw him go outside like that with her still here in his house!

"I'm going for a run, Hope," he said. "Thanks for straightening up my bedroom. I went ahead and put that picture Marla brought with her in my bedside table drawer. I found it facedown, so I'm guessing it bothered you?"

"I did not want Adam looking at it." She thought perhaps this might be an opportunity to let him know that she did not appreciate the way he was dressed, either. "We try to teach our children to dress modestly."

"Of course you didn't want Adam looking at a woman in a bathing suit. I apologize for that, too. Marla can be very thoughtless sometimes. She should never have brought that picture here."

With that, he was out the door. She peeked out the window and saw him bounding down the road with his shorts and his long, embarrassing bare legs. She let the curtain drop and shook her head. It was just like each time she tried to make sense out of the little colored cards taped all over her old bedroom. The *Englisch* were crazy people. That's all there was to it. In her opinion, it made no sense for a grown man to run around on the roads unless it was an emergency.

Because it was starting to be winter, and chilly outside, Logan had recently purchased what he called a "stationary bike" as well as something he called a Bowflex. These items now sat in his front room, taking up space and needing to be dusted.

He told her that he sat so much at a desk, he needed to stay in shape, and so he had started running—when there was no reason to run—and on especially cold days, he used that silly bicycle that pedaled to nowhere, and then, presumably, he'd use that thing with the pulleys and ropes.

She agreed with him that he needed to move his body after

sitting at a desk for so many hours, but she did not understand expending that much energy to accomplish nothing.

Amish men bicycled, but they bicycled to work every morning and home every evening. It was more convenient and kind to park a bicycle outside a woodworking shop than to keep a horse and buggy there. Amish men lifted weights, but usually in the form of bales of hay or lumber or firewood, and they used their muscles holding a plow steady against the pull of a team of horses.

If Logan had told her he needed exercise, she would have been happy to recommend a few chores to him. She would have handed him a shovel and had him turn over the garden she intended to plant. Or she might have suggested he get himself a nonstationary bicycle and ride it to the antiques store each day instead of burning gasoline everywhere he went.

Amish men had common sense, and plenty of it. *Englisch* men . . . well, from what she could see, not so much.

She liked her employer, but she did not understand him. How could a married man act so cheerful with his wife so far away? After meeting Marla, she wondered if he was relieved to have an excuse not to be living with her. It was a puzzle.

On the other hand, when he was home, she could frequently hear him upstairs in that room with the index cards on the wall, talking to himself. Sometimes he'd storm down the stairs, look at her with wild eyes, and say something crazy like "what's another word for *infectious*?"

She would shake her head in bewilderment and he'd turn and stomp back upstairs.

He was a very nice man. He paid her well and treated her with respect, but had he been an Amish man, she would suspect that he had some screws loose in his head. As it was, she simply wrote it off to his being *Englisch*.

chapter FIFTEEN

"Everything looks good," Grace said. "You and the baby are doing well."

Levi's wife, Grace, took the stethoscope from around her neck and stuck it into the pocket of her smock as she helped Hope off the examining table.

"That is such good news." Hope adjusted her clothing and glanced around the comfortable room. Claire and Grace had done a good job of making the examination room feel homey, with Amish quilts hung on every wall, but also easy to keep clean, with its shiny wood floor and sparse furnishings. "It is wonderful to have this clinic so close to home."

Grace took a bottle of prenatal vitamins out of a pine cabinet and handed them to her. "When I was working as a military nurse in Afghanistan, the last thing I would ever have imagined myself doing is running a home birthing center in partnership with my Amish mother-in-law."

"It's working out well for you?"

"Claire is such a skilled midwife that I have learned a great deal from her."

"Thank you." Hope put the vitamins in her purse. Grace gave her a thirty-day supply every time she came for her once-a-month visit. "I'm certain Aunt Claire has learned much from you as well."

"We make a good team, but we had to get over quite a few hurdles first."

Hope glanced into an antique wall mirror to make certain her hair and *Kapp* were tidy. "Like what?"

"It took a while for her to stop resenting me for being part of the reason her son left the Amish church. Then it took me a while longer to stop resenting *her* for being so good at absolutely everything! The woman can grow anything, cook anything, sew anything, make a living for her family midwifing, *and* raise a houseful of kids at the same time. There's no way on earth I could ever measure up. It was easier on my ego to just go to work at a hospital where no one expected me to turn a half-acre of cucumbers into pickles."

"Aunt Claire can be a little intimidating," Hope said. "She caught me in bed one morning a few weeks ago, with my cow still unmilked!"

"Gracious!" Grace exclaimed in mock surprise. "I'm shocked Claire didn't call the sheriff."

Hope could see the humor in it now, even though it hadn't been much fun at the time. "I got a good talking-to!"

"I'll just bet you did! What time was it, anyway?"

"Seven-thirty."

Grace burst out laughing. "Claire probably already had the week's wash hung out on the line, done her spring cleaning, and had plucked and butchered a chicken for dinner!"

"I don't know about that, but she had already baked an apple pie from scratch. It was still warm when we had it for breakfast."

"See what I'm up against?" Grace pulled off the sheet of paper upon which Hope had been lying and put a fresh one on the examination table. "The woman truly is remarkable."

"How did you get over your problems with her?" Hope asked.

"I made myself stop feeling like I had to be in competition, and just started appreciating the amazingly talented woman she is. Besides, when you work as a team day after day helping bring the miracle of new life into the world—it tends to draw you closer. We've turned into pretty close friends."

"It is a great relief to have you so close . . . and family," Hope said.

"When Elizabeth proposed that we combine our skills, it felt like an answer straight from God. It still does. I don't know why we didn't see earlier that we could join forces and make a difference for the women of the area."

"I bet Levi didn't mind doing the carpentry necessary to turn this house into a clinic. I know he was not happy with you working at the hospital."

"I never saw a man so focused. Didn't he do a good job?"

Grace opened the door of the examination room and led her out to the front room. It was interesting to see how Levi had remodeled Elizabeth's old house. He had somehow found room to create three birthing/examination rooms without taking anything away from the large, old, original kitchen, which was fitted out now with comfy chairs in addition to the central table. There was enough room for at least five or six women to nurse babies or just have a cozy place to visit.

"Doesn't Elizabeth mind using her house for this?"

"You don't know my grandmother," Grace said. "She comes over and spends part of each day sitting here chatting with the women who come to see us and handing out advice right and left. She's in her element and feels like her home is being used for something important."

"Are you seeing *Englisch* patients, too?"

"No."

This was a surprise to Hope. "Why not?"

"We would never be able to afford the insurance on this

place if we accepted *Englisch* patients. The chance of a lawsuit with non-Amish people is simply too great. It would take only one lawsuit to shut us down. We trust the Amish and Mennonite women of this area not to take us to court. It's against their beliefs. That's why Claire and I can afford to charge really modest rates. If we had to insure this place, we could never have afforded to open it."

"Well." Hope picked up her purse. "I am glad you are doing this. How much do I owe you?"

"Oh, sweetie, you know I don't charge my family."

"Then you will not get rich around here," Hope joked as she reached into her purse. "We're pretty much all related, and I do have a job now."

"I'm serious." Grace put out a hand to stop Hope from handing her cash. "There are plenty of pregnant women around here with husbands who can afford to pay our fees. I'm not charging a widow with small children for the honor of helping her through her pregnancy. I know it is hard to go through this without your husband at your side, but I hope that knowing Claire and I will see you through it helps a little."

"It grieves my heart not to have Titus here to see our new little one, but having you and Aunt Claire so close does help a lot. I can pay you for the vitamins?"

"You can pay me for the vitamins," Grace said. "Next visit."

Hope closed her purse. "Levi made a good choice when he married you."

"Even though I was *Englisch*?" Grace teased.

Hope smiled. "Even though you were *Englisch*."

As she left, it struck her that both were speaking in the past tense, as though Grace was no longer *Englisch*, even though neither she nor Levi were exactly Amish. What were they now? It was a great puzzle. She suspected that it was a puzzle to Levi and Grace as well. Where did one go to church after coming from such different backgrounds? She was grateful that she did not have to make that decision.

In the meantime, the big news was that all was well with her and her child. The baby's heartbeat was strong. She felt physically well. Grace continued to offer her services for free—which was a great blessing, and she was beginning to feel that she had a good friend in her cousin's wife.

She did not want to take Grace's services for granted, and had saved back part of her salary just in case her cousin's wife decided to charge her this time. Now that she had a little extra money, she considered stopping at the Scratch 'n' Dent store up the road and stocking up on what groceries she could find there.

The only problem was, Abimelech and his older children ran that store, and she was trying her best to avoid him. That was a sacrifice, because sometimes she found good bargains there.

Every Amish woman in the Holmes County area worth her salt had her favorite Scratch 'n' Dent store. They were discreetly tucked away in various hollows and hills all over the area along back roads, usually where no one would think to look. The Amish knew where to look, though, and many grateful local mothers frequented these stores and filled their buggies with good deals.

It was sometimes a challenge to use up everything before the expiration date came around—but it was worth it in savings. Today, however, she could not make herself face the possibility of seeing Abimelech again. She did not know for certain if the bishop had talked with him yet, and it would be exceedingly uncomfortable if there was no one else in the store and she had to shop with him staring at her.

Even though her buggy ride home took her straight past his store, she decided to not stop in. She would simply spend a little extra money at Walmart in a couple of days when her mother and aunt shared the cost of a van to go do their weekly shopping. They always invited her and the children to go along.

Unfortunately, she was not able to get past Abimelech's store without him seeing her. He was outside, stacking boxes in front, and waved her down.

She was too well trained in politeness not to stop. He seemed happy to see her, and acted as though their conversation at Logan's house had not happened.

"It has been a long time since you have been in the store." He put a foot on the bottom step of her buggy and leaned toward her. He had been working hard and sweat droplets had collected on his forehead. In the bright sunlight, she could see the large pores on his nose, and the discoloration of his teeth. She did not hold his lack of beauty against him, but she could not help recoiling a bit.

"I—I have been very busy," she said.

"Too busy cleaning an *Englisch* man's house." His voice held contempt.

"*Ja.*" Her back straightened. "I have been cleaning two houses, my employer's and my own. Plus I have been caring for two children."

"And what were you doing down at Grace and Claire's clinic?" His eyes dropped to her stomach and lingered.

She gasped. The man really was too much. At five months, she knew she was showing—but he did not have to stare!

"That is none of your business." She clicked her tongue at the horse and tried to leave. Abimelech grasped the reins and held the horse back.

"I have a gift for you and your children," he said. "Some overstock. The truck brought too much. I will load up the back of your buggy with some extra food."

"No, thank you."

"It's a gift, Hope. You and your children have to eat and I

doubt the Parker man is paying you all that well." His voice took on that cunning sound again. "Or is he?"

She lifted her chin. "I make a modest salary."

"Modest." He let loose of the reins. "Don't be foolish, Hope. There's no need to turn this food down. Just keep the buggy still, and I'll put these boxes in."

"I will pay."

"It is a gift."

"I will pay," she insisted.

He ignored her and loaded several boxes of canned and boxed goods into her buggy. "There. That should keep you and the children filled up for now."

"How much?" She fumbled for her purse, hoping she had enough cash to pay for all those boxes.

"Like I said. It is a gift. From a widower to a widow." With that, he left her sitting there and went back inside. Unless she followed him inside, which she did not want to do, she had no choice but to leave with the boxes.

All the way home, she thought of things she could have and should have said to him. The man made her skin crawl these days, and she was suspicious of his sudden generosity—from a man who her father had once said was so parsimonious that if a fly accidentally landed in his milk, he would demand the fly spit out whatever it had drunk.

Yet for all she knew, today he was simply trying to be kind. She had been trained by her gentle mother to give people the benefit of the doubt, and she tried to give Abimelech the benefit of the doubt as she drove home.

She also tried to give Abimelech the benefit of the doubt while she carried the boxes of canned goods into her home and began stacking them on the table so she could see what she had gotten.

It was only after she had laboriously unloaded every last can and box and was beginning to place them on her pantry shelves that she thought to check the expiration dates.

What she discovered was insufferable. Her father once said that Abimelech's new venture of selling damaged goods was a good fit for the man's personality. But even she was surprised to find out that every last can and box had passed its expiration date by at least three months.

Abimelech had given her things he had pulled off the shelf and had probably intended to throw away until he saw her trotting by. Was he paying her back for refusing him? Or was this his strange attempt to court her? Either way, she was stuck with having to dispose of a pantry's worth of items most people would not feel safe eating. Especially not a pregnant woman with small children!

Being a young widow was turning out to be a whole lot more complicated than even she had imagined.

chapter SIXTEEN

"And how is this job of yours going?" Ivan Troyer had a scythe in his hand, evidently intending to clear beneath the split-rail fence that separated his field from Logan's backyard.

Hope had known Ivan Troyer and his wife, Mary, for as long as she had been alive. She had grown up with their children, played inside their house, and hunted Easter eggs in their backyard. Even though Ivan and his wife had become Mennonites several years earlier, their families had always been supportive of one another.

"It is going well enough." She pegged the last wet sheet and dried her hands on her apron.

"Is my new neighbor treating you well?" Ivan chopped at some weeds beneath the fence.

"He is. Have you met him?"

"Not yet. I wasn't sure if someone from New York would welcome a visit. Many city people want to keep to themselves. I was afraid he might get annoyed if I just showed up. I had hoped he would make the first move and drop by."

Ivan had never had any neighbors from the city that she knew of. "How do you know city people are like that?"

"Our youngest told us. Helda had to move from Sugarcreek

to Chicago last month with her new husband. It was because of his job. She says none of her neighbors seem all that anxious to speak to her."

"Oh, I am so sorry that Helda had to move." Hope placed a comforting hand on Ivan's arm. This was indeed terrible news. The worst things besides sickness, death, or having a loved one leave the church, was having family move far away. "I had not yet heard. How is Mary taking it?"

"Crying her eyes out some days, on other days accepting it as the Lord's will."

His light blue eyes looked off into the distance, and his chin trembled slightly. For the first time since Hope had known him, Ivan looked old to her.

She clucked her tongue in sympathy. "I will come visit with Mary soon."

"She would like that," he said. "We still have Caleb, William, Charlotte, and Leah living nearby, plus their spouses and all the grandchildren—but having Helda move so far away still hits hard."

Hope truly sympathized. She could not imagine living in a world where she could not go visit her *Maam* and younger siblings several times a week.

"Helda cried so hard when they left. We are praying that they will find a good Mennonite church to attend soon. At least then we will know that there is someone close who will help them if there is need."

"I shall add that to my prayers, as well," Hope promised.

"Sometimes I think . . ." He hesitated, as though unsure whether or not to say what was in his heart.

"*Ja?*"

"If only the other . . . terrible trial had not happened to our family. Perhaps Mary would be a different person now. Stronger maybe."

"Your family has endured great tragedy with much faith," Hope said. The sad business had been many years ago, but it was easy to see that it still affected Ivan and Mary. "How is Esther doing since Helda's move?"

"Mother?" Ivan smiled. "My mother does as she always does about everything . . . she prays. Even with her painful joints, she gets down on the floor beside her bed every day and prays that Helda's husband will find a job that will bring them back here where they belong."

"I will pray extra hard as well, and I will write to Helda. Maybe that will help her with homesickness."

"That would please her so much." Ivan pulled out his handkerchief and blew his nose. Then the twinkle in his eyes that she knew so well returned. "Or it will make Helda even more homesick than ever to hear from you."

Hope laughed. "I will tell her all the bad things I can think of. Including the fact that you are as lazy as ever—allowing your fencerows to get in such bad shape."

"That is true," Ivan agreed. "I should be horsewhipped for my lazy ways."

For years, it had been a running competition and joke between Ivan and her father to see which of them could keep the cleaner farm. Both were excellent farmers and they vied constantly to see who could make the straightest furrows, Henry with his team of horses, or Ivan with his old blue Ford tractor.

"Speaking of fencerows," Ivan said, "has your employer given any thought to what to do about the farm? It's good for a field to lie fallow for a short while, but he'll have scrub pine shooting up before he knows it if he doesn't have someone come in and mow things down."

"I do not think Logan thinks of these things. He seemed surprised when I told him that come spring, he will have to buy a lawn mower."

"What does the man do for a living?" Ivan asked.

"He's a writer," Hope said.

"Him and every other person I meet in this county these days." Ivan laughed. "Ever since writers discovered the Amish, everyone wants to write about our people—including our own people. I heard the other day that Carlisle Printing over in Walnut Creek can hardly keep up with the new demand."

"Are there not other printing places for our people to use?"

"None that I know of that will accept a manuscript written out in longhand." Ivan put on a mock-serious face. "I have been thinking about publishing Mary's shopping lists she's let pile up over the years. I'd call it *A Mennonite Woman Buys Toilet Paper and Eggs*. Caleb's eldest girl could illustrate it. I think tourists would probably buy it in droves and make us rich."

"I would not bank on that project succeeding." Hope giggled. "And our Amish ways are not what Logan Parker is writing about."

"Oh? What is he writing?"

"I think he is writing a war book."

Ivan's eyebrows rose. "A war book!"

"I am afraid so. He has been talking with old soldiers."

"Will the *Englisch* never see the wisdom in putting away their weapons and living at peace with their fellow man?" Ivan shook his head, as amazed with the *Englisch* preoccupation with war as she. "It is the one thing upon which your father and I have never disagreed—the necessity of our Amish and Mennonite churches continuing to hold fast to our practice of nonresistance."

"I do not know how Logan feels about war, all I know is that he is enjoying writing a book about it."

"Perhaps it would be better if he tended to his fields."

"Perhaps it would be better if you met the man and told him yourself," she said. "I believe he would profit from your advice, and my father refuses to have any input into the running of this farm. He says it hurts his heart too much."

"No doubt."

They were both silent, pondering the tragedy of her father's weakness, then Ivan heaved a sigh and said, "Now is as good a time as any to meet the man who lives across the fence from me. Will you go get him?"

"I think you will like him," Hope said. "He pays me more than my work is worth. He allows me to bring the children with me, and he has forbidden me to climb on chairs to clean the high cabinets until after the baby comes. Sometimes there is even extra pay in my envelope, which he calls a 'bonus.'"

"And this man who pays you well . . . he leaves you alone?"

She could hear the suspicion in Ivan's voice.

"He is very respectful," she answered. "I would not continue working for him if there was the slightest problem."

"Then I would be pleased to meet him," Ivan said.

From the upstairs window, he watched Hope hanging out laundry. She was using the gasoline-powered wringer washer she had asked him to buy. He could not believe how rough and stiff his towels were—he had never used wind-dried towels before, but there were trade-offs. He also had never slept beneath such sweet-smelling sheets.

Actually, there was another trade-off—getting to watch Hope hang the laundry from an upstairs window like he was doing now. The woman was a study in gracefulness, even while engaged in the most mundane tasks. Who would ever have thought that the mere domestic task of pinning sheets to a clothesline could be so mesmerizing?

Hope made it a thing of beauty, even in early March, when the fields and trees were still gray with late winter. She was wearing a dark blue dress, with the sleeves folded back over a black sweater, and a simple white kerchief holding her hair back.

Her pregnancy had become quite noticeable beneath her modest clothing. He saw her stop several times, put a hand upon the small of her back, and stretch. It was obvious that she was growing uncomfortable with the extra weight of the baby.

He remembered back to the day when she had confessed to him that she was pregnant. She had been afraid that he would not allow her to work for him anymore, and he had told her that he wouldn't think of letting her go.

It surprised him how destitute he had felt at the mere idea of her not showing up every day. Hope and her children had brought light and life into his life in many small ways. It delighted him when he found a small toy tractor beneath his kitchen table and knew that Adam had been playing there. Once, he found a sheet of paper where Carrie had drawn a picture of a horse. That picture now hung above his desk. It was purple and made him smile every time he glanced at it.

Hope had seemingly gotten over her inhibitions about being there while he was at home. She had worked for him now for nearly four months and was no longer skittish. To make sure she stayed that way, he spent a lot of time working in his office whenever she was there. To hang on to her, he also routinely overpaid her to make it possible for her to survive without having to take on more hours somewhere else.

Sometimes, while he was in his office, Hope would forget that he was in the house and she would sing as she went about her tasks. Of all the sounds in the world, he decided, a woman singing as she went about doing her housework had to be one of the most comforting. He had never heard Marla sing and didn't know if she could. She tended to listen to some sort of hybrid techno music when she was home. Carrie and Adam's voices laughing and chattering while at play were also music to his ears.

One of the biggest revelations he had experienced since moving here was that a pregnant woman could be so beautiful. He watched her, holding that tiny life within her, and felt a strong desire to protect her. It was everything he could do not to run outside and carry the heavy basket of wet clothes that he saw her lugging to the clothesline.

He realized that he was falling into the habit of comparing everything he saw Hope doing to the life he knew Marla was living, and his fiancée somehow always got the short end of the comparison.

In the real world—the world not of the Amish—Hope would have had many options when her husband died. In many cases, there would have been at least some life insurance. For an Amish woman, there was none. A woman in her circumstances would have qualified for food stamps and welfare. He knew from talking with Hope that she and her people accepted no government help.

In regular society, she would have qualified for Medicaid for the children. Hope barely seemed to realize it existed. Instead, she treated her children's colds and small illnesses with various elixirs that she concocted. He'd asked about doctors, and she'd explained that she tried to use them as little as possible. Not for religious reasons, but because of the cost. He was grateful that she had the inexpensive birthing clinic to go to.

He found her and her way of life utterly fascinating, and he wondered why. Was it because it was so totally different from anything he'd ever known? Or was it because of a deeper pull—that of a culture trying to live upright and godly lives in a society that they felt was falling to pieces around them?

This baby was also beginning to consume his thoughts. He kept wondering if it would be a girl or a boy. He wondered how

Hope would manage after it came. He admired her more and more as the baby grew and he realized that even under hard circumstances, Hope was happy about its impending arrival.

Marla would have swept it from her life. There was no doubt in his mind. Babies were messy, she'd often said. They smelled bad. They ruined figures and careers.

Hope treated the idea of having this baby as though it were a holy thing. He had asked if she was worried.

"Oh no. It will be so good to have a new baby in the house." Her eyes lit up every time she mentioned it.

It was as though he were watching an entirely different species from the one among which he had lived.

It occurred to him that few of his and Marla's friends in New York had children. Those who did tended not to be invited to social events once the child appeared unless they had no issues with hiring a babysitter. It was easier, Marla explained as she'd made out a guest list, not to be bothered with the presence of children when adults were trying to have conversations. He had to admit, the few children he had been around as an adult tended to be annoying, demanding little things.

What he saw between Hope and her children was entirely different. Hope, in spite of the grief he knew she still bore, noticeably enjoyed her children's company.

Five-year-old Carrie was a tiny replica of Hope, and he was entranced by the picture the two of them made together as the little girl helped her mother at whatever task Hope had set for herself that day. If her mother was washing windows, then Carrie handed her dry rags for polishing them. If Hope was washing dishes, then Carrie dried each dish and carefully set it on the kitchen table for her mother to put away in the cabinets.

The whole time they worked, he was treated to the music of Hope's gentle conversation with her little daughter. She spoke to her in what she referred to as German, but what he heard others refer to as Pennsylvania Deutsch. He had always thought German an unattractive, guttural language, but when Hope talked with her children, it became something lovely.

The relationship between mother and daughter was mirrored in the bits of interaction he saw between Hope and her own mother, Rose. There was a mutual respect in the way they spoke to each other. Even when they were speaking in German, he could tell from the tone of their voices that it was respectful and kind.

Adam was given more masculine tasks to do, carrying scraps of food out to the compost pile Hope had started, or taking kitchen trash to the garbage can out back.

Hope represented a way of life to him that was so alien and yet so compelling, he was beginning to have a hard time staying away when he knew that she would be at the house.

He refused to see this as a danger to himself. The cultural gap between the two of them was entirely too great to harbor any romantic thoughts, and besides, he was committed to Marla. Eventually the contracted book would be finished, his need for this extended period of retreat over, and he would go back to his old life. He and Marla had patched things up, and she'd begun to move forward with their wedding plans. She had set a date for October. Her design firm was going through a dry spell and she was using the extra time to create a memorable wedding. She had recently purchased an elegant black wedding dress. Black was the "new white," she had informed him.

He didn't really care what she did for their wedding. It was hard to muster any enthusiasm for it. Marla told him that his role would be to nod his head, look handsome, and murmur agreeable words. She said it in a joking voice, but he knew she was not entirely joking.

Often, he reminded himself of Marla's good qualities. She was smart. She was witty. She was elegant. She was beautiful and fashionable. She could turn an apartment into a work of art. When she was in the right mood, she could light up a room with her smile.

As Logan stood at the window musing about his upcoming marriage while admiring the picture Hope and Carrie made hanging laundry together, he saw his neighbor, a man in his early sixties, walk through the pasture and approach the fence line near Hope.

He had not yet formally met his neighbor, but the man always waved each time he drove by. The problem with living in the country was that he wasn't always sure what the rules were. Was he supposed to go meet his neighbors first, or wait for them to meet him? His experience in the city had been that it was wise to avoid even making eye contact with strangers.

Hope glanced toward the house and saw him standing in the window. She gestured for him to come down, and he was happy to do so. Throwing down the pen with which he had been trying to make notes, he grabbed his coat and headed down the stairwell and outdoors.

chapter SEVENTEEN

Logan had never met anyone quite like Ivan Troyer. He wasn't Amish, but he wasn't exactly *Englisch*, either. He said he was Mennonite, which was yet another religion Logan knew little about.

"I used to be Amish," Ivan explained. "The problem is, I was never a great hand with horses. Not like Hope's father. Henry can practically talk a horse into plowing a field all by itself. He makes farming look easy. Seemed like I was always fighting with horseflies, or getting kicked or bit, and I almost got killed when a four-horse team decided to run away with me. Horses don't like me and I don't like them. When I turned forty, I decided that if the good Lord really wanted me to fool around with horses, He would not have invented cars and tractors."

"I think it was Henry Ford who . . ."

"Ivan is making a joke," Hope said. "That's his latest Mennonite joke. *Daed* does not think it is funny."

"Henry doesn't think much is funny anymore," Ivan said. "I'm worried about him."

"He is humiliated and sorry," Hope said. "The problem is,

nothing can be done about it. He still has to live with his deci-sions—even if the church and his family have forgiven him."

"Your father is a good man," Ivan said. "And he was a good neighbor. The best."

Logan heard the grief in the man's statement and wondered if he was expected to apologize for living in Hope's family's house. Sometimes it felt that way around here.

"Take a walk with me over to my place," Ivan invited. "We'll let Hope get back to her chores. I'd like for my wife to meet the man who bought the house next door . . . just for the pleasure of living beside us."

"I didn't . . ."

"I know." Ivan chuckled. "You were probably passing through and fell in love with the old house. Outsiders some-times do that here. They see the pretty farms and think they'll find peace just by living here. I've talked to a couple of them. They have no idea how much sweat and tears goes into keeping those farms going. The other thing most of them can't figure out is that peace can be found anywhere if you have Christ in your life. Peace isn't about pretty. It isn't about where you live. It's about who you live with, and who you live *for*."

The man said this in such a matter-of-fact tone that Logan could not take offense.

Ivan's wife, Mary, was setting food out on the table when they arrived. She was a small, round woman whose face lit up with a sweet smile when Ivan introduced them.

"You'll have to stay for supper," she announced. "Thanks to my husband's hard work, we always have plenty."

Logan was a little taken aback by the invitation. Dinner parties were one thing. Being invited to sit down and eat in someone's home whom he'd just met—that didn't happen in his world.

"I'm sorry. I couldn't."

He realized his mistake when he saw the look of disappointment on Mary's face. The woman truly meant her invitation.

"Although . . . I suppose I could stay for a few minutes. Something smells really good."

"I'll set a place!" Mary whirled around and began pulling dinnerware out of a cupboard.

At that moment, an elderly woman wearing a gauzy head covering and a loose-fitting plain dress shuffled into the kitchen. "Is that you, John?"

"No, Mother. This isn't your brother. This is our neighbor, Logan Parker." Ivan helped her get seated. "Logan, this is my mother, Esther."

The old lady extended her hand. He was gentle when he shook it because she seemed as fragile as fine china, and he was half afraid that if he squeezed too hard, he might break something.

"I must be getting old," Esther said. "I could have sworn I heard my brother's voice just now."

"John's been dead for over fifty years." Ivan's voice was gentle.

"Oh, I know that." Esther flapped a hand at her son. "I'm not *senile*. I've been napping and got a little confused for a moment, that's all."

"It's good to meet you, ma'am," Logan said.

Esther turned to her son. "And who is he again?"

Ivan responded with patience. "He is our next-door neighbor, Mother."

"Henry and Rose are our neighbors," she argued. "What happened? Did this young man marry their daughter Hope?"

"No, Mother," Ivan explained. "Henry and Rose moved away. Logan is from New York City. He bought the house and moved here."

"Supper's ready!" Mary announced brightly. "I hope the others come in before it gets cold."

Within a few minutes, the rest of the family began to appear. A tall man, whom they introduced as their eldest, Caleb, came through the door along with his wife. A daughter named Leah arrived with her husband, Seth. They had two small children with them. William was the second oldest son. His wife, Prudy, was hugely pregnant and complained of swollen ankles. Another daughter, Charlotte, had a baby in her arms and her husband carried a toddler.

Altogether, Logan counted fourteen people seated around one long table. Ivan explained that there would be more except that Caleb's youngest three were teenagers attending a youth function and that their oldest was serving the Lord in Haiti.

It seemed so strange to Logan to hear someone say "serving the Lord" as easily as if he were talking about the weather. It would have sounded self-conscious in most people's mouths, but from Ivan it sounded as natural as breathing.

"It's not always like this," Mary explained after Caleb had said grace. "It's usually just me, Ivan, and Esther and only one or two of the grandkids. But we try to make it a priority to eat together once a week just to get caught up on what's happening in each other's lives, and"—she wiped the chin of the toddler who was slurping up buttered corn from his place on her lap— "to keep the children close to our hearts."

"What a wonderful tradition." Logan meant it. His eyes swept the table, watching the easy camaraderie between brother and sister, brother-in-law and sister-in-law, grandparent and grandchild . . . and he envied it. To his surprise, he was not at all the center of attention. They didn't exactly ignore him, they just seemed used to having a stray in their midst, and after a few polite questions, they settled in to their own conversations about everything from Braxton-Hicks contractions—which apparently the pregnant wife was having—to the new tooth the fussy baby was sprouting, to what vegetables they were thinking of planting as soon as the earth warmed up.

It was a pleasure to sit there, listening, even if he didn't have much to contribute.

Then it happened again.

That feeling of déjà vu came over him.

Everything about this house, those cabinets, that view out the kitchen window felt familiar.

There was a staircase leading upstairs from the kitchen. Built into the wall beneath the staircase was a small, child-sized door that caught his attention. As he looked at the unusual door, the feeling was so strong, he had to put down his fork while it washed over him, leaving him nearly dizzy from the intensity, while inside his mind flashed an image of shelves filled with children's books and a few toys.

"Excuse me," he said, pointing, "but do you mind if I ask what's behind that small door?"

He knew it was an odd question, but he had to ask. All conversation dropped and all heads turned to look at him. He was sorry he had stopped the flow of their conversation, but the need to know was too compelling to keep quiet.

"I turned that space into a playroom when Caleb was a child," Ivan answered. "All the children have enjoyed that little hidey-hole, along with their friends."

"Does it have a small shelf of children's books?"

"It did," Mary said. "Most have been borrowed or lost since our children were small. Why do you ask?"

"I don't know. I wish I did, but I just don't know. I can't explain it. I don't understand it myself, but with this house and my own, it feels like I've been here before. Maybe when I was very young."

"Were you ever in Holmes County when you were a child?" Ivan asked.

"I've asked my mother. As far as she knows, I've never been in Ohio at all until recently."

"You probably saw some pictures of Amish farmhouses." Caleb's voice conveyed finality, as though he did not want to discuss it further. "There is a similarity to many of them."

"Oh well." Logan was uncomfortable with the puzzled looks he was getting. "I don't suppose I'll ever know for sure, and it probably doesn't matter." He left it at that, and they all went back to eating. After he had finished and thanked Mary for the good meal, he started out on the walk home, when Caleb called out for him to wait.

"What were you trying to pull in there?" Caleb asked, catching up with him.

Logan stopped in his tracks, surprised. "I don't know what you mean."

"I hear you're a *writer*." Caleb could have inserted "serial killer" for "writer" and the contempt in his voice would have been the same.

"I am."

"What were you really doing in our house?"

"Your father asked me to come meet your mother. She invited me to stay for dinner. It's as simple as that."

"You were pretending to have knowledge about our home . . . like there's some mystical connection. That's cruel. My family has been through enough."

"I do feel a connection . . . at least with your parents' house and with my own. I have no idea why."

"Hope loved playing in that room beneath the stairs when she was a little girl. It doesn't take a genius to know that she's mentioned it to you."

"She never said a word." Logan was appalled at the ferocity he saw in Caleb's face. "Why would you even say that?"

"Let's just say that I would appreciate it a great deal if you would leave my parents alone. They've been through enough. They don't need someone like you coming along and stirring things up."

"I have no idea what you're talking about, but that's okay by me."

Logan had thought he was having a pleasant dinner with neighbors. Obviously there was something else going on. There were currents of emotion he did not understand. He wasn't sure exactly what he was being accused of, but he had no plans to go back.

"Good." Caleb gave him a long look. "I'm glad we have an understanding."

Logan wasn't exactly sure what the understanding was, but the warm feeling he had experienced sitting around Ivan and Mary's kitchen table had evaporated.

Later that evening, his mother called to check on him.

"Anything new?" she asked.

"As a matter of fact, I had an interesting encounter with my next-door neighbors today. They invited me to eat dinner with the family, and I did."

"Are they Amish?"

"They used to be. Now they are Mennonite, which from what I can tell, is an interesting story."

"How so?"

"Something to do with not liking horses."

She chuckled. "That could most definitely be a deal-breaker for an Amish man."

"Oh, I think it was probably a little more complicated than that." From his upstairs window, he glanced over at the Troyers' home.

"I had that feeling again when I was there. Like I'd been there before."

"Oh?"

He told her about his innocent comment about the children's closet, and Caleb's accusations afterward.

"Did you say his name is Caleb?"

"Yes."

"What is this family's last name?"

"Troyer. Ivan and Mary Troyer . . . and a bunch of their children and grandchildren whose names I didn't catch."

"Oh," she said. She paused. He waited, and then she said, "I need to go now . . . someone is trying to call in."

"Sure. Talk with you later." He hung up, wondering if his mother had gotten a new phone. Always before, he heard the slight disconnect when people called her while they were talking.

He was glad he had a visit to New York planned soon. It would be good to catch up with his mom as well as spend time with Marla. At least in New York, he knew the rules.

"You're here a lot earlier than I expected." It might have been his imagination, but Marla appeared to be less than thrilled when he arrived unannounced at her workplace.

He tried to tease her out of her mood. "Don't you love me anymore?"

"Of course I love you." Her voice softened. "But you know how I get when I'm on a big project. Everything scheduled down to the last minute."

"Ariela always said you were the only person she'd ever met who carried around a thicker day planner than her own."

"That was something we had in common. I like to have a schedule and get things accomplished. So did she."

"As opposed to, say, being a writer who lounges around all day, sipping coffee, looking out the window and thinking deep thoughts?"

"I *know* you work hard, Logan."

"Guess I'll go back outside and wait then." He pretended to check her calendar. "Exactly what time did you have me scheduled for?"

"I'm sorry. It's just that we got this big client last week. Do you remember me telling you about him? Jebulan Steele? The actor who wants us to restore that old brownstone he just purchased? My boss put me in charge of it and I've been pulling my hair out trying to get everything in place to start the project."

"I'm sorry to hear that." He knew she'd worked for a couple of other actors in the past and neither had been easy. "Can I take you out for an early dinner?"

"Well"—she tapped her lovely nails on the desk—"there *is* a new Middle Eastern place that just opened up that I'd like to try. Let me make a couple phone calls first. Why don't you go out to the foyer and wait for me." She waved him away and smiled sweetly as she picked up the phone. "I can't concentrate with you standing over me."

Somewhat deflated, he went to go wait.

When Marla came through the elevator doors a few minutes later, she was a different person, relaxed and happy to see him. He decided that it might be best to not surprise her with an early visit from now on.

She was a woman who turned heads, and several men pivoted to watch her as they stepped out onto the sidewalk and made their way to the new restaurant a couple blocks away.

In the restaurant, she pointed out that he had not yet admired her new handbag.

Marla did not shop for bargains. The large, red purse had cost four figures. He couldn't begin to fathom from looking at it why it had cost so much.

"I guess you'll have plenty of room for your stuff," he offered lamely.

Marla looked hurt. "You don't like it?"

"I don't like it or dislike it."

"Then what is your problem?"

"I don't have a problem. It's just a handbag. I don't care what you buy."

"I suppose you want me to walk around carrying some old, black, cheap thing like that housekeeper of yours." She speared an olive. "I saw her purse sitting on a chair when I was there."

For the life of him, he did not know what was eating at her, but suddenly, he regretted his decision to waste the hours he'd spent driving from Ohio to New York. He was tired from driving, disappointed in her reaction to his arrival, and on top of that, he had never liked Middle Eastern food. Marla always forgot that he did not share her love for exotic cuisine. He was hungry, and a hamburger is what he wanted. Instead, he would be paying the earth for a meal he didn't want. Yet again.

He didn't know why any of this bothered him so much except that last night Hope had asked permission to take home a chicken carcass she had roasted for him the day before. When he asked why, she told him that she could boil it down into broth, make some egg noodles, and get another meal out of it . . . for her children.

"Hope could feed a family for six months on what you just spent on that ridiculous handbag."

It was not what he had intended to say, but he was tired, his guard was down, and it was what flew out of his mouth.

Marla gasped and stared at him round-eyed. "I *cannot* believe you just said that!"

Actually, he couldn't either, but he had no intention of backing down. What he'd said was the truth.

When he didn't apologize, she threw down her napkin and stood. "I'm going home."

"Fine." He picked up a fork. "I'm going to stay here and eat this overpriced meal you just ordered. Did that one olive fill you up?"

Wow! Where had *that* come from? His resentment of all those meals he'd bought that she barely touched had finally risen to the surface.

She stormed out without another word. He watched until she had hailed a taxi. Then he proceeded to eat his meal and hers, too. Strange how ravenous he felt after that exchange. He decided that Middle Eastern food wasn't so bad after all.

An hour later, after walking off his anger, he let himself into the apartment. Marla was sitting in bed, her ever-present laptop perched on her knees. Her eyes were red from weeping. "I don't understand why you were being mean to me. All I did was buy a new purse. It's not like the money was coming out of *your* pocket."

That was true. Not only did Marla have her own job—thanks to her grandfather, she also had a modest trust fund. She could buy a purse like that out of her monthly allowance and not feel the pinch too much. Especially since he was taking care of all her other living expenses.

His Amish housekeeper did not have that option and he resented it for her. Hope worked hard so that she could feed and clothe her children. Marla worked so she would not be bored.

Evidently it was best that he had come back to the city for a visit. He had been spending entirely too much time with Hope. Even though there was nothing at all between them, seeing her struggle to raise her children was changing his point of view in ways that were not healthy. Especially if he was to maintain a good relationship with his fiancée.

"Marla," he said, "I was tired from the trip and said things I shouldn't have. I'm sorry."

She sniffed and nodded, then slid off the bed to have her bath and do her nightly beauty regimen. He went to his dresser to get his pajamas and found his things shoved over to one side. That was so like Marla—trying to eke out a little more room for her possessions. Ever since she'd moved in, there were times when he felt like the space he controlled within his own apartment was diminishing rapidly. Truth be told, being able to spread out in the farmhouse had felt nice.

He went to his closet to hang up his clothes and found that his suits had also been shoved to one side. This seemed a little strange, considering that Marla had already taken over the entire master closet, which she guarded like a pit bull.

Worn out from the drive, and the fight, he fell asleep long before Marla completed her nightly beauty ritual.

chapter EIGHTEEN

One of the pleasures and banes of Amish existence was hosting church services at one's home at least once a year. A family cleaned out barns, homes, workshops, basements—wherever there was space to seat upward of two hundred people on backless benches.

Under normal circumstances, it would soon be Hope's turn. Unfortunately, these were not normal circumstances and she was worried. The house she and Titus had rented last year was small, but it was all they could afford. The maximum she could seat in her living room was maybe thirty people. The barn was old and decrepit. There was no basement beneath her house.

Titus had intended to build a workshop this winter large enough to hold everyone, but that had not happened, for obvious reasons. She was grateful he'd not gotten around to it before he died or she would be saddled with a debt she couldn't pay. That was one of the problems with the Amish dependence on home church services—couples often felt forced to go into debt for a building they could not afford and did not really need except for hosting church obligations.

Hope had heard of an Old Order Amish church that had recently built what they called a "community building" to take this burden off their young families—but they were being criticized for it, and some now accused them of being New Order Amish for taking that extreme step.

There was a lot to be said for the fellowship a church enjoyed when they were packed together inside one another's homes every other Sunday, but with the prices of homes being what they were these days, it was becoming more and more of a financial burden on their people.

Young couples were usually given a pass for a year or two until they could get settled, but there always came a time when an Amish family had to start taking their turn or deal with the annoyance of other members who were shouldering the responsibility for them.

As a widow, she knew she wouldn't necessarily be expected to host right now, but there was a stubborn streak in her, and she was determined to find a way. Perhaps she could rent a wedding tent for a day if the weather was fine . . .

"Is everything okay?" Logan was lying on his stomach on the living room floor, playing tractors with Adam. He and Adam had built a road with ramps from a pile of old books and her son was loving every minute.

She had grown comfortable with having Logan around while she worked and considered him a decent, caring man. In fact, as her pregnancy progressed, he had surprised her by growing quite solicitous. She suspected he made sure he was around when she came each day, just so he would be on hand if she needed him to lift something heavy.

This was not behavior she was used to. Titus was a good husband, but he considered childbirth an everyday thing, and tended to treat her exactly the same as when she wasn't pregnant. She would never have admitted it, but having Logan worry a little about her was . . . nice.

Maybe a little too nice.

She still missed Titus terribly, and cried at night when the children were asleep. But as she watched Logan racing his toy tractor along the makeshift book-road, entertaining Adam while she and Carrie worked in the kitchen, a stab of longing came over her.

She had thought him nice-looking the first time she met him, but as she had gotten to know him better, he'd become more and more handsome to her. Funny how that was.

He was so different from the Amish men she'd known, and not in a particularly good way. He was useless when it came to repairs, or carpentry, or anything else an Amish man would consider of importance. He knew nothing about livestock, or seed and harvest.

What she found attractive about him was the way he treated her. It was as though he thought she was as smart as he was, or smarter. He asked her opinion about things, and then pondered the things she said, as though they had weight. He questioned her about her people and beliefs and treated the things she told him with respect.

Sometimes he bought thoughtful toys for the children. Like this new set of tractors. He seemed to know better than to buy Adam little automobiles.

There were moments when he looked at her, when her children were doing something especially clever, and their eyes would meet and it was as though he was sharing in her pride in them.

She hated to judge anyone, but in her opinion, his wife was a very foolish woman not to move here. Unfortunately, she was beginning to fear that she might be equally foolish for continuing to work for a man she found so . . . likable.

"Are you okay?" Logan repeated.

"Yes," she said. "Everything is fine."

"You've been standing there staring at the living room for an awfully long time. That's the same look Marla gets right before she hires painters to come repaint our apartment. What are you thinking?"

"Actually, I was thinking about church. My turn is coming up soon to host it, and I was wondering about renting a tent. Do you have any idea how much they cost?"

"I don't. But what does that have to do with my living room?"

"Not a thing. I was just remembering how nice it was when we had church here with enough space to seat a couple hundred people."

He glanced around the room. "It's a nice-sized room, but it isn't *that* big."

"Do you see this wall here?" She pointed to the one separating the room from the kitchen. "It can be moved. That's what we always did. *Daed* would move the wall back and open up a space large enough to seat everyone."

"Then why don't you just have church here?" he said.

"Here?"

"Why not?" He shrugged and went back to playing with Adam.

She tapped a finger against her lower lip, considering the possibilities. Having church here was not something she would ever have asked for, but it could be a solution. It would most definitely be a much cheaper solution than renting a tent.

"Are you sure you wouldn't mind?" she asked.

"Of course not," he said. "I'll stay away if you need me to."

"Oh, no," she said. "I would never ask you to leave your home. I'm sure the bishop would allow you to stay if you wanted." This would be a wonderful answer to her problem. "You're sure?"

"I'm absolutely sure," he said. "I can't wait to see two hundred Amish people inside my house. Will we need to rent chairs?"

"No," she replied. "The church has benches the men will bring and set up, and the wraparound porch is perfect for laying out the food afterward. You won't have to do a thing."

"It's settled, then."

"Do you mind if we use the barn for the horses?"

"Hope," he said, "use whatever you want. You know a lot more about what your church needs than I do."

"My people will help me get ready."

"You do realize that other religions just show up at a church building, right?"

"Those other people aren't Amish. The harder it is for us, the more we think God likes it," she joked.

She turned to her daughter. "Come, Carrie. I'll need to make a list of everything that will need to be done."

With Carrie holding her hand, she went to check out the barn. She might need to bring in some hay. As they approached, she heard a noise that sounded like a low moan. Logan had no livestock so there shouldn't be any sounds coming from there. Perhaps a wounded stray dog had gotten in. She would have to be careful.

She made Carrie stand back while she opened the door. It took a moment for her eyes to adjust to the semi-darkness of the large, empty barn, but when they did, what she saw was appalling. Simon Hochstetler, the older teenage boy who had done some work for her father the past two summers, sat hunched over in a corner, his arms around his legs. It looked as though he had been badly beaten.

"Simon?" she asked. "Is that you?"

"*Ja.*"

After one glance at his face, she turned her daughter's eyes away from the young man. "Carrie, run to the house and tell Logan to come quick."

She watched as the child scurried up the hill. Then she

rushed over to Simon, fell to her knees, and examined the bruises on his face, arms, and neck. "Who did this to you?"

"*Daed.*"

"Your father?" Hope felt a lump come to her throat. "No one deserves to be treated like this. Certainly not a good boy like you, but why come here?"

"I thought the *Englisch* man might not come to the barn—not like Amish men who are always there." He hid his bruised face in his arms. "I am ashamed. I did not want anyone to see."

She thought her heart would break. This gentle seventeen-year-old boy had often helped her father put up hay and do chores around the farm. He had such a gentle way with their animals, she had always had a soft spot for him.

"Tell me what happened, Simon."

"I had our horse team out, getting them conditioned for spring plowing. One of them got spooked. Both tore away from me and went through a fence. I could not stop them. I tried."

"Did you get the team back?"

"I did, and I fixed the fence, too, but the mare's leg is bad swollen and the gelding is limping."

Getting the crops in was nearly a matter of life or death for the Swartzentruber Amish. More than any other Amish sect, they made their living from farming, supplementing their income with handwoven baskets or carpentry. Still, she could not understand why Simon's father would beat him for something he could not control.

"So he beat you because he thinks you were responsible for two horses going lame?"

The boy wiped his nose and nodded. "And *Maam's* having another baby."

"Ah." That would make nineteen children in Simon's family, a family that was already impoverished. Did Simon's father not know how babies got here?

"I thought he would kill me." Simon choked out another involuntary sob. "Wilma got between us and told me to run."

Wilma? Hope tried to remember all the children of that family. She was pretty certain that Wilma was the eldest, about twenty or twenty-one.

"Is Wilma in danger?" she asked. "Will he do this to her?"

"He about wore himself out hitting me." Simon shook his head. "She'll probably just get a few good slaps."

The commonplace tone of his voice gave Hope chills. This must be a fairly common occurrence.

"Does your *Daed* hit you a lot?"

"Got to keep us respectful, *Daed* says."

Hope had never liked Moses Hochstetler. When Simon had worked for her father, Moses always came and collected his son's wages, as though he did not trust the boy to turn them over to him. He always refused to do business with her or her mother if Henry happened to be gone. Still, she never dreamed he could be this brutal.

"What's going on?" Logan came rushing to the barn at a dead run, Adam in his arms, Carrie running behind. "Are you okay? Carrie grabbed my hand and told me to *kommen*. I figured that meant 'come.'"

In her shock over Simon's condition, Hope had momentarily forgotten that at five, Carrie would not have the English words to give Logan her message. Hope switched from English to German so easily, she was barely aware she was doing it. Fortunately, the little girl had gotten her point across anyway.

"We have a visitor, Logan, and I think he might need medical attention."

Simon looked scared. "*Daed* doesn't allow doctor bills."

"Can you walk?" Logan asked. She saw a look of recognition in his eyes. She realized Logan must have met Simon while the boy was out peddling firewood.

"I made it here." Simon stood up and took a couple steps to prove it. Then he staggered and nearly fell. Logan caught him with one arm while holding Adam with the other.

"I'm calling the police," Logan said.

"No!" Simon sounded terrified. "*Daed* will kill me!"

"I'm calling an ambulance." Logan sat Adam down and pulled out his ever-present cell phone.

"Not yet. Let's take him up to the house," Hope said. "I want to clean him up and see how bad it is first. Then we'll decide what to do."

"I forgot," Logan said. "No medical insurance. But isn't there a church fund of some kind?"

"The Swartzentruber churches are much poorer than the Old Order Amish. Paying for an ambulance and emergency room visit could take everything their church has. Let me check him out first, and if necessary, we'll call Grace."

As Hope expected, the boy's cuts and bruises were bad, but they were not life-threatening. Logan gathered together some of his clothes for Simon to wear and she ran bathwater for the injured boy.

Adam watched it all with wide blue eyes. "Simon is hurt?"

"Simon's hurt," Hope said, "but he will get better."

While Simon was in the bathroom, Hope and Logan stood in the hallway outside the bathroom door and debated what to do.

"I still think we should call the police," Logan said. "Who does that to a kid?"

"I know," Hope said. "But you don't understand what a tightrope some of the Swartzentruber Amish families walk or the kind of stress the fathers are under. Those two horses that were made lame? If they don't get better soon, they could make the difference between the children eating well this winter or having empty bellies. A good plow horse is worth a lot of money. Moses probably just snapped from stress and frustration."

"And the fact that his wife is pregnant with her nineteenth child! Who *does* that!"

"The Swartzentrubers live on farms and have huge families. Extra hands mean more help on the farm, just like it used to for your *Englisch* ancestors as well as ours."

"I don't understand," Logan said. "You talk about the Swartzentruber Amish as though they are from a different culture, and yet they are Amish—like you."

"The Swartzentruber Amish make the Old Order Amish look like . . . like we are modern people." Hope smiled sadly. "I know that is hard for you to understand, but it is true."

"So Simon's father gets by with this behavior? No police are called?"

"The police probably would not be able to do much anyway. Simon would never testify against his father. He would only tell the police that he got kicked by a horse or something. A policeman is like a person from another country to them."

"Then what can we do?"

"I'll talk to my father. He likes Simon and will be upset at what has happened. He will pay a visit to Simon's bishop. The bishop will look into the condition of the family and see what can be done. The bishop's word will be more effective than anything you or I can do. It will be more effective than anything the police might do as well."

"How about if we leave your father out of it and I go to see the bishop. I'm the one who saw that boy tonight and the shape he was in."

"An outsider like you?" She shook her head. "No, it is better handled by my father." A sound of singing and splashing came from inside the bathroom.

"For someone as beat up as Simon, he certainly seems to be enjoying his bath!" Logan said.

There was the sound of more water being run into the tub, and more splashing.

"It's probably the first time he's ever gotten to take a real bath in a bathtub. The Swartzentruber do not allow running water or indoor toilets."

"You're kidding!"

"I am not."

"So what do we do with him after he comes out?"

"Do you mind if he stays here for the night?" Hope asked. "I know him well. He is quite harmless and you have extra beds. I think it would be best to give his father time to cool off."

"Of course he can stay here. He can stay as long as he likes. It's a big house."

A few minutes later, Simon came out of the bathroom, announcing, "I'm done," carefully dressed in Logan's clothes. He was shorter and had to roll his pants legs up, but he'd tucked in the shirt, which was also too large, and tightly cinched the waist of the chinos with the belt Logan had loaned him. His hair was plastered down, and he'd been liberal with Logan's shaving lotion.

His face, however, looked like it had been used as a punching bag. One eye was swollen entirely shut. Hope saw that Simon, in spite of his pain, had tried to leave the bathroom clean. Two damp towels were neatly folded over the edge of the bathtub. It tugged at her heart that the battered boy had tried to tidy the bathroom.

"Are you hungry?" Hope asked.

"I can always eat." Simon rubbed his stomach. "It's a little hard to get filled up at my house."

"Then we will see if we can find you something," Hope said.

"You've already cleaned the kitchen, Hope," Logan said.

"And Simon and I met a few weeks ago when he brought firewood. I've seen how much the boy can pack away. Instead of you cooking again, how about I pick up some pizza? Does that sound good to either of you?"

"Pizza?" As much as possible with the bruises, Simon's face lit up. "I *like* pizza!"

Hope knew he probably rarely got it, too. Take-out pizza was far too expensive for a large Swartzentruber family to purchase often.

"Then, if you don't mind waiting a few minutes," Logan said, "I'll go make a pizza run. Shall I get enough for all of us, Hope?"

"If you don't mind."

It did sound like a good idea. She was tired. Running two households and raising two children while pregnant was not easy. Not having to cook for herself, Adam, and Carrie tonight sounded heavenly.

Logan thought for sure that he'd gotten enough pizza to feed the five of them twice over, but watching Simon pack it away made him wish he'd ordered more. He didn't know if the boy was actually that hungry, or if he just thought he might never get to eat pizza again in his lifetime.

Adam sat on his mother's lap and ate one whole piece. Carrie ate one with dainty small bites. Hope managed three pieces. She seemed so grateful to get to sit down and not have to cook that he decided he needed to pick up take-out food more often for her and her little family . . . and him. He enjoyed having company while eating.

"You can spend the night, if you want," he told Simon. "I've got plenty of room."

The look of gratitude on the boy's face was worth the small inconvenience it might be.

"I'll work for you," Simon said. "I'm a *gut* worker."

Logan racked his brain trying to think up something for the boy to do. It was hard enough coming up with enough work to keep Hope busy a few hours each week.

"What are you good at?" he asked.

"Livestock," Simon said. "And I could put in some crops for you if I had a team." The boy grinned self-deprecatingly. "As long as one of the horses don't get spooked, I do pretty good."

Livestock. Plowing. Crops. Subjects about which he knew nothing.

"It would be nice to work away from home," Simon continued. "*Daed* wouldn't get so mad if I could work here for you."

"You might as well ask me to launch a rocket into space," Logan said. "I know nothing about such things."

"I know what you need." Hope's voice was eager. "I know exactly how this farm should be run. I could easily find a couple of good plow horses and the equipment to go with them. Simon does know how to do this. He's worked putting in crops and caring for livestock since he could walk . . . and so have I."

With two sets of hopeful eyes looking at him, Logan felt a little railroaded. "Can I talk to you out on the porch, Hope?"

While Simon happily polished off the last piece of pizza and chatted in German with Carrie and Adam, Hope followed him out to the front porch.

"I can't hire that boy to farm this place," Logan said. "I have no idea how to oversee him. I don't know a plow horse from a racehorse."

"I disagree," Hope said. "Simon is a terribly hard worker, and we both know what we're doing, even if you do not. Give us land, and we know how to work it. If the crops do well, he'll make his own wages come harvest. You have to do nothing except pay for two horses and some equipment and seed. We can do the rest. Simon will have a job that will keep him away from his father. Let him live here with you. It will keep him safer than telling the police like you wanted. Besides"—she waved a hand out toward the field—"this land will soon turn to scrub if you don't do something with it."

Hope's lovely face, framed by her white *Kapp*, was so earnest as she argued the subject. He was struck once again with how her eyes were an unusually deep shade of gold-flecked brown. It was becoming more and more difficult to ignore her beauty. A man could lose himself gazing into Hope's eyes. Her reasoning made complete sense, but he knew that, sadly, if he kept his word to Marla to come back within the time they'd agreed upon, he would not be staying here long enough to even see the harvest.

When had the thought of leaving created a permanent ache in his heart?

"I'll think about it." He gave himself a mental shake and forced himself to look away. "That's all I can agree to right now . . . I'll think about it."

chapter NINETEEN

Logan was having his morning coffee on the porch when an Amish man drove in, pulled his horse around, and stopped in front of the house. He was seated on the hard, wooden seat of what looked to be a homemade farm wagon. There was no red safety triangle on the back, which Logan knew probably meant the man was Swartzentruber.

"I have come for my son."

So this was Simon's father. He was a large man with big, raw-looking hands. It made Logan's blood boil to think of what those hands had done to Simon.

If there was one thing Logan had at ready command, it was words. There were hundreds of words he wanted to fling at the man. His fingers itched to call the police. Show them the bruises on the boy's face and body. Have the man thrown in jail for domestic abuse.

What he wanted most, what he *craved*, was to climb up onto that wagon and slam his own fist straight into the man's face.

Instead, he heard Hope's voice in his head, cautioning him, reminding him that he was dealing with a different culture with different rules and different outcomes.

Let my father and the other men deal with him.

He had looked in on Simon earlier. The boy was curled into a ball in bed, sleeping off the trauma of the beating. With any luck, he would sleep through his father's visit.

"How did you know he was here?"

"I did not," the man said. "But now I do. I think . . . he runs to *Englisch* man's house who gave him doughnuts. Where is my son? He has work at home."

Two things struck Logan. One was that English sounded more foreign on this man's lips than in the mouths of Old Order Amish people he'd met. He spoke slowly, sounding as though he were having to stop to translate every word before he spoke. Hope had told him once that the Swartzentruber stayed much more isolated than the other Amish sects.

The other thing that struck him was astonishment that, as badly beaten as Simon was last night, his father still expected him to work this morning.

There was only one way he could think of to keep Simon safe.

"I have work for him, too," Logan said. "I want to hire him to . . . to help around the farm."

"This?" The man looked around him in contempt. "This is not a farm."

"Exactly." Logan still wanted to smash the man's face in, but for Simon's sake, he kept his voice even and reasonable. "I'll pay him a small wage, and give him room and board. You and your wife will have one less mouth to feed."

Simon's father contemplated the offer. "Let me talk to my son."

"Sorry. He's not well enough to get out of bed this morning." The anger and contempt he felt for the man crept into his voice in spite of his best efforts. "I was going to take him to the hospital yesterday, but he said his *father* would not approve. I also considered calling the police, but my Amish housekeeper talked me out of it."

The man's eyes did not quite meet Logan's. "He must bring his pay home each week."

"I'll tell him."

After the man had left, Logan went back inside and found Simon trying to scramble eggs, in spite of the fact that now both eyes were nearly swollen shut.

"You don't have to do that, Simon," Logan said.

"I must earn my pay."

"Yes, you do." Logan gently took the spatula out of the boy's hand. "But not today. Not now. Sit down. I'll fix your break-fast."

"Thank you." Simon collapsed onto a kitchen chair, put his head down on his folded arms, and sobbed.

"Would it bother you if I had electricity brought into the house, Hope?" Logan approached the subject carefully after he'd filled her in on what had transpired between him and Simon's father.

Hope had arrived early with both Adam and Carrie and had immediately attacked the few dishes he and Simon had used for breakfast.

"It is your house." She placed a dish in the drainer.

"I mean, would it . . . bother you?"

"Because I'm Amish?"

"Yes."

"I don't see why it should. We do not expect *Englisch* people to live as we do."

"So you wouldn't feel offended if you had to use, say, an electric washer and dryer?"

Hope shrugged. "It is not a matter of using electric devices. Many of us do that in our jobs. Some of our people are also beginning to use solar power on our farms. Many of us own gasoline-driven generators."

"You are aware that this doesn't fit into most people's views of Amish life, right?"

"Then they do not understand. We are not ignorant of technology. It is our hooking into the electric grid that our bishops forbid. It is one of the many ways we try to be separate from the world."

"And you agree with their decision?"

Hope paused to give this some thought, her soapy hands dripping into the sink. "I feel sorry for our bishops for all the hard decisions they are constantly being called on to make. A cell phone, for instance, can be a life-saving tool for an emergency or nothing more than a plaything tempting our young people to access things they should not."

The struggles of Amish church bishops were not his problem. His immediate need was to make a decision about his own house. He had held off having electricity put in for several reasons. He liked the glow of kerosene lamps and the quiet and peace of a house that didn't constantly hum. This was Hope's childhood home and built by her ancestors. Later, when Hope came, he held off because he didn't want to create a situation that would make her feel she was compromising her faith.

The problem was, as Hope continued to work for him, he kept thinking of how much easier it would be for her if she didn't have to wrestle with a wringer washer and heavy, wet clothes in laundry baskets, and didn't have to wash every dish by hand. Although he had gotten weaned away from needing the noise of television to work by, he did miss having classical music playing. He also missed having a really good light to read by. Besides that, it was getting old having to recharge his laptop and cell phone from his car battery. One thing was for sure, Marla would certainly love it if he brought the house into the twenty-first century.

"I wonder who to get to wire the place," he mused.

"Oh, that is no problem," Hope said. "You should call my cousin. He will bring in his crew and have it done in a very short time."

"You have a cousin who is *Englisch*?"

"No. He is Amish."

"He is Amish but he knows how to rewire a house for electricity?"

"Oh, yes." Hope was matter-of-fact. "Do not worry, he does not have electricity in *his* house."

"Give me his number and I'll give him a call." He walked away, amazed at the inconsistencies among the Amish people.

Over the next few days, his house experienced quite a few changes as electricity was brought in. Hope's cousin Silas was indeed very good. He seemed to understand exactly what the old house needed. Simon was entranced with the changes and followed the Amish electrician around, soaking up everything. As the days passed, the bruises on the teenager's face and body began to heal.

Once the work was complete, and the outlets installed, Logan enjoyed purchasing and bringing in new, labor-saving devices and explaining to Hope how each one worked. She was quick to learn and it took only one or two demonstrations for her to have it down.

"With all these things, you will no longer need a housekeeper," she said, after he'd introduced her to the joys of the dishwasher and an electric iron. "You will be able to do everything for yourself so easily."

"Of course I'll need a housekeeper," he quickly reassured her. "I just thought a few new things might make your work a little easier."

"Do I have to learn how to use a computer?" she asked.

"Of course not," he said. "That's one thing I can handle all on my own."

To his surprise, she seemed disappointed.

"That is too bad," Hope said. "I think I would have enjoyed learning how to use the computer."

"I'll be happy to teach you . . ."

"How is your wife?" Hope abruptly changed the subject. "Will she move here now that you have electricity?"

"Why are you asking?"

"I ran into Verla Grayson again yesterday. I told her that the three children and the pregnancy were a joke Marla had played on her."

"How did Verla take it?"

"She was surprised, but relieved. She said she had been worried about those children being raised without a father."

"I'm sorry we worried her."

"That's okay, she's not worried anymore."

Hope appeared to lose interest in the conversation as she inspected the new coffeemaker.

He was wrong. Hope had not lost interest in the conversation at all.

"So, *will* Marla be moving in now that you have electricity? Perhaps if she does, you could give her some real children instead of your wife having to make up joke-children."

She smiled to let him know she was teasing him, but he had been around her enough to know she wasn't really joking. If there was one thing she was passionate about, it was children.

It was one thing for Marla to tease him in front of a stranger. It was entirely another thing to live a lie to a woman whom he saw almost on a daily basis. "Seriously"—Hope was unpacking small containers of coffee from the box the coffeemaker had come in—"do you plan to have children anytime soon? You are very good with them."

Really? It surprised him that Hope felt that way. He knew the Amish had high standards for fatherhood.

"No. Marla and I won't be having any children."

Hope blinked. "What did you say?"

"Marla doesn't want children."

"Your wife does not want *children*?" Hope was genuinely astonished.

He decided it was time to come clean with Hope about his and Marla's relationship, even if it *would* offend her religious sensibilities. The better he got to know Hope, the more he felt it was wrong to keep this from her. He was sick of pretending.

"Marla's not exactly my wife."

"What does 'not exactly' mean?"

"We are planning on getting married in a few months. Marla is making the wedding arrangements . . . and we've shared an apartment for a while."

"You two have been living together?" Hope's voice rose in shock. "Without being *married*?"

"Yes."

"But that is a sin!"

"Well, we aren't very religious," he explained.

"I do not understand. You do not want children together. You do not have a problem with living in sin together. You are not religious." Hope crossed her arms over her chest. "Why bother to get married at all?"

He'd been wondering that himself recently, only for different reasons. The longer he spent in Holmes County around Hope, the less attractive he found the idea of marrying Marla.

"I will be more careful to keep the children out of your way from now on!" Hope said. "I did not realize you did not like them."

"I never said that I don't like children, I said that Marla doesn't want any."

"Then you *do* want children?" Hope shook her head as though to clear it.

"Yes, I do, but it isn't fair to ask her to bear children that she doesn't want."

"Oh—it is a *very* good idea for her not to have children she does not want," Hope said. "A very good idea indeed! Children should be wanted and loved."

"You wouldn't understand, Hope. Marla and her friends . . . they are different from you."

"You are right. I do not understand. When we can't have children, we adopt. There are many children who need good homes. Or we take in a relative's child if that child needs a good home. To us, children are our hope for the future and a gift from God."

He knew these were not just words to her.

"You're a good mom, Hope," he said. "Your kids are lucky to have you. I don't think Marla would make a very good mother."

The look Hope gave him was an interesting mix of pity and scorn.

"A visiting bishop spoke with Titus and me before we were married," Hope said.

"And what did this visiting bishop have to say?"

"The bishop said, 'Do you know the best time to get a divorce?' Titus and I were surprised by his question. We said that we didn't. The bishop told us that the best time to get a divorce was before we got married. He warned us to be very careful in choosing our spouse."

"Are you suggesting I should not marry Marla?"

"You do not act like a man who is happy about the woman he is supposed to love."

That stung. Of course he was happy. "You don't like her."

"It doesn't matter if I do or not. All I know is, if I were married to a man like you . . . I would *never* value my job over my husband." Hope gasped and put her hand over her mouth. "I didn't mean . . ." A miserable look swept over her face. "Really, I didn't mean anything by that. I—I just miss my husband very much."

"Of course you didn't mean . . ." His mind was whirling. What exactly *had* she meant? Was it merely an unfortunate slip of the tongue, or had she begun to care for him?

The possible ramifications that someone like Hope was possibly falling for him were mind-boggling.

"Marla's okay." He backed away from the emotional precipice they were teetering on. "We'll be fine."

"Of course you will." Hope scrambled to hide her embarrassment. "And if you are not . . . well, that is none of my business. I need to go finish my chores now."

As she walked away, he wondered if this honesty thing was all it was cracked up to be. He'd told her the truth, and he didn't feel a bit better for having done so. All he'd managed to do was upset both of them, find out her negative feelings about Marla, and maybe even caused the girl to trip up and accidentally confess that she had feelings for him. He had no idea what to think about that. The ramifications for both of them if he ever allowed himself to return those feelings were staggering.

The conversation he'd thought would purge his soul had not exactly been a success.

chapter TWENTY

Logan was hard at work a week later when a small army of Amish men and women showed up to prepare his house for church. Most were Hope's relatives, who—from what he could tell—cleaned every square inch of his house. With all of Hope's hard work, he wondered what they found to clean. Then he found several women standing on stepladders and realized they were actually washing down all the walls and cabinets. Cleaning for church was apparently serious business.

With Simon's willing help, the men started in on the yard. Weed eaters were pulled out of buggies and gasoline-powered push lawn mowers were fine-tuned and added their whir to the general noise as they cut the tender spring grass that had sprung up in uneven clumps.

Men worked in the massive old barn with pitchforks. Hay bales arrived on flatbed buggies, and were distributed to the various stalls. Small children seemed to be everywhere. Teenagers worked harder than he had ever seen teenagers work. It was as though everyone had been assigned a job by some unseen church foreman, but Hope told him that had not happened. They just all knew what needed to be done and did it.

Logan was left with nothing to do but watch in wonder as

Hope's father and some others moved the partition out of the front room. Everything they did was accompanied by talk and laughter. He was wandering around, offering to help and finding nothing to do that wasn't already being accomplished, when Hope's mother took him in hand.

"We know you need to write," Rose said firmly. "And we don't want to disturb you, so we've set you up out under that tree where you can watch what's going on and still get some writing done."

He was astonished to find that someone had actually carried his writing desk out to the tree and his laptop was on it. An extension cord was curled beside it, long enough to reach a house outlet if he ran out of battery. Someone had even poured him a cup of coffee and set it beside the laptop. Freshly sharpened pencils were placed in a decorative cup, along with a new notebook. A sturdy piece of plywood was laid on the ground, to create a flat surface for his office chair.

In other words, they did not need him, were not thrilled with him trotting around offering his help, and were giving him something to occupy himself with so that he would stay out of their way. Adam and another little boy were sitting beside the same tree, each with three crayons grasped in their hands as they colored together in a single picture book with farm animals on the front.

"So—you've been sidelined, too, huh?" he said to the children.

In reply, Adam held the book up and showed him a badly colored green house.

"Good job!" Logan said. "Whatever you do, don't color in the lines. It's supposed to be bad for your creative development."

Adam tilted his head to one side, and then once again became absorbed in his coloring book.

Logan could not begin to concentrate with all this activity

going on around him, so he simply typed "All work and no play makes Jack a dull boy" over and over again, trying to look busy, while he watched the ultracompetent Amish take over his house.

Hope was so cute directing foot traffic. She was seven months pregnant now and glowing with health. He studied her, thinking of how he would describe her if she were a character in one of his books.

Hope Schrock was barefoot, modestly dressed, and pregnant. A preparer of food, a lover of children, an encourager to the elderly. Her name fit her well. Wherever she went, whomever she touched, she brought a lifting of spirits. In other words, she brought with her wherever she went . . . hope.

He read the words aloud and then deleted them, deciding that they did not do the woman justice. She was the most competent woman he'd ever met, and she managed to do it all with patience and a ready smile.

It was a pleasure to watch her with her children, or with the other women. He saw her touch an elderly woman's arm and lead her to a rocking chair on the porch. Solicitous and kind. That was his Hope.

He caught himself. She was not *his* Hope.

A problem was developing and he did not know what to do about it. He had trouble taking his eyes off her. What if she were religiously free to marry whom she wanted? Would she consider him as a candidate?

Sitting here was giving him entirely too much time to watch and think about her, and yet it was a great pleasure to do so.

Then he saw Hope's mother, Rose, staring at him with a concerned look on her face, as though she had read his thoughts. Immediately he dropped his eyes and began to write in earnest.

"You have an interesting job, my *Englisch* friend." The man who had been introduced to him as Bishop Schrock startled him by dropping a copy of one of his own books onto his desk.

Logan picked it up. "Where did you get this, Bishop?"

"Hope brought a copy to me."

"Why?" Logan was not ashamed of his books, but he wasn't exactly thrilled with the idea of an Amish bishop reading one.

"Because when she told me who you really were, I asked her to. It is possible to learn much about a man's heart by what he writes."

Logan hoped the bishop hadn't come to the conclusion that he was a dangerous psychopath just because he wrote about them!

"I'm a storyteller," Logan said. "I make things up. I don't experience or believe in everything I write."

The bishop nodded at this and said nothing.

"Did you finish it?" Logan probed.

"*Ja*," the bishop said. "I finished it."

Logan waited for him to say something else about it. Good or bad. The bishop seemed in no hurry to speak. He simply stood there, towering over him.

"So . . ." Logan prompted. "You hated it?"

"I did not hate it."

"Then what?"

"I am wondering what good they do, these books you spend your life writing."

"What good?" Logan felt the sting of the bishop's words. "They are how I make my living . . . just like building a house or shoveling manure."

"Ah," the bishop said. "That is true. Our honest labor does little except provide goods for others and food on the table for our family."

"Then why do you ask what 'good' my books do? Why do they have to do 'good'?"

"Like all Amish, I was only educated through the eighth grade," Bishop Schrock said. "I am no judge of literature, but even I can see that God has given you much talent. You put words together in ways that pulled me in and kept me reading much later at night than what was good for me."

Finally, some praise. "So what is the problem?"

"I admit, I am a little envious of your ability with words." The bishop shook his head as though with wonder. "To throw them away on books that mean nothing . . . it seems like such a waste."

Books that meant nothing? The Amish certainly didn't pull any punches.

"Your book left me with a dark feeling in my heart for many days. It was not good for me to be inside a bad man's head for so long. Through your words I saw things I should not have seen. I would like to forget them but now I cannot."

Logan wished Hope had asked permission before she loaned the bishop one of his books.

"The Bible says that there is a great spiritual battle going on around us that we cannot see. It says that there are forces of evil to be fought with whatever weapons we are given. After I read your book, it felt like the forces of darkness had won a small battle in my heart."

That hurt.

His mission accomplished, the bishop blithely walked away, leaving Logan to drum a pencil on his desk and seethe. When everything the bishop said was stripped down, he believed that he had just been accused of being a tool of Satan.

While they worked together, Hope enjoyed showing the other women the new appliances that Logan had purchased.

"You just put this little cup in, pull down on the handle, and . . . out comes a cup of coffee or tea!" She demonstrated the new Keurig coffeemaker Logan had purchased. Compared to the labor involved in using the drip coffeemaker on the stove, the Keurig seemed magical to her.

She handed Rose the cup of coffee she had just made and watched as her mother took a sip.

Rose's eyes widened. "This is really good!"

"I *know*!" Hope wiped off the counter and dropped the little spent Keurig cup into the new trash compactor.

"But very expensive, is my guess," Rose said.

"I don't know how much it cost," Hope said. "Let me show you the washer and dryer now."

Hope's mother was suitably impressed with the new water-saving laundry appliances, but she seemed to grow more and more worried.

"You are enjoying these modern things a little too much, I think," Rose cautioned. "And maybe the man who bought them?"

"I have done nothing wrong," Hope said.

"Of course you haven't," her mother soothed. "But you are without a husband, and he is too much without a wife. There is danger here. You must protect yourself. It would be easy to have your head turned by so many expensive things. Before long you might not want to be Amish anymore."

Hope hurried to reassure her.

"I am just doing my job," she said. "You remember how Titus had to use electric tools when he worked in the furniture factory? It did not change him. He still used the old ways when he came home. So do I."

There was a part of her that felt guilty saying this to her mother. The truth was, she had enjoyed getting to use modern things.

"I suppose you are right," Rose said. "But watch yourself, Daughter. Satan is sneaky and he creeps into a person's life so quietly."

"I will be careful, *Maam*," she promised.

"*Gut*," her mother said. "Now I must go and see to the set-ting up of the tables on the porch."

What she had said to her mother was true. She would be very careful. Even more careful now that she had discovered that Logan was not truly a married man. Thinking he had a wife had created an extra wall of protection around her heart. That wall of protection had crumbled with his confession. She had recently begun to feel his admiring eyes on her and some-times it warmed her heart in spite of her best intentions. Most of the time she shoved that warmth out of her heart by remind-ing herself that he had been, and probably still was, living in sin with Marla whenever he went to New York. Still . . . her mind had begun to think of things that it should not.

Her conscience and training told her that she must flee temp-tation immediately, but her practical mind reminded her that she needed the income he provided. Where else could she work for such an easy boss, who paid so well and who welcomed the idea of her children being with her? What other employer would offer to allow her to bring the new baby with her after it was born?

And so, she did what she had been warned against doing her whole life. She pretended that there was no temptation, while deep down inside, her attraction to this *Englisch* man deepened every day.

Her *Daed* came into the kitchen at that moment and her sin-ful thoughts scattered like scurrying mice.

"Could you draw a glass of water for your old father?" he asked. "Cleaning the old barn is thirsty work."

She grabbed a drinking glass from the cupboard. "But you are not yet fifty. You should not say you are old."

"Being here makes me *feel* old." He accepted the drink from her hand as he glanced around the kitchen. "It was a fine place we had here once. I hope the *Englischer* is enjoying it."

She heard so many emotions in his voice. Bitterness, anger, shame.

"I know it hurts you to be here."

"It hurts to see the good earth that I tilled and enriched my entire life growing into nothing but weeds!"

She saw tears come to her father's eyes, but there was nothing she could do or say. The situation was what it was, and he had been the one to bring it about. He could blame no one except himself. She ached for him, but there was nothing she could do.

"What's the *Englisch* man going to do with my land?" he asked. "Sell it to developers?"

"I don't know for sure. I hope not."

She deliberately changed the subject. "Did you talk with Moses Hochstetler?"

"I did."

"Did he listen?"

"He listened, but . . ." Her father hesitated. "It was one of the few times in my life I wished I was not forbidden to raise my hand against another man. He does not deserve a son as fine as Simon."

Hope was grateful for the restriction their faith put on violence. She hated to think of what might have happened had her *Daed* and Moses fought. *Daed* was powerfully built, with work-hardened muscles as strong as steel—but Moses was strong, too. Had the men actually fought, one or both would have ended up in the hospital and that would have devastated two families.

"I also spoke with Bishop Weaver, the Swartzentrubers' bishop, about what Simon's father had done," he said. "He was not happy. He said not to worry, that he will deal with Moses."

"I am certain he will, then. Thank you for taking care of this for me."

He smiled. "That is what fathers are for."

"And *Gott* gave our family a *gut* one in you."

He caressed the surface of one of the fine cherry kitchen cabinets that his own father had built. "I am grateful that you still think so, Daughter."

A look of deep regret crossed his face. She could only imagine how hard it was for him to remember all that he had lost.

"It is only wood, *Daed*." Hope's heart broke at seeing his grief and she gave him a rare hug. "It's only wood."

chapter TWENTY-ONE

A low, slow, humming sound rose through the floorboards of his upstairs bedroom. He paused in the act of tying his necktie and listened. The singing was made up predominately of male voices and reminded him of the otherworldly drone of a bagpipe he had once heard played at a funeral.

He had not worn a suit for months, but when he asked Hope if a white shirt and dark suit would be appropriate, she seemed relieved he'd brought the question up. Her enthusiastic approval made him wonder if she'd been fearful he would show up in jogging shorts and a T-shirt.

He slipped his suit coat on and checked outside the window. The assembly of buggies had grown in the past ten minutes. From his vantage point of the second story, it looked as though the field beside his house was carpeted with black buggy tops. And horses. Lots and lots of glistening, dark-brown horses.

Hope had suggested he wait until services were starting before coming downstairs. There was a prescribed way to enter the room, she explained, a matter of respect. The bishop walked in first, regardless of his age. Then the ministers filed in according to their age, with the oldest going first. The deacon followed. Then the rest of the men came in turn, from the oldest down to the youngest, teenage boys bringing up the rear.

Working an *Englisch* man into the traditional entering and seating situation, she explained, was going to be a little awkward, especially since he deserved respect for his generosity in allowing them to assemble beneath his roof. Hope wasn't sure quite what to do, and so they agreed that it would be best for him to simply come down a few seconds after he heard the strains of the first hymn.

He glanced at himself in the mirror and nervously straightened his tie. One thing he did not want to do was embarrass his housekeeper.

Unfortunately, he was also a little worried about staying awake. The writing on his thriller novel had been going unusually well last night, the story finally unraveling in his head, and he hated to stop, so he went on late into the night, afraid that if he did stop, he would never get back into the writer's zone that was so hard to achieve. It was looking like he might have a book ready to turn in to his publisher by deadline after all. It might not be his best, but it was by far not his worst. The house, the people, Hope, his extracurricular writing at the antiques shop, had somehow, someway, rescued him.

What time had he gone to sleep, anyway, 5 a.m.? All he remembered for sure was that the last thing on his mind when he crawled into bed was that it was Sunday morning. The thought that on *this* Sunday morning there would be a houseful of guests had been a pleasant one. It occurred to him right before he closed his eyes that he did not enjoy being alone nearly as much as he had always tried to tell himself.

Hurriedly, he ran a brush through his hair, took a deep breath, and then headed downstairs.

Spread out before him when he got to the bottom was a scene that he would never forget. Black-bonneted, black-cloaked women and children sat on one side of the room; bearded men on the other.

The singing stopped and he stood there, wondering how to go about finding a place to sit. It appeared that every available seat was already filled. He sought out Simon, but the boy was nowhere to be seen. So many eyes were turned on him.

He was about to sit on the stairs themselves, when several men scooted over and a spot opened up. The bishop waved him toward the seat. As he squeezed himself in between two Amish men about his own age, the bishop launched into what sounded like a sermon or a harangue—Logan wasn't sure which. He just hoped that Bishop Schrock was not informing everyone that the owner of the house was a writer of dark novels and therefore the spawn of Satan.

The Amish were not an openly affectionate kind of people, from what he had seen, but their personal space when it came time to worship was far less than what he was comfortable with. He couldn't so much as take a deep breath without the man sitting next to him feeling it.

Someone—he couldn't tell who, but someone sitting close to him—had obviously missed their Saturday-night bath, or it could have been several Saturday-night baths. He found himself wondering if deodorant was against some obscure Amish rule.

The sermon, as Hope had warned him, was in German. He did not understand a word. Soon, the novelty of being in an Amish worship service began to pall, and he found himself wishing that he'd taken the time to use the bathroom before rushing down.

He also wished he had gone to bed at a reasonable hour last night, gotten up earlier, and had enough time to grab a cup of coffee. The lack of caffeine and lack of sleep made him feel like he might topple over if he wasn't careful.

The next thing he knew, everyone—men and women—rose

as one, turned around, knelt in front of their benches, put their elbows on the bench, and bowed their heads. Once he saw what was happening, he scrambled to his knees as well.

Not a word was said. The praying was silent and it went on for a long time. At first, he was simply grateful for the chance to move into a different position. Backless benches tended to make a body ache. Then he grew uncomfortable with being on his knees. Finally he found himself rising with the rest of the group and he sat back on the bench with the other men.

That was how the next three hours went, alternately sitting in a half-daze while various men addressed the group in unintelligible German. Then sudden movement as they all kneeled in prayer. Then everyone would sing from a hymnal he could neither read nor understand, as his bladder grew more and more uncomfortable and his desire for a cup of coffee grew, and his back and bottom ached from the hard benches.

With all his heart, he wished he had never asked to take part in an Amish worship service. They didn't even have so much as a band to break up the monotony—just that strange, in-unison singing where each song seemed to go on forever.

He had his elbows on his knees and was leaning with his chin resting on his steepled fingers, trying to give his back a break. His eyes were closed and he was far away in his mind when he realized that a few of the words had just made sense to him.

He sat up quickly and looked around. Had someone spoken in English?

No, the preacher was droning on and on in impenetrable German.

He leaned over again, closed his eyes, and let his mind wander.

There it was again! He sat upright and received sideways looks from his seatmates. He knew the meaning of that German word. It was not English being slipped in at all—it was his brain processing the German into an image he knew and understood.

How had this happened? He closed his eyes again and concentrated. He could not understand a word, no matter how hard he tried. It was only when he allowed his mind to slip into neutral that he understood some words and phrases.

He had heard that there was a method of learning a language that consisted of simply being around it long enough that eventually one's mind began to understand it.

He didn't give the idea much credence, and the method took days, months, years, as far as he knew. It didn't happen in a couple hours.

He leaned forward into his original position, and cleared his mind by concentrating on the grain of the wooden floor beneath him. The German words flowed over and around him. It took all his discipline to keep himself from trying to process them, but when he came out of his self-imposed trance, he knew that it was not his imagination. He was hearing individual words and some phrases that made sense to him. He actually had a smattering of an idea what the preacher had been talking about.

How could this happen?

He didn't believe in multiple lifetimes, but some of his new age friends did, and some even had put themselves under hypnosis to try to ascertain who they had been in ancient times. It was always interesting to him to note that these friends never had lived previous lives as slaves or ditchdiggers or coal miners. Without fail they all had been princes or kings or some kind of important personages in their previous existence. One of Marla's friends was convinced that she had been a mistress of Genghis Khan.

But for himself? A past life that involved being a humble, German-speaking Amishman? He doubted it.

And yet . . . why the strong déjà vu again? Why this strange and sudden ability to understand a few German words?

The déjà vu feeling was not at all uncomfortable. Instead, it brought with it, just like when he'd first entered this house, a feeling of peace.

The singing started up again, and the melody of it sounded vaguely familiar. Church ended and even the rustle of the women's dresses sounded familiar. He heard conversations starting up all around him in another language, and understood snatches of what he was hearing.

Worst of all, or best of all—he didn't know if it was good or bad—he felt some sort of wall break down inside his heart and he had a terrible and pressing need to just . . . cry. Not from a feeling of pain, but from *relief*.

It was as though all his senses had opened up, little by little, as he sat there bookended by two Amish men, and he couldn't figure out why it felt so *right* to be with these people. Was this what a religious experience felt like? Was this what people who became Christians experienced?

He didn't know, but he didn't think so. This wasn't about God or Jesus. This was something else entirely.

He realized that if he didn't get out of there *fast*, there were going to be a few Amish people getting an eyeful of an *Englisch* man sitting there sobbing . . . and worst of all, if anyone inquired why, he had no idea what to tell them!

The minute services ended, he made his way politely toward the stairway, as quickly as possible.

"Aren't you having dinner with us?" Hope asked, just as he made it to the foot of the stairs.

He shook his head, so choked up he was unable to speak, and then bolted up to the second floor and the bathroom. After relieving himself, he splashed water on his face. There was a polite knock, and he opened the door to half a dozen Amish women who had lined up at the door.

Nodding to them, he went to his bedroom, closed the door,

and sat down in a rocking chair beside the window. As he looked out over the rolling fields, the flock of black buggies, and the people now milling about on his lawn, another flood of "memories" came pouring in. He had the sensation of being very small and being held in someone's arms as the two of them gazed out this very window. A wave of grief hit him so hard it nearly took his breath away.

Grief? How could he experience grief from simply being part of an Amish church service?

Perhaps his mother had forgotten something. Perhaps there was a reason for this after all.

He fumbled his cell phone out of his pocket. His mother usually spent Sunday afternoons volunteering at the local food bank or doing pro bono work at one of the domestic violence shelters she helped support. Some parents complained that their grown children never had time for them, but not Deborah Parker. She had her own agenda unless he needed her. But if he needed her, he knew she would drop everything. He dialed the phone, knowing that wherever she was, and whatever she was doing, she would answer when she saw his name on her caller ID.

"Logan!" She picked up on the first ring. "It's so good to hear from you."

"Hi, Mom. Are you busy?"

"Not at all. How are you?"

"I'm not good."

He could almost feel her grabbing her purse and reaching for her car keys.

"What's wrong and what can I do to help?"

"Are you absolutely certain that I've never been in Ohio Amish country? Is there *anything* you might have forgotten?"

There was a long pause. "You need to chalk this déjà vu thing up to one of those unexplained happenings in a person's life."

He tried out an idea that had been floating around in his

mind. "Mom, if you say yes to this, I won't think any less of you. It won't change anything between us, but is there any chance that I was adopted?"

"I swear to you, Logan," she said. "You were not adopted."

"Oh." He had begun to hope that he *was* adopted. That was far preferable to the suspicion that he might be losing his mind.

"Why are you asking me about this again?" Her voice grew tight with concern. "Tell me what's happened."

He sighed. "This morning I was in an Amish worship service and I realized that I was starting to understand some German words."

It sounded ridiculous, even to him.

"A lot of foreign words resemble English."

"They were not English-like words, Mother. And even though things were completely alien to me at first, everything in the worship service started feeling familiar, as though I'd been part of an Amish church before. By the time it ended, I wanted to start bawling, and it's been a lot of years since I cried about anything. Ever since I lost Ariela, nothing ever seemed bad enough to waste tears on."

"Perhaps it's time for you to come home." She warmed to the subject. "You've probably been working too hard. Take a break and we'll go somewhere nice together. My treat. How does Ireland sound? We could rent a cottage for a couple weeks and just relax."

His mother had talked about going to Ireland for years, but something always came up at work. She must be very worried if she was offering to actually take time off and go there.

"It sounds great, Mother. We'll talk about it after I meet this deadline. Thanks."

They said their good-byes and he leaned his head back against the hickory rocker he had purchased for his bedroom. If his mother had no answers, there was no one else left to ask.

He would be tempted to think he was losing his mind except for the fact that he'd done enormous research into deviant mental behavior for his psychological thrillers, and not once had he read about a phenomenon where someone suddenly, for no discernible reason, started understanding a foreign language.

There was a cautious knock on the door.

"Are you all right?" Hope looked in on him, her face pinched with worry. "Am I intruding?"

"You are never an intrusion, Hope. Come in."

She closed the door behind her and leaned against it. "I know our services last a bit long for *Englisch* people. I'm sorry if we wore you out."

"The service wasn't too long."

She got a good look at his face. "Logan! You've been crying! What is wrong?"

"I have no idea. Hope, I . . ." He hesitated. Should he risk telling her what had happened when even he didn't understand it?

She sat down on the edge of his bed. "You can tell me."

"You should be downstairs with the others," he said.

"I am fine where I am. The others and the children are fine where they are. All are eating their lunch. You are not fine. Tell me what is wrong. Did one of my people say something that offended you?"

"No. Your people have treated me well. It's just that either I'm having a mental breakdown, or I'm having some sort of past-life experience—which I don't believe in—or I have been in an Amish service before. The more time I spent sitting in that service, the more Amish words and phrases I began to understand. Even the melodies of the hymns started sounding familiar. Then I was hit with such a deep feeling of grief that I had to get out of there before I made a fool of myself. It's all somehow connected to the feeling of familiarity I had when I first saw this house, and the weird knowledge I had about the Troyers' home when I ate over there."

"Have you tried talking to your mother again to see if she remembers anything?"

"I just got off the phone with her. She is as mystified by this as I am."

"Forgive me, but could your mother be lying?"

The thought had never entered his mind.

"I don't think so. One thing I have always been able to depend on is her integrity. She's always been deadly honest. I just got off the phone with her and she denies I was adopted."

"Then that is that." She held out her hand and urged him to his feet. "We have a mystery we cannot solve. Give it up to God for now, and let us get some good food in you and some coffee— I know you didn't have any this morning, or breakfast—and let's see how you feel then. Maybe it is just weakness from lack of food?"

"Maybe." He liked the feel of her hand in his. It was the most she had ever touched him. He knew it was simply a gesture of sympathy and compassion, but it meant a great deal.

Such an overwhelming rush of appreciation for her kindness washed over him, he pulled her toward him, enfolding her in an embrace that was meant, at first, to be nothing but a brief hug of gratitude.

That's all it would have been except for one thing. Once he had her in his arms, he never wanted to let her go.

He pulled her tight against his chest, one arm around her shoulder, his hand on the back of her bare neck. A small curl had escaped her *Kapp*. He suddenly wanted to kiss that curl, and that neck, and that lovely face.

For a brief, breathless moment, she melted into him, as though she had been waiting for this embrace. Then he felt her stiffen in his arms and pull away.

"Tomorrow, I will find someone else to work for you," she said. "Go home to your almost-wife, Logan. There is no future for us."

He ate, but only by trying to swallow food past a huge lump in his throat every time he glanced at Hope. How foolish he had been!

Now she was leaving him. He could not allow this to happen, but he did not know how to keep her from it. She had trusted him, and he had broken that trust.

"Go back to your almost-wife," she had said.

The idea of going back to Marla now left him cold. It was as though a fog had parted in his brain and now he clearly saw that marriage to his fiancée would be a disaster. He cared for her, he was grateful to her, but he simply did not love her as a man should love his wife.

Today he finally admitted to himself that he would rather have this pregnant Amish woman in his life, no matter what the price.

He watched as Hope sat at one of the long tables holding Carrie on her lap, bending her head to listen to some small request by Adam, smiling at something the older woman on her right said. He felt a wild surge of protection toward her and her children.

The truth was, he was desperately in love with his housekeeper. He already loved her two little children and her unborn baby. His very soul resonated whenever she entered the room, and he had been lying to himself about it for a long time.

Dreams and doubts rolled in his mind as he worked his way through a piece of apple pie that he did not taste.

He heard his name being called, and saw Ivan Troyer wandering over from his home, evidently just back from his own

at Ivan and his family had left the Amish for the
made him wonder.

rned his attention back to Logan. "Mary sent me over
en you're coming to see us again."

n't know. Caleb is uncomfortable with my being there.
nder the impression that I'm planning on exploiting you
ary by writing about you in a book."

re you?" Ivan asked.

No."

"Too bad." Ivan preened a bit. "Personally, I think writing
out me would make an *excellent* book. You can ride on the
actor behind me while I do my spring plowing and I'll give
you the benefit of my years of wisdom." This time Ivan elbowed
Henry sitting on the other side of him. "By the way, Henry,
that tractor of mine is a sweet, sweet ride. You don't have to
do a thing except turn it on and steer. Doesn't require any hay,
doesn't kick you in the rear end when your back is turned . . ."

"Does not reproduce itself," Henry replied. "Requires expensive gasoline. Compacts the ground. Too many fumes."

"Don't mind him," Ivan said in a stage whisper to Logan.
"Henry's just jealous of my superior farming skills."

"And you are too lazy to train a horse to plow well," Henry
retorted.

Logan watched the back-and-forth and kept quiet. He
couldn't tell if they were joking or if they were serious. If Ivan
had left the Amish church for the Mennonites only because he
didn't want to fool with horses, there had probably been some
hurt feelings somewhere along the way. He didn't think Amish
people left their faith quite so lightly.

Hope would never leave, and he would not ask her to. The
impossibility of the situation made him half sick. He shoved his
plate away.

"Do you mind taking a walk with me down to the barn,

Ivan?" Logan said. "I think Simon Hochstetler might be hiding out down there. I haven't seen him all morning and I want to check on him."

"Simon? Of course I don't mind." Ivan grew serious. "Excuse us, please, gentlemen."

Simon was in the barn when they arrived, currying one of the horses.

"Have you been down here all day?" Logan asked. "I didn't see you in church."

"I'd rather be here in the barn than in church," Simon said. "I've had enough preaching to last me a lifetime."

"Simon's been staying with me for the past few days," Logan explained to Ivan. "We found out that his dad has a bit of a temper."

"I don't know your father well," Ivan said, "but I can imagine that being the case."

"Why don't you go eat," Logan said to the boy. "It looked like there were plenty of leftovers."

"But I didn't go to church. *Daed* always said if we didn't go to church we didn't get to eat."

"That isn't the rule at my house," Logan said. "I'm certain Hope would want you to come eat whether you went to church or not."

Without another word, Simon loped off, his lanky frame looking like a scarecrow in Logan's larger clothes. He made a note to go purchase something in an appropriate size for the boy, since it looked like he'd be staying around for a while.

"So, you're taking in strays now?" Ivan said.

"Simon was pretty banged up when Hope found him in the barn last week. I have plenty of room and he's good company. I don't mind."

Ivan leaned over a stable door and stroked the nose of one of the horses that had been stabled there.

"I thought you didn't like horses," Logan said.

"Just working with them. They're still nice to pet," Ivan said. "You said that Caleb wanted you to stop coming around? That concerns me."

"He took offense when I said that I felt like I'd been in your house before," Logan said. "I never did quite figure out why that upset him so much."

"Caleb's my eldest son," Ivan said. "And sometimes an eldest son takes the responsibility for the family on his shoulders, becoming a little more protective than necessary. Ever since Caleb was sixteen and . . . made a mistake that ended up hurting the entire family . . . it's as though he thinks he has to be the family watchdog. Sometimes he takes it too far. It is my house, not Caleb's, and you are welcome anytime. My wife sends her greetings as well."

"Sixteen is a tough age. It is easy to make mistakes then."

"It's even tougher when you allowed your little brother to accidentally drown." Ivan, so quick with a joke, turned deadly sober. "His name was Joseph, and Caleb has never forgiven himself."

"I'm so sorry," Logan said.

"Our baby is with God," Ivan said. "I often think of him sitting on Jesus' lap with our Lord's arms about him. It comforts me and Mary to envision that."

Logan was impressed with Ivan's reaction to his loss. What a comfort it must be to think in terms of a God who would cradle a loved one.

"With Simon living here, are you going to put that boy to work on some of these fields of yours?" Ivan quickly changed the subject. "It's almost time to plant."

"Hope suggested it, but I think it would be difficult to go about getting the equipment that he would need. According to Simon, he only knows how to farm with horse-powered equipment."

seen it over and over again. It is just about all I think about these days."

Logan was intrigued. "And you actually go yourselves to do this?"

"Two or three times a year at least one of us is somewhere helping supervise, carrying equipment, or simply making arrangements for well drillers to come into the area. Once we get the water situation under control, we can teach people how to grow crops where there weren't crops before. Sometimes the right knowledge and a few packs of seed is all it takes to make a big difference in a family's life."

Ivan glanced at his watch. "Well, I need to get going. Mary will have dinner on the table by now, and Mother will have put her teeth in. The kids are all coming over today. We're planning our next mission trip to Haiti. You should join us."

"Me?" Logan was surprised. "I'm not Mennonite."

"You don't have to be." Ivan chuckled. "You can use a shovel, can't you? Don't worry, we'd never let you loose with the Gospel without a driver's license anyway. If there's any Bible teaching to be done, we usually leave that up to William. He's the scholar in the family."

Logan was baffled. "A driver's license?"

"That was a joke, son." Ivan clapped him on the shoulder. "I'll ask Mother to pray about it. She always was a formidable force at praying. Now that she's half-blind, it seems like she puts in double the time. She says there's nothing much else she's good for anymore, so she might as well pray. She has such a strong hold on the Almighty's ear, the rest of us step real careful around that woman. You don't want to get on the bad side of her. No telling *what* she might pray for."

With that, his neighbor went whistling off, pausing every few steps to talk to people he knew.

Logan saw Carrie with her head against a nearby tree, eyes

closed, counting. Then suddenly the little girl took off running after her playmates. Logan could hear squeals and giggles as she tagged other children. Some of the older ones allowed her to tag them even though they could easily outrun her. Some pretended to stumble or ran comically slow. Several minutes into the game he saw a sweaty, flushed Carrie run to her mother and whisper in her ear. Hope poured her daughter a glass of water, and Carrie drank thirstily. Then she gave the cup back, wiped her mouth, and ran off to play again.

What would it be like to love a child and not have the ability to quench its thirst? He couldn't imagine.

"What good do your books do?" Bishop Schrock had asked only yesterday. What good, indeed, compared to the Troyer family's pure water ministry. Or compared to what Hope was accomplishing in raising her sweet children. Or his mother with her pro bono work at the shelter.

He'd always considered himself one of the good guys. He had taken loving care of his wife during her final days. He had never deliberately hurt anyone. He didn't cheat or steal. He voted and paid his taxes. But was that enough?

Here he found himself surrounded by industrious, caring people who raised food, created homes, nurtured children, helped their neighbors, and made the world a better place in every way possible. He remembered the joy the elderly quilter with arthritic hands took in the extra-special quilt she told him she planned to donate to an upcoming auction for Haitian orphans. Even the WWII soldiers lived with the knowledge that they had done something to save the world.

He, on the other hand, had spent most of his life sitting at a computer making stuff up. No wonder it had finally resulted in such a paralyzing writer's block.

He watched Bishop Schrock, standing in a corner of the yard in deep conversation with Simon as the boy poured out his heart. He saw the bishop put a comforting hand on Simon's shoulder.

He could see, across the field, all of Ivan's family's cars parked around the house, planning their next trip to make certain other people's children got safe drinking water while William taught those who wanted to learn about Jesus. What kind of courage did that take? What kind of sacrifice? What kind of *faith*?

Marla had been wrong about him. He didn't need a shrink. He needed God.

The cleanup after church seemed effortless with so many people helping. Before he hardly knew what had happened, the benches were gone, the partition and furniture put back in place, the house and yard swept clean of any lingering debris.

It was a little astonishing to have dozens of people laughing and talking with him one minute, and be standing there completely alone the next. With Hope and the children also gone and probably not coming back—he was left with a feeling of such aloneness that it was physically painful.

He looked longingly across the field to where the Troyers were still having their weekly family get-together. Ivan had said he could come anytime. He understood better about Caleb now, and Mary had been so welcoming the last time he was there.

He decided to chance it and walked over. When he arrived, Esther was sitting on the porch alone, a blue and white afghan thrown around her shoulders.

"Who's there?" she asked as he approached.

"It's Logan, ma'am. Your next-door neighbor."

"Oh, how nice." She patted the rocking chair next to her. "Come have a seat. I hear you hosted church today. How did you like it?"

He obediently sat down beside her. It had not been his plan to visit with Esther, but ignoring the old woman would be rude. "I enjoyed it very much."

"I'm glad to hear it. The rest of the family are all inside working on their plans for the next trip to Haiti," Esther said. "My job, as I see it, is to pray for them."

"What do you pray for?"

"For safety. For wisdom. For the project to succeed if it is God's will, for it to fail if it is not. For my family to bring honor and not shame to the name of Christ."

"That sounds like a tall order."

"No. It is not a tall order. It is my job, and an honor."

"Do you ever pray for other people?"

"All the time," she said. "Why do you ask?"

"Would you consider praying for me?"

She stopped rocking and listened intently. "In what way?"

"I feel like I've been wandering around in a dark forest for a long time." He struggled for words. "And I don't know how to find my way out."

"Ah." She nodded and resumed her rocking. "Then it has begun."

"What has begun?"

"Your finding your way out of that forest. I've been praying that might happen for you ever since I learned that an *Englisch* man had moved in next door."

"Why?"

"Oh, I don't know." Her voice held a hint of humor. "It just seemed like the neighborly thing to do."

"Can I ask you something?"

"You can ask me anything," Esther said. "I may not know the answer, but I'll answer honestly."

"I have a problem." He wondered if he was being foolish, but something told him that Esther could be someone who might have an answer. He briefly described what had happened during the church service. "Do you have any earthly idea what might be going on?"

Esther was silent for a long time. "Hope came to visit me the other day. She said that you were rather broken when you first came. She says you are getting better. By any chance does your mother pray for you?"

"Yes. Why do you ask?"

"Because a mother's prayers can be a powerful thing. I wonder if God might have answered them by leading you here. Do you suppose He might have deliberately brought you to this place where you might find this healing?"

He found Esther's faith sweetly innocent and childlike. He didn't want to hurt her feelings, but he was a little disappointed in her answer.

"I can't imagine God telling me where to live," he said. "I'm sure He has better things to do with His time."

"I don't know about that," Esther said. "I've found that it is unwise to put God in a box and try to define what He will and won't do."

"Mother?" Mary came to the screen door holding a sweater in her hand. "Are you chilly?"

"Come out and say hello to our neighbor, Mary," Esther said. "He finally got the courage to come back to see us."

Mary came out and handed the sweater to Esther—who obediently put it on. Then she sat down beside Logan. "I'm glad you decided to come back after that interrogation Ivan tells me Caleb put you through."

"That's okay. Frankly, I'm a little envious that your other children have had a big brother who is that protective of them."

He saw a shadow pass over Mary's face, but then she put on a determined smile. "Our Caleb has had his struggles, but he is a good man."

Logan did not ask what Caleb's struggles were. He already knew. It could not be easy to forever carry the burden of responsibility for a child's death. He searched his mind for a less emotional topic.

"Ivan was just telling me about your family's upcoming trip to Haiti. Are you going?"

"No, I'm not," Mary said. "I have the best job of all. I get to stay home and be the grandmother. Someone needs to be available if children get sick or Prudy has her baby. I help make it possible for Ivan and the boys to go. Ivan says he invited you to go along."

"Yes, but I doubt I could be much help."

"You should go." Mary put her hand on his arm. "Honestly, Logan. You should. They could use the help and it would change your life."

"You need to go." Esther echoed Mary's words.

"Mom?" Now it was Caleb at the door. "Who are you talking to? Oh, hi, Logan."

The next thing Logan knew, the entire family had come out to the porch and he was surrounded by a well-meaning, enthusiastic family who seemed to think that the thing he needed most in life was to get his shots, update his passport, and join them on the trip to Haiti.

He made no promises, but deep down he was beginning to think that it might be wise for him to go. Maybe it would help him find his way out of the forest.

chapter TWENTY-TWO

T he girl that Hope had chosen to take her place as housekeeper showed up the very next morning. He was surprised that Hope had taken so little time to find her replacement. She must have made the arrangements while having dinner with the church.

Agatha was awkward and shy. The poor girl could also have used a good dermatologist. She burned his toast, the bean soup was unsalted, and the potatoes she fried to go along with the beans were dripping with grease.

If Hope was not such a person of integrity, he would be suspicious that she had chosen Agatha deliberately so that he would miss her all the more—which he did.

It turned out that Simon *could* cook, and over the next few days the boy took it upon himself to help Agatha. At first, Logan thought it was merely a matter of survival on Simon's part. Then he realized that Simon and Agatha had taken an immediate liking to each other and there was much awkward flirting going on in his kitchen. This worried him. He had never expected to find himself in the position of having to be a chaperone for two Amish teenagers, and he wasn't sure how to go about it. As the week drew on he realized that he needed to find something to occupy Simon besides the new housekeeper.

He knew that morals had changed for society at large, but he had a strong suspicion that they had not changed at all for the Amish and that if his new housekeeper ended up getting pregnant on *his* watch, he would have some explaining to do.

He left several messages on Hope's phone shanty answering machine, but she did not return them. He understood her reasons, but he really needed help with the developing situation between Agatha and Simon and he didn't know who else to ask. He also needed recipes. Lots and lots of Hope's recipes. He had not thought it possible to find an Amish girl who couldn't cook, but Hope had managed it.

Finally, when she continued to ignore his phone calls, he gave up and decided to take a different tack. She'd given him no choice.

"What are you making, *Mommi*?" Carrie asked as they sat together in their kitchen.

"I'm making a card to try to get some work." Hope finished the little flower border she'd made the first time.

"It's pretty."

"Thank you, Carrie."

"Can I help?"

"I'm finished now, but you can play with these." She gave Carrie some crayons and blank cards to color.

It broke her heart to stop working for Logan, but that was the point. Her mother had been right to warn her. She had grown too attached to him, just as her mother had feared. Talking with him was a pleasure that she had looked forward to from one day to the next. When he went to New York, her heart felt the void, and her heart lifted the minute she saw his car in the driveway. She was treading on very thin ice.

Until he had pulled her into his arms, she had been able to pretend to herself that there was no danger. The day of worship at his house had changed all that. She could pretend no longer. Now she had no choice.

The problem she faced was, who else would want to hire a pregnant woman with two small children in tow? Silently, she bowed her head and prayed for God to intercede in her life. All she asked for was the means to care for her family.

She thought through her marketable skills again. She could cook, sew, do housework, and raise children. Perhaps after the baby came, she could babysit for others, although that did not pay very well. Once again her mind went to the dream she'd had since she was a little girl trotting around the farm behind her father. Having her own land. Making her own decisions about livestock and crops. She had always subscribed to two farming magazines and read every word—not because she thought anything would ever come of it, but because the subject fascinated her.

She'd tried to interest Titus in a sheep breed she'd read about that produced not only marketable meat but decent-quality wool. There was a market for lamb in Cleveland and Columbus in the ethnic restaurants. With all the interest in sustainable farming practices and a growing market for organic, grass-fed meat, she thought there might be a business opportunity there.

Plus, she was fascinated with the idea of having wool to work with. Her mother had an old spinning wheel that had belonged to her grandmother and still knew how to use it. Hope longed to spin her own wool and dye it with natural substances. The tourist market being what it was in Holmes County, she had a suspicion that hand-spun wool might bring in a modest income, especially if the tourists could purchase it at a real Amish home where they could see the grazing sheep from which the wool had been produced.

It would involve purchasing a different breed, but sheep milk could be made into a rich soap, good for the skin, that could also be sold. Making soap and yarn would be something her children could help with. Creating a strong work ethic in their children was key to their survival as an Amish people, and her mind naturally worked that way.

The good thing about sheep, also, was the fact that sheep manure contained more nitrogen, phosphorus, and potassium than horse or cow manure. It could be used to help build up the land to produce better crops.

An Amish schoolteacher she knew was doing well with an organic chicken farm. Both chickens and rabbits produced excellent, rich manure for vegetable growing. She'd recently read that there was also a growing market for rabbit meat.

Ideally, an organic farmer could create a sustainable cycle in which rabbits thrived on the discards from the vegetables that their very waste helped produce. Of course, there was the possibility of selling baby bunnies as well—another potential job for Adam and Carrie.

Sustainable farming practices and diversity. That's what she believed would keep the small family farms in business.

The problem was she could raise only four ewes per acre, and this small piece of land she was renting was simply not big enough. There was also the problem that those ewes, chickens, rabbits, chicken houses, rabbit cages, and feed, cost up-front money that she did not have.

It was so terribly frustrating. She knew she had the knowledge, energy, and will to create a healthy living for herself and her children. Except for two things. She did not have enough land, and she did not have enough money to get started. Unless God gave her a miracle, she would be eking out an income by cleaning houses for other people the rest of her life.

She asked God for forgiveness for her rebellious heart! Since she had quit work at Logan's, she missed the ease of the electric lighting and appliances at his house, and every time she pulled out onto a busy highway with her children in that buggy, she questioned the wisdom of their bishops' decision to forbid cars. She had no doubt that good Mennonites like Ivan and Mary and their families were going to heaven, too, so why did she have to put her children in danger?

Quickly, she said another prayer asking for forgiveness for her bad thoughts. Yes, she was tired. Yes, she was frustrated. Yes, she was uncomfortably pregnant, but that did not give her the right to be angry about her position in life. The Amish believed that the way things were was the will of God. Unless He showed her differently, she would try to stay on the path He had chosen for her.

"See, *Mommi*?" Carrie held up her crayon drawings. Hope tried to admire her little girl's efforts, but all she wanted to do was cry.

Her mother was planning to come by this morning, and Hope was not surprised when there was a knock on the door. She didn't even bother to put on her head covering before answering it.

To her shock, it was not her mother. It was Logan—the last person she expected to see standing on her doorstep. The last person she *wanted* to see.

"You either need to write out all of your recipes, in *detail*, or that housekeeper you gave me has to go," he said.

"Why?" She tried to look innocent, but she had known all along that Agatha's cooking was substandard. It served him right for breaking through the fragile wall they had built between them. "Is her cooking not to your liking?"

"You must have had to look very hard to find an Amish woman who can't cook!"

"Not really." Hope tried to hide a smile and failed. "Many

in our Amish community have learned to avoid Agatha's con-
tribution to potlucks. She needed a job and I hoped her cooking
would improve with time."

"Time is the one thing I can't afford. Her cooking is slowly
improving, but it's her affection for Simon that's beginning to
worry me. I'm assuming the Amish are not thrilled with an
unwed pregnancy."

"Agatha is *pregnant*?"

"Not to my knowledge. She's only been working for me a
week, but if you don't get her out of there and away from Simon,
I think it could become a strong possibility. I didn't sign up to
be a babysitter for two Amish teenagers with raging hormones."

"This is indeed a problem." She tapped her lower lip.

"Come back to work for me," he pleaded. "I'm sorry, Hope.
I know I stepped over a line last Sunday. I've kicked myself a
hundred times for it. You were right to walk away. If you'll
just come back I promise to stay in my office when you're there
working. Or, if you prefer, I'll leave the house completely when
you're there. Just tell me what I need to do and I'll do it."

"Agatha's cooking must be worse than I thought," Hope
said. "I had better hurry with those recipes!"

"It isn't just the cooking and you know it. Hearing you talk
to your children, or sing as you work around my house. It's . . .
it's important to me. I haven't been able to write well since you
left. I miss hearing the chatter and laughter of your children.
The house feels lonely without you coming in every day."

"It would not be wise for me to continue to come."

"Of course it would be wise," he argued. "You need a job. It
will be hard for you to find one you can manage with the baby
coming. At my house you can take breaks whenever you want
and put your feet up, or take time off when the baby comes and
start back slowly whenever you feel up to it. The one thing I
can't bear is for you and the children to go without because I

was upset, and you were kind. It was a moment of weakness. It won't happen again."

She knew this was a bad idea. Going back there went against all her training. She shook her head. "No, Logan. I'm sorry, but . . . no."

Gently, she closed the door in his face and locked it, shutting him out of her life.

Then she watched from behind a curtain as he walked away and climbed into his car.

But he didn't leave. Instead, he sat in the driver's seat with his head thrown back against the headrest as though he was napping . . . or thinking. She grew nervous. Was he never going to leave?

In a few minutes, he opened the car door and walked back to her house. He knocked again.

She opened the door a crack. "I have given you my answer."

"I don't think you have."

She was ready to slam the door shut and lock it again if necessary. He had never been anything but kind to her, but one never knew *what* an *Englisch* man might do. Perhaps she didn't know him as well as she thought. Sunday had certainly been a surprise.

"I promised you I would think about something. That's what I've been doing while you were peeking through the curtains. Keeping my promise. Thinking."

"About what?"

"Do you think you could gather together whatever you and Simon need to make your father's farm productive again?"

"Of course, but why?"

"I see farmers starting to till their soil. Evidently they think it's warm enough to start planting. Seems to me like it would be a good idea to put some crops in, and I don't have a clue."

"Wait a minute." She was incredulous. "You are offering to make me, a pregnant Amish woman, your farm manager?"

"I sure am. You can manage the farm, Simon, Agatha . . . and me for that matter."

"But why?"

"Here's the problem, Hope. I have a deadline coming up in a couple more months and this book has to be stellar. I *have* to concentrate, and I can't with Simon and Agatha mooning around in my kitchen. I can't send Simon back to his father to get beaten up again. I'm tired of people asking me if I'm planning to let my property grow into scrub. I'm sick and tired of hearing about what a good farmer your father was and how straight he made his corn rows."

She was stunned. "Why did you not offer this before?"

"Because I was afraid you'd overwork yourself."

Hope tried to wrap her mind around his offer to let her farm land that she knew like the back of her hand.

"You can oversee all the planting and sowing and manure spreading or whatever else it takes to grow crops. Purchase the livestock you need. Hire the workers you need. One restriction, though. I don't want you doing anything stupid like getting behind a plow. The idea is for you to *manage*—not work until you drop."

She swallowed. "You are serious about this?"

"Dead serious."

Was this an answer to prayer? Or a temptation straight from the devil?

She couldn't help it. Excitement flared in her heart at Logan's words.

"My father made a good living for us on that property," she said. "He used the old farming methods and cared for the soil."

"I'll give you complete freedom."

Her mind was already whirling with calculations. "You would be willing to back me financially and work on shares?"

"I would."

A terrible thought struck. "What if I put time and effort into getting the farm up and running again, and you decide to sell it?"

"I won't. I'll put it in writing if you want."

She could feel her resistance melting. It would be foolish to pass up this opportunity. It would probably never come around again.

"I have so many ideas! If my methods and crops are successful, there is a good chance I might be able to buy my own farm in a few years!"

He smiled, enjoying her enthusiasm. "You seem to have given this a great deal of thought."

"I have been thinking of better ways to make a living off the land since I was ten and started reading my father's farming magazines."

"Farming's a gamble. What if the weather doesn't accommodate your plans?"

"I have in mind a diversification of crops and animals that could see us through any weather. If hail takes our wheat crop, then our organic chicken business would create a stream of income. If a weasel gets at the chickens, the corn crop will still bring in some money. Sheep can bring in profit several different ways. This land is good at growing briars and wild blackberries. Why not take advantage and plant the new hybrid, thornless blackberries? With all the new knowledge of the benefits of blackberry juice, I know I could sell any amount. It's a perfect summer job for two children. And blueberries! They are so easy to grow and so healthy. People would drive miles to pay for a chance to pick their own. You have two hundred prime acres. You won't *believe* the various businesses, crops, and livestock I can work with on that much land!"

Her words came to an abrupt stop. Too many dreams and

thoughts had just poured out of her mouth. He would think she was talking foolishness.

She was reassured by the kindness in his eyes. He was pleased with her joy.

"Your father gambled on blackjack and horses," he said. "I think he would have been wiser—so much wiser—to have gambled on you."

While Hope and Simon made plans about which crops to plant and where, Logan headed back to New York. It was time to break things off with Marla.

His reasons had little to do with Hope. Any fantasy he'd had about Hope was just that . . . a fantasy. Still, the feelings he had for her made him realize how very wrong he and Marla were for each other. It would not be fair to allow her to go ahead with wedding preparations.

Even if Hope had not been in the picture, he needed time to sort out where he was spiritually.

He felt so bad about initiating this breakup that he was seriously contemplating allowing Marla to keep the apartment. That would be quite a consolation prize to her and she probably deserved it. It also might ease the awkwardness of the breakup. Marla had her grandfather's trust fund to blow on expensive handbags and clothing for herself, but she would never have the funds to purchase an apartment like the one in which they lived.

On the other hand, the apartment would bring quite a substantial price. *If* he decided to sell it. He wasn't sure he was ready to relinquish all ties to New York—only his ties to Marla. It had been his home for a long time. Still, visions of the good that even part of that equity could do for Ivan Troyer's thirsty children made him feel selfish for thinking about hanging on to such a valuable asset. Plus, he had no idea how much start-up money Hope would need.

The doorman at his building seemed a little agitated when Logan showed up, which surprised him. He'd purposely not called Marla ahead of time because she was astute when it came to reading the tone in his voice, and he was afraid she'd know that something was wrong and start interrogating him over the phone.

He wanted to be face-to-face with her when he explained. It would be cowardly not to.

He stepped into the elevator that would take him to the top floor, thinking about the fact that he would miss the view from his apartment if he sold it, but not much else.

He opened the front door and threw his keys on an antique table, walked into the living room, and stopped cold. There, wearing one of his own bathrobes, sat a man so famous that grown women had been known to faint when he walked by.

He had met a few actors, he'd even been on movie sets when three of his books were made into movies, but Jebulan Steele was like a demigod to moviegoers. At least he had been. Movie stars tanked quickly, and Jebulan's past two movies had bombed.

But still . . . he didn't know whether to be upset or ask the man for his autograph. Jebulan Steele was right here, drinking coffee and eating a bagel with cream cheese. In fact, the movie star had a smudge of cream cheese on his upper lip. Both of them stared at each other in openmouthed surprise. Jebulan found his voice first.

"*Who* are *you!*" His impressive voice was imperious. "And what are you doing here!"

"I happen to own the place," Logan said. "The question is, what are *you* doing here?"

At that moment, Marla came out of the bedroom. She

quickly belted the flimsy robe she was wearing, leaving no doubt as to their relationship.

"Logan! What are you doing here!"

It was like a very bad comedy routine.

As his shock drained away, Logan felt a great calm come over him. There would be no need for explanations, no need for recriminations. His reason for breaking off the engagement had been handed to him on a silver platter.

A part of his brain also recorded the fact that there was a reason things had felt strange to him when he'd been here before. That's why his suits had been shoved to the side, and the contents of his drawers moved. That's why Marla had wanted him to go out to the foyer while she made a phone call. She had given Jebulan a warning to clear his things out. This affair had apparently been going on for some time.

But why hadn't she broken off the engagement if she was in love with another man? Jebulan was famously single.

"I've been decorating his house," Marla said. "It's—it's not finished yet."

He could see her eyes darting around the apartment as though searching for an alibi. "His apartment is being renovated. He needed someplace to stay and . . ."

In spite of his initial shock, her attempt to give him an innocent explanation struck him as funny, as did the caught-in-the-act look on the movie star's handsome face. It wasn't as though Jebulan couldn't afford to stay in an upscale hotel while his apartment was being renovated. Both of them seemed to be holding their breaths, waiting for him to react.

He had been so geared up about breaking up with her—finding her with this man—he had to collapse on the couch while he reevaluated everything he'd been thinking up to this point.

Strangely enough, his first thought was that real estate was in a slump right now, but the apartment was primo. It should sell within the year.

"I hope the renovations are about done," he said.

"We're close to the end. Why?" Marla said.

"I want to sell this place as soon as possible. I have no desire to hang on to you and your boyfriend's love nest a minute longer than necessary. I want you to move out as soon as possible."

"We will, but for what it's worth, Logan," Marla said, "I am sorry you found out this way."

"Are you in love with him?"

"Very much so. We're talking about getting married."

"Well, at least you already have the wedding dress." He was surprised at the bitterness he heard in his own voice.

"Don't be that way, Logan. I took good care of you for a long time."

"You did," he conceded. "But were you ever truly in love with me?"

"I care deeply about you, but . . ." She hesitated.

"Go ahead and say it," Logan said. "Let's be completely honest with each other for once."

"I may have my faults, but I keep my promises," she said. "I always have. You know that."

"What does that have to do with anything?"

Marla came and sat down on the overstuffed hassock directly in front of him. "Before Ariela died, she asked me to take care of you. She wanted me to try to love you as much as she did."

It sounded just like his wife. "And you actually promised?"

"Of course I did. Ariela was my friend, and she loved us both. She thought she was giving me and you the gift of each other. I tried, Logan. I'm really sorry, but I did try."

He leaned forward and smoothed his hand over her hair. She really was quite lovely. The crying shame was that he felt so little pain over the breakup. Instead, it was beginning to feel as though someone had just given him a get-out-of-jail-free card.

"You do realize old Jeb over there will cheat on you, don't you?" he said in a low voice. "You deserve better than that."

"I hope he won't." She glanced worriedly over her shoulder. "I do love him."

"Then I wish both of you well." He rose from the couch. He'd never particularly liked that couch. In fact, there were a lot of things in the apartment he didn't care for. All were things that Marla had insisted on. Chrome. Glass. White leather. White rug. Stainless steel. Art on the walls that cost the earth and looked like a kindergartner had painted it.

"Take anything you want when you move out," he said. "I don't want a thing."

"Where will you go if you sell this place?" she asked.

"Holmes County, of course." He was almost surprised she would ask. "Home."

Then, putting his hands in his pockets, he sauntered down the plush hallway, rode the elevator all the way to the main floor, and tipped the nervous doorman as he left.

It felt as though the weight of the world had been lifted from his shoulders. Tonight he would take his mother out for a nice dinner, if she was free, and spend the night. Tomorrow, he would make his way to his Realtor's office and put his 2.5-million-dollar apartment up for sale.

Then he would head home to his old farmhouse, where a child's fingerprints wouldn't cause a meltdown and where he could put his feet up on his sturdy oak coffee table if he wanted to. Where Hope and the children and Simon and his friends would come and go and fill his life with laughter.

He and Hope might not be able to be together as man and wife, but getting to watch her doing what she loved as she brought his farm back to life would be joy enough for now.

chapter TWENTY-THREE

The next few weeks reminded him of the days leading up to Hope's family hosting church in his house. It seemed as though he could not walk out to his porch without tripping over one of her relatives or some workman she had hired. He wasn't quite sure what-all was being accomplished, except that once a week Hope would knock on his office door, sit down with a notepad, and explain everything that she had done or hired done, then hand him a bill for things he needed to pay for. Considering all the activity going on around his home, he was frequently surprised at how little it was all costing. The same amount of activity in New York City would've bankrupted him.

He still had no idea why he'd had the strange reaction to the Amish worship or to Ivan and Mary's home and this house, but as he spent time around his new friends, he found himself wondering if their faith in the idea that God was in control of their lives was valid after all, and if perhaps God might even be in control of his. Had God deliberately drawn him to this place? It was hard to believe that the Creator of the universe would care enough about him to do something that personal, but it gave him a good feeling to think that perhaps God had known how badly he needed this place and these gentle people and in His grace had brought him to it.

He found that it was a lot easier to believe in God when one was surrounded by the vibrant, natural world he saw around him now that spring was here. The awesome variety of it all was staggering. He saw Hope and Simon planting tiny seeds and admired the miracle of programming within them.

"Come see what we've got, Logan!" Hope waved at him from the back of a van that had just pulled into the driveway.

He hurried down, wondering what type of miracle she'd purchased for the farm this time.

"It's our baby chicks!" she called. "You have got to see these. They are so cute!"

He got there just in time to see her holding what looked like a yellow ball of fluff up to her cheek, a look of ecstasy on her face.

"So that piece of fluff is the start of your chicken farm?" he asked.

There were three heavy cardboard boxes in the van with holes in them from which he could hear a chorus of tiny chirps.

"*Ja*," she said. "This is my chicken farm. Do you want to hold one?"

"No."

"You will be sorry," she said. "Baby chicks are like children, they don't stay little for long."

She seemed so disappointed, that he obediently held out his hand, and she deposited a slightly distraught chick there. He wasn't sure what he was supposed to do with it, but after cupping both hands around it, he had to admit that it did feel rather soft and nice.

As Hope got her organic chicken business started, he was fascinated with the process.

"These we will not eat," she announced. "These are going to be our laying hens."

This he was relieved to hear. He had not relished eating something that had already captivated him with its cuteness.

A barn swallow built a nest on his porch and he forbade Simon to remove it. He decided the bit of mess was a small price to pay for getting to watch the intricate nest-building process, and frantic feeding of baby birds.

All this land bursting with life was beyond miraculous to him. The wonder with which small children marveled at the natural world was nothing compared to Logan's awakening to God's great gifts. The marvel of man's engineering accomplishments in building the great skyscrapers of Manhattan were nothing, in his opinion, to the mysterious instincts that brought the migration of songbirds to the North.

Hope's cousin Levi heard about Logan's fascination with barn swallows, and arrived one day with a large volume about birds under his arm. Logan found Levi to be a strong, quiet man with an encyclopedic knowledge of birds. They spent several early mornings together watching and listening. Levi was able to mimic many of the birdcalls and patiently taught him to discern between their songs. He also introduced him to the pleasures of formal bird-watching, and helped him begin his own life list.

With nice weather, Hope's extended family seemed to be stopping by almost on a daily basis to help her with something or just to chat. One by one, he got to know these gentle people. He reveled in the fact that no longer was his connection to humanity based primarily upon a good morning from a doorman or a luncheon date with his editor, or waiting for Marla to come home from her job.

He realized now why the reviewer had called his characters cardboard. It was hard to sit in a room year after year and make people up out of thin air. A writer, he discovered, needed to be part of the rich stew of humanity if his characters were ever to become living, breathing people.

These days he could hardly write fast enough. The writer's block was gone and floods of ideas kept him awake nights churning words and scenes in his mind.

"Living here was exactly what I needed, even when I didn't know what was missing," he said one evening on the porch when Ivan and Mary strolled over after supper. Mary had brought a fresh blueberry pie still warm from the oven. He'd added ice cream from his freezer, and they were enjoying the treat out on the porch. "Have you been thinking any more about going on that trip to Haiti with us?" Ivan asked. "We could use the help."

"What you really want is for me to become Mennonite." He laughed. "Just admit it and quit beating around the bush, neighbor."

"When have I *ever* beat around the bush?" Ivan asked. "I admit, having you become a Mennonite wouldn't exactly hurt my feelings, but it can get complicated. Especially in this neck of the woods."

"How so?"

"Deciding on which Mennonite church to attend is a lot like this ice cream. There's a lot of different 'flavors.' Some are pretty liberal. Women can dress in jeans, cut their hair short, and the people get to drive whatever they want. Some churches have strong opinions on what their people can wear and what kind of car they can drive. You have everything in between, down to the ultraconservative horse-and-buggy Mennonites. About the only pillars of faith left holding us together are a belief that Jesus is the son of God, adult baptism, the Bible being the Word of God, and nonresistance—or pacifism. We stand alongside the Amish in the belief that a man should not lift his hand against another. Including not participating in war."

"There's another thing we have in common," Mary added. "Our relief organizations."

"True," Ivan said. "Helping people has been our way for centuries.

"Our son William once made a study of the teachings of Menno Simons. That's one of our leaders from five hundred years ago. The name 'Mennonite' comes from him. He was a Catholic priest who converted after his brother, an Anabaptist like us, was killed for believing in adult baptism. I memorized this one quote because it gets to the heart of what we stand for.

"Menno said, 'True evangelical faith . . . cannot lie dormant, but manifests itself in all righteousness and works of love . . . it clothes the naked; it feeds the hungry; it comforts the sorrowful; it shelters the destitute.'"

"In other words, a cup of pure water," Logan said.

"Exactly," Ivan agreed. "That's our answer to pretty much everything, including war and political strife. We go in and we try to help others in the name of Jesus. We are most definitely not perfect. We stumble. We fall. We say stupid things. We wrangle over doctrinal issues sometimes—just like everyone else, but we *try*. We really do try to serve others."

Logan had seldom heard anyone speak so passionately or honestly about their faith. The man and his family were truly living lives in service to God and others. He felt himself drawn to the ideal that Ivan had described.

"I think I'll go ahead and get those shots," Logan said. "You never know. I might just actually go with you sometime."

chapter TWENTY-FOUR

H ope felt guilty. She couldn't help it, she just did.

It was so much easier running a farm with electricity . . . not to mention a house. Logan had put in a dishwasher, and she loved using it. The electric range was a flick of a button. A food processor cut down on so much time chopping and dicing.

The best things of all were the washer and dryer. She didn't have to depend on the caprices of weather to know if she could do a wash. No more mad dashes outside when it rained. She could toss a small load of the children's clothes into the washer every morning, then at lunchtime dry them with no more work than throwing them in and pushing a button.

Logan had been the one to suggest that she bring her and the children's clothing to wash when she came, and she took full advantage of it. She had learned to pull clothing out of the dryer still damp and let it dry on the hangers—which meant no more ironing for her! Compared to filling a wringer washer with buckets of water and line-drying a week's worth of clothes, and then sprinkling and ironing everything in sight, it felt like laundry had become no work at all. She could hardly believe how fluffy the towels came out—amazing!

Taking home a small basket of clean clothes with her each afternoon had, literally, freed up nearly a whole day each week. It was also convenient not having the entire world looking at her laundry and evaluating it every Monday. There was always the problem of how to dry unmentionables on an outdoor clothesline. Some simply put them right out there for God and everyone to see. Others—like her—dried their underwear inside, away from prying eyes. The last thing she wanted to see was pictures of her underwear showing up in some tourist photograph of Amish country!

Yes, a clothes dryer was a wonderful invention. She was Amish, but she wasn't so Amish that she couldn't appreciate the savings in time. She had also learned the joys of using a slow cooker. There weren't enough hours in the day to accomplish all she wanted to do before the baby came.

Logan had been as good as his word. He seemed to be completely absorbed in his writing these days. She rarely saw him except when she went over the expenses with him.

This savings of time in using his appliances was a huge benefit, because it enabled her to spend more time implementing the changes she wanted to bring about on the farm. And all her industry was a godsend, because it wore her out and allowed her to fall into bed exhausted each night. It also occupied some of the time she might have spent thinking about Titus. Some days were better than others, but she found herself aching over what they could have accomplished on this property together!

Her grief was like an emotional toothache, always there, dull and throbbing, but she found that it was possible to plan and work in spite of that ache in her chest. Her love for her children and her unborn child helped her focus all her energies on creating a life for them.

She had taken to reading the description of the virtuous woman in Proverbs 31 every morning, and it helped give her the energy to continue her fight toward a better life for her family. It talked about how the virtuous woman considered a field, and bought it, and planted a vineyard on it. Hope could not yet buy a field, but by the grace of God, Logan had given her permission to use his land as she wished. She did not have to plant a vineyard, there were several that had already been planted by her father, but they had become neglected. She personally pruned them, affixed them to better supports, dug around the roots, and fertilized them.

She redug the asparagus plants, mulched the flower beds, replanted the strawberry beds she had so loved as a child. She hired help to come redig post holes and repair the fences. There was a forty-acre pasture where she intended to run beef cattle again.

Now that she was spending so much time there, she brought her little Jersey milk cow over one day tied behind her buggy, and fixed her up in a nice, clean stall. It was handier this way.

The spring weather was perfect in every way. She and Simon tried putting in a different rotation of crops than her father had ever used, and she had high hopes. There was every reason to believe there might be a good harvest.

Her mother, worried that she was doing too much, cautioned her about the baby, but Grace told her to do what she felt like doing except for heavy lifting and to rest if she got tired. She chose to follow Grace's advice instead of giving in to her mother's worries. All Hope knew was that she felt healthier and happier than ever as long as she was outdoors with her bare feet planted firmly on freshly plowed ground. Like one of those solar-powered outdoor lights her people were starting to use, the more she was outside in the sunlight, the better she felt.

Chicken wire, plus a design for two new chicken houses on wheels that Simon made for her, created a home for her little biddies, who could now feast on worms and bugs and scratch the earth with their little feet like they were meant to do. Every morning, Simon would hitch one of their two horses to the portable chicken houses and slide them a few feet farther along in the field, giving the chickens fresh ground to work, and fertilizing the ground with chicken manure.

She'd looked into the purchase of some ewes, and would soon have her rabbit business up and running. With any luck, she would have extra vegetables to sell soon. She made a note to have Simon build her a small roadside stand.

The possibilities were just endless.

Logan had not criticized anything she had done or spent so far. Well, maybe one thing, and it wasn't really a criticism, it was more like a joke. When he looked over the receipts she gave him for the money she used to pay drivers to deliver various items to the farm, he commented once that it would be a lot cheaper to buy a truck and teach her how to drive it.

The idea of actually owning a pickup truck and having the skill to drive it was an idea that just kept niggling at her. What freedom that would give her! She did not mind using a horse-drawn plow instead of a tractor—in her opinion the horses were better for the land than the heavy tractors anyway, although that was a subject debated all over Holmes County. But to be able to run to the feed store at a moment's notice without having to call and make arrangements for some *Englisch* driver?

The idea just wouldn't let her go.

At that very moment, Ivan drove by and waved. She waved back, as he went by with one elbow hanging rakishly out of the open window. He still wore a summer straw hat like he had when he was Amish, and he had never given up the suspenders. He was a godly man in every way, and she simply could not see where having exchanged horse and buggy for a truck had made that big a difference in his service to God.

Ivan had been like a surrogate parent to her most of her life.

His sons were like brothers to her and his daughters like sisters. She knew the family's integrity and admired their faith.

They attended worship much more frequently than her Old Order Amish church. Ivan and his family even attended what they called "Bible study" every Wednesday night.

Her father and mother had disapproved of Ivan and Mary's choice to leave the Old Order church, but they had more compassion than most about the reasons behind that decision. Henry and Rose, themselves, had chosen to leave the more conservative Swartzentruber church and had endured being shunned by both their church and their families for a while because of that change.

Of the two men who had helped raise her, it was her poor father who had gotten caught up in the sin of gambling—in spite of appearing to obey the *Ordnung*.

"Do you mind if I don't take supper with you tonight?" Simon asked, as they finished up the day's work.

"Not at all." Hope was a little surprised. It wasn't as though Simon had an active social schedule or didn't have an appetite. "Where are you going?"

"Agatha invited me to take supper with her folks." Simon blushed scarlet.

So, those two were still in contact. That was interesting.

"You go ahead," Hope said. "Have a nice time and tell Agatha I said hi."

If Agatha was in her *own* home when Simon came to call, then she was her family's problem and not Hope's. Agatha was a sweet girl and a hard worker—even if she was a poor cook. Simon could do a lot worse.

chapter TWENTY-FIVE

"**I**s there anything you want from New York?" Logan asked.

"Why?" She was on her knees planting cabbage.

"Because I'm planning to drive there tomorrow morning."

It bothered her when he went to New York. It always hurt to think of what might be going on between him and Marla when he was there.

"There's nothing I need, thanks. I hope you have a nice time."

"I'm not going there to have a nice time," he said. "I need to sign some papers. My Realtor called yesterday and said he has a solid buyer for my apartment."

Except for discussing expenses, they had seldom been alone together since the day he'd come to her home with his astonishing offer. She had no idea he had put his apartment up for sale.

"Have you and Marla purchased another apartment?"

"No."

"Then why are you selling?" She gently patted the earth around the last tiny seedling. She loved the act of planting.

"Because I'm going to live here full-time."

She glanced up at him. "I don't understand."

239

He helped her to her feet as she struggled to stand. The baby was due in about three more weeks. It was getting harder and harder to get up unassisted.

"Marla and I broke up the last time I went back."

She gasped. "You're serious?"

"I'm serious."

"What on earth happened?"

"Among other things," he said, "she has a new boyfriend."

"How do you know?" She brushed the loose dirt off her hands.

"Well, for one thing, a man was there at my apartment wearing my bathrobe last time I showed up."

She cared nothing for Marla, but her heart broke for him. "That must have been very hard for you."

"To tell you the truth, Hope, when I had time to think it over, I realized that I was relieved."

"Are you sure?" She studied his face. "I thought you loved her."

"I do love her . . . in a way. She was a good friend to my wife and a good friend to me when I needed her. I guess we finally figured out that we didn't love each other enough to build a life together."

"You said nothing to me about it all this time?"

"I've been on deadline, Hope, working practically day and night. You've been on deadline, too, trying to get things in place here before the baby arrives. Plus, I needed time to process everything that had happened before I told you."

"So, you've processed it all now?"

"To an extent. Even better, I've finished the book."

"What happens now?"

"I leave it alone for a few days and then go back and edit it."

"I didn't mean the book. I meant about Marla."

"Like I said . . . I'm going over tomorrow to see if she's

moved all her things out. Then I'll get rid of whatever else is left and sign the papers. I'll be home soon. This time to stay."

"Daughter," Bishop Schrock said. "People are talking."

Hope paused in the act of tacking chicken wire onto the frame Simon had built. "And what are people saying?"

She placed her hand on the small of her back and stretched, relieving the deep ache that had settled there this week. The baby was growing heavier every day.

"At least three of our women at church have come to me saying that you are giving the impression to the world that you are living with this Logan Parker."

"But I'm not," Hope said. "I rarely see him. I'm working outside most of the time."

The bishop removed his straw summer hat and fingered the brim, obviously uncomfortable with the conversation. "There are some who say that it is unseemly for a pregnant woman wearing Plain clothes to be seen working in an *Englisch* man's fields like a hired hand."

"Unseemly? Doing honest work?" Hope felt her dander rise. "I've seen pregnant Amish women work like mules in their husband's fields and no one took offense."

The bishop ignored the comment. "I have found you appropriate part-time employment at Mrs. Yoder's restaurant. You can greet people and seat them. It is an easy job. Thelma and I will care for the children while you are there."

Hope felt a sense of desperation settle over her. "I am bringing this farm to life," she pleaded. "Logan has invested much money in seed, livestock, and equipment. Simon now has a job helping me that puts money in his father's pocket to use for the rest of the family. I cannot walk away from all I've begun here."

"From the beginning, I was not pleased with you working here," the bishop said, "but you assured me that it would only be for two hours a day. Now the job has grown until you are working here full-time. People driving by see your buggy here many hours a day. I would never have advised you to begin this work had you asked."

Which is why I could not ask, Hope thought.

"I have an opportunity to provide a good living for my children here," she said. "To give them a future."

The bishop cleared his throat. "The Scripture says that we must give no appearance of evil."

"Scripture also says that women should be keepers at home, caring for their own families, not running around gossiping— like those women have apparently been doing," Hope said. "Perhaps you should talk to them about tending to their own business instead of mine."

"If only my son were alive." A look of grief passed over the bishop's face. "Then we would not be having this conversation."

Everything within Hope warned her to be careful with what she said next, but her back hurt, her feet hurt, and she was very tired. She should have been holding the reins on her tongue more tightly, but was so angry she could not hold it back.

"If only your son had listened to me and gotten rid of that bull," Hope snapped, "*then* we would not be having this conversation. I would be at home with my feet up knitting a baby's cap instead of building chicken coops trying to make a living for my family."

"There are alms . . ."

"I have a job and a skill," she retorted. "I don't need alms."

"Don't do this," the bishop pleaded. "I have loved you like a daughter from the moment our son brought you into our lives, but I'm a bishop first and a father-in-law second. Don't put me in the position of having to put you under the ban."

"For what?" Hope felt a chill go through her body. "For trying to make a living for my family?"

"We must avoid the appearance of evil. You know that, Hope. If you continue spending so much time here, you risk bringing shame upon our religious community."

"I have done nothing wrong," she repeated. "Nothing! Raising chickens and planting crops does not bring dishonor to the name of Christ."

She felt a gust of wind whip at the hem of her dress.

The bishop glanced worriedly at the sky. "I think there is a bad storm brewing. You should take the children home. We will discuss this later."

Logan was sitting on the back porch talking by cell phone with his Realtor when he felt the fine spring weather they had been having start to change. At first it was nearly imperceptible. Then a strange stillness and an unnatural light settled over the place. Gusts of wind made the weather vane on the barn spin. He probably would barely have noticed had he still been in his New York apartment—but he was much more tuned in to the weather since moving here.

Concerned, he went in, turned on the weather radio, and heard that they were under a tornado warning. He started to go check on Hope, and saw that her buggy was already gone. She must have decided to go home early.

Simon came in from the fields, unhitched the horses, and let them out to graze, all the while glancing nervously up at the sky.

"What do you think?" Logan called. "Are we in for a storm?"

"I think there might be funnel clouds before long," Simon said. "Maybe not here, but close."

Logan grew more worried.

Ivan went by in his truck, and he was going fast. He put

on the brakes in front of the house. "You and Simon better get down to the cellar, son," Ivan shouted. "This weather isn't looking good."

Then suddenly, Ivan pointed. "Dear God, look at that!"

Logan turned to look just as Simon came running. He could see the black funnel cloud far off in the distance, and it was a big one.

"Get to the cellar!" Ivan yelled and spun gravel as he took off toward his own home.

Simon practically shoved him through the front door. "We've got to take shelter."

Hope had never really liked the little house in which they lived, but it was what they could afford, and so she made the best of it. The thing that bothered her most about it was not how small it was, but that there was no good place to shelter during storms.

A phone rang in her phone shanty as she drove up to her house and she ran to answer it.

"Your *Daed* says for you to take cover right now," her mother said. "He says there is a tornado coming. He has seen this kind of weather before."

"Where am I to take cover?" Hope looked around in a panic. There was nothing except the small barn and their house. Not even a root cellar stood between her and her children and whatever might be coming.

"Henry is yelling for me to come to the cellar now, I have to go," her mother said. Hope hurriedly unhitched her horse while frantically looking around for a place to shelter.

"Over here!"

She whirled and saw Mr. Lemon gesturing at her to come toward his house.

"Bring the children!" he yelled. "Hurry!"

Without wasting another moment, she grabbed her children out of the buggy and they all scrambled up the small rise toward Mr. Lemon's house—their nosy *Englisch* neighbor.

Mr. Lemon had the sort of old-fashioned root cellar built separately into the side of a hill. It was the kind that people used to dig back when they had only shovels and no heavy equipment. The door to it was flush with the ground, and he stood there holding it open for them as the wind whipped at his clothes and sparse white hair.

He held it while she and the children clambered in, and then he closed the door tightly above them and secured it with a long pole threaded through clamps attached to the inside of the door.

She crouched on the ground with the children huddled around her. A lamp had already been lit and hung from the low ceiling.

"I saw you coming and waited," Mr. Lemon said. "I helped build the house you live in and I knew it had no basement or cellar."

"Thank you," she panted, nearly breathless from the exertion. "Thank you so much for waiting for us."

At that moment, she heard the sound of a freight train where no train should be. The door rattled above their heads. Dirt sifted down from the low ceiling and the lantern shifted and swayed with the force of the wind that roared over them.

"I'm scared!" Carrie clutched at her.

Adam's lower lip began to tremble.

"We will be fine," Hope soothed, gathering them close. "Close your eyes. It will be over soon."

Then the hail came, sounding as though baseballs were being thrown upon the cellar door.

Every second seemed like an hour. Beside her, the children sobbed from fear. Mr. Lemon clung to the door above them, as though he could somehow manage, with human strength, to keep it from being torn out of his grasp. A moment later, something heavy crashed into the door, knocking Mr. Lemon to the ground.

Simon closed the basement door behind them as Logan flicked on the cellar light. It was nothing but a bare bulb in the middle of the bare floor joists, but it was better than nothing.

The cellar smelled of earth, and was large and empty. All the walls were lined with shelves that Hope's mother and grandmother had probably once filled with canned goods. He was grateful there were no glass jars there now.

As the wind increased, the old house began to creak and complain. It was sturdy, but even a well-built house was no match for wind like this.

Then he heard what sounded like a large aircraft overhead, and there was pounding on the outside, as though a giant were trying to get in. The light went out, and he and Simon sat on the bottom cellar step in total darkness. The scared teenager instinctively grasped his hand and Logan did not pull away. Instead, he wrapped a protective arm around Simon and they clung together while waiting out the tornado with hammering hearts.

The one thing thrumming through his head, stronger than even his concern for his own safety, was his worry over whether Hope had made it home all right, but there was nothing he could do for her now. He could feel the house above him rising and settling, like a giant accordion.

Beside him, Simon was muttering something in German. He could not understand all the words, but it was no trick to understand that the boy was praying and praying hard when every other word was *Gott*.

Falling back upon his years as a small boy kneeling beside

his mother in St. Patrick's, Logan also began to pray. It was awkward and halting, but he prayed.

A giant tree limb had broken through the cellar door, sending Mr. Lemon sprawling, and tearing open a hole through which torrential rains now poured, churning the packed earth floor of the small cellar into mud.

Carrie whimpered against her shoulder, and Adam buried his face in her skirt, his little body trembling with fear.

"Mr. Lemon is hurt." She pulled their clinging arms away from her. "Sit here against this wall. I must help him."

In the pouring rain, ducking beneath the wet branches intruding on their tiny shelter, she crawled on her hands and knees toward the valiant older man. He was unconscious and his head was bleeding. She was strong from all her hard work, and he was not a large man. She was able to tug him out of the rain, to the area of the cellar that was still intact, where she and the children had been when the limb came crashing through.

As she wiped the blood off his face with her apron, she gave thanks for the light the lantern still managed to throw off. At least she could see what she was doing, and the worst of the storm was over. Soon she would try to force a way out through the debris of the broken door.

It was then that a nagging stitch she had been ignoring in her side went away and a wave of pain washed through her abdomen. This pain was familiar. To her horror, she realized that the trauma of the tornado had thrown her into labor.

After the wind and torrential rain died down, Logan and Simon crawled up out of the cellar to a changed landscape. They walked around the yard, stunned and silent, assessing the damage. His home was fairly intact, with the exception of some roof damage, but all the pots of flowers Hope had so lovingly planted were blown away, and the chicken coops she and Simon had built had disappeared. A few bewildered and bedraggled half-grown chickens huddling on the ground near the house were the only evidence left of Hope's dream for an organic chicken business.

Several trees in the small peach and apple orchard behind the house were twisted and torn. The promising blossoms that Hope had said indicated a good harvest now lay on the ground, blown in all directions. Carrie's pink tricycle was twisted around one of the top limbs of the giant oak tree. Adam's blue one was nowhere in sight.

It had happened so quickly—in a matter of a few minutes.

He glanced next door, and saw that Ivan's house was basically intact as well, but as he stood on the hill beside the oak tree and looked out over the countryside, he could see the path the tornado had taken. It had skipped all over the land, knocking down a tree or building as its tail flipped this way and that, destroying wherever it landed.

On one hillside of trees near his home, a circular bare spot had been dug out by the twister's tail where it had apparently settled for an instant before coiling into itself and moving on.

The thing that worried him most was that it looked like it had come from the general direction of Hope's house.

"Simon!" he yelled. "Let's go!"

Simon didn't ask where they were going. He knew.

As they headed toward her home, Logan's heart pounded with fear.

The contractions were growing harder, and Mr. Lemon had not yet regained consciousness. The tree limb was massive. In spite of the hole it had driven through the cellar door, the remaining part of the door was held tight by its weight. She had struggled with trying to shove it open, but she'd managed only to make her contractions worse. She was terrified of what might happen if she did not get out of here, and soon.

Adam and Carrie had both been born after a very short labor. Her mother had teased her that most women would be jealous of the easy time she had. She had been grateful to be spared the agony she knew some women experienced, but right now, she wished she could be one of those women. Otherwise, unless God intervened, there was a very good chance she would have to give birth on this muddy floor with only Carrie and Adam to help her. She shuddered at the thought.

"Mr. Lemon?" The contraction eased up for a moment and she leaned over and patted his face with her hand. "Please wake up, Mr. Lemon. I need you."

"There." Simon pointed and Logan slammed on the brakes. The area around Hope's home had changed so drastically that he barely recognized it. He jumped out of the car and tried to take it all in.

Hope's house was gone. The barn was gone. There was no horse. No buggy. Some of the fence posts that had once graced the property and the barbed wire fencing was tangled in the tops of some young trees. Several older, larger trees had been uprooted and lay tossed upon the ground. Her next-door neighbor's house had disappeared.

There was no sign that an Amish woman or her children had ever lived here.

"Do you hear that?" Simon put one hand behind his ear.

"Hear what?"

"That," Simon said. "It's really faint, but I think I hear a child crying."

Logan held his breath and listened. He heard it, too. Was his mind playing tricks on him?

"Over there!" Simon pointed. "Look!"

It was Carrie. She was crawling out from beneath the tangle of some giant trees. Her *Kapp* was gone, her hair hung in tangles, her face was smeared with dirt and tears, and her little dress was torn—but she was alive.

"Carrie!" Logan ran to her and gathered her up in his arms, kissing her tear-stained face, overcome with gratitude. "Where are *Mommi* and Adam?"

His heart stood still when she pointed at the massive tree from beneath which she had just crawled. Hope and Adam were beneath that?

"Hope?" he yelled. "Can you hear me?"

"Logan!" Hope screamed. "Get us out! Please! Get us out!"

He could hear Adam crying out in fear now, from the sound of terror in his mother's voice. It would take something terrible for Hope to scream like that with a child beside her. She must be hurt.

Using their bare hands and a broken two-by-four, he and Simon managed to pry away enough of the broken cellar door to pull Adam through. Then Simon, with his scarecrow build, lowered himself into the hole and lifted Hope up until Logan was able to grasp and pull her out.

"Thank God you're okay," he kept repeating as he pulled her into his arms. "I thought I had lost you. Thank God you are okay."

The moment she felt his strong arms around her, she knew that she was safe. Finally she was safe. She clung to him, her face pressed tightly against his chest. The very scent of his body gave her a feeling of security. The knowledge that she didn't have to be strong anymore washed over her. Logan was here. Logan would take care of her. She could melt into his arms and let the contractions come. Logan would see that she got the help she needed. As he held her, half-kneeling on the sodden ground, it seemed as though he were trying to shelter her with his own body against any more pain.

"I knew you would come for me." She said it over and over. "I knew you would come for me."

Then she felt another great pain grip her belly, stronger this time, and she writhed with the intensity of it.

"What's wrong, Hope?" There was panic in his voice. "Where are you hurt?"

She could not answer him. She held her breath until the contraction eased.

He helped her to her feet. "I'm taking you and the children straight to the hospital!"

"No." She drew a deep breath. "You passed Levi and Grace's place on your way here. Is the birthing clinic intact?"

"Yes. Levi and Grace were outside."

"Good." She gasped. "Please, Logan. Take me there!"

"Is the baby coming?"

Another contraction hit and all she could do was nod and bend over until it passed.

He helped her walk toward the car. "How long have you been having contractions?"

"Too long." She panted. "I think there may be little time . . . please . . . take me to Grace. Then get Mr. Lemon to the hospital. I think he may have a concussion."

"Simon!" Logan shouted. "I'm taking Hope to the birthing clinic."

Simon poked his head up out of the cellar. "Her neighbor is waking up. I think he needs a doctor."

"Not as badly as she needs a midwife. Stay with him. I'll be back soon." He tried to help her walk to the car, but another hard contraction hit and she could not move.

"Kids, get in the car. Hurry." He swooped Hope up in his arms and deposited her on the front seat while the children tumbled into the back. "Mommy needs to visit cousin Grace's."

chapter TWENTY-SIX

B oth Aunt Claire and Grace were standing outside inspecting the damage to the clinic's yard when Logan pulled in.

"Hope is having her baby," he yelled. "The contractions are coming fast!"

They came running, and within minutes they had helped her out of her muddy clothing, given her a quick sponge bath, put a clean nightgown on her, and covered her with a warm flannel sheet.

"Now *you* get to do the rest of the work," Aunt Claire made a gentle joke. "Are you ready?"

Hope's body answered with a primal desire to push. There was pain, and there was pressure, and she wished with all her heart that Titus were there with her . . . but God was good. He had provided her with two women who cared about her to help her through the next intense minutes. She knew that she and her baby would be fine with Grace and Claire watching over them. She knew Adam and Carrie would be fine with Logan watching over them. Her heart sang with gratitude as her brand-new baby girl entered the world.

• • •

"How are you feeling?" Logan brushed a wisp of hair away from her face. "I hear you have another beautiful daughter."

She opened her eyes and roused from the dreamlike state of relief in which she had been floating. Her new baby had been born healthy and safe in one of Grace and Claire's fresh, clean birthing beds instead of on a muddy cellar floor.

"Where are Adam and Carrie?" she asked.

"I took them to your mother's. I'll go get them whenever you want."

"Not yet. Is Mr. Lemon okay?"

"Levi drove him to the hospital while you were having the baby. We've not heard anything yet."

"He saved our lives, Logan." She grasped his hand. "That old man saved our lives."

"I know. I'll make sure he's taken care of."

"Have you seen her?" she asked.

"I have. I made the acquaintance of that little lady while she was getting her first bath. From all the racket, I am pretty sure she was not happy about it."

"Thank you for taking care of us."

"Not a problem." He straightened the sheet. "Have you given the baby a name yet?"

"Esther Rose."

"Esther Rose Schrock." He said the name slowly, testing the sound. "I like that very much. Let me guess. You decided to name her after Ivan's mom and your own mother."

"I did."

Their eyes locked, and the intimacy of having him sitting here beside her made her heart beat faster.

"Do we have a farm left?" she asked.

"The house and land are still there. We can replace the rest."

"Are my chickens gone?"

"We're still finding a few here and there that are still alive.

I don't know chickens very well, but these seem a bit nervous. Oh, and your buggy horse managed to somehow find shelter. Simon caught him and rode him to our barn. The buggy is gone, though."

"When I get my strength back, I'll start to rebuild."

"And when you get your strength back," he said, "I'll help."

"Are you still leaving for New York tomorrow?"

"Yes, but I'll be back as soon as I can. In the meantime, take good care of Esther Rose."

As he left, Hope felt such a strange mixture of emotions. Happiness that her delivery was over and the baby was safe. Sadness that Titus had not lived to see his little girl. Happiness that Logan was returning to Holmes County permanently. Guilt about how happy she felt that Logan and Marla had broken up.

Her life was turning out to be so much more complicated than she had ever dreamed when she was a girl.

Marla had abandoned his apartment, but only after taking every stick of furniture out of it that she deemed worthy. That meant she took anything that had been crazy expensive. That also meant she had taken with her most of the uncomfortable, unattractive pieces that he had never liked. Left behind were his bed, a recliner she had frequently threatened to throw out, a comfortable old couch he kept in his office, and his desk, chair, and bookcases. Gone was every piece of art from the walls. Left behind was every first-edition book he had collected. Gone were all the crystal and designer dishes. Left behind were his good camera and his collection of antique writing pens. She had also taken the drapes—which made no sense because they were custom-made—but he was grateful. He had never liked those heavy things anyway.

The Realtor brought cleaners in after Marla got her things out, and painters, so the apartment looked bare, but pristine.

All in all, he was well satisfied.

His plan was to spend a few days signing papers, making the final arrangements for moving the few possessions he wanted to keep to his home in Holmes County, and dealing with financial and business issues.

He also wanted to have lunch with his long-suffering literary agent. They had kept only in loose contact these past eight months, and it was time to let Harry know that his advice to buy the house had been wise.

"Long time, no see." His agent arrived at the restaurant they had agreed upon and took a seat across from him at a small table. "You're looking well. How did your country idyll go?"

"Better than I expected."

"Were you affected by that tornado that passed through your area yesterday?"

"Not badly." Logan didn't elaborate.

He knew that Harry would not be interested in the details of the tornado, or the last-minute rescue of Hope, or the birth of Esther Rose, or Mr. Lemon's injuries. His agent would only be interested in those details if they were written in a saleable manuscript he could broker to a publisher.

"So." Harry glanced at the menu and then laid it aside. "How is the writing going?"

Logan thought his agent sounded nervous. He also knew that he had given him ample reason to be. It felt nice to have good news.

"The last novel in the psychiatrist/stalker series is finished. A week more to polish it and I'll email it to the publisher."

"Your two-month extension was a help?"

"A great help. You were right. I was burned out."

"Is the book any good?" Harry fingered his fork and didn't look at him.

"I think so. It's definitely better than the last two."

Harry breathed a sigh of relief. "And the drinking?"

Logan nodded at the pitcher of iced tea he'd had brought to the table instead of the wine he'd always ordered in the past. "It was a struggle at first. Now I rarely think about it."

"Good!" Harry did not even try to hide his relief. "I'm almost afraid to ask if you have any new proposals for me to pitch."

"I do, actually." Logan reached for his briefcase and pulled out the manuscript of the war novel he'd started at the antiques shop. He laid the carefully typed pages on the table between them.

"You're kidding," Harry said. "No one uses hard copy anymore."

"I do," Logan said. "At least I did with this one."

Harry lifted the top page of the manuscript and started reading while they waited to order lunch. Logan remained silent, wondering, waiting. His agent wasn't always the most encouraging person in the world, but Harry knew good writing when he saw it.

Harry turned the first page facedown on the table and started reading the second page. Logan's hopes rose. This was a very good sign. Someone as experienced as Harry could tell if a piece was saleable after just one paragraph.

He sipped his tea and waited. Harry kept reading. The waitress took their order, and his agent kept reading. When she brought their salads ten minutes later, Harry laid the page facedown on the pile he'd just finished and glanced up.

"This is not at all like anything you've written in the past."

"I know."

"This is a wartime love story."

"It is."

"People expect a very specific reading experience when they buy a Nate Scott novel and this isn't it."

"I know."

"Publishers aren't going to want to touch it." His agent loosened his tie. "It would be like buying a Stephen King horror story and finding out you just bought *Gone with the Wind*."

"I know."

"You do realize you're nuts for wasting your time on this. Right?"

Logan shrugged. "I don't care."

It was the first time he had ever seen his agent at a loss for words.

"Here's the thing," Logan said. "I'm not trying to sell a million copies of this novel. I'm just trying to make a few very special people happy—and the sooner the better. I'll publish it under my real name, Logan Parker, instead of Nate Scott, so there will be no preconceived ideas. You can shop it around and take your fifteen percent or I can self-publish, have fifty copies made for my friends, and then let it drop out of sight. It doesn't matter to me."

His agent fidgeted with the dinnerware. "You know how good this book is, don't you?"

"To tell you the truth," Logan said, "I don't really care."

Harry sat back in his chair and gave him a long look. "Living in Amish country is changing you isn't it?"

Logan broke apart a dinner roll. "You have no idea."

After leaving his lunch with Harry, Logan elbowed his way through the after-lunch crowd in Manhattan, but all he could think about was how badly he missed Hope and the children. He even missed Simon. He was so homesick that he probably would have grabbed and hugged Agatha if she had walked by.

It was a different culture, a different place, and often felt like an entirely different world. No longer did he feel like he belonged here. He called home to check on Hope and Esther Rose, and Grace told him they were fine and staying with them at the clinic for another couple of days. He was relieved. Hope and the baby couldn't be in a better place. He left word that if Hope and her children needed a place to live, they could use his place until they found something else. He'd rent a room somewhere.

He realized that he was as nervous about Esther Rose and her mother as a brand-new father, and he wasn't the father, but he couldn't help it. He'd lost his heart the moment he held that baby girl in his arms.

His heart was so sick with longing for Hope, and her children, and the life he might be able to have with them, that he actually tried on the idea of becoming Amish.

He could rip out the electricity, buy a buggy, grow a beard, wear suspenders. He had lived in a nonelectric house for several months. He could do it again if it meant having her and her children in his life. He could easily endure a three-hour worship service twice a month if it meant having Hope and helping her raise those children.

He could easily imagine himself sitting on the front porch with Hope thirty or forty years from now, watching grandchildren play in the front yard, hosting church in his house, enjoying close friendships with these decent and gentle people.

In some ways, becoming Amish would be a relief. He longed for the faith he saw in their lives, their acceptance of God's will. He longed for the decency and goodness he saw in Hope and her family. He admired the simplicity of their lives. If becoming a spiritual man involved studying the Bible, he could do that. If it involved praying daily, he could do that, too.

It wasn't just Hope. It was a longing to belong to something bigger and better than himself that was drawing him to this decision.

Even if Hope did not want him . . . he wanted to belong to her people.

Everything within him wanted to jump in the car and go home, but his meeting to complete the sale of the apartment was tomorrow. There was no way he could leave before then. He was taking care of having dinner with his mother tonight, so there would be nothing keeping him from heading home the minute the papers were signed. He couldn't wait.

"She is such a fine baby." Thelma Schrock looked fondly into Esther Rose's tiny face. "She looks like you, but I also see a bit of Titus there as well."

It was the day after Esther Rose was born, and Hope was grateful to be able to recuperate at the birthing clinic for a few days. It was such a homey place. At the moment she was seated in a padded rocking chair in the kitchen, having a snack of ginger cookies with her mother-in-law and Grace.

"I'm so glad you won't be working over at your father's old place anymore," Thelma said.

"What do you mean?" Hope asked.

"Well, now that the baby is here . . . and after all the damage the tornado did. We heard that it had destroyed everything that you and Simon had built. Certainly you won't be going back now."

"I never intended not to go back."

"But my husband said he told you about getting you that job at the restaurant."

"I'm not interested in that job."

Thelma looked hurt and confused. "You would disobey the bishop's counsel?"

Hope tried to put her feelings into words that would do the least damage. "Bishop Schrock is a good and wise man. He has been an excellent father-in-law, and I could not have asked for a better mother-in-law than you, but I have plans to turn my father's old place into a productive farm. Logan has already put too much money into seed, equipment, and livestock for me to walk away now. I made a business deal. I gave him my word. It would not be honest or fair to suddenly stop working there."

"You would honor an *Englisch* man's financial concerns more than your own bishop's counsel?"

"Of course not, but I cannot go back on my word."

She could tell that the idea of having a different opinion than the bishop was mind-boggling to his wife. This, no doubt, had made the bishop's life much easier.

"I—I should go." Thelma handed the baby back to Hope and headed out the door as though frightened by their conversation.

"Wow," Grace said, after Thelma had gone. "You are certainly brave."

"Not brave," Hope said. "A little rebellious? Probably. But not brave."

Grace glanced at the clock. "I have a client coming in a few minutes, but I'd like to ask you something first. Do you mind if I get a little nosy?"

"After all you've done for me?" Hope said. "Of course not."

"Sometimes where there's smoke, there's fire. Is there any chance you are interested in Logan Parker romantically? He's a good-looking guy, and the way he looked at you when he was here makes me think he wishes he had the right to be Esther Rose's daddy," Grace said. "It worried me to see that, because I thought he had a wife back in New York."

Hope knew that her cousin's *Englisch* wife was not interested in gossip, but was truly concerned.

"Not a wife. A fiancée. He told me yesterday before the tornado came that they have broken up. He is in New York right now selling his apartment. When he comes back, he plans to stay here permanently."

"That's very interesting." Grace busied herself putting away the cookies Thelma had brought. "So, how do you feel about him?"

Hope knew that Grace did not have the same mind-set as the people in her Amish church. She would not judge her harshly for having feelings for Logan. Because of that, she felt free to voice something that made her cheeks grow pink with embarrassment. "If Logan were Amish, I would not mind being courted by him."

"Ah," Grace said. "That's what I was afraid of. Let me ask you this—have you ever considered jumping fence and becoming a Mennonite? Seems to me that might be the easiest solution for everyone."

"I have given it some thought."

"If I understand how things work around here, your Old Order Amish church would not shun you as long as you become part of another conservative, Anabaptist church. Right?"

"Sometimes I do wonder what it would be like to have more freedom," Hope confessed. "But my family and church would be so very disappointed if I left."

"My husband tells me that Logan is not a nonbeliever. He thinks that there are possibilities there. If both you and Logan were to join, say, Ivan's church—wouldn't that solve everything?"

Esther Rose opened her eyes, started to root around. Hope began to nurse her.

"I know that would seem like an easy solution to you, Grace. You were raised *Englisch*. You truly can't understand what me jumping fence would do to my parents, my brothers, my sisters, and Titus's parents. It would break their hearts." She stroked the baby's downy head. "And because it would break their hearts . . . it would break mine."

"Instead of having dinner tonight"—his mother's voice sounded strained over the phone—"could you meet me at St. Patrick's in a few minutes?"

"Sure, Mom." What an odd request. He glanced at his watch. It was only two o'clock in the afternoon. Normally she would be in her office. He'd never known her to go to the cathedral in the middle of a workday. "Is something wrong?"

"Yes, Logan." There was a long silence. He couldn't be sure, but he thought he heard her crying. "Something is very, very wrong."

"Where are you, Mom?"

"Already there."

"I'm on my way."

He didn't bother to hail a cab. It was only a few blocks. He could get there quicker if he ran.

chapter TWENTY-SEVEN

I t had been a long time since he'd walked up the steps of the famous cathedral. He had been little, and still holding his mother's hand. Now he took them two at a time.

His mother was sitting in her usual pew. In the right corner, far back. Even though it had only been a few weeks since he'd last spent time with her, she seemed . . . smaller.

He slid in beside her, and grasped her hand. She gripped it hard.

"What's wrong and why are we here?" he asked.

"I needed courage, and I needed you." She dabbed her eyes with a tissue.

"Are you ill?"

She nodded and his heart nearly stopped.

"How ill?"

Her eyes, when she turned to look at him, were not only red-rimmed from crying, they were haunted. "Less than a year."

"Dear God!" His world collapsed. "No!"

"Cancer almost got me over thirty years ago, Logan, and I beat it. Now it's come back."

Then she dropped another bomb.

"I've had a good run. There's little I wanted to do that I haven't done. I can face death. It's facing you that is going to be hard."

His mind was whirling. "Courage to face me? I don't understand."

"Ever since I left the doctor's office, there's been only one thing on my mind . . . and that was you. I don't know how long I have, and I need to tell you some very important things before I go."

"Mom, if it's about finances . . ."

She shook her head. Impatient. "You've had power of attorney for years. Everything is in order. I need to tell you about your father. And Logan? It is not going to be easy."

It had been quiet and peaceful in the cathedral when he arrived, but a tour group had come in and their voices, under the circumstances, grated on Logan's nerves. "Let's go back to your apartment, Mom," he said. "Please."

"Perhaps that would be best."

She walked to the sidewalk, then stopped and looked back at the massive building. "I've walked here at least once a week for most of my life. Now I think it would be best if you caught us a cab."

There was an ebb and flow of mothers at Grace and Claire's clinic and, two days after the birth of Esther Rose, a small crisis when four women arrived and gave birth within hours of one another. Levi brought in a cot and set it up for the fourth mother while Hope got ready to go.

"Thank you for everything," she said to Claire on her way out the door. "And thank Grace for me. I know she's a little busy right now."

At that moment, they both stopped and listened to an angry

wail as Grace ushered a newborn into the world. Another healthy set of lungs. All was well.

"I'll come to check on you later today." Claire turned and hurried toward the sound.

"Please take me to Logan's," Hope said as Levi helped bundle Esther Rose into the tiny car seat he'd placed in the back.

"I thought I was taking you to your mother's."

"Logan called Grace and said to tell me that I could stay at his house if I wanted to while he was gone. He said he would be gone a few days longer than he expected. I want to see what damage the tornado did and get Simon started on the repairs. He's pretty good at what he's doing, but I'd feel better if I could supervise a little at this stage."

"And how are you going to do that so soon after giving birth?"

"The weather is nice. I will spend a great deal of time on the porch."

"People will talk. They will expect you to go stay at your mother and father's."

"People *always* talk," Hope said with exasperation. "My mother has her hands full taking care of both her family and mine right now. I'll stay there until Logan gets back. The baby and I will rest better there than at my parents' for now. Then I'll make other arrangements."

Logan brought the glass of ice water his mother had requested and handed it to her.

"Thank you, dear," his mother said. "Would you mind if we went outside on the balcony while we talk?"

"Whatever you want," he said.

After they were seated, with the panorama of the city from Deborah's high-rise apartment laid out before them, she began.

"First of all, you must promise me something," she said. "You must promise me that once I begin, you won't interrupt and you won't ask questions until I'm finished."

"Why not?"

"Because I'm afraid if you stop me, I won't be able to start again. I have to take a run at this thing. When I'm finished, I'll let the chips fall where they may."

"I promise," he said.

She took a deep, shuddering breath, and then began telling him a story that he suspected would probably change both of their lives.

"I was thirty years old," his mother said. "That can be a hard year for a woman. It was also the year the doctors discovered cancer. My fiancé left me within hours after finding out. He was a man who couldn't stomach sickness of any kind."

"Was he my father?"

"Oh, heavens no. It's much more complicated than that."

"I'm a grown man, Mother." He took her hand in his. "I don't care who my father was. A married man maybe? A criminal? It's all in the past . . ."

Then she started laughing, but her laughter was on the verge of hysteria. Soon the laughter turned to sobs. Finally, her sobs subsided and she wiped her eyes.

"I will probably end up in the hospital before this is over, Logan, but I've accepted the fact that what I've deserved for a long time is prison."

"Mom . . ."

"Please, dear. Don't interrupt. I have to tell this my way."

It was so hard to see her like this, but he sat back and let her tell her story her way.

"The worst part about the cancer was that it was ovarian and when it was all over, I knew I would never be able to have children. I was an only child and I had always wanted children.

When the surgery and chemo were completed, I was not in good shape physically or mentally. I craved sunshine and air, and so I rented a cheap beach house in Florida with my last bit of savings. I had the idea that watching the ocean would be peaceful and I thought it would help me heal."

"Did it help?" he asked.

"Please don't interrupt, Logan." She took a sip of water. "It helped for a while, until I was treated to the sight of a large, happy family playing together on the beach."

Far below, they heard the sound of an ambulance wailing. His mother waited for the sound to fade away before she continued.

"It was an isolated beach. They wanted privacy and so did I, but I became obsessed with watching them. I kept wondering how some people managed to have all the luck. The woman had so many lovely children, and I had nothing. I brooded on this, which was not a wise thing to do in my condition.

"The littlest boy caught my eye. He was a beautiful child, about three years old. They left an older brother in charge one day—a teenager. He soon grew bored with his job as babysitter. He kept swimming farther and farther out while keeping only half an eye on his brother. The little boy was so happy playing in the sand, he didn't notice at first when his brother didn't come back."

"What happened? Did the brother drown?"

"That's what I feared. I saw this child all alone on the beach, and I knew it was dangerous for a child that young to be left alone near water. So I walked down to where he was and simply sat down beside him. That was all I intended to do. Just watch after this sweet little boy until the family returned. He was hot and sweaty. I took his hat off and laid it on the beach. No one came. I had sat there for over an hour.

Logan wondered what this had to do with him and his

father, and wished she would get to the point, but he didn't interrupt. It was her story, and she needed to tell it the way she wanted.

"I should have called the police or the coast guard to hunt for the older brother. I should have done a lot of things. Instead, I decided the little boy had spent enough time in the sun and I took him indoors with me. A wind had begun to blow up by the time I picked him up and started carrying him, and I saw that it was erasing my footprints. It occurred to me that this was a good thing. When I got him back to the beach house, I fed him applesauce, which he gobbled up like a hungry little bird. I was entranced. He was so trusting, sweet, and innocent."

Logan began to realize where this was going. For the first time in months, he found himself craving a drink.

"After he ate, he climbed up onto my lap and I rocked him to sleep. There is something magical about having a child lying, sleeping, in your arms. I studied his eyelashes, his tiny mouth, his eyebrows, the flush on his cheeks, and I fell in love. I had been through too much. I was weakened by my ordeal, both physically and mentally. Something snapped. I told myself that fate had given him to me to help heal the terrible hurt. It was a long time before I realized that I was not entirely sane for a while."

The blare of a fire engine filtered through to his consciousness. Somewhere there was a fire. Somewhere down below people were going about their jobs. Somewhere there were people who were eating and sleeping and doing normal things. He longed to be normal, to go back to before this terrible day began. It occurred to him that "normal" was vastly underrated.

"The local police came to my door. They said two kids had gone missing. They said they'd found the youngest child's hat at the edge of the water. They feared both had drowned. They wanted to know if I'd seen anything.

"The little boy was sleeping on my bed in the other room while I talked with them. I could have brought him out then and been a hero. Instead, I lied. I told them that I was still recuperating from chemo, had spent the day in bed, and had seen nothing. I was very apologetic. I was also very pale and thin, still wearing the turban women who are cancer victims sometimes do. I looked every bit like the sick woman I was. No one would have suspected me of being capable of anything like what I had done."

Logan listened in horror. It was exactly what he had feared. She was describing a kidnapping.

"They thanked me and left. I knew the minute they were gone that I had crossed a line and that there was no turning back. I waited, but there was no follow-up. I watched the rest of the investigation from behind a drawn curtain. It didn't take long. The family, in their terror over their two missing children, had walked up and down the beach, obliterating any footprints or possible clues. I watched the mother crying, and the father trying to comfort her—and I felt great sympathy for her because I knew exactly how she felt—I had been feeling the same kind of grief myself until this angel-child came into my life like a gift from God.

"As I said before, I was not entirely sane.

"The family left and did not come back. I stayed two more days, so that no one would get suspicious. The little boy did not cry at first. I had never seen a more contented child. I was fascinated with him. We played little silly games all day long with me on the floor with him, stacking everything from canned goods to toilet paper. Someone had left a toy truck behind, and we played with it endlessly. I made a game, also, of cutting his hair. He'd worn his hair rather long for a little boy. Straight bangs across the forehead, and a straight cut at the earlobes. When I was finished he could have been a miniature Marine."

Her voice, he noticed, had gotten singsong and had begun to

sound as though it was coming from far away. It was almost as though she were describing someone other than herself doing these things.

"The one thing we did not do was go outside. The risk was too great. I left the blinds closed and we played together in a sort of twilight world."

Who was the child? Was *he* the child?

"There did come a time when he began to cry. He spoke a different language than me, so it was impossible to communicate with him in words. He missed his mother and kept saying something that sounded like *mem*.

"In the middle of the second night, while he was deep asleep, I packed up the car and drove him to my mother's home in New York City."

"Please tell me this story has a happy ending, Mom," he said. "Please tell me you regained your sanity and gave him back to his family."

"Please be patient, Logan. I've waited a long, long time to tell you what happened. You see, I had graduated at the top of my class from Columbia law school, right before the surgery, and had gotten offers of three different jobs before I got sick. I figured that gaining employment from one of those offers was about the only real chance at a normal life I had.

"My mother was a painter. As you know, she was not a particularly good one. We had always lived a bohemian lifestyle and moved around a great deal when I was young. Like you, I never knew my father. I've often thought that her lifestyle is why I chose to study so hard, get good grades, and go into law. Nothing could have been more different from the way I had been raised.

"My mother was not happy with me showing up with a stolen child, but she did not want to see me go to prison. Her own past was not without legal blemishes. She preferred no one look into her life too closely, either. She was estranged from her family, and her few friends were not the kind of people who would find a child appearing out of nowhere particularly suspicious. Many of them were living in a sort of substance-abuse fog anyway. I had worked two part-time jobs to put myself through law school. Between studying, going to classes, and keeping myself afloat, I had not made any close friends. We made up a story about the child and people bought it.

"On my way out of town, I had bought a newspaper. A three-year-old child drowning off the coast of Florida was not big news, although there was a brief mention of his disappearance and a paragraph about his brother being found later on that day when a fishing boat had discovered him clinging to a large piece of driftwood.

"As my strength returned, my grief over my illness and faithless fiancé diminished, and I began to regain my emotional stability. By that time, I had landed a job with a good law firm. I knew I could not confess my sin without destroying my future. The way I saw it, there was nothing I could do to make atonement except love the child as my own and give him the best life possible."

She stopped talking.

He waited. "Is something wrong?"

"Just gathering my thoughts. It seems like I've spent my life dreading this moment."

"Take your time, Mom," he said. "This is a lot for me to take in, too."

After a few minutes, she began her story again. "Because I had studied criminal law, I had a great deal of book knowledge about the mechanics of committing crimes in general. I had the legal knowledge necessary to obtain a birth certificate for the child and I applied for a social security number for him. I gave him a name that I thought sounded strong and brave."

"You named him Logan."

She nodded. "I named him Logan, after the great Indian chief."

He wondered if he would ever rid himself of the sickness he felt in his stomach over this terrible tale. Where was the family from whom he had been stolen? Who were they?

"It wasn't long before I realized that caring for a child was not all giggles and kisses. Little boy Logan needed supervision and constant care. Fortunately, the bit of language he had learned by three years old dissipated under a steady diet of English. It was all he heard, and eventually, it was all he remembered.

"I've read that taking away a child's native tongue also helps take away his memory. This was not something I deliberately did, but I genuinely had no idea what he wanted when he asked me for something in that foreign language. If he used any form of English, I praised him lavishly.

"As he got older, he seemed to have forgotten everything he'd experienced before the age of three. If he mentioned some vague memory, I told him that it had been a dream. When he turned into a man, I braced myself to be accosted with his knowledge of what I had done, but he never did. He had been a good child, and he became a good man.

"I was never a good mother. I tried, but I could never give him what he truly deserved . . . the truth. I also could not give him one other thing he always wanted, a sibling. Sometimes in the beginning, he would cry himself to sleep repeating what sounded like his brothers' and sisters' names. He was lonely, and each time that happened, I would hold him, trying to comfort him, and shedding silent tears over what I had done. I loved him, I still love him, very much."

"You were an excellent mother." It was true. At least, apart from the fact that she had stolen him from someone else, it was true.

"I've often thought it was no accident you became a writer who explored criminal and psychotic behavior. Subconsciously, you must have realized you had been living with 'crazy' most of your life," she said. "Looking back, I realize that I have tried to make up for the terrible wrong I committed by going out of my way to do pro bono work. I've helped a lot of people, innocent people wrongly accused who did not have the money to hire a really top-notch criminal attorney.

"I kept innocent people from dying inside prison where they didn't belong. I also put psychopathic killers behind bars with so much evidence and expertise it would take a hundred years for them to get out. I built, brick by brick, a reputation for integrity so thick, strong, and high that I thought with luck it might protect my son and myself for the rest of our lives. Even though I was raised with zero religious training, I began going to St. Patrick's every Sunday morning to pray. I was not Catholic, but I have never wavered from that one habit. Even when I was traveling, I would find some kind of a chapel somewhere and pray."

She drained her water glass and set it down on a small glass table beside her chair.

"One of the great ironies of all of this mess is the fact that in trying to make up for what I had done, I became a very good person . . ."

With that last sentence, she was done.

Logan left her sitting on the balcony while he wandered into the kitchen in a sort of daze. Trying to comfort her, he microwaved a cup of water for tea. She liked tea. He had gotten his Earl Grey habit from her. It was only after he absentmindedly took a sip before giving it to her that he realized he had neglected to put a teabag in the water. He did not bother to go back.

He sat back down beside her, trying to take it all in. He was not his mother's son. Not his grandmother's grandson. He looked down and rubbed the skin on the back of his hand, wondering whose DNA he carried. Who did he belong to? Were they still living? Were they dead? Did they love him and long for him, or did they have so many children that they had gone on with their lives and forgotten him?

He tried to wrap his mind around the fact that everything she had told him about his existence was a lie. Deep down, he had never known who he was. Deep down was a memory of something else, someone else, an entire family from whom he had been ripped away.

He had no idea how he should feel about this revelation. On one hand, he felt so very sorry for his mother—for the guilt and pain she must have felt all these years.

On the other hand, what kind of a person steals an innocent child?

"Who were they?" he asked. "Who did you take me away from?"

Her answer staggered him.

"I thought your writer's brain would already have filled in the details by now, Logan. For many years, Sarasota has been a popular Amish vacation destination. The Sarasota newspaper said their names were Ivan and Mary Troyer, an Amish family from Holmes County, Ohio. You haven't been experiencing déjà vu all this time, Logan. From the moment you saw that fork in the road that looked so familiar, you've been experiencing actual suppressed memories."

"Ivan and Mary Troyer?" His mind was spinning. "Are you talking about my *neighbors*?"

"I am."

He could not sit still another minute. He leaped to his feet and began pacing, trying to assimilate everything his mother had revealed. "How could I remember a turn in the road? I was so young. Children that age don't pay attention to roads."

"Maybe not a modern child riding in the backseat of a fast-moving car, but the Troyers were still Amish when you were a child. So—a smart little Amish boy riding on his mother's lap sitting in the front seat of a slow-moving buggy? Yes, I think that fork in the road and many other places would be pretty well imprinted on your brain over a span of three years."

It was all so difficult to imagine. If he hadn't agreed to go with Marla on that furniture shopping trip . . . If she had not insisted on going to see that pottery place . . . It was amazing how random actions could impact a person's life forever.

"You were lying each time I asked you if I'd ever been in Ohio."

"That's my whole point. I've been lying to you your whole life."

chapter TWENTY-EIGHT

They were both exhausted. His mother was drained from voicing such a painful confession. He was drained from dealing with so many emotions warring inside him. The idea of being Ivan and Mary's son was hard to take in. It was even harder to accept the fact that his mother was a criminal. And then there was the horrible news that she was terminally ill. How much could one person absorb? He longed for some normality.

"Can you eat?" he asked.

His mother looked at him in surprise. "I think so."

"Let's shelve all this for a bit and go out to dinner like we planned."

"Do you hate me?"

"Mom, I have no idea how I feel right now. All I know for sure is that I'm hungry . . . and that I still love you."

"Thank God for that. Could we maybe talk about the weather while we eat? I think I need a break from our present topic."

"I think we both do. I'll tell you all about the tornado and little Esther Rose."

"It's a deal. And . . . thanks."

"For what?"

"For not storming out and never speaking to me again."

And so they talked about Esther Rose, Carrie, Adam, Simon, Mr. Lemon, Hope, and the terrible storm. They discussed bedraggled chickens and damaged roofs. The one thing they did not discuss were the terrible things she had told him.

When he got his mother home, she took a bath and put on blue silk pajamas and a matching robe. Then they sat up and talked deep into the night.

He had never heard his mother talk so much or so openly. It was as though thick stone walls had tumbled down and he was allowed to see the brilliant but fragile girl who had fought her way through law school, fallen in love, overcome cancer and rejection, only to discover that an act so heinous could lock her away forever—not in a prison of mortar and bricks, but in a prison of her own making. She had waited for years to be found out. He saw the naked truth in her eyes that she had loved him desperately. "You know that I will have to face them," she said, after their long and lingering conversation.

"That's your decision to make," he said. "I won't force you."

"No. I'm done keeping secrets. It is time for me to face the Troyers. They can press charges, of course, and I will give them my full cooperation. Under the circumstances, I doubt I'd do prison time. That's at least one benefit of being terminal. It isn't as though I'm a flight risk." She grinned, an echo of her old self emerging. "I do happen to know a rather good criminal attorney."

He was grateful she was not asking him to keep her crime a secret. He had seen the Troyers' grief. Knew a little about Caleb's ongoing guilt. It could be healing to tell them.

He did not expect, as a grown man, to be made part of the family. Attempting to become a Troyer after all these years would be a little silly. All he hoped for was to take away some of their pain.

"Are you feeling strong enough to make the trip tomorrow?"

"Honestly? Now that I know that you do not completely hate me for what I did, I feel strong enough to face anything."

There was a peace on her face that he'd never seen before.

Hope was surprised when Logan drove in with an older woman beside him. She and Simon had just sat down to the simple supper of bean soup that her mother had brought over, when she heard the car.

She handed Esther Rose to Simon and went outside.

Her ewes had been delivered today and she was dying to show him, but knew this wouldn't be a good time for bringing up farm issues.

"How are you feeling, Hope?" he said.

"I'm doing well."

"I'm glad you decided to stay here while I was gone."

He did not inquire about the baby or the children and seemed very distant and distracted.

"Who do you have with you?"

"My . . . mother," he said, as the woman climbed out of the car. "Deborah Parker."

Hope wondered at the hesitation. Something was not right here.

"Mom, this is Hope. I've told you about her."

His mother had the bruised look about her face that a person got after crying very hard for a very long time. "Are either of you hungry?" Hope asked. "I have some bean soup."

"Mom?" Logan asked. "Do you want to eat first?"

Deborah shook her head. "No, I want to get this over with. I won't be able to think of anything else until I do."

"We have some business next door that needs tending to," he said. "Then maybe we'll have some if Mother is hungry."

Deborah was very quiet. She kept staring at the Troyers' home while Logan quickly carried her two small suitcases inside.

"We'll be back in a while." He took his mother's arm. "Pray for us, Hope."

"Of course I will." Something was terribly wrong here, but she had no idea what.

She watched as he walked his mother across the pasture toward the Troyers' home. Even though Deborah was not all that old or infirm, he kept his hand on her elbow the entire time, as though she needed steadying.

Hope could not begin to imagine what "business" he and his mother had with the Troyers that could cause them to act so worried. She went straight back into the house, took Esther Rose from Simon so he could finish eating, and then sat down to rock the baby to sleep while she prayed.

When Logan and his mother arrived at the Troyers', he discovered that they had come on the one night a week the family tried to all eat together. He wished the timing was better. He would have preferred for his mother to face Ivan and Mary alone.

They had all finished supper and were sitting around on the porch, visiting and watching the children play. It was remarkable to Logan to realize that most of the people he was looking at were his blood relatives.

Perhaps as a holdover from their Amish heritage, Logan's brothers and Ivan all wore some form of beard, although they were cut much shorter than the untrimmed beards of the Amish. This had kept him from noticing any family resemblance before now. As he approached this time, though, he saw that Caleb's eyebrows were formed much like his, and William had the same color eyes, and Charlotte's hair was the same shade of brown as his own. A nephew playing catch on the lawn reminded him exactly of his fourth-grade school picture.

It could have been a wonderful moment for him, the moment when he got to lay claim to this amazing family, as well as give them the gift of knowing that the child they thought they had lost had not drowned. But everything was overshadowed by the fact that his mother was standing beside him with a lifetime of regret in her heart.

"Don't you dare feel sorry for me," she whispered. "I deserve whatever they say, whatever they do. I don't want you telling them I'm sick, either. I don't want them to think I expect them to feel sorry for me."

"Hello," he said, as they approached the porch. "I'd like for you to meet my mother, Deborah Parker."

There was a flurry of introductions and welcomes. Two chairs were drawn up, creating a sort of large, meandering circle.

"Would you like something to drink?" Mary asked, always the caring hostess. "I have fresh cookies, too, if the children haven't eaten all of them."

"Nothing, thank you," his mother said.

"So tell me all about yourself." Mary sat down next to her. "We've enjoyed having your son as a neighbor so much."

"Well, I'm an attorney," his mother managed to say.

"Mother is one of the top criminal attorneys in the country," Logan said, wanting them to know that she was, in many ways, a remarkable woman.

"My, my, my," Mary said. "You must be good at what you do."

"She's the best." Logan wanted them to love his mother—in spite of what she had done. It was, of course, impossible, but he couldn't help wishing.

"I can't take any more of this, Logan." His mother looked at him with those haunted eyes again. "They are too nice. They don't deserve what happened to them. I have to tell them."

"Tell us what?" Caleb said, suspiciously, always the protective, responsible one.

"I've always found that it's best to say things straight out," Ivan said. He looked at Logan. "Just tell us the truth, son, and it will be okay."

It was that "son" that undid his stalwart mother. Her head dropped. She sat there shaking it back and forth while the Troyers looked at one another with concern.

He had thought long and hard on the drive over here about what he was going to say and how he would say it. He was, after all, a wordsmith. Now he realized that no manipulation of words could help this situation.

"Do you remember the first time I came here and thought I remembered about that little play closet?"

"I remember," Mary said. "I've thought and thought about that, wondering how you could have seen it, but we've had so many guests through the years."

"I've recently discovered that I was in this house and I did play inside the little room with the books." He turned to Caleb. "I wasn't making it up."

"Did I babysit you?" Mary frowned, perplexed. "I used to babysit some *Englisch* children from time to time."

"No . . ." There was no way to say it except to just say it. "I'm . . . Joseph."

Several members of his family had been rocking comfortably throughout this conversation. Now all rocking ceased. All movement ceased. All sound ceased, except the faint voices of children now playing tag in the backyard.

"One-two-three . . . you're IT," a childish voice called.

"Huh-uh . . . *you're* it!" another voice answered.

Beside him, Logan's mother stared at the ground, a woman condemned by her own heart. Mary stared at him wide-eyed. Caleb's mouth hung open. Ivan threw both hands in the air in disbelief, then grasped his thinning hair, with both hands—a stunned expression on his face.

Esther was the first to break the silence. "I *thought* you sounded like my brother John. I may be half-blind, but I am not deaf."

"*Sis ken fashtaut!*" Mary whispered, as though to herself. "I can't believe it."

"Wait a minute." Caleb got his wits back. "Are you trying to tell us that you're my little brother who drowned while I was supposed to be watching over him?"

"I didn't drown."

"Then how . . ."

"Because I *took* him!" His mother finally lifted her head and faced them. "I saw him. I wanted him. I took him. And I raised him. I would give my life not to have done so, but I did. If it does any good, with all my heart, I apologize for the terrible pain I have caused this family."

Everyone was silent for a few seconds, absorbing his mother's outburst.

"He does have a bit of the look of our Elias about him," Caleb's wife said. "But I don't know . . ."

"I'll need better proof than that," Caleb said. "We aren't rich people, but there are some who might think we have money. If that's what you're after, you've come to the wrong place."

"I don't need your money. Nor does my mother. We're telling the truth."

"You think these people are lying, Caleb? Why would anyone do such an evil thing?" Mary laid a hand on Logan's knee. "*Are* you the baby I lost? *Are* you Joseph?"

Then his mother spoke, and she was once again an accomplished attorney stating a case.

"You *were* supposed to be watching him." She looked straight at Caleb. "But you got bored. You started swimming farther and farther out. Then you got caught in some sort of current and disappeared. Your baby brother was left completely alone. I did not intend to take him. I thought I would simply watch over him until the family came back. But no one did. There were no cell phones back then, and my cabin did not have a phone. I was still recuperating from chemo and did not have the strength to carry him far. I barely had the strength to get him to my cabin and then I thought I would rest before I put him in the car to drive him to town to the police station.

"He was so adorable and trusting. He had started trying to drink the ocean water and I could tell he was thirsty. I had some juice back at the beach house that I gave him. He fell asleep in my arms and I pretended that he was my baby . . ." His mother looked down at her hands, folded now in her lap. "That was my mistake. I allowed myself to pretend that he was my baby."

Again there was silence as everyone tried to absorb the impact of her words.

"Did you know about this?" Ivan asked him. "Have you known all along? Have you been lying to us about who you are?"

"I only found out two days ago." Logan shook his head. "I had no idea."

"I still don't believe it," Caleb said to his father. "They could have gotten the information from the newspaper."

"I'd eaten some bad food at a restaurant and was taken ill," Mary said. "And Ivan was worried. Two of the other children were starting to feel unwell, too. He and the rest of the family helped walk me back to the cabin we were renting so I could lie down. Caleb did not want to come in yet, and offered to watch over his baby brother. Neither of them had eaten the food. Caleb was always such a responsible boy, we thought we could trust him to watch after little Joseph . . ."

"But he was just a teenager," Deborah continued where Mary left off. "And the ocean current took him farther out than he could swim back. The baby was wearing Amish clothing, except for some little sneakers that had tiny Velcro fasteners. It was the first time I'd seen a child's tennis shoes fastened like that, and I found it strange that an Amish child would be wearing them."

"*Englisch* friends had given them to me," Mary said. "Their child had recently outgrown them."

"He had a little cut over his eye that did not heal for several days. I worried about that cut. It had gotten slightly infected—I think by the sand."

"He had fallen in the cabin against the coffee table," Mary said. "The furniture was unfamiliar to him and he stumbled over a throw pillow that had fallen to the floor."

The realization seemed to finally hit Mary that he truly was her lost son. With a sob, she rose from her chair, and fell to her knees with her arms around his waist and her face pressed against his chest.

He did not know what to do. He awkwardly patted her back. This was, in truth, his mother. That man over there was his father. The old lady was his grandmother. These were his brothers and sisters.

As Mary cried, Ivan looked from Logan to Deborah, and then back to Logan again. He, too, was having trouble taking it all in.

"You stole my son?" he asked.

"I am so sorry," his mother said. "I was young and half-crazed from illness and grief."

"All those years you kept him? You knew what we would be going through, but you kept him!"

"I am so sorry," his mother kept repeating. "I had worked so hard for so long for my law degree. I knew that if I gave him back and people found out that I had . . . taken a child, I would never be able to get a job with any reputable firm anywhere."

"You allowed my parents to go through the agony of grieving a child because of your CAREER!" Caleb jumped out of his chair and came toward her, his hands clenched into fists.

Logan rose and stood between his brother and the woman who had raised him. "Don't touch her," he said. "She's suffered enough."

"*She's* suffered?" Caleb exclaimed. "She doesn't know the *meaning* of suffering! I was there! I watched my mother cry her heart out night after night. I had to live with the pain that I had caused it all by swimming too far out and leaving my baby brother alone . . ."

Stalwart, protective, prickly Caleb broke down at that point. Terrible, harsh man-sobs racked his frame. When his wife tried to comfort him, he shook her off.

"I think it might be wise for you and your . . . mother . . . to leave now." His grandmother, Esther, who had been listening in silence, pulled herself upright on her cane and took charge. "I believe our family needs time to think this through. You should leave now before any more harsh words are said that cannot be taken back."

"No!" Mary was on her knees, her arms outstretched toward Logan. "He is my son. I want to talk with him."

"There will be plenty of time for that later," Ivan said firmly. "He's not going anywhere. My mother is right. We need time to absorb this information, think about it, and pray about it. Go on home . . . Son."

Logan noticed that this time, Ivan stumbled over the word.

"I won't fight you on this," his mother said. "I know what I deserve and I won't fight whatever the court decides."

"Go on home, Logan," Ivan repeated. "Give us some time. Please."

Logan thought he had never heard a better suggestion in his life. The one thing on earth he wanted right now was to get off this porch.

As he helped his mother across the field and into his house, he glanced back and saw that the entire family, including the children, had disappeared into the Troyers' home, except for Esther, who seemed to be standing vigil on the porch, an old lady leaning on her cane, facing his house.

Hope saw them coming back, and it reminded her of pictures she'd seen of refugees. Logan's mother was bent over, and his arm was thrown around her protectively. He kept looking back over his shoulder at the Troyer house. She didn't know what had happened over there, but from the look of things . . . it wasn't good.

Simon had finished his soup and had gone out to the barn. With Esther Rose in one arm, she hurried into the kitchen and turned on the electric teakettle, then she started the oven warming. Mary had brought over cinnamon buns a few hours earlier for their breakfast tomorrow morning. They would be good warmed up.

"I have water boiling for tea," she said as Logan and Deborah came in. "And cinnamon rolls. If either of you are hungry now."

"Mother?" Logan asked solicitously. "Can you eat something?"

"No."

Deborah fell into a kitchen chair and buried her head in her arms. She seemed utterly exhausted.

"Please let me make you some tea, Mother. Or coffee. Or . . . please, just let me do *something*."

"Did you see her?" his mother said. "Did you see Mary's eyes when she found out? I'll never forget that look as long as I live. And your brother Caleb. So much pain!"

Hope heard only one word. "Brother?"

Almost as an afterthought, Logan said, "Yes. Caleb is my brother. I'm the baby who drowned. Except I didn't. My mother here found me and took me home with her . . . and kept me."

Hope decided that *she* needed a cup of tea, even if Deborah did not. With plenty of sugar. She was a strong woman, but she'd just given birth three days earlier. This was way more than she could take in while standing up.

"Logan. Am I hearing this correctly?" She plopped down on a kitchen chair, a sleeping Esther Rose cradled in one arm. "You're Joseph?"

"Yes, I am."

"If you are Joseph, then my mother used to babysit you," she said. "It was at a time when she was newly married and didn't have any children yet. Mary was older and a little overwhelmed with her large family. My mom said she would go get you nearly every day and play with you to give Mary a break."

She sat there, piecing everything together in her mind. "That's why this house was familiar to you, Logan. My mom used to take care of you here."

"I'm sure that's the reason," Logan said. "But right now . . . that's the least of my concerns. Mom's not well, and everyone over at the Troyers' is in shock."

"How bad was it over there?" Hope was very concerned about Ivan and Mary. They were not young.

"It was bad. They're talking it over now to decide what to do. I don't know when they'll contact us again. Tomorrow maybe?"

"My guess is tonight," Hope said. "I know those people really well. They do not believe in allowing the sun to go down upon their wrath. Unless I miss my guess, they are deep in prayer right now. They will come here once they feel they have had an answer from the Lord."

chapter TWENTY-NINE

I t broke his heart to see his mother waiting, waiting. The tension in the room practically roared in his ears as he waited. Simon came back from the barn, took one look at their faces, and went right back outside without saying one word.

Esther Rose began to grow fussy, so he took her from Hope and walked the floor with her. It hit him that Ivan and Mary had probably walked the floor with him in their arms. It was all so very strange to try to imagine.

Would he continue to call this woman who had raised him "Mother"? Would Mary want him to call *her* that? He had no clue how to deal with any of it.

And then Hope, who was looking out the window toward the Troyers' home, gave a small cry.

"They're coming!" she said.

He strode over to the window, and sure enough, they were coming . . . the whole tribe of them. Even Esther was with them, and with a grandchild's help, seemed to be leading them. She steadied herself by holding on to the child's shoulder, her cane grasped in the middle like a drum major. The wind was blowing, and her long, gray hair streamed out behind her. She wore a plain, brown dress and reminded him of some sort of prophet as she marched across that field.

Mary stumbled along behind her with Ivan. His arm was around Mary's waist. Children scattered out on either side. All the rest walked together in a loose group.

Why was it necessary for the entire family to come? he wondered. Why the children? Why all the in-laws? Why the grandmother? Couldn't just Ivan and Mary tell them whatever it was that they wanted to say?

He and his mother walked out to the porch to face them.

Esther sat down in one of the many porch chairs and gestured for him and his mother to sit as well. The others grabbed chairs and scooted them into a circle around them. The children sat on the floor, their arms draped over fathers' and mothers' knees, some crawling onto laps. One young teenage girl sat with a toddler on her lap on the porch floor with her back against a porch column. He remembered the girl's face, but not her name or which of his siblings she belonged to.

All waited, including him and his mother, for what appeared to be a pronouncement. It reminded him of waiting in court for a judge to assign a sentence after a person had been found guilty.

"We've talked," Ivan said. "My mother insisted that all the children be here to hear what we've come to say. She says we need to set up stones of remembrance after crossing this Jordan."

"I have no idea what you are talking about," Logan said.

"Joshua was instructed to set up twelve stone monuments, after he and the nation of Israel crossed the River Jordan, so that when the children of future generations asked what they were there for, the adults were to tell them the story about how God had performed a miracle. How their people were saved when the river parted and they walked through on dry land."

"You want me to erect a stone monument?"

Ivan looked a question at Esther, who nodded.

"It might not be a bad idea," Ivan said. "You tell me if you think you should, after you hear what my mother has to say. Go ahead, Mother. You are the one who is responsible for all of this coming to light."

"I still don't understand," Logan said. "How is Esther responsible for anything related to any of this?"

"Explaining it would require another Bible story," Ivan said. "About a judge who gets pestered to death by a widow. The judge gets sick of her and gives in, just to shut her up."

"I'm sorry, but I'm very confused," Logan's mother said.

"I think I understand," Hope broke in. "Esther has prayed for the return of Joseph every day for as long as I can remember. Even though the police were certain that he had drowned, Esther never let up. It became a sort of sad little joke among her grandchildren and great-grandchildren. How their grandmother didn't even eat breakfast each morning until she had prayed for the return of her missing grandchild."

Esther pointed her cane at Deborah. "And I also prayed for *you!*"

"Me?" Deborah gasped.

"I prayed that someone kind had come along and found him and saved his life. I prayed that he was being raised by good people. And I prayed that someday, somehow, he would find his way back to us."

"Are you saying that your prayers *drew* me here?" Logan said.

"Of course they did. I am growing very old. I wanted to see you again before I had to leave. I've been praying doubly this year for you to come back to us."

Logan looked into her clouded eyes in wonder. All these years, this woman he hadn't even known had kept him in her heart and mind?

"I—I did not pray," Mary confessed. "I could not. I did not

think I could continue to care well for the other children if I tried to keep hope alive in my heart. I was afraid it would eat me up. I am so sorry, Logan, but I gave up on you in order to survive."

"You should probably call the police now," Deborah said. "I don't think I can bear much more of this."

"Police?" Esther grasped the handle of her cane tightly. "Who said anything about police?"

All the Troyers looked at one another with discomfort written on their faces. Logan saw his brothers shift their feet and glance away.

Ivan cleared his throat. "Like the rest of the Amish and Mennonites, we try not to get police involved unless it is absolutely necessary."

"But I committed a crime," Deborah said.

"We believe that God can bring triumph out of tragedy," Ivan said. "We believe that it is possible for His will to triumph over evil where His people are involved. We are a people who believe in practicing forgiveness."

"I don't deserve forgiveness."

"You've got *that* right!" Caleb's voice was bitter.

"Hush, Caleb. You stop that right now," Esther said, then she turned back to Deborah. "You seem to want to be punished. No doubt you need to make amends for what you did and you should, but I think we can find a better way than by putting a perfectly good attorney behind bars."

"Mother?" Ivan said. "What are you doing? I thought we had agreed about this."

"Shhh, Son. This is a woman who needs to make restitution. I'm going to give her something to do."

"Anything," his mother said. "I will do absolutely anything you ask. Just name it."

"Logan says that you are very good at what you do," Esther said.

"It is rare for me to lose a case."

The old woman seemed to be thoroughly enjoying herself. "Do you know anything about international law?"

"Not a lot, but I could learn." Deborah's voice was puzzled.

"Do you, by any chance, speak Spanish?"

"I have a working knowledge of it." She looked perplexed. "What does this have to do with me taking your grandson?"

"Mother, that is brilliant!" Ivan exclaimed. "I know exactly what you're thinking, and you're right."

Esther sat back and smiled as Ivan explained.

"We are having trouble with legalities about one of the wells," he said. "Logan might have mentioned that our family has worked for years to bring clean water to third-world countries. It is not terribly hard to get volunteers who will help dig wells or teach people how to use filtration devices or pass out purification packets, but the red tape we have to go through to get permission is sometimes a great headache. If we had someone who knows how to do the legal maneuvering to get things done—and would be willing to work for free—that would be a gift straight from God."

His mother's eyes grew wide. "Are you saying that you and your family would forgive what I've done for nothing more than some pro bono work?"

"Oh, no." Esther shook a finger at her. "You will not get off so easily. We need funds for what we do. We're assuming you have made good money in New York and have influential and wealthy friends?"

"I have made excellent money in New York, and I have dozens of influential and wealthy friends."

Logan could hear hope dawning in his mother's voice.

"Wouldn't it be something," Ivan said, "if what Satan intended as evil turned out to bring about a great good?"

"You truly believe that?" Deborah asked.

"We do," Esther said.

Deborah's shoulders straightened and her chin lifted. "I would need to know more about what you do. A lot more. I'd love to be part of something as practical and necessary as providing pure water to people who have none."

"What you did was a very grave wrong," Ivan said. "You should have given our boy back to us immediately. You should never have kept him. On the other hand, had you not been there, the chances are very good that he would have drowned. A three-year-old does not have good sense. He might have tried to wade out to where he had last seen his brother. That beach was very isolated and we were gone a very long time. God used Pharoah's daughter to save Moses' life when he was a baby. We believe God might have used you . . . and your weakness . . . to save our son. We'll never know, but . . . we forgive you. 'Weeping may endure for a night, but Joy cometh in the morning.'"

It was then that Mary opened her arms to him, and he truly hugged his . . . other mother . . . for the first time.

"I—I have pictures," Deborah said cautiously. "Back in New York. So many picture albums. One for each year. I will have copies made and bring them to you."

"Thank you," Mary said. "We would appreciate that very much."

Logan noticed that Hope had disappeared for a few minutes. Now she came out on the porch. "I still have all those cinnamon buns you made, Mary, and I just made some fresh coffee. I also have milk for the children. Please, everyone, come in."

"Before we do," Ivan said, "Mother, would you lead us in a prayer of gratitude?"

Esther, who had been so faithful in her prayers for so long, lifted her nearly sightless eyes to the sky, raised her hands above her head, and prayed a prayer of thanksgiving to the Lord so pure and heartfelt that Logan could feel the power of it.

"And this," Ivan said to the children gathered around, "is who we are, and this is what we do. Our family serves the Lord—no matter what comes—and when He answers our prayers, no matter how he answers them—we give him praise."

Logan wiped moisture from his eyes as he watched his family file into his house. Except for Caleb, who walked off the end of the porch and went over to the large oak tree. He leaned one arm against the tree and looked off toward his father's house.

Logan followed him.

"You were adorable," Caleb said, without turning around. "And I loved you like only a big brother can love a baby brother. I would have given my life for you . . . and yet because of my foolishness, all these years I thought I had caused your death."

"That's a terrible burden to carry," Logan said. "But I *am* still here."

Caleb turned to look at him. "And I'm glad. It's going to take me a while to forgive that woman—your 'mother'—but I'll work at it. I agree with my parents, it will do none of us any good to make a public thing out of this. What's done is done. Punishing her will accomplish nothing."

Then he hooked an arm around Logan's neck, drew him near, and gave the top of his head a good, hard scrubbing with his knuckles.

"What was that!" Shocked by his brother's actions, Logan put his hand on top of his stinging scalp.

"As the eldest, I figure we've got about thirty years of "noo-gies" to make up for, little brother," Caleb said. Then he hugged him hard. "You have no idea how good it is to have you back. Maybe I can sleep without nightmares now. We all tried to pretend we were okay . . . for each other . . . but we weren't. Now maybe we can begin to heal."

"Did your grandmother really pray for me every day all these years?" Logan asked as they walked back to the house, their arms resting upon each other's shoulders. "That's kind of crazy."

"We thought so. Now we're figuring out that she was crazy like an old fox. I think the rest of us learned a thing or two about prayer tonight."

His mother had a restless night. Not from pain, which had not become a big problem yet, but apparently from sheer astonishment. She couldn't get over what had happened earlier in the evening. She kept pacing back and forth across the living room floor, occasionally glancing out at the window toward the Troyers', although it was too dark to see anything except their porch light.

"I've never seen anything like it," she kept saying. "What an amazing family you've come from, Logan. I never dreamed it would turn out like this. Never!"

He was beyond exhausted, but he wanted to stay up as long as she needed him. "You need to get your rest, Mom."

"I'll rest when I'm dead," she snapped. "Until then, I need to work. I promised I'd help with their well project. They don't yet know I only have a limited time to work. I want to accomplish as much as possible for those good people for as long as I can."

"Can you keep your voice down, Mom?" He rubbed his eyes. "Hope and the baby are asleep. So is Simon. I wouldn't mind getting a little sleep, myself."

"Is she going to be staying here permanently?"

"No. She doesn't want to. That was just a temporary fix while everyone knew I was in New York. I'll take her to her mom and dad's tomorrow. If you remember, she doesn't have a house to live in anymore. A tornado destroyed it three . . ." He glanced at his watch. "Make that four days ago."

"I have to get back to New York." His mother wasn't listening. "You need to take me home."

"Now?"

"My time is short," she said. "I have an office to close down. Research on international law to begin. You can help me polish my Spanish along the way."

"I don't know any Spanish."

"Then I'll review mine by teaching you. You can catch a nap at my place before you head back."

He knew his mother. When she got like this, a protest was futile. "Whatever you say, Mom."

Sick or not, the powerhouse known as Deborah Parker was back, at least for now.

chapter THIRTY

"Hold still!" Logan shouted from inside the barn. "Please!"

Hope wasn't sure what was going on, but she thought she'd better investigate.

"Not like that, like this." Simon's calm voice overrode Logan's frantic one. "You have to move this over here, and . . . uh-oh . . ."

She heard Logan let out a yelp.

"I was afraid that was going to happen," Simon said. "You're trying to do too much too fast."

"I want to surprise Hope."

"She's going to be surprised, all right!" Simon chuckled.

Hope stepped into the barn, worried about what she was going to find.

"*Vas ist letz?* What's wrong?"

The last thing she expected to see was Logan lying in a stable that needed a good cleaning, where he had apparently been kicked by her buggy horse.

"Are you all right?" She rushed in and squatted beside him.

"No, I'm not all right," he gasped. "That horse of yours just kicked me!"

"That's what horses do. You have to be on your guard."

"Where did you get him, anyway?" Logan asked. "He's always so good for you and Simon, but he's done everything but roll over and play dead trying to keep me from hitching him to the buggy."

"That's Copy Cat," she said. "Claire gave him to me a few months ago. She said she had a little trouble managing him, but I've never had any. You should have known better than to stand behind him. Why on earth were you trying to hitch him to the buggy anyway? Don't you have better things to do?"

Logan had been lying prostrate, now he sat up and gingerly felt his ribs. "I don't think anything is broken."

"Copy Cat is smart," Simon said. "He pulled back at the last moment. He knew he had an amateur behind him so he didn't kick as hard as he can."

"What I don't understand is what you're doing out here bothering my horse at all," Hope said.

"You tell her, Simon," Logan groaned. "I'd rather not right now."

"I'd rather not, too," Simon said.

"Well." Hope put both hands on her hips. "*One* of you had better tell me, and fast."

"I was trying to learn how to harness the horse to the buggy. I asked Simon to teach me."

"I already got that part. What I want to know is why on earth you would want to harness *my* horse to *my* buggy when you have a perfectly good car sitting outside."

"That's the part I don't want to tell you," he said. "Not yet." She tapped her foot. "I'm waiting."

"Well, I sure didn't want to tell you while I'm lying here in a pile of manure."

"Logan . . ." Hope allowed some real anger to enter her voice.

"Oh, okay!" Logan's face turned bright red. "I wanted to see if I could hitch a horse to a buggy because if I turned Amish I'd need to know how to do things like that."

"Turn Amish?" Hope was puzzled. "What on earth are you talking about?"

"You know . . . become Amish. Like you."

"Have you lost your mind?"

"No. Have you lost yours?" His voice was much too defensive, and she didn't know why. It sounded like they were having an argument when all she wanted was to figure out what was causing Logan to try to hitch up her buggy. Now he was saying he wanted to become Amish. Nothing he was saying or doing was making a lick of sense to her.

"You aren't even all that religious," she said.

"I could be," Logan said defensively. "You don't know what I think about God."

"That's because you never mention Him."

"That's because you never ask."

"So . . . let me get this straight . . . you're trying to hitch my horse to my buggy because you believe in God now?"

Logan pulled himself out of the muck. "Of course I believe in God. I asked you to pray for me and my mom, didn't I?"

He stood up. Simon handed him a handful of clean straw and he started wiping his pants off with it.

"So you think you're going to become Amish? Do you know how ridiculous that sounds right now?" Hope said. "You've purchased every electric appliance and gizmo known to man, and now you're going to go completely nonelectric? Amish people become *Englisch* sometimes, but *Englisch* people do *not* become Amish."

"Is there a rule against that?"

"No. It's just that it's too hard. Only a few who try it ever make it. It's a difficult life, even for those of us who have been raised in the faith. Usually people join the Amish church not for religious reasons, but because they've fallen in love with some Amish person and think they have to become Amish in order to get married . . ."

Her voice trailed off because Logan was standing there looking at her with the strangest look on his face.

"You're not . . . you couldn't be . . . are you . . . oh no." She stuttered to a stop.

Simon watched avidly and safely from the front end of the horse.

"I had planned to propose *after* I'd mastered the horse and buggy," Logan said. "And I certainly didn't intend to propose covered in manure, but yes . . . that's what I'm thinking."

It was not exactly a romantic moment. Logan sounded decidedly grumpy, and he smelled . . . well, like horse manure.

He dropped the handful of straw and wiped his hands off on the front of his shirt, which had managed to remain somewhat clean until that moment. The man was a mess.

"I love you, Hope. I think you've suspected that for a long time. I want to marry you and help you raise those sweet children. *But,* I don't want to be a laughingstock in front of all the other Amish men, so I was trying to learn a few things ahead of time before I started to court you. That's what you call it, isn't it? Court?"

Childbirth hormones were unpredictable things. It had been less than two weeks since she'd given birth and they kicked in big time now. She didn't know whether to laugh or cry or scream in frustration, so she just stood there gritting her teeth. He would never have the knack to do a tenth of the things Amish men learned from birth up. The man was a storyteller, not a horse wrangler, or anything else that was needed on a working farm.

"It would never work."

"I've already met with Bishop Schrock about this situation and he's going to try to explain some things about the church to me . . ."

"You did *what*?" The idea of him meeting with her father-in-law appalled her. What must the bishop think of her when she had kept reassuring him that there was nothing between her and her employer?

"I know I can be a good husband to you, Hope. And I'll cherish your children like they were my own. Besides, I was born Amish. That must count for something."

"You would teach my children the *Ausbund*, and the *Ordnung*, and how to speak German?" Hot tears came to her eyes now. Angry tears. "You have sat through one worship service and met one time with my father-in-law and you suddenly think you know what it is to be Amish? You have no idea what you are talking about. You would become bored with our ways within a year!"

With that, she stomped out, leaving him to deal with his messy self alone. All she could think about was *now* what was she going to do? She had been a foolish, foolish woman to put all her eggs in this basket. There was a summer to get through and a harvest, Lord willing, to arrange. With the harvest, along with her savings, she might have had enough to put a down payment on a small place of her own.

Now she had to deal with an employer who had proposed to her! She couldn't allow herself to consider his proposal—not for a minute. He was crazy. There was no way that he could do what he was suggesting. Some men, perhaps, but not him.

It broke her heart that he would even try, and it made her angry, too, because of the sheer hopelessness of the situation.

Thankfully, he did not follow her. Instead, she heard another yelp, and Logan's voice complaining, "Good grief! The blamed thing just bit me!"

Copy Cat obviously did not enjoy being harnessed by an amateur.

She knew that Simon was probably sniggering in a corner somewhere and trying to hide it, and she wished she could laugh at the situation as well, but she just couldn't. The whole community had watched Grace and Levi struggle with *their* marriage, and they were still working out what to do about church the last time she checked. Hope was not going to endanger her children's eternal souls, or hers, by bringing this New Yorker into their family as the father and spiritual leader.

Even if he was one of the kindest most thoughtful men she had ever known. Even if those eyes of his did melt her heart every time she allowed herself to look into them.

She marched into the kitchen and began preparations for dinner. She would not eat with him and Simon tonight. She would leave the food on the stove and they could serve themselves. The less time she spent with the man, the better! She'd find another job to do after the harvest and hopefully never run into him again.

But she would miss him terribly.

She hoped he and Simon would manage to get poor Copy Cat harnessed soon. She didn't want to go back out there after the scene she had just been through, and she had an appointment with Grace in an hour for Esther Rose's checkup.

It would be good to ask Grace for advice.

Being in Grace and Claire's home birthing clinic was always soothing. She loved going there. Elizabeth was frequently in attendance, making hot chocolate, handing out advice, or cooing over babies. If Claire had a few minutes between clients, she would rest her feet by putting them up on a footstool and turn out yet another knitted cap for a newborn. Grace's baby girl either slept in a crib in a corner, or rode around on her mother's hip while Grace consulted with the various mothers.

It always smelled good in the home birthing clinic, usually from something Claire had baking in the oven. Sometimes mothers brought extras from their own baking day. There was nearly always something good to eat, and a cookie for a tag-along child.

It was a comfortable and comforting woman's place where subjects like nursing, childbirth, or postpartum blues could be discussed frankly and without embarrassment.

Hope wondered how Levi withstood the almost constant onslaught of Amish and Mennonite women who came to the clinic. She guessed that he probably pretty much lived in the barn or fields during clinic hours.

She was a little early when she pulled into the driveway of Elizabeth's house. To her delight, Levi was in the barn with the doors wide open, working on his car with his new stepfather, Tom, her aunt Claire's husband.

Tom had been raised Amish, joined the military, then came home to his roots twenty years later after recuperating from wounds sustained in combat. Hope figured he was probably the only Amish man in the world who could fly a helicopter. Claire and he had fallen in love and the whole Amish community had rejoiced.

Tom saw her and came to take charge of her horse.

"And how is our little mother?" His battle-scarred face was wreathed in smiles. "Isn't it awfully soon for you and Esther Rose to be out riding around?"

"I'm feeling well enough," Hope said.

"I hear the baby was almost born in a cellar."

Hope shuddered. "It was too close for comfort. I don't know what I would have done if Logan Parker hadn't found me."

"Got you here just in time for Grace to deliver the baby, from what I hear," Tom said.

"He did."

"Come see what I'm doing!" Levi called out to her. "Tom is teaching me how to replace a transmission."

She walked over and peered into the open hood of the vehicle. What Levi was doing looked complicated. She wondered how in the world he could learn such things when he had spent most of his life using nothing but hand tools and horses.

"It'll drive like a dream again when I get this fixed." Levi grinned at her with a grease-stained face. She had never seen her cousin happier.

"It must be so nice to go where you want to go without having to hire *Englisch* drivers," she said.

"Is that envy I hear in your voice, Cousin?"

"Maybe a little," she answered. "I have no desire to run around all over the countryside, but it would be nice to have a pickup to drive to get farm supplies when they are needed. *Englisch* drivers are sometimes unavailable when you most need them."

Levi's eyes narrowed. "Are you thinking about jumping fence, Hope?"

"Of course not," she said. "Just because it was the right decision for you doesn't mean that it's the right decision for me."

Still, she couldn't help running a hand over Levi's car just for the sheer enjoyment of it. The finish was as smooth as glass. She had heard that secreted in the body of the car were air bags that could save a life if there was an impact. But being able to drive a car was a shallow reason to leave a church. Even if it was tempting to have strong steel and air bags to protect her children.

She had faith in God. A lot of faith. But it was hard to believe that it was God's will every time one of her people's lives was lost because of a careless *Englisch* driver. It hadn't bothered her so much before she had children. Now it was on her mind constantly whenever she was on the road and *Englisch* cars were passing by so fast they made her buggy sway.

Levi wiped his hands on a rag. "Something is bothering you. What is it?"

"Logan Parker asked me to marry him," Hope burst out. "He said he would become Amish in order to do so."

"Oh!" Levi's eyebrows lifted. "Now that is news, indeed. And how do you feel about this?"

"I think he is being very foolish."

After tying her horse to the railing, Tom, who had overheard their conversation, weighed in. "You're right, Hope. The man has no idea what he's saying. I was actually raised Amish and yet it has been a struggle for me to go back to the old ways after being in the military for so long. Being married to Claire and enjoying the close fellowship of my people again has made it worth it, but that's a terribly hard decision for someone like Logan to make." Tom paused. "He must love you very much."

"I know," she said miserably. "He loves my children, too."

"I've gotten to know him pretty well these past few months. I like the man and I trust him," Levi said. "How do you feel about him?"

"I love him." It felt a little strange having this conversation with two men, but she had always valued Levi's opinion, and was learning to value Tom's. "But I don't want to go through what you and Grace have. It wouldn't be fair to put the children through that."

"But what we've been through has been worth it," Levi said. "Yes, we had our bumps along the way while we got some things figured out, but our commitment to one another never wavered. When you and I were little, Hope, of all the cousins, you were always the one who took the most risks, climbed to the highest limb in the tree, tamed the meanest barn cat. I always thought you were fearless."

"I never thought of myself that way."

"You were, though. I always admired that in you. What you've taken on since Titus died is pretty impressive, too. The marriage counselor Grace and I finally agreed to talk to taught us that the root of anger is almost always fear. That was a surprise to both of us. We discovered that most of our fights were fear-based. I was afraid she would leave me; she was afraid I would control her to the point of losing her identity.

"Now you seem to be angry about the fact that a man you love is willing to join the Amish church in order to marry you." He slammed the hood of his car so hard it startled her. "What is it that you are afraid of?"

"That's easy to answer," she said. "I'm afraid that Logan won't be able to live Amish, that it will be too hard, and he'll give up and leave me. That the children and I will have our hearts broken when he leaves. I'm about half afraid that he'll get himself killed just trying to harness my horse. The poor man has no business around farm animals. Logan is a writer, not a farmer."

"Well, if that's the case," Levi said, "there's something else the counselor taught us that's been a big help to me and Grace."

"I'm listening."

"Compromise."

"How can I compromise?" she asked. "Logan is either Amish or he's not."

Levi bent over and started wiping off his tools one by one and placing them in his tool box. "I wasn't saying that Logan was the one who needed to do the compromising."

"How . . ." Hope stopped midsentence. She thought she knew exactly what Levi meant. "Have you and Grace settled on a church yet?"

Levi straightened up. "As a matter of fact, we have. We've started going to the one where the Troyers go. Grace likes it there. I like it there, and most importantly, as far as I can tell, it's Bible based. The people there aren't perfect, I doubt that their doctrine is perfect, but they're trying awfully hard to love each other and follow Jesus. Truth be told, it's a relief to have found a place to worship. Grace and I are doing great."

He looked at her and she looked straight back at him. In silence, they had a weighty conversation without saying a word. Could she compromise? Would she?

She knew what Levi had gone through leaving his Swartzentruber church. From what she had seen of Grace, the woman was worth any sacrifice Levi had made for her. To give up one's soul for another was wrong. To give up five hundred years of tradition? Maybe that was not so wrong. Levi had made it plain to everyone that although he had questioned his church's *Ordnung,* he had never lost his faith in Christ. Grace had considered herself a Christian as well. A Bible-based church. People who loved one another and tried to follow Jesus.

"I'll give it some thought," she answered. "Thank you for the advice."

Levi did a half salute with a monkey wrench. "Let me know if you ever need someone to teach you how to drive, Cousin."

As she walked away from the two men, her head was spinning with questions. What was at the core of her belief in God? Doctrine? Tradition? Martyred ancestors? Or was it nothing more than a pure and simple faith in a resurrected Christ?

Millions of people came to Holmes County every year, from what she could tell, at least partially because they longed for a simpler lifestyle, but she knew the truth. There was nothing simple about her people's lifestyle. Not when their various *Ordnungs* prescribed everything down to the width of ribbon a man could wear on his hat. Rules on top of rules. Yes, it brought about an enviable vision of unity—but were her people unified in heart? Not always. People were human. There were always those who gossiped and judged. Those who strayed. Those who were so small-minded they became mean-spirited.

If Titus were alive, she wouldn't be having these thoughts, but she *was* the spiritual head of her home now. It was she who had the right to decide what her children would be taught and where. She remembered years ago, when she had attended a Sunday school class with some of the Troyer kids. How she had loved it! Classes taught on a child's level. Coloring little Bible pictures. A story taught with a fascinating object they called a flannel-graph. Even as a child, she had wondered why such a thing could be wrong.

Once considered, it was as though a floodgate opened in her mind. If one of the children was to become ill, and she had a truck, she would be able to drive to the hospital so very quickly. If she were Mennonite she could have a telephone in her home or even carry a cell phone with her. Not for frivolous chatter, but for business and emergencies. If she were Mennonite, she would have a greater choice of fabrics with which to make her clothing and her children's clothing. If she were Mennonite she could . . . oh my! . . . take classes in agriculture or animal husbandry!

Her thoughts were so radical, they scared her, and yet, having entertained these rebellious thoughts, she could not manage to shove them away.

Ivan's church did not require one iota less moral accountability than her Amish church. In fact, the church Ivan's family attended met together twice a week instead of twice a month, like her Amish church.

Changing churches was not something to be done lightly. Ivan and Mary had done so only after much prayer and consideration. She had been a child, playing with their children, and had heard many of their heartfelt discussions as they wrestled with the decision.

If she ever did make that change, and right now it seemed too radical to seriously contemplate, she wanted to make certain it was for the right reasons, and not just because she thought it would be convenient . . . or might make it possible to be with Logan.

Still . . . the idea that she had the right to purchase a car with seat belts and air bags was a heady one. Isn't that what a good mother did? Protect and teach her children?

Levi called her fearless. She was not fearless anymore. Except when it came to her children. Then, she would face anything and anyone, if it meant protecting them or giving them a better life.

Her mind was roiling so badly with these new thoughts that she sat down on Elizabeth's porch swing for a moment to try to pull herself together. If Logan was willing to become Amish for her sake, then becoming part of the Troyers' Mennonite church would not be all that much of a stretch for him—and he'd have the added advantage of his brothers and sisters and Ivan and Mary there to encourage and strengthen him. She believed that with all that behind him, he could go the distance as a Christian.

She straightened Esther Rose's tiny *Kapp* as she lay sleeping in her arms. Then she arose and entered the clinic Grace and Claire had created. There was a lot she wanted to talk to Grace about, and not all of it was medical.

Becoming Amish had made perfect sense to him when he'd been lying on his bed daydreaming about how thrilled she would be with him for making such an extreme decision in order to be with her.

He had not factored in the possibility of angrily shouting a proposal at her while still in pain from a horse's kick . . . and covered in fresh manure.

Nope—it had not been his finest moment by a long shot.

Still, her negative reaction surprised him. It was like she thought he was stupid or foolish—and he wasn't. He'd been reading up on the Amish, trying to learn everything he could. He'd already made an appointment with the bishop to start whatever sort of catechism thing they made people go through.

He wanted Hope, he wanted those children, and he wanted God in his life. He also wanted to belong to the community of people he saw around him.

Giving up was not an option. He would show Hope that he could do this. He could become Amish. Others had done it. It hadn't been easy, but they had done it.

It was his custom to shower and shave before he went to bed each night. Tonight he followed the same routine, except for one thing. He put his razor away on the top shelf of the bathroom cabinet.

It was time to start growing a beard.

chapter THIRTY-ONE

There were a lot of changes involved in becoming Mennonite, Hope thought. But there were also many similarities. Like the Amish, the Mennonites were pacifists. Like the Amish, the Mennonites believed in adult baptism. Like the Amish, the Mennonites believed the Bible was the inspired word of God. That was pretty much where the similarities ended.

One of the spiritual differences that she found herself drawn to was that the Mennonite church the Troyers attended was much more grace-driven than the particular Old Order Amish church that her parents and the Schrocks attended.

The idea that Ivan and Mary introduced her to—that God's grace was ever-present in a believer's life—drew her like a spiritual magnet.

The other changes she would like to make were not spiritual ones, but they still involved a certain amount of thought on her part. She had seen Mennonite women wearing jeans, and wondered how that would feel. Her guess was that it would make working in the fields easier, but she didn't know. Some women claimed that dresses were a lot cooler outdoors than pants.

She didn't know how she would wear her hair, either.

Women who did not wear their hair beneath head coverings had to take care of it in a different way. She wasn't sure she wanted to drop the idea of a head covering entirely. Perhaps a kerchief instead of a *Kapp*. At least a kerchief would be easier to wash and keep clean, not to mention a lot cheaper.

A big problem was that now that Logan had come home, she was having to live with her parents until she could make other arrangements. How was she to change when she was still beneath their roof? There were going to be some terrible fights when she told them what she had planned, and why.

Perhaps she was taking too much for granted. She should probably see if Logan was okay with this. Perhaps he actually *did* want to become Amish.

But she did not think so.

She tossed and turned for two nights after her conversation with Levi, trying to gather her courage to do this thing she realized she had been wanting to do for a long time. The problem was, she did not know how to be anything but her father and mother's obedient daughter, and Titus's obedient wife, not to mention Bishop Schrock's not quite so obedient daughter-in-law.

Oh, it was going to cause such a stir! People would talk about her, and much of that talk would not be kind.

But was she doing anything wrong in God's eyes? She did not think so. She wasn't so shallow that she would give up her soul for a man. All Logan had done, with his proposal and ridiculous attempt to be Amish, was to precipitate a decision that had been simmering in her subconscious for a long time.

"Simon?"

"*Ja?*"

"I need to learn how to push a plow today."

"Push a plow?"

"You heard me."

Simon scratched his head. "The plowing time is over for now."

"There must be *something* I can do."

Simon began to sidle away.

"Stop that!" he said. "I need to learn how to do an Amish man's work. Teach me how to pick corn or bale hay or *something*."

"Corn's not ready yet. Hay's not ready, either." Then Simon brightened. "There's always manure to shovel."

"No." Logan shook his head. "I've had enough of manure. How about hoeing something?"

"Already done." Simon looked up at the sky. "Already getting too hot to hoe today anyway. You need to get up really early to get that done while it's still cool."

"I could shear sheep, maybe."

"Hope would throw a fit if you touched her ewes."

"Feed cattle?"

"They're pretty happy grazing where they are."

"You really aren't any help, Simon," he said. "How am I supposed to become Amish if I can't even hoe?"

"I have an Amish friend who works on a computer at Keim's Lumber," Simon said hopefully. "Maybe you could get a job there."

"I don't need a 'job,' I have a 'job.' I want to learn to do something . . . Amish."

"We have some fences that need tightening, some posts that need straightening. You could help me work on the fences."

"Great!" Logan was ecstatic. Building fences. Now *that* was something that sounded Amish!

"Did you forget to shave?" Simon asked.

"No. I'm growing a beard."

Simon sighed.

By the time Hope arrived, he had smashed his thumb, ripped a hole in his pants, cut himself on barbed wire, and discovered that growing a beard was one itchy proposition.

"You look like you've had a hard morning," she commented as she lifted Esther Rose out of the buggy.

He was happy to see her. "Me and Simon got nearly thirty feet of fencing fixed," he boasted.

Something told him to turn around, and he did . . . just in time to catch Simon in the middle of an eye-roll.

"Simon is fully capable of putting up fencing without any help."

"I told you." He stood his ground. "I'm turning Amish."

"Is that why you didn't shave?"

"Yes. I'm growing a beard. All Amish men wear beards."

"Not all of them. Did you notice that Simon doesn't have one? Amish men grow beards *after* they get married, not before."

He had not known that.

"You mean I can shave it off for now?" He hoped his relief didn't show.

"You and I need to talk," Hope said. "Do you care to babysit, Simon? This might take a while."

"Sure thing." Simon accepted Esther Rose into his arms. "Sure beats fixing fences."

It wasn't until they were inside the house that Hope spoke. "I've been giving some serious thought to the idea of leaving the Amish church."

"Whoa!" He was floored. "Why?"

"I have many reasons, but what I want to know right now is . . . would you consider going to Ivan and Mary's church with me if that is where I started going?"

"After what the Troyers did for my mom? I'd be happy to!"

"Good."

"Are you really serious about this, Hope?"

"I talked with Levi. And with Grace. It won't be easy. The bishop and my parents will want to talk to me. People will say I'm doing this just because I'm in love with you, but yes, I'm serious."

He heard only five words. *I'm in love with you.* And suddenly, he felt ten feet tall. "Are you saying you'll marry me?"

"Of course. Isn't that what you were getting at the other day in the barn when you were trying to hitch that poor horse to the buggy?"

"Hope, I . . . I don't know what to say." He took a step toward her with his arms outstretched.

"Please don't get mushy." She held up a hand. "One of my childhood friends married an *Englisch* man and she said the worst thing about him was that he was always saying mushy things to her. Amish people don't do that."

"But you aren't going to be Amish anymore. Right?" He took another step toward her. "Isn't that what you're saying?"

"Well, I'm not exactly going to be *Englisch,* either." She put her hand on his chest.

"Do you suppose a not-Amish/not-*Englisch* woman might consider kissing the man she's just agreed to marry?"

He took the hand she had placed flat against his chest and pulled her to him.

"Logan, I . . ."

He stopped her protestations with a kiss. Then he pulled back, checked to see how she was taking it, saw a sparkle in her eyes that told him that she was taking it *very* well, and then he bracketed her face with both of his hands and deepened the kiss.

When he pulled away, she was breathless and her cheeks were flushed.

"I believe we might have discovered something besides storytelling," she said, "that you do extremely well."

He laughed out loud and pulled her into his arms once

again. He was going to get to be a father to adorable Carrie and stalwart little Adam. He was going to get to carry tiny Esther Rose into church and seat himself among his brothers and sisters, his father, and maybe both of his mothers. He would get to visit with Esther after they shared Sunday dinners together and learn everything he could possibly learn from that woman.

It was apparently going to be okay if he didn't know how to plant a field, or drive a buggy, or milk a cow. He was going to have a wife who was expert in all of that, and such a wife she would be!

"It isn't going to be easy," Hope warned. "Nothing about this is going to be easy."

"Except that loving you and the children will be easy," he said. "That has always been easy."

"*Ja*," she said. "It was the trying to pretend that we didn't love each other that was so hard."

Epilogue

H e walked into the antiques store where it had all begun. Where he had found the ancient typewriter that had changed his life. That was where the chance meeting with the brave woman trying to find houses to clean had taken his life in a direction he never would have dreamed possible.

As he had hoped, Violet was seated behind the counter. As usual, she was wearing a high-necked collar, a long, dark skirt, and a cameo broach at her throat.

"Logan!" she exclaimed. "You are back from your honeymoon? Where did you go?"

"New York."

"Did Hope like it?"

"Not a bit, but I wanted her to see where I'd lived. Then we flew to Sarasota, Florida."

"What did you do there?"

"I rented a small beach house. A place my mother stayed a long time ago."

Violet beamed. "How nice."

"I thought so. I brought you a present."

"A present?" Her face lit up. "For me?"

"I thought you might enjoy this." He handed her a hardback copy of his latest book.

"What is this?" She looked at the title. *"To Ride the Dark Wind."*

Then she opened it and read the inscription. "To Violet. One of the courageous women pilots who helped save the world . . ."

"Is this . . . is this . . ."

"The book you and your friends helped me write." He grinned. "Everything is fictionalized, but the essences of the stories I heard are there and woven into the story."

"I can't wait to read it!"

"Oh—and by the way. It came out while Hope and I were gone, so I just found this out. It's getting excellent reviews—even though it was written by this unknown new author named . . . are you ready for this? Logan Parker."

"Oh, Logan." She cradled the book against her chest. "Thank you so much."

"By the way, I made arrangements for the advance and royalties to go into a special account for our local veterans. It won't be huge, but it'll do some good."

"But don't you need . . ."

"It isn't my book, Violet. It's yours, Frank's, and the others who told me their stories. You have no idea how important all that was to me."

"You can leave now." Violet made a shooing motion with her hand. "I have a book to read!"

As Violet excitedly dipped into the book, he left the antiques store, stuck his hands in his pockets, and walked down the sidewalk, whistling—a teetotaling, Sunday-school-going Mennonite man with a lovely, strong wife, a prosperous farm, and three healthy, happy children to go home to.

He also had work to do. Important work. Work that he loved and was good at.

There would be other books, a lot of them, and they would be good ones. Possibly even ones that Bishop Schrock might enjoy reading. He could already feel one bubbling up, begging to be written. It would be about an awkward, bookish missionary to Haiti, and God's impact on his life.

He would be doing the research firsthand. He and his mother had a trip planned in one month's time to Port-au-Prince along with his brother Caleb. There was a well to dig, and his mother had negotiated and paid for the land upon which it would be dug. In the past few months, she had sold her law firm and started a nonprofit organization for the work that she intended to devote the rest of her life to. Neither he nor she knew if that would be years, or months, but as far as he could tell, she was fighting the cancer with as much single-minded purpose as she had done everything else in her life, and fighting it well. He could not help but believe that her new focus was giving her the fight she needed.

A few of the Troyers, Mary and Caleb especially, had struggled with forgiving his mother, but as her heart and basic decency was revealed day after day, they accepted her for what she was. An amazing woman who would bring an infusion of strength and purpose and financial resources into their family mission for as long as she was able. They would fight back, as a united family, against the misery some people had to endure.

"Did Violet like her gift?" Hope asked when he got home.

She was barefoot, wearing a sleeveless, loose-fitting print dress that came to her knees. Her shoulder-length hair was held back from her face with a simple kerchief, her skin kissed by the sun. She held a basket of eggs in one hand, and six-month-old Esther Rose on her hip with the other.

How could any woman be so beautiful?

Esther Rose had a thumb-sucking habit that worried Hope, but that he found adorable. Little eyes sparkled at him from over her tiny, curled fist. He smiled at her. The little minx—she knew exactly what she was doing.

"Violet was very happy with her gift. It did my heart good."

"I went over to Grace and Claire's this morning."

"Oh?" This worried him. She had been a little tired lately. "Is everything okay?"

"Can you paint a room?"

"Probably, why?"

"That fifth bedroom—the small one next to ours—needs a good coat."

"I'll be happy to give it a try. What do you have planned for it?"

"Nothing much." She set the basket of eggs on the ground and pulled Esther Rose's thumb out of her mouth. "But after you get it painted, I'll also need for you to go over to my mother's and borrow back that cradle that Esther Rose outgrew a few months ago. It's up in their attic."

"Cradle?"

She nodded. It was then that he realized that her eyes were twinkling as she waited for his reaction.

He grabbed her and Esther Rose in a bear hug. He thought it might be possible to burst with happiness. God was indeed so good.

"I have more news," Hope said, when he let her go.

"And what would that be?"

"Guess who I saw having her first examination at Grace and Claire's clinic?"

"I have no idea. Is it a secret?"

"Shouldn't be. She's a properly married woman now."

"Are you talking about Agatha?"

"Sure am. She told me that Simon is nervous as a cat over this pregnancy, but she's never been happier. They're awfully young to be starting a family, but I think they'll make it."

"I hope she can manage to feed the poor little thing."

"Me, too!" Hope laughed. "Speaking of food, supper is ready. Oh, and Claire and Tom and the kids are coming over later."

"Good."

As they walked into the house together, he skimmed his hand over a shoulder-high granite stone he had asked the local stonemason to install near the front porch.

It wasn't fancy. He had not wanted it to be fancy, but chiseled into the rough stone were these words: *This is who we are, and this is what we do.*

When his children asked him what the words meant, he would tell them about the night their great-grandmother Esther's prayers brought healing to their family. The same night their grandfather, Ivan, defined their family for future generations by saying,

"Our family serves the Lord . . . no matter what."

A Howard Reading Group Guide

Fearless Hope
Serena B. Miller

From beloved author Serena B. Miller comes another Amish love story set in Holmes County, Ohio. The third novel in the series, *Fearless Hope* tells the story of the title's namesake, Hope Shrock. A young mom of two with another baby on the way, Hope is forced to take on work as a part-time housekeeper after she loses her husband suddenly in a tragic farming accident. But working for the new *Englisch* man in town—Logan Parker—in the house she grew up in proves to be more complicated than Hope could ever have imagined. Together the pair face a tornado, town gossip, and a secret from the past that could make or break their future together. A love story with characters you will recognize from the first two novels, *Fearless Hope* promises to give the reader hope that love really can conquer all.

DISCUSSION QUESTIONS

1. "But it was the running of a farm that fascinated her. It always had . . . [her father] often commented about what a wonderful farmer she would make . . . if she were a man" (page 5). In these first few pages of the novel we meet Hope, a woman who knows she has what it takes to run a farm, but who must work as "an obedient wife" (page 5) and not as a farmer. Does Hope believe in the assigned gender roles in her community? Does she follow them?

Are there moments when she relies on her own judgment instead of following the rules of her culture? Had she ignored Titus and insisted she run the farm, do you think her husband would have lived?

2. Compare and contrast the two settings of the novel: Holmes County, Ohio, and New York City. What does each of these settings represent for Logan? Do the differences between his two homes symbolize the differences between Marla and Hope?

3. Logan buys the house in Holmes County ultimately because he feels like he belongs there. Is a sense of belonging, a sense of origin, what Logan was missing from his life? Is there any irony to be found in the fact that Logan feels less alone in a big house in the country than in a crowded city apartment?

4. Why do you think Logan is finally able to overcome his writer's block in Violet's store? He describes the store as "energizing" (page 66)—what do you think that means?

5. Throughout the novel Hope mentions the importance of family, saying "she could not imagine living in a world where she could not go visit her *Maam* and younger siblings several times a week" (page 140). Do you think that having a family, knowing your roots, is a theme of the novel? Consider both Hope's and Logan's points of view in your answer.

6. Revisit the tender scene on page 143 when Logan watches Hope hang laundry on the line from the upstairs window. He thinks that "Hope made it a thing of beauty" to work around the house, that she "was a study in gracefulness" (page 143) no matter what her task. Is this the moment where Logan falls in love?

7. The novel is titled *Fearless Hope*. In what way or ways is Hope fearless? Does she give hope to others in the story? How so?

8. Consider the ways in which Logan's old-fashioned home filled with high-tech appliances symbolizes the marriage between Logan and Hope, between modern life and Amish culture. Do the two ways of life complement each other? How so?

9. Discuss the character of Deborah Parker, Logan's mother. Do you like her? In what ways does her character change throughout the story?

10. Even before we learn that Ivan Troyer is Logan's biological father, he serves a father-like role for Logan, giving him advice, discussing his faith in God, and inviting him into his home to share a meal. Seemingly out of the blue, Ivan tells Logan, "Peace isn't about pretty. It isn't about where you live. It's about who you live with, and who you live *for*" (page 150). Do you think Logan's journey is about finding peace within? Is he successful? In the end, who does Logan live for? Is this a different version of Logan from the Logan at the start of the novel?

11. "I am wondering what good they do, these books you spend your life writing" (page 186), the bishop tells Logan. What do you think he means by "good" in this context? Does Logan learn to make his books do something good? How?

12. Discuss Logan's conversion to faith. Do you agree with him that it is "a lot easier to believe in God when one was surrounded by the vibrant, natural world" (page 230)? Does Holmes County alone open Logan's eyes to faith, or is it something (or someone) else?

13. In what way(s) do Logan and Hope "weather" the storm in the novel? Do you read the tornado as a symbol for their unlikely love? Is the tornado ultimately responsible for finally bringing them together?

14. Revisit the ending of the novel. In what ways does the story come full circle? Do you think Logan and Hope will manage to overcome the difficulties ahead?

ADDITIONAL ACTIVITIES: WAYS OF ENHANCING YOUR BOOK CLUB

1. So many of the characters in *Fearless Hope* are characters who have their stories told in the other novels in the series. Have your book club read Serena Miller's other two Holmes County novels, *An Uncommon Grace* and *Hidden Mercies*. What lessons can be gleaned from all three of the novels? Which story did you feel most connected to and why? In your opinion, is there one character who stands out among the crowd as the real hero?

2. On page 212 Logan confides to Esther that he's felt like he has "been wandering around in a dark forest for a long time" and can't find his way out. This line alludes to Dante's *Inferno*, which famously begins "midway on our life's journey, I found myself in dark woods." Have a movie night with your book club and watch the 1935 classic *Dante's Inferno*. How is Dante's journey similar to Logan's journey? How are they different? What do Dante and Logan have in common?

3. Hope reveals that she had taken to reading about the "virtuous woman in Proverbs 31 every morning" (page 235)

in the hopes that she would find strength and guidance in her fight for running Logan's farm, a job her community feels is inappropriate for any woman but especially a widow with young children. Read Proverbs 31 aloud to your book club and afterward meditate in silence on the passage. Then, share with your book club the message as you understand it. Does it make sense that Hope would use this passage for guidance? What do you need guidance on in your life? Does Proverbs 31 help you as it helped Hope? Share your feelings with your book club.

4. When Logan and Deborah Parker confess the truth to the Troyer family, they are shocked to discover that Deborah is forgiven, that the family believed "God might have used [Deborah] . . . and [her] weakness . . . to save our son" (page 295). The Troyer family really believes that God works in mysterious ways, and despite their heartache, they forgive Deborah for taking their son and even appreciate that she likely saved him from drowning. Over dinner, share with your book club a time when you felt God was working in mysterious ways in your life. Did it take time for you to realize God's presence?

QUESTIONS FOR SERENA B. MILLER

You choose to tell the story from both Logan's and Hope's points of view. What drove this decision? What effect does it have on the story? Ultimately, does this story belong to Logan, Hope, or the two of them?

Serena Miller: I always enjoy getting deep into both my main characters' heads. I think this helps keep the writing fresh—especially in a love story. Ultimately, I felt like this story belonged to Logan, but perhaps that's only because as a writer I identified more strongly with him. Hope was harder for me because I'm not a farmer. I do, however, have an older sister who can grow absolutely anything and has spent most of her life running an organic farm.

Fellow author Ann H. Gabhart has said of your work that you breathe "such life into [your] characters they almost leap off the page into your imagination." Are any characters based on real people, or are they entirely fictional? Which character is your favorite in the story and why?

My characters are mostly fictional except for where I drew heavily upon my sister's skills in developing Hope's dreams for the future. Logan's mother was based on a passage I ran across years ago about mental compartmentalization and how some people who have done very bad things sometimes compensate by becoming ultragood in every other aspect of their life. My favorite character was the grandmother who diligently prayed for her lost grandson even when common sense would have made most people give up. She reminds me of my mother-in-law, who has diligently and successfully prayed for family members when most people would have given up.

Along similar lines, where do you get inspiration for your characters? Do you interview your neighbors in your local Amish community?

Actually, I spend a lot of time in Holmes County, Ohio, which is the largest Amish community in the world. It is only three hours from my home and has a greater diversity from which to draw than the small, new settlement near me. I have many close Amish and Mennonite friends in the Holmes County area. I try not to "interview" my Amish friends, but I do care deeply about their beliefs, struggles, and dreams.

Do you consider Hope something of a renegade in the Amish community?

I don't think of her as a renegade as much as a mother who is desperate to provide a better life for her family—even if not everyone approves of her choices.

Like the Troyer family, you and your family have been involved in ministry work. Briefly describe the work you've done with your husband. Did this ministry inspire the Troyer family's?

In 2005, my husband and oldest son went to Haiti to help show Haitians how to use an inexpensive water purification system. Their report, upon their return, encouraged our home congregation to become a much more mission-oriented church. Our church has now sent multiple mission groups to both Haiti and Honduras. Our immediate family created a common bank account into which we contribute windfall money to make it possible for family members to go on mission trips without having to ask our church for financial help. We are far from the level of involvement of the Troyer family, but we're working toward that goal.

Fearless Hope **is a story full of light and dark, happiness and sadness. Do you think it's necessary in fiction to have a mix of both? What about in real life? Can we have love without hate, peace without unrest?**

I would be uncomfortable writing inspirational fiction that gives the reader the impression that the Christian life is easy. This life was never meant to be easy—but God does make it possible to have great joy and hope in spite of experiencing the inevitable sorrows and challenges of life.

Share with us your literary influences. Who do you read for inspiration?

I seldom read fiction anymore. Now that I've studied the writing craft for so long, I find it hard to lose myself in a story without analyzing structure, etc. I've heard other writers complain of the same problem. There comes a point when it is difficult for a writer to suspend the critical brain long enough to be swept away. As a younger woman, though, I saturated myself with so many wonderful authors: Willa Cather, Margaret Mitchell, Marjorie Kinnan Rawlings. Later in life I discovered Allan Eckert's scholarly historical works and read all of them. Now, with time so limited, most of my reading involves research.

Why do you think it is important to share stories of the Amish? Do you hope to break any stereotypes with these novels?

If I can break stereotypes, I would be very happy. One of the biggest mistakes tourists make when they come to Amish country is to assume that uniformity of clothing means a uniformity of personality. My Amish friends are varied and interesting. Many have a great sense of humor. Most struggle with many of the same problems the rest of us have. The difference is that, as a people, they consistently try to apply godly principles to their lives in practical ways. I think there are good things we can all learn from them. I certainly have been blessed by my association with them.

Have you ever experienced writer's block like Logan? How did you overcome it?

I came so close to burnout this past year that I was afraid I would never write again. For most of my life I loved the process of writing and I dreamed of becoming a published writer. Then the reality of meeting deadlines, doing PR, keeping up with social media, and worrying about reviews hit and I almost allowed it to destroy my desire to write. How did I overcome it? Like Logan, I began to write completely outside my genre. It happened accidentally. I took a train trip to visit a relative and was on Facebook talking with friends about the experience, when someone suggested that I write a story called "Murder on the Texas Eagle." For the sheer fun of it, I began writing a cozy mystery about an old, opinionated Kentucky woman. Suddenly, writing was enjoyable again. I knocked out a ten-thousand-word story before the trip was over. That led to another cozy mystery and another. Are they award-worthy? Nope. They aren't even serious writing. But the "Accidental Adventures" of old Doreen Sizemore helped me start writing again. I've recently put them up as e-stories just to entertain my friends. These tongue-in-cheek stories fed something inside of me as I wrote them out by hand on yellow legal pads instead of my computer—kind of the equivalent of Logan's antique typewriter.

What would you name as the major theme(s) of this story? What do you hope readers will remember about Hope and Logan?

Hope had to learn to trust her own vision of what obedience to God looked like instead of relying on others to define it for her. Proverbs 31 does talk about a woman buying a field and planting it and selling the produce. Hope depended on the scriptures to determine what was right and wrong and to determine what God's plan was for her—instead of relying on other people's opinions. Logan had, in his own way, a similar discovery. This is a story about spiritual obedience in the face of criticism, the incredible power of prayer, and the healing power of forgiveness. Ultimately it is—like all my other books—a story about hope.

Is *Fearless Hope* the last book in the series? Do you have any plans for a new writing project you can share with us?

This is the last book that will use the characters of this series. I doubt this will be my last work of fiction involving the Amish. However, at the present time I'm deeply involved in writing a nonfiction book entitled *The Wisdom of Amish Parenting*, which I hope will give non-Amish parents some pointers about the peace I've seen in Amish homes that I think would help us manage our own stress-filled lives a little better.

AN
Amish Wedding
INVITATION

AN eSHORT ACCOUNT OF
a REAL AMISH WEDDING

SERENA B. MILLER

HOWARD BOOKS
A DIVISION OF SIMON & SCHUSTER, INC.

NEW YORK   NASHVILLE   LONDON   TORONTO   SYDNEY   NEW DELHI

AN
Amish Wedding
INVITATION

AN eShort Account of
a Real Amish Wedding

"So, how many chickens do you think we'll need to butcher in order to feed everyone?" Luke Beachy asked the group seated around the yard as we relaxed and visited after supper. Everyone was close kin to him, except me.

Luke was the father of the bride-to-be, and the wedding was weighing heavily on his shoulders. This was his eldest daughter's wedding, and she was the first of his many chicks to leave the nest. As with most *Englisch* weddings, there was a bittersweet quality to discussing the upcoming event. They liked the boy, but Luke and his wife, Deborah, grieved the fact that the daughter was moving so far away.

Five miles.

"I know that doesn't seem like so much to you," Deborah

had said to me earlier, "but with a horse and buggy, it is a lot to us."

At the moment, we were watching a group of young cousins, ages five to twenty-one, playing volleyball in the front yard. The girls were barefoot and wearing Old Order Amish dresses made from pastel-colored fabric. Two of the older boys were dressed *Englisch* and had short, modern haircuts. Their cars were parked discreetly behind the barn. They were having their *Rumspringa*—their "running around" time—before settling down. All were laughing and having a good time. It was a pretty sight.

"Well, we'll need to feed around five hundred people before the day is over," the grandmother said.

No one ran for the calculator, because Luke's question was rhetorical. They knew exactly how many chickens they would need, and how many quarts of home-canned green beans, and how much celery and flowers and everything else they would have to grow or gather or borrow. The Amish are experts at marrying off their children, and the chicken would be one of the greatest expenses. Fortunately, the father of the bride was a chicken farmer, which, under the circumstances, seemed a lucky thing.

There were ten of us relaxing in folding chairs around a small campfire beneath the comforting shade of an ancient maple tree. We had come together to celebrate the successful publication of my first book, *Love Finds You in Sugarcreek, Ohio*, which was a story set in a nearby town and had involved Amish characters. This family had been kind enough to allow me to spend months pestering them with questions, trying to truly understand their culture.

The book had debuted to great reviews, but the opinion that mattered most to me was theirs. Had I gotten it right? Had I portrayed their people accurately?

Yes, they said. I had gotten it exactly right. Deborah especially enjoyed it. She commented that she wished I could speak German.

"Why?" I asked. Her comment puzzled me.

"Because then I could tell you what is in my heart," she said. "It is so hard to say in English the things I feel."

This was intriguing. "Can you try?"

"Because you did not make our people look . . ." I could see her translating in her mind, "Weird."

"Weird"? This was not a word I had ever heard an Amish person use.

"After I read your book," she explained further, "I felt a lot better about being Amish."

"Oh." Her comment was unexpected and felt like a gift to me. "I am so glad!"

I was beyond grateful to this Old Order family who had allowed me, an *Englisch* woman with jeans and short hair, to enter their world and become part of their lives. As a small thank-you, I was giving the women a break from cooking supper and had ordered a towering stack of pizzas. I wanted to make sure everyone could eat their fill, and they had—including the children, who broke away from their play from time to time to run over and grab another piece. Deborah had brought a large sheet cake.

We were eating outdoors with the food stacked on makeshift plywood-and-sawhorse tables. This was not for want of room inside. This is the land of ultralong dinner tables and homes built large enough to seat two hundred church members. We were outside tonight because it was a pleasant day to watch the children play volleyball, and a small campfire is always a cheerful thing even if you don't need it, and, well, outdoors is a cooler place to be on a summer evening when you don't have air-conditioning.

"The publisher is interested in more books," I said. "Do any of you have any stories you can think of that you would want me to tell?"

"What kind of stories?" Deborah asked.

"Love stories about the Amish."

"Oh, lots!" Her sister-in-law Mary practically jumped up and down in her seat. "We have lots and lots of love stories."

I grabbed my ever-present notebook and pen.

"But we can only tell them to you in German," she teased, and everyone laughed.

They laughed because I had recently entertained them with a story about my experience taking a high school German class from a teacher with an unfortunately deep Southern accent. I had demonstrated the extent of my knowledge of their language by drawling an exaggerated, "*Danke schön*, y'all."

Susan, Mary's five-year-old daughter, ran up to her mother and rattled off a question.

"We have a guest," Mary gently reminded her. "You are interrupting."

The child glanced over her shoulder, gave me an apologetic grin, and switched smoothly to English as she asked permission to have another piece of cake.

"Such a sweet tooth," Mary said fondly, and gave her permission.

It is unusual for a five-year-old Amish child to speak English so fluently. Usually they speak only German until they begin school at six, but Susan had grown up playing with a little *Englisch* boy her mother babysat. She was a bright child and picked up this "foreign" language of English very quickly.

Our conversation turned once again toward the fascinating subject of the upcoming marriage. This visit was the first time I'd heard anything about a wedding, and I wanted so badly to go. I assumed it would be an informal affair along the lines of a barn-raising, a sort of come-as-you-are function with piles of food laid out potluck-style on makeshift tables. I envisioned, after a brief ceremony, the couple riding off in a buggy decorated with flowers.

I figured it wouldn't be too much of an imposition to ask if I could attend. I mean, what's one more person at a big church potluck. Right?

"I apologize for asking," I said, "but would it be rude if I came to the wedding? I've been thinking about putting an Amish wedding scene in my next book."

There was a hesitation as they pondered my request. I attributed that hesitation to what my husband and I call "the Amish pause." These people take time to think before they speak, so it came as no surprise that my abrupt question required a few beats of quiet contemplation before answering. I have read that this is a matter of humility with the Amish. They do not want to be like *Englisch* people, who answer off the cuff as though they already know everything.

To me, whose talking style has frequently been described by my family as "shooting from the hip," this pause is fascinating. Try as I might, I can't seem to achieve it.

It is a full two months later before I realize that this particular hesitation had more to do with the fact that the father and mother of the bride were mentally shifting seats around in their heads while wondering where on earth they would put me. They had not expected an *Englisch* woman to suddenly pop up and invite herself, but they politely agreed that it would be fine if I wanted to come, and I eagerly wrote down the date.

Sometimes it seems as though I have a great talent for making a dummkopf of myself around my gracious Amish friends. I never mean any harm, and so they have made a habit of forgiving my ignorance. At the time, I had no idea how carefully planned out this wedding already was. To this day, I wonder who gave up their seat for me.

The largest settlement of Amish in the world resides in the Holmes County, Ohio, area. In the heart of Holmes County is the small town of Berlin. In the middle of Berlin is German Village, which is a lovely group of shops that sell local products. Anchoring this small shopping area is the German Market, a local grocery store.

This store is a busy place, and it caters to both *Englisch* and Amish clientele. There are usually at least a dozen horse buggies tied up at the hitching posts. As you go into this building, you see the grocery store on one side and a large open space in the front where many rocking chairs are placed. Usually these are filled with older Amish men waiting patiently for their wives to finish their shopping. This sometimes involves quite a wait, because there is a lower level where Spector's Dry Goods stocks fabric, sewing supplies, sturdy wooden clothes-drying racks, Amish men's hats, and fresh, white prayer *Kapps*.

In the middle of the grocery store, on the main floor, there is a piece of bibliophile heaven called the Gospel Bookstore. This is where Eli Hochstetler, the enthusiastic owner, proves that it is still possible to run a profitable, independently owned bookstore.

The foot traffic into Eli's place is enviable, especially since much of it is composed of Mennonite or Amish customers who have not yet acquired the habit of ordering books at the click of a computer button. Instead, they browse, taking their time, examining the books they are interested in, and more often than not, conversing comfortably with Eli in their own language.

The day after the Amish pizza party, I had my very first book signing ever in the front of Eli's bookstore. I was enjoying discussing books with the handful of locals who were kind enough to talk with me. I was especially delighted when my friend Joyanne walked in.

Joyanne and her husband, Clay, are transplants from Texas who run a cozy bed-and-breakfast and hire out to drive the Amish. She had driven Deborah and her daughter Rebecca to the book signing, and they also planned to pick up a few groceries while they were there.

"This is for you." Rebecca handed me a thick, high-quality envelope, which I opened. Inside was an elegant, professionally printed invitation to her wedding. This is the first I realized that the Amish purchased and mailed out wedding invitations. I had assumed Amish weddings would be a simple word-of-mouth thing.

After they left, I showed the invitation to Eli, the bookstore owner. He was excited for me.

"An Amish wedding?" he says. "Oh, you are going to eat so well on that day!"

Later, when I got home, I attached the wedding invitation to my refrigerator with a magnet, and the next morning, I glanced at it again and did a double take. There was an obvious printing error. The invitation said that the wedding was to take place at 8:30 a.m. on a Thursday morning.

I put on my reading glasses. Yes, that's exactly what it said: 8:30 a.m.

I have been a preacher's wife for many, many years and I've been to a *lot* of weddings. I've sung for several of them and decorated for others. I've helped pin brides into borrowed wedding gowns and eaten more wilted salads at receptions than I care to count. I've been to afternoon weddings, right-before-noon weddings, evening weddings, late-afternoon weddings, weddings in the woods, weddings on the beach, second weddings, fourth weddings, renewing-of-vows weddings. And never, *ever*, had I seen a wedding take place at 8:30 a.m. on a Thursday morning.

I immediately phoned Joyanne and asked if they had printed the invitation wrong. She laughed and said that this was the customary time for Amish weddings to take place. I asked why on earth they would begin that early in the morning. She gave me the same answer she had been given when she had asked. It was a "tradition."

She also told me that there would be about three hours of preaching before the actual ceremony took place at around noon. That was when the realization first began to dawn that there was a whole lot more to this Amish wedding business than I had ever dreamed.

As the time for the wedding drew near, I made my plans. The Holmes County community is three hours from my home. Getting up before dawn to drive all that distance did not seem like a good idea, so I stayed overnight in Oak Haven, Joyanne's farmhouse B&B, which has become a home away from home for me. It doesn't take a whole lot to give me an excuse to go stay an extra day or two if she has room. When I arrived, she filled me in on a few of the things that had been happening over at the Beachy family farm this past week.

The Thursday before the wedding, Deborah's sisters and friends had arrived to help clean house, paint, and weed the garden.

On Friday, the mobile kitchen had arrived, and it had taken a great deal of maneuvering to make the large, metal, wheeled structure fit in behind the house.

Saturday, the men had erected the tents that would extend the seating room in the barn, and another that would provide shade to the kitchen workers. They had also given the barn a thorough cleaning.

Monday, the women had begun all the prep work that could be done that far in advance. The bride had been particular, with definite ideas about the spices she wanted mixed into the coating for the chicken. She had spent a great deal of time adding and mixing and adding and tasting large bowls of coating until it was perfect. Large amounts of celery had been chopped and refrigerated.

On Tuesday, the women had toasted all the bread for the bread dressing, and had mixed the salad dressing and put it into bottles. Pizza crust had been baked for the fruit pizza dessert. Green beans had been put into kettles. Ham had been chopped to add to the beans. All had been stored in the giant walk-in refrigerator built into one end of the mobile kitchen.

The day I arrived, Wednesday, was a very big day. Two hundred and fifty pounds of potatoes had been peeled. The ingredients for the bread dressing had been combined and stirred in a dozen large bowls. The bride had also perfected the exact seasoning she wanted to use for the dressing and had taped a recipe card beside one bowl.

When the dressing was finished, it was put into storage containers until the next morning, when it would be cooked. There had been an animated discussion on the merits of starting the frying of the chicken at 5:30 a.m. the morning of the wedding, but Deborah had decided to fry it the day before to make it easier for the women assigned to that task. Pineapple was cut up and blueberries thawed for topping the fruit pizza. Gallons of mint tea, an Amish favorite, were made and cooling.

Joyanne informed me that we had been invited to take part in their work frolic "haystack dinner" that would start in an hour. I could hardly wait to get over there and witness everything . . . and take notes.

I love the Amish phrase *work frolic*. To my mind, it conjures up a joyful time—which also incidentally involves work—and that is exactly what it is. One of the things that surprised me most about the Amish is that the women, at least the ones I have met, are not drudges. Even though they don't have all the time-saving appliances that we have, and usually a lot more children, somehow they don't seem to be as weighed down with responsibilities as most *Englisch* mothers I know. I believe that a large part of that is because of their work frolics.

Work frolics are called for whenever a woman is scheduled to host the church on Sunday. Walls will be washed, floors scrubbed, stables cleaned, and grass trimmed. If peach trees have a bumper crop, it's time to break out the canning jars and have a work frolic. A barn needs painting? Someone is ill and has crops in the field to harvest? Work frolic!

A work frolic is always accompanied by talking and visiting, much laughter and gentle teasing, lots of food, and plenty of children running about. The younger children play, and the older ones watch after the smaller children or learn a new skill at their father's or mother's elbow. The Amish believe that many hands make light work. From what I have seen, many hands also make for light hearts.

When we arrived, we found the haystack dinner being served in Deborah's spacious basement, where most of the food preparation for the wedding was taking place. With an outside door and plenty of windows, it felt surprisingly light and airy.

"This is my canning kitchen," Deborah explained, when I commented on the enviable fact that she had an entire second kitchen in her house. "It makes things so much easier during canning season. When I'm canning, I can work all day and still be able to run upstairs and prepare meals for my family without having to clean up the mess. Then I can come back downstairs and finish whatever I've got started."

I've done quite a bit of canning myself, and this second kitchen struck me as an absolutely brilliant idea. There was nothing fancy about it. Everything was plain and utilitarian, but

I couldn't help but be envious of all that counter space and the large bank of cabinets.

In the middle of the room was a huge, old, scarred wooden table that had been pressed into service as a serious worktable. A few old couches and various chairs were scattered about. That day, every chair, every couch, every place at that table was filled with Amish friends and relatives helping Deborah prepare for the wedding.

Deborah is one of the most serene women I've ever known, even under these circumstances. I marveled at the fact that the day before the wedding, a mother of the bride could be so calm about having so many people in her home. I would have been a nervous wreck, but these were her Amish sisters and aunts and mother and daughters. They knew exactly what they were doing and were being an enormous help. It probably would have seemed exceedingly strange to her if they were *not* there helping.

Lunch was not a formal affair. Women filled their plates whenever they came to a good stopping point in their work. A haystack dinner has become the preferred work frolic meal, at least in Holmes County. This meal consisted, basically, of piling every sort of salad-type food item imaginable in layers onto your plate as though mounding up a haystack.

My plate held layers of crumbled Ritz crackers, rice, spaghetti noodles, taco meat, shredded lettuce, chopped tomatoes, cucumbers, salsa, crumbled Doritos—all seasoned with a ladleful of a delicious, thin cheese sauce. The best way I can describe a haystack dinner is to say that everyone brings a big bowl of whatever they have on hand. The cheese sauce blends the various foods together and makes mixing rice, spaghetti noodles, and Doritos seem like a good idea. It's a little like creating a do-it-yourself taco salad spread, but with more varied ingredients. It was delicious.

Joyanne explained to me that this has become the favorite

meal for raising funds for various charity events, too, such as helping out a neighbor with medical expenses or raising funds for one of their schools. Everyone contributes a dish and then donates money as they go through the food line.

In addition to all the women working there today, there were children. Always children. Having spent days at a time with my Amish friends, I am convinced that Amish children are the happiest children in the world. I hear no bickering, no tattling, and definitely no fights or back talk. I don't even see any spankings or sharp glances from mothers. Instead, the children simply . . . play. Cheeks grow ruddy from playing tag and hide-and-seek outdoors, as well as investigating every activity in which the adults are involved.

One toddler looked as though she could pose for a painting of a Victorian cherub. Curly blond hair, round, rosy cheeks. She'd just learned how to walk and held on to a couch for stability as she watched all the activity with round, solemn blue eyes. She wore a miniature blue Amish dress exactly like her mother's and was so adorable I ached to cuddle her. I refrained from doing so because I was concerned that being scooped up by an *Englisch* stranger would frighten her. The last thing I wanted to do was to make this enchanting child cry.

The conversation swirled around me and I wished I knew enough German to join in. Considerate as always, the women switched to English in order to include Joyanne and me. They might as well not have bothered. The intricacies of various relationships and babies being birthed, and who was ill and who was recuperating, were almost as incomprehensible as they would have been had they been speaking in their mother tongue.

One kind lady took pity on me and asked how my writing was coming along. I cut my answer short because I could tell that it was a sacrifice for her to pull away from the more fascinating Amish topics floating around us. She kept losing concentration, which I found amusing—but I appreciated her effort.

The Amish women teased Joyanne by pretending to talk about her to me behind her back.

"Joyanne is our favorite driver." A young matron named Tabitha shielded her mouth as though telling me a great secret. "We make sure she gets to go shopping a LOT!"

Joyanne's eyes sparkled as she joined in the fun. "Do you know how many Amish women you can get into a van?" she asked.

"I have no idea."

Joyanne held up a finger. "Just one more."

This brought on peals of laughter, but I didn't get the joke.

Joyanne explained it to me. "The van driver is paid by the mile, not by the number of passengers, so the Amish women, being the frugal people they are," she said, grinning at them, "always make room for 'just one more' friend to help share the expense. They also pack a picnic lunch and make an event out of it."

"But we always pack extra for Joyanne," Deborah said.

"They have to. I've been driving these women for so long, I've started to think I'm half Amish. I used to have short hair, wear jewelry, and never go out of the house without makeup." She patted her hair, which she wore in a bun. "Now look at me!" Her face was devoid of makeup and she wore no jewelry.

"We think Joyanne looks a lot better now," Tabitha said.

I couldn't tell if Tabitha was joking or serious, but as a harried writer with many deadlines, I immediately started calculating how many minutes of writing time per day I could salvage if I gave up curling my hair, digging through my drawers for matching earrings, and putting on makeup every time I went out the door. I decided that this idea would bear closer examination to save for a future time.

"So, what is your favorite store when Joyanne takes you shopping?" I asked.

This involved some serious discussion as they pondered some of the possibilities. I fully expected them to name one of the local stores that catered to the electricity-avoiding Amish, or possibly Walmart, where I'd noticed they frequently shopped.

Tabitha finally said, "I like Kohl's the best."

The others nodded in agreement. Yes, Kohl's was most definitely a favorite among these Amish women.

"Um, Kohl's?" I was surprised by their choice. All I could picture were the jewelry, makeup, and clothing departments that greeted me each time I walked into that particular store. What could they possibly find to purchase in Kohl's?

"Shoes, bed linens, purses, towels, kitchenware . . . oh so many things," Tabitha said. "Sometimes they carry nice black cardigans, too."

Eventually, we began the cleanup and everyone assigned themselves a job. I grabbed a broom and dustpan. Unless one is sick or extremely pregnant, it is taken for granted that all will pitch in after a meal to make sure the hostess doesn't have anything left to clean after the guests leave. I noticed that Deborah's sisters and other relatives knew exactly where every item went—they didn't have to ask. They were completely familiar and at ease in one another's kitchens.

Afterward, Deborah took Joyanne and me to check out the mobile kitchen they had rented for this affair. From this extra kitchen, Deborah's friends and family would provide around five hundred meals before the day was over.

These large mobile kitchens are a necessity during wedding season in Amish country. One end is devoted to an eighty-square-foot walk-in refrigerator lined with sturdy shelves. The rest of the space is filled with a well-designed commercial kitchen. There are five stoves, three sinks, and what looks like acres and acres of cabinets and drawers. It is fully equipped with dishes, pans, utensils, dish towels, dishcloths, and potholders. Everything anyone could possibly need to feed large groups of people has been provided, down to the serving spoons. For a household that has no electricity, this mobile kitchen, arriving with its own generator and propane tank, is a welcome addition.

Deborah told us that it might be best for us to wait an hour or two before coming to the wedding the next morning. She explained that since the entire three hours would be conducted in German, we might enjoy the experience more if we came halfway through the service instead of trying to grit it out for the entire three hours. I protested that it would be rude to show up so late. She assured me that no one there would consider it so. Besides, she added in typical Amish no-nonsense bluntness, it would be better to come in late than to fall asleep halfway through the wedding service.

Suddenly, we discovered there was a crisis. Rebecca's carefully tended flower garden had not yielded enough flowers for all the vases she intended to place on the tables. The flower supply would have to be supplemented. Joyanne and her van were pressed into service so that the bride and her friends could make an emergency trip to a nearby florist.

The next morning, we arrived at the Beachys' large working farm and parked alongside dozens of black buggies in a field across the county road from the house. Dozens of horses were tethered there beneath a line of trees.

It was a gorgeous fall day. The preferred wedding month for the Amish is October, but this wedding took place in September. There are only so many Thursdays to go around in the month of October, and with so many young people having weddings, September has also become a frequently scheduled wedding month.

With a community as interconnected as the Holmes County Amish, there are many, many weddings to attend in the fall.

Weddings are not taken lightly by the Amish. It is my observation that most are total romantics at heart. From the oldest to the very young, they believe in an enduring love between one man and one woman for life. Old women and old men can, and often do, lovingly recount details of their own courtship—even if that courtship took place sixty years ago.

"Do you see that clock on that shelf on the wall?" The bride's grandmother pointed out a wooden clock as we sat in the living room of her *Daadi Haus.*

"It's beautiful."

"My husband made that for me before we got married."

"There was a lot of love put into the making of that clock," I remarked.

"*Ja,*" she said, smiling happily. "There was."

All Amish believe that a marriage should be celebrated with gifts, food, laughter, great joy, plenty of people, and various silly wedding tricks played on the bride and groom by the *youngies.* Everyone who can come will come. One never knows when a groom's courting buggy might just "accidentally" end up on the roof of some outbuilding. A wedding is not to be missed.

We climbed out of the van that morning and carried our gifts through the field, across the county road, and up the sharply inclined driveway. As we approached the house, we heard singing coming from the nearby barn. This was something I had longed to experience. I knew that the hymns the Amish sang had been, for the most part, written by their martyrs five hundred years ago. The Amish hymnbook, the *Ausbund,* is the oldest continually used book of hymns in the world. I also knew that they sang the songs extremely slow, in respect for those martyrs who, while singing hymns in their prison cells, were mocked by jailers who danced to them. Showing typical Amish pacifist ingenuity, those early ancestors solved the problem by simply slowing their songs down until it was no longer feasible for the jailers to dance.

The beauty of the day and the rural scenery about me made it feel as though I'd walked straight into an Amish movie, complete with authentic background music. The timbre of the German words, sung in unison, resonated throughout the valley with a haunting quality unlike anything I had ever heard. Their music, to me, sounded so very holy.

I had given much thought to purchasing a practical gift for a new bride, finally settling on a large cast-iron Dutch oven with a yellow baked enamel surface. What I had not realized was that I would be carrying it quite so far. The thing was heavy, the package awkward, and the driveway steep.

Fortunately there was a handful of little boys waiting alongside the driveway to relieve the guests of gifts. This was their job and they seemed pleased to be doing it. They were dressed in the same traditional black hat, white shirt, and black coat of their fathers, and their eyes were sparkling with excitement over being part of the wedding. I was worried that the little guy who came for mine was too small to carry it.

"Be careful, it's heavy," I cautioned him.

The child didn't even grunt when I handed it to him. Instead, he flashed me a grin as he trotted off. He knew that I was impressed.

We were met by Luke, the father of the bride. He was handsome in his new black coat, vest, and pants, and with so much responsibility, he was more serious than usual. He politely showed us to the seats that had been waiting for us.

The barn, where the actual wedding would be held, was built into the hill, close enough to the house to require only a short walk. It was a large, sturdy barn. There was a second story below that Joyanne told me had been cleaned within an inch of its life. Several horses were stabled there; others took their ease in the shade across the road where they had been tethered. The main level of the barn was so clean it practically shone. Brothers and uncles and grandfather had cleaned it so well over the past week, there was not so much as a spiderweb in view. Square bales of hay were piled to the rafters along the sides of the barn as well as in the haymow to make room for guests. It smelled amazing—the scent of fresh hay permeated the air. I took a deep breath and for an instant, I was transported back to my own childhood on a farm in southern Ohio. A sudden great nostalgia for the hours I spent playing with my cousins in our own barn washed over me.

Hanging from one beam was a single, perfect hanging basket of blue petunias. It was the only floral decoration in the barn. The wooden floor had been swept clean, and was in its own way a work of art. The weathered flooring had been built from planks of wood wider than any I'd ever seen. My father was a sawyer. I knew just enough to recognize virgin timber, built so long ago that there were still forests of giant, ancient trees available.

As large as this working barn was, the family did not think it would be large enough to seat everyone. There was a white three-sided tent placed against the open double doors of the barn, in order to expand the seating. We were placed here, along with a handful of other *Englisch* guests. Luke expressed disappointment that Joyanne's mother, a woman in her nineties, had not felt well enough to join us. He had made certain that there was an especially comfortable chair for her.

I wished I could take a picture of all of this, but I respected my friends' beliefs against the making of graven images. Instead, I tried to imprint the scene before me on my mind, memorizing details, savoring every moment. Inside the barn, sitting sideways in front of us, were two groups. All the women sat to my right, facing the men, who were on my left. They turned their heads and watched with friendly curiosity as we entered, but then their attention was caught again by the preacher, who stood between the two groups with his back to us as he spoke to the church.

There would be three ministers who, taking turns, would preach for nearly three hours by the time this wedding was finished. Several preachers were needed to get through the long wedding service. I recognized a few words—"Noah" and "Moses" and "Abraham"—but the rest of the service was incomprehensible. This was as it should be. The wedding service was not for us, and it was not for show, it was for the Amish. We *Englisch* were allowed to watch, but it would never occur to them to switch to English for our benefit. Nor would Joyanne and I have expected them to do so. This was their culture, their church, their beliefs, their traditions. I was honored and grateful simply to be allowed to observe.

When one preacher wore out, another one took his place. One of them used a sort of singsong cadence in his preaching; another, who was younger, was more impassioned and seemed to hold the crowd's attention a little better. Later I heard comments about what a good speaker he was.

Interspersed with the preaching was the singing. I had recently purchased an *Ausbund* songbook at Eli's bookstore. It had been printed locally, with the English translation right beside the German. In the *Ausbund*, there are no notes, only words. These songs were now sung with every note, timing, and nuance executed from memory. They are not simple melodies. I was amazed that the music to all these words could be passed down, one generation to another, through five centuries.

These songs are not easy to describe, but they were most definitely not happy, bouncy songs. I cannot imagine anyone ever clapping along with the rhythm, because there was no rhythm. The music, with its long, sustained notes, reminded me a little of the mournful wail of a bagpipe. As I said before, the songs were composed by martyrs. They are songs about faith and God and perseverance, written by a people who were hunted down and persecuted for their faith. The church sings in unison, men and women together. Harmonies are considered prideful. A solo would be unthinkable. No instruments of any kind are ever used.

I noticed that the oldest women sat in the back, where, even though they were seated on backless benches, they could rest themselves against the wall of hay. On the men's side, it was different. The old men sat toward the front, and the teenage boys sat in the back. I raised three sons. It amused me that Amish boys looked about as miserable and bored as most *Englisch* teenagers would look if expected to sit through an entire morning of preaching.

Children were sprinkled throughout the group. There is no babysitting service at an Amish church. A little boy who had been sitting with his mother decided that he wanted to sit with his grandpa, and with her permission, he scampered across the open space where the preacher was standing. No one seemed to care. At one point, a young mother, frustrated with a squirming toddler, carried the child over to the men's side and plunked him down upon his father's lap. Then she returned to her seat and crossed her arms. She had not spoken a word, but her actions spoke for themselves. "Here," her body language said. "*You* take care of this kid for a while. He's wearing me out."

The grandfather, seated up front on the men's side, welcomed his little grandson, who was holding a toy tractor and proceeded to run it over the grandfather's knee and large Bible throughout the rest of the service. The grandfather looked dour to me, and I expected him to make the child stop. Instead, he fondly patted the little guy's head and went back to listening to the preacher, unconcerned that he was being used as a runway.

As the service continued, I noticed that the children's trips to the rented Porta-Jon were becoming more and more frequent. Also, a great thirst had apparently overtaken many of them. Several walked in and out of services, using the bathroom, drinking out of a large Igloo cooler situated at the back of the tent. It surprised me to see that the health-conscious Amish had provided only one cup for this community water supply. I wondered if it was because they considered themselves such a close family unit that they did not deem it necessary to provide individual paper cups.

The preaching continued unabated throughout all this activity. Although the preachers paused often to gather their thoughts, the children wandering in and out did not seem to upset their concentration.

The bride and the groom sat together in the front row, along with their carefully chosen witnesses—usually the bride's best friend or sister and the groom's best friend or brother. These "side-sitters," along with the bride and groom, do not do anything except listen intently. This bride, a naturally happy person, was more solemn than I had ever seen her as she absorbed the words of the preacher. She wore a dark navy-blue dress with a white apron. She also wore a black bonnet. This was to emphasize the solemnity of the occasion. After the wedding, she would once again wear the white head covering. She carried no bouquet. There would be no exchange of rings.

Suddenly I heard the preacher say a complete phrase in English. "Divorce is not an option," and I wondered if he spoke these words for the benefit of the bridal couple, or was trying to make a point to the *Englisch* visitors.

Then the whole church rose, turned around, and knelt in front of their bench, bowing their heads and engaging in silent prayer. The preacher apparently had given a cue that I did not understand.

This was not the first time I had experienced the Amish

way of praying silently even within a group. I don't know why
they do this, nor does the husband of one of my Amish friends,
whom I asked later. I was used to being "led in prayer" at my
church services and at shared meals. My guess is that they believe for one man to attempt to "lead" the prayers for the many
would be arrogant.

I like their custom of silent prayer. Having allowed my mind
to wander too many times during public prayers, I notice that
when I am with my Amish friends and left to my own devices
to pray in silence for a few moments, I truly do pray.

So, kneeling, I gave thanks for being allowed to be in this
place, at this time, with these good people. I asked God to help
me portray their culture accurately and with respect. I also
prayed for this young couple, that they would learn early in
their marriage the importance of being kind to each other—
whether they felt like it or not.

We rose and seated ourselves again. The steady stream of
the foreign language lulled me into a pleasant, dreamlike state.
I was startled when the preaching abruptly ended, and the bride
and groom stood up. The preacher said a few words directly to
them. They answered and nodded and then suddenly the wedding was over. The actual wedding ceremony itself, after three
hours of preaching, took less than three minutes.

Now that the wedding was over, the feasting and visiting
began. We walked outside, and I noticed men plucking their
hats out of the mountain of black hats stacked in a pile outside.
They looked identical to me, and I wondered how they knew
whose was whose, so I asked.

"They write their name inside the brim, of course," Deborah told me. I laughed at such an obvious answer. Deborah was
already rushing around in the cool September weather. Her
cheeks were flushed and her eyes were alive with the excitement
of hosting this wedding. In spite of having so many other people

around, she took time out to make sure Joyanne and I were inside her house and comfortably seated before she rushed off to check on last-minute food preparations.

The main floor of her house has two large rooms. One is a well-appointed kitchen. The other is lined with chairs in which many older women were sitting quietly visiting with one another. In the kitchen, I met with a young cousin who I understood to be in nursing school.

"How will your people respond to you becoming an RN?" I asked.

"An RN?"

"You know . . . a nurse."

"I'm not getting an RN," she said. "I'm getting certified to be a nurse's helper."

This made sense. Certification is allowed by the Old Order Amish. High school and college are, like divorce, not an option. I apologized for having misunderstood.

Our semiprivate conversation was cut short, since privacy is apparently not part of the Amish culture. Seeing an *Englisch* woman sitting alone talking with an older cousin is a curiosity. A group of children soon joined us, drinking in every word of our conversation. I realized that my mere presence was entertainment to the little ones.

A few moments later, after she'd swept the sidewalks, Mary, an aunt of the bride, took me aside. "So, what did you think of the wedding?"

"I enjoyed it, but I only understood about five words," I said. "What were the preachers talking about?"

"They were telling the stories of biblical marriages down through the ages. That's what they do at every wedding," she said.

"I thought I recognized the names of some of the biblical patriarchs."

"Were you bothered by the children coming and going so much during the preaching?"

"No," I said. "The children at my church seem to need quite a few drinks and trips to the bathroom during worship, too."

"Oh." She gave a sigh of relief. "I'm so glad. I was worried you would think badly of us."

It was a revelation to me that she had been worried about this. I'm always concerned about what visitors will think of our church. It never occurred to me that the Amish would feel the same way.

People began to gravitate toward the large workshop, where tables and benches had been set up. Luke came and ushered us to the correct table. We were among the first to enter, and the sight made me gasp. Snowy tablecloths covered long stretches of tables. Golden-colored mint tea glistened in narrow goblets at each place setting. Fresh flowers were positioned at intervals on each table between the lovely dinnerware, along with candles, white netting, and gold-colored ribbons. Sunshine streamed through sparkling windows and winked back at us from the polished silverware. I was absolutely stunned at the simple, tasteful elegance. This was nothing at all like the church potluck affair that I had once envisioned.

Over the years, I have developed a private, extremely judgmental, and nonscientific predictor about marriages. I have a theory that the longer the guests are made to wait for the bride and groom to appear at the reception dinner, the shorter the marriage will last. This hypothesis was developed one Saturday afternoon as I and the other guests waited at the reception dinner for nearly three hours, while the bride insisted on a picture-taking marathon. That marriage didn't last even to the first wedding anniversary.

With no wedding pictures to pose for, it took less than a half hour to get everyone in place. It felt like I'd barely had time to get seated before there was a silent prayer. Then the group sang a song that had been printed on a card left on every plate, and the food began to arrive. Dish after dish was handed down the table as people helped themselves to the bowls and platters of steaming home-cooked food.

Sprinkled throughout the salad was a new type of tomato I had never seen before. It was sweet and approximately the size of a blueberry. Those tiny tomatoes looked so pretty sprinkled among the various greens that I asked about them later, and was told that Deborah had discovered this particular seed and had made sure to grow plenty.

The chicken was so tender it could be cut with a fork; the bread dressing that the bride worked so hard to season was perfection. The two hundred and fifty pounds of potatoes had been whipped into fluffy clouds; green beans were passed, seasoned with ham raised and cured on a relative's farm. Homemade rolls arrived, along with fresh-churned butter. We were plied with coffee and water in addition to the mint tea. Two kinds of dessert arrived, along with ice cream.

Competent, smiling Amish young people—friends of the bride and groom—glided up and down the aisles and saw to everything. I had never seen even a professionally catered dinner served as smoothly or as gracefully.

The bride and groom were seated in a corner called an *Eck* with what we *Englisch* would refer to as their wedding party. Their table and surroundings were carefully arranged. Not only were there flowers and a wedding cake, but even the walls behind them were decorated. I noted a prayer plaque hanging behind them.

The words to a song had been professionally printed and placed beside each place setting. At some point during the dinner the guests serenaded the couple with what I think was another hymn. Apparently everyone except me and Joyanne was familiar with this song, written in German, and they sang with enthusiasm, the strong voices echoing off the walls.

I was seated at the very end of a long table. A little girl approximately nine or ten years old stood at the end beside me. From what I could tell, her job was to watch and make sure everyone at our table had everything they needed. She took her responsibility very, very seriously and stood proudly. I noticed that there were other children her age assigned to each table. I saw them also carrying empty bowls to the kitchen to be refilled. From what I could see, every child over the age of eight seemed to have some small job.

There was a short space of quiet as we concentrated on eating, then a second round of food began. Fresh platters of chicken, dressing, green beans, and baskets of rolls were all carried in from the kitchen and started down the table so we could have seconds.

Through a window, I saw the canopied area where a dishwashing area had been set up. It involved three tubs on one side of a table and three tubs on the other. There were six women washing dishes. I could see that they were having a great deal of fun. Even though I could not hear their words, I could see them chatting with one another and laughing. I was impressed with the practicality of this dishwashing system. Six sinks, six faucets, six women up to their elbows in soapsuds. How quickly a potluck at our church could be cleaned up if we had such a station! Everyone who was helping seemed to have a deep sense of belonging. The organizational skills being exhibited were impressive. Everything worked like clockwork. No one seemed to be overwhelmed. There appeared to be real pleasure on the face of everyone who was serving in some capacity.

This did not happen by accident. It's part of the Amish psyche. Service to one another and to others is deliberately modeled for the children from early childhood on.

I had also seen the impressive planning behind this well-oiled wedding machine. The day before, Rebecca had shown me her bride's notebook. It was approximately three inches thick, filled with hand-lettered tabs. One section dealt with job titles: *Eck* servers, parent table, wedding coordinators, water servers, coffee servers, guestbook, dishwashers, gift receivers, babysitters, and hostlers. Beneath each title was a list of family members and friends who had agreed to be responsible for the job.

Cooks headed another section of the wedding book, with a list of each item of food and who would be responsible for preparing it. Another section had instructions for each dish. These pages had been copied and posted all over the house from the kitchen to the basement to her grandmother's nearby *Daadi Haus* so that everyone would know exactly what they were supposed to be doing, and when they should be doing it. There was information on where to order the invitations, where to find the vases for the simple flower arrangement on each table, where to purchase the netting and ribbons to be used to decorate each table. Even the children's jobs were listed, along with the name of each child who would carry out that function.

As I flipped through this bridal book, I couldn't get over the amount of planning that goes into a "simple" Amish wedding. My preconceived idea of a couple standing up in a barn in front of the bishop and saying a few words seemed incredibly naive. I was convinced that there had been wars fought and won with less planning than had gone into this wedding.

After the meal, everyone was welcome to follow the bride and groom back into the barn, where there was a table set up with gifts. Not everyone came to this. Most of the men stayed outside and visited. Many of the women were involved in the cleanup.

I was seated between Joyanne and Frieda, the bride's grandmother. Frieda is one of my favorite people in the whole world. She has twelve children and seventy-three grandchildren. At the moment, the number of her grandchildren exactly matches her age. She is a small, slender woman and it is hard to imagine her having given birth to all those children—but it certainly does not seem to have hurt her. She is as nimble and hardworking as any of her daughters.

As we sat and watched the couple opening their gifts, I noticed a line of six or seven little boys perched upon the top board of a stable, watching. They were all dressed in identical outfits, of course. Black pants, black suspenders, white shirts, black hats—all miniatures of their fathers. They reminded me of little birds lined up on a wire. It was obvious from the smiles and whispers that they were enjoying watching the proceedings.

The opening of gifts was different from anything I'd ever observed at non-Amish weddings. It appeared that it was traditional for the groom to open each gift, and that it was his responsibility to thank the giver. There was no effusive, over-the-top gratitude for an especially nice gift, but merely a dignified nod and thank-you. Every gift was equally appreciated. The bride silently read and kept track of the cards. She seemed content to allow him to take the leading role.

The gifts were remarkable only for their practicality. There were tools for him, an ironing board and new canning jars for her. A mailbox. A bucket filled with cleaning supplies. A basket of garden tools. A rake, shovel, and hoe tied together with a big bow. A wheelbarrow, a nice grill, a garden hose. There was a step stool, and a pressure cooker for canning. Everything that people had deemed necessary to start the young couple off on a good footing was there. My favorite gift was one they accidentally got multiples of—the WhirleyPop, a handy and practical device for making lots of popcorn on top of a kitchen stove. After they opened three of them, Frieda leaned toward me and whispered, "I sure do hope they like popcorn!"

Her dry wit struck me as hilarious and I had to cover my

mouth to keep from bursting out laughing. Joyanne, on the other side, wanted to know what Frieda had said. I told her, and then we both had a problem. The opening of wedding gifts is a serious thing, which made the need to laugh become contagious. Before long, Joyanne, Frieda, and I were trying so hard not to laugh that we were practically crying.

Fortunately, Frieda's comment came near the end, and in a few minutes, the gifts had all been unwrapped and it was time to leave. Another wave of guests needed to be fed—the young adults, who would stay until very late. They would also be served a large meal. The women were already preparing it.

As we said our good-byes, I noticed that the bride and groom were helping with the cleanup. This is expected among the Amish. It would seem arrogant and thoughtless to the family and friends who have worked so hard if the bride and groom simply left. Just as the bridal couple was up before dawn helping to set up for the wedding, they would stay and work until late on their wedding night. To my knowledge, Amish have not yet begun to have formal honeymoons. These two will traditionally spend the night in the bride's parents' home, then get up early the next day to finish taking down the tent and putting everything to rights on the farm. Sometime tomorrow, they will load up their gifts to take to their own home.

The bride's family is pleased with their new son-in-law. He is known as a worker and a saver, a steady man who will make a good husband and father. Like most Amish youth, he has held down a job since he graduated from eighth grade. They will use and value the practical gifts they have been given. There is every expectation that a new baby will grace their home and church within the year. Babies are greatly valued. Not only because the Amish deeply love their children but because each child born to a steady, God-fearing couple like this helps secure the future of the Amish church.

I can't help but admire the things I saw emphasized that day. Three hours of preaching about God and His will for the marriage, and less than three minutes focused on the bride and groom as they pledge their commitment to each other. The very firm expectation by everyone there, including the bride and groom, that this marriage will last for life.

Instead of comments about how beautiful the bride was, I heard people remarking on what a good mother she would make, what a good homemaker she would be. I heard comments about what a hard worker he was, and how well they were suited for each other. Unlike a few unfortunate *Englisch* weddings I've attended, no one speculated unkindly upon how long the marriage would last. Amish do divorce, but the actual statistic hovers right at approximately one percent.

There is something touching and valiant about this young couple and about the Old Order Amish in general. They are not an ignorant people. They are well aware of technology and the world around them. I've heard some of the young people on *Rumspringa* casually mention that they have sold items on eBay and craigslist. Many of the young people, before they commit themselves to the church, own cars, enjoy various kinds of music, and carry cell phones. I am even told that they tend to prefer the cell phones with all the bells and whistles. They wear their hair stylishly cut, purchase modern clothing . . . and all the while, they ponder the biggest decision they will ever make in their life. Will they, or will they not, follow in the steps of their ancestors and become members of the Amish church?

One of the most extraordinary things I've learned about the Amish is that an estimated nine out of ten, after having these freedoms, will choose to be baptized into the Amish church. This statistic flies in the face of all conventional wisdom and makes the retention rate of every other religious body pale by comparison. One would expect a religious group whose lifestyle is so backward and old-fashioned to be dying out by now—especially when there is such an enormous gap between our society and the Amish culture. How in the world can the Old Order Amish church be one of the fastest-growing churches in the world? To put that retention rate of 90 percent in perspective, according to a study by Georgetown University, even the Muslims have only a 76 percent retention rate.

Instead, the Amish population is doubling approximately every twenty years, one of the highest religious growth rates in the world. Also remarkable is the fact that this is the highest retention rate they have experienced in their entire history. Eventually most of these modern, technologically savvy young people will choose to sell their cars, put away their *Englisch* clothes, disconnect themselves from phones and television and rock music, have a wedding much like this, and begin raising a family exactly in the same way they've been raised.

I wonder how this can be. This is a church where the members routinely endure two- to three-hour church services. They sit on hard, backless benches. They have no paid, trained clergy. They have no church buildings. Instead, they meet in homes, barns, and basements. No church is allowed to grow beyond approximately two hundred members. Instead of allowing a church to get too large, a new church is established a few miles away. They have no praise team, no instruments, no Sunday school program, no vacation Bible schools or revivals. They are not at all evangelistic. (One older Amish man commented to me once that in his opinion, living a truly godly life is the most important form of evangelism possible.) Young adults who choose not to be baptized into the Amish church are not ostracized. Their rules of unity, known as their *Ordnung*, are complicated, and in an *Englisch* person's eyes, even unreasonable.

To me, it is a miracle that a church like that survives at all, let alone thrives!

The answer, I think, lies partially in the fact that in general these kids are allowed to see and experience the world just enough to know that they want to turn their backs on it. They long for the decency and honesty of their parents' lives. They want the close-knit fellowship and support with which they've grown up. They look at the commitment to God and to one another other, and they are willing to sacrifice a few conveniences. While *Englisch* people are becoming more and more attached to artificial friendships and socialization, the Amish continue to enjoy close, satisfying, and meaningful fellowship with one another.

Are they perfect? Far from it.

Are they biblically sound? Probably not on every tenet.

Are they more spiritually mature than other Christians? No.

I think the root of the success of the Old Order Amish can be observed in the microcosm I've observed of their society as it is exhibited in this wedding. Close, nurturing family and church relationships. A deep commitment to honoring God. A work ethic that puts them head and shoulders above most of our society, and an ability to support themselves. The security of knowing that a crowd of competent hands will be willing to help whenever help is needed.

In a world that frequently seems to be going crazy, I find great comfort in my visits with my Amish friends. There is a steadiness in the rhythms of their lives, so closely attuned to the seasons of nature. There is an enviable feeling of peace in their homes unmarred by the cacophony of TV sets or ringing telephones. The only music I've ever heard in their homes is the happy laughter of children playing—and that is music enough.

This modern young couple has made a choice today and I

am inspired by it. They have vowed to remain faithful to the traditions of their ancestors, to God, and to each other, for life.

I pray the Lord will bless their union and that their home will be filled with children, love, and good memories. Most of all I pray that they will be able to continue this decent life they've chosen. Our broken world could stand to have many more families just like theirs.

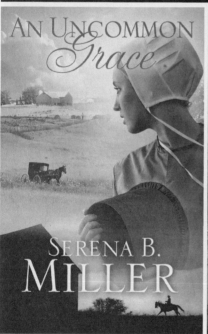
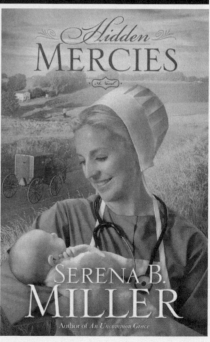